SoulShares
Firestorm
Book Four

Rory Ni Coileain

Firestorm© 2015 by Rory Ni Coileain
Book Four of the SoulShare Series

For more information contact:
Riverdale Avenue Books
5676 Riverdale Avenue
Riverdale, NY 10471.

www.riverdaleavebooks.com

Design by www.formatting4U.com
Cover by Insatiable Fantasy Designs Inc.

Digital ISBN 9781626012097
Print ISBN 9781626012103

First Edition July 2015

Prologue

The Realm
July 12, 1991 (human reckoning)

Cuinn would have clenched his fists in frustration, if he'd had any. It was probably a bit much to expect the new Queen of the Demesne of Fire to quit cooing at the fussy bundle of hair-at-one-end-and-the-smell-of-sulphur-at-the-other who had elevated her to the throne just by being born. But she'd been doing it for going on two hours, and if she didn't put the brat down and find something else to do, he, Cuinn, was going to miss a very important appointment. Either that, or he was going to have to add regicide to the list of crimes he was pulling off tonight, and he was reasonably sure his friendly overseers in the Pattern would be unhappy with his lapse in diplomacy.

As if kidnapping a baby stood much higher on any moral scale than killing the baby's mother.

Cuinn shrugged. Mentally, anyhow. Hard to do that physically when his physicality was Faded. *Come on, your newly-minted Majesty. Put down the brat and back away slowly. Or turn and run. I'm easy either way.*

1

His fellow Loremasters had concocted a system, more than two millennia ago, to ensure that the elementals among the Fae kept breeding, and in so doing feed elemental magick into the Realm. While a chosen four thousand slept through the final battle with the *Marfach*, Cuinn's fellow Loremasters had, not to put too fine a point on it, fucked with their heads. When they woke up, they all recognized the formerly reclusive and rare elemental Fae as their rulers. Not only that, but the new rules of Royalty required the throne of each Demesne to have two occupants at all times, a King or Queen and his or her opposite-sex offspring. A single Royal, or a childless Royal couple, was just killing time, until a female gave birth and the offspring's sex determined who would be ruler and who would be Consort. So when Nuala, here, had popped out baby Rian, she had given herself one hell of a promotion. Hence, all the fussing and cooing and gurgling.

Well, the promotion to Queen probably had a lot to do with it, yes, but there was also that whole love-of-blood-for-blood thing the Fae had going on since before the Sundering. Good thing he had lost all his own blood kin a long time ago. Not to mention the fact the squab's ensouling ceremony had been this morning, so no doubt Mama Queen was feeling even more maternal. Fae didn't suffer from illnesses, and wounds not mortal healed quickly, but more than half of all infants died, inexplicably, within two weeks of birth. So tradition said that a newborn Fae didn't receive his or her soul until two weeks had passed safely. *Too bad this one's going to lose half of his, right after he got it.*

Oh, fuck, not another lullaby. Cuinn tried to pace,

2

but when he was in this condition, he could only drift. He was good for another three or four hours of this, but every minute he spent Faded increased the chance he would get careless and look into one of the many mirrors scattered through the palace to trap Fae foolish enough to attempt what he was doing. Royals were paranoid, all of them. Perhaps rightfully so.

The Queen made a lovely picture as she bent over her son, he admitted grudgingly. Her long blonde hair was done up, and fastened with strands of fire opals; her diaphanous scarlet gown moved as she swayed with the infant in her arms, clinging to her in ways that under other circumstances would have had Cuinn conjuring a bucket of water to soak her to that creamy skin. At the moment, though, all he wanted was to see her put her precious Rian into his cradle and tiptoe out of the nursery.

SIMPLE ENOUGH. He'd groaned out loud, reading the shaping that had sent him off on this idiotic venture. *ENTER WHILE FADED, TAKE THE CHILD, AND LEAVE BY THE NEAREST EXIT.* At least the other Loremasters had understood he couldn't just Fade out of the palace with the kid, not with the way Royals had taken to warding their residences. Unless he wanted to be turned inside out. Which he didn't, particularly.

What the fuck had the other Loremasters been smoking, to come up with this? Not that immortal souls bound in a matrix of pure magick were likely to smoke anything, but still —

The Queen bent, carefully placing the swaddled infant in his cradle. She kissed his forehead, and Faded without straightening.

3

That's the last time she'll ever do that. The thought startled Cuinn. His conscience, such as it was, picked the damnedest times to rise from the dead. He had an assignment to complete, and if he was lucky he could do his duty and be back in San Francisco before the bars closed.

Drifting out of the curtained recess where he'd been lurking, he took form. Just to be safe. Which was fortunate, because when he approached the cradle, he saw the mirror at the head of it even before he saw the sleeping baby. One last soul-trap. The Fire Royals were thorough; he had to give them that.

All their precautions weren't going to help them, though. Cuinn reached into the cradle and lifted out the infant, swaddling clothes and all. The kid would probably need the blanket, though Cuinn hoped the Pattern would drop him someplace where it was summer.

No, now was not the time to be thinking about what he was going to be doing to this helpless baby. Now was the time to be getting the fuck out of here before someone spotted him. Yet he lingered, looking at the child asleep in his arms. One thing he'd learned, over his twenty-five hundred something years of life, was that people who gushed about beautiful babies were, for the most part, either talking about their own children, or just being polite about someone else's. Babies all tended to look vaguely sinister to Cuinn, as if they weren't quite finished being formed yet and were looking around for some nice tasty life essence to absorb to fill up the corners.

This one, though, really was everything a proud new parent had ever bragged about. Perfect features, a fuzz of blond hair, one tiny hand curled up in a fist under his chin, and fuck if his lips didn't look just like a little rosebud.

Cuinn wished his conscience would shut the hell up. He was spending too much time around humans. Almost time for a sabbatical, back here in the Realm, anonymously banging everything over the age of consent that moved, and a few select things that didn't.

The baby's eyes opened. Rian Aodán had the bluest eyes Cuinn had ever seen, the blue faceted like a cut gemstone. Perfect blue topaz. He got the distinct impression those eyes were accusing him.

Cuinn grimaced, and deliberately turned his thoughts back to the route he'd taken to get to the Royal nursery. Shielding the baby with his arms —not that it would hurt him to be Faded by someone else, at least not until he came of age and came into his birthright of power, but dropping him now would be the textbook definition of a Very Bad Thing —he Faded to the closest exit he remembered, a bay window set into the wall of a corridor, with a velvet-cushioned window seat.

Said window was set seamlessly into the stone wall. *Son of a syphilitic bitch.* Cuinn thought about trying to break the glass. Then he thought about trying to climb out of a shattered window over jagged shards of glass, unnoticed, carrying an infant. Not happening.

The next window he tried presented the same situation. The next one, too. Worse, his Royal Highness was starting to get restless, his face working as if he was about to either cry or fill the Royal nappie. Worse still, he could hear the voices of what sounded like a gaggle of servants heading his way. He'd been incredibly lucky so far. Maybe it was time to stop counting on luck.

There was a scullery entrance almost halfway around the perimeter of the palace. He hadn't wanted to use it to get in, mostly because it was too damned far from the nursery and it would have taken him hours to drift incorporeally to his target. But the door had been open when he passed it yesterday, scouting the place out, and he'd caught a glimpse inside. Enough to let him Fade there without ending up half inside a stone wall?

I sure as shit hope so.

He could hear footsteps now, as well as voices. *Time to go.*

Holding the infant tightly, he Faded.

Taking form in the Royal kitchen, he found himself staring straight at what had to be the delivery entrance. All the way through the curtain wall, wide enough to allow for the unloading of a wagon, bolted with a counterweighted latch the thickness of a tree trunk. *It's a door. Good enough.*

"Who are you?"

The female voice came from behind him. Which meant she hadn't seen his face, or the Royal brat in his arms. Without turning, he made sure matters would stay that way, closing his eyes and drawing on his inner store of magick to channel a pulse of brilliant white light that would leave anyone, even a rapidly-healing Fae, blind for at least a minute.

The female screamed. Unfortunately, so did Rian.

Fuck me backwards. Too late to deafen the female as well. Cuinn sent the magick arrowing straight for the door, channeling the counterweight up, opening the double doors wide with a silent blast of power.

He was greeted by darkness. He caught a glimpse of the yard outside, bare earth churned by the hooves of horses and the wheels of wagons, and the torchlit wall of the enclosure around the postern gate, off to one side.

And the deep, angry baying of at least a half-dozen hounds. The Royal Fade-hounds.

Cuinn sprinted out the door into the darkness, the screaming infant clutched as close as he dared. The bellowing came from the area the gate, so he took off running in the other direction.

He tore through the torchlit darkness, not even daring to spare the magick to snuff out the torches as he fled, much less speed his flight or do something about the fucking dogs. Fade-hounds scented magick. If the hounds had his scent, they'd be able to follow him when he Faded. Which would mean an untimely end to his role in the Pattern's ultimate plan for the Realm; unless there was something he could do while each of his limbs was being carried off triumphantly by a different dog.

Rian squalled in his arms. Cuinn didn't dare spare a glance as he hurdled a watering trough set out for the cart-horses, but he was sure that perfect little face was screwed up like a monkey's and a brilliant shade of red. *Shit, could we possibly be any more obvious?* He had to get far enough ahead of the hounds to be able to spare the time to stop and Fade, and between the dogs and the brat, it was only a matter of time before the Royal Defense cut him off.

The rounded shape of a giant stone cistern loomed ahead of him.

I am fucking insane.

Cuinn leaped to the tongue of a wagon drawn up beside the cistern, and from there to the driver's seat. One more leap brought him teetering to the edge. His luck, such as it was, was holding; the basin had no cover, and it was nearly full. Looking down at the screaming baby, he clamped a hand over the tiny nose and mouth, drew a deep breath, and jumped into the dark water.

Fuck, I hope water kills magick-scent. Though it was a bit late for that particular concern. Rian kicked and wriggled in his arms as the two of them settled to the floor of the cistern. The instant his ass hit the stones, he reached within, found his magick, tapped it. One last Fade.

Water came along with the Loremaster and the infant Prince Royal, spilling away from where Cuinn sprawled on the floor, the baby still cradled against his chest. He heard a tiny cough, a gasp for air. A pause, as if to consider options. Then the caterwauling started up again.

Cuinn gritted his teeth and slowly, carefully, got to his feet. The black floor gleamed under him like polished crystal. No barbaric splendor of torchlight this time; the chamber was lit only by the moonlight from the single window over his head, and the silver-blue shimmering of the complex knotwork of lines under his dripping bare feet.

The lines changed, shifted into a shaping. *YOU'RE WET.*

"No shit." This was the only place in two worlds where he could talk directly to his fellow Loremasters, whose souls formed the matrix embedded in the Pattern. "The next time you decide a felony needs to be committed, you can fucking well do it yourselves. Or at least tell me if I need to bring drugged meat for the dogs."

The shaping under his feet ignored him entirely. Which was typical. *TIME IS SHORT. LEAVE THE CHILD AND GO.*

Rian was still crying, but the shrill, fingernails-down-chalkboard quality of most newborns —Fae or human —was gone. Babies this small were too young to weep, yet it seemed as if this one did.

But what the hell did he know about babies?

"You'll let me know where to find him on the other side?" Normally Cuinn didn't ask where a Fae was going, didn't really care. A lot of them didn't survive the transition. This one would —whenever the Pattern told him to get involved with a transition, the Fae involved lived through it —but there was usually no point to getting attached to a stray Fae. The infant Prince was making himself an exception, though, and the Pattern could usually find out if it tried.

NO. YOU MUST NOT KNOW. NEITHER CAN WE.

"*What?*" The edge to Cuinn's voice set Rian off again. "You expect me to just dump a newborn into the human world and walk away?"

YES. This shaping had the gentler curves that meant Aine had been delegated to handle the conversation. She was the one Loremaster who could usually get through to Cuinn. *YOU CANNOT TOUCH HIM, AND NEITHER CAN WE.*

"Why?" Cuinn was starting to get irritated. He wasn't going to lose sleep over this, given that even a newborn Fae would be immortal on the other side of

9

the Pattern, but was a straight answer every once in a while really too much to ask?

THIS IS A PART OF THE PLAN WE HAVE BEEN UNABLE TO FORESEE. The silver-blue light flickered, the Pattern's equivalent of a sigh. *YOU COULD REFUSE, OF COURSE. BUT IF YOU DO, YOU PUT AT RISK EVERYTHING WE HAVE ALL WORKED FOR. THAT MUCH, WE DO KNOW.*

Cuinn glanced involuntarily at the window. A shaft of moonlight shone in, the full moon nearly framed in the chamber's one tiny window. He had set this channeling up himself, twenty-three hundred years ago, his own little secret, a magick no one but him understood, creating a pathway between worlds that didn't draw on the Realm's ambient magick. All he had to do was put the baby on the floor in the path of the moonlight, and let the moon do its work.

Once again, Rian's crying was subsiding, though tears still spilled from the corners of his eyes. Cuinn couldn't shake the feeling that they were angry tears, and that those faceted blue eyes were glaring at him. *Shut up, conscience. This is not my fault.*

He shifted the little bundle in his arms. Paused, frowned, feeling something small and hard and heavy in the blanket that wrapped the little Prince, something that hadn't been there before. Peeling back the blanket, his brows arched at a glint of gold, the color visible even in the pure white moonlight. The color meant it was truegold, formed of magick and possessed of a purpose all its own.

He reached into the blanket and caught up the object, just enough to see what it was. The Royal signet, the stylized *Croí na Dóthan*, Heart of Flame, carved deeply into the flat surface. He'd be willing to swear it hadn't been there when he took the child. Obviously, it had decided to come along, for its own reasons. Cuinn hoped it hadn't just vanished off the Prince Consort's finger. At least, not while its owner had been looking.

NOW, CUINN. The shaping flared, almost as bright as the moonlight.

Cuinn growled in response, tucking the ring back into the blanket. Rian was still glaring at him, fair wing like brows drawn together into a scowl. "I'm not stealing the damned thing. I couldn't if I tried."

Two steps took him to stand in the path the moonlight was marking across the wet floor. He bent, set down the infant, and straightened.

Shit. The tiny chin was quivering, fists smaller than Cuinn's thumbs were flailing.

Cuinn looked down at the infant, surrounded by the intricate bluish-silver network of loops and whorls that made up the Pattern, and every single fucking memory he'd been trying to suppress since he Faded in here came back in a rush. Watching his best —his only — friend test the new-formed Pattern, only to be stuck halfway through, in utter agony. Testing it again, himself, after making changes to the channeling that powered it, and discovering that the agony was only slightly less when the damned thing worked the way it was supposed to. He'd had nightmares for months afterward, as had every Fae he'd ever seen pass screaming through the Pattern over the millennia since.

And he was going to do that to a baby?

GO. NOW. OR YOU WILL BE CAUGHT YOURSELF.

11

The circle of moonlight on the floor was brushing the finely stitched hem of the blanket that swaddled the Prince Royal. Around him, the floor was beginning to go transparent, the lines to brighten, to glint like the blades they were, keen enough to divide soul from soul. The baby stared up at him, now silent, his faceted eyes wide. Not pleading, it was as if he knew pleading would be useless.

Memorizing. Remembering.

Rian Aodán was about to take Cuinn an Dearmad's face to hell with him.

Cursing, Cuinn Faded, and found himself leaning against the outside wall of the little round tower he had built himself, over two thousand years ago. Unable to stop listening, he waited.

Wind howled within the tower.

The baby screamed. Cuinn flattened his hands over his ears, but it wasn't enough to stop the sound. Nothing could be worse than the uncomprehending terror in that sound.

Nothing, except the silence that came after.

Chapter One

Belfast
Present day

Rian rested his forehead against the rough wooden bench, taking a moment to catch his breath. The air he gasped in carried the scents you'd expect in a club like OTK, fags and sex and lube and blood. But there was more, and his fecking sensitive nose was just the one to be picking it up. Gunpowder, cordite, probably decades old. All buildings in Belfast of a certain age had probably been bombed, or used to store explosives, or both. Down here in the cellars, it was more likely the latter. And wasn't that fitting, a pyro such as himself, coming to a place like this to get what he needed?

Though he wasn't getting it so much of late. His man Feargal could usually be counted on for the pain, he was a good hand with a whip and sweet Jesus his cock was enough to make a man's arse scream for mercy. But lately the big Scot was beginning to show some reluctance. As did most of the men Rian went to, sooner or later. His appetite for pain was always greater than their ability, or inclination, to deliver.

"I said, knees apart, ye—"Feargal choked off whatever it was he'd been about to say, and settled for kicking Rian's knees further apart on the concrete. Fresh meat that came into OTK looking for the thrill of an S & M session usually got more verbal abuse than physical pain, at least until Feargal or one of his friends got their measure. Rian, though, had been straight up about what he wanted, needed, right from the start.

Hurt me. Don't you worry about how much, I'll heal.

He always did. Except for his mind, which kept getting madder and madder.

Feargal dropped to his knees behind Rian, grabbed the unruly forelock hanging in his eyes, and used it to haul his head back. Reflexively, Rian fought the pull, groaning as the bear yanked. And he groaned again, at the feel of the cock that fell into the crack of his ass, heavy and solid and all business. Being fucked by Feargal when he was in a mood was nearly as much pleasure as having a nightstick shoved up your arse. High praise, but the man deserved it.

"Having trouble getting it up, lad?" His voice was a little strained, from the strange position his head was in, but he could no more refrain from taunting Feargal than he could fly. In fact, given the fecking insane things that had been happening to him since last July, flying was probably more likely. "D'you need me to hold your wee ballbeg for you?"

"Is that what ye think ye're gettin'?" Feargal's laugh was short, harsh, and rough as black whiskers rasped against Rian's cheek. "Think again."

Rian gasped as two thick, blunt fingers invaded

14

his ass, then withdrew. Next time it was three, and out again. By the time four had worked their way in, Rian's arms were braced against the splintered bench, and his cock was as hard as iron in anticipation of what was coming next. Which just might be himself. His man Feargal had a massive fist.

By the time the Scot's thumb had joined its fellows, Rian was sweating. As the fist tightened, his thigh muscles started to shudder. And when that hairy, burly forearm started to disappear, sweet Jesus his arse screamed bloody fecking murder and his cock could have been used to hammer nails. "Oh, God." Short breaths tore out of his chest. "Oh, fuck yes. Yes. More."

Feargal grunted, and let go of Rian's hair to grip his shoulder. A bit of a disappointment, but Rian couldn't spare time to think about it just now, not when he couldn't fecking breathe and the beat in his cock put the Lambeg drums to shame. Sweat poured down his face, down his chest, over the trail of stars inked into his flesh that spiraled from shoulder to abs and pointed straight to his throbbing erection. In and out, slow and massive.

Rian's low moan felt like it started at his toes, and the burn was as close as one such as he was ever going to get to Heaven. Even better, this pain was touching the buried place that craved the hurt. He never knew when he'd catch that wave, what new or old torture would start that rush. This was going to be one of the magical times. Each slight movement of the clenched fist in his arse was bringing him closer, not to one release, but to two. Bliss, pure and uncut.

Until the movement stopped.

"Jesus feckin' Christ, finish what ye started!"

The response wasn't what he expected.

"Get that arm out of him unless you can live without it."

The voice was not Feargal's.

The strange thing started to happen again. The fire thing. Rian's hands were getting hot, and if he didn't make it stop, he'd soon be burning whatever he touched. Just like he'd torched the little chapel at the convent, the night Ma died, the night God had turned a deaf ear to his pleas. Only difference was, this time he welcomed the fire, and whoever had interrupted Feargal could have a flaming high colonic, courtesy of Rian Sheridan. He twisted around, feeling Feargal slip out of him but right now too pissed to do aught but grind his teeth at the loss.

Rian fell back against the bench. Standing just behind Feargal —*in a room that is feckin' well supposed to be locked*—was a man, all in black leather and chains, with sandy hair that fell in tangled waves almost to his shoulders, and a body to kill for. Pouting lips that were pure sex. Eyes so pale a green the color almost wasn't there at all.

He had never wanted a man more desperately in his life. All twenty-one years of it.

He didn't think he'd ever been more pissed off at one, either. "What the feck d'you think you're—"

"Fuck off, Sasquatch, he doesn't need you anymore." The other man ignored Rian, glaring at Feargal with something like murder in his eyes.

Feargal's brows drew together, both hands clenching into fists, and Rian held his breath. Close on to twenty stone of angry Scot could leave this cocky

16

son of a bitch using his last breath to call for an ambulance, and Rian wasn't entirely sure he wanted to see that.

The other man raised a hand and gestured. Rian's jaw dropped at the sight of the air around that hand starting to glow, with a kind of light he'd never seen before. The glowing air flowed from the man's hand to Feargal's mostly bald head and wrapped itself round it, settling into it somehow and disappearing.

Then, to Rian's continued astonishment, the frown vanished from Feargal's face like candyfloss when water melts it. The big man nodded placidly, got to his feet, unlocked the door, and let himself out, wedging the ill-fitting door back into its frame. Rian only managed to stop staring after him at the sound of the lock shooting home again from the outside.

He turned back to the intruder, the heat returning to his hands. "What the God-damned hell did you just—"

"Take it easy, *buchal dana*." The sandy-haired man waved Rian back and leaned against the far wall. He slouched, almost lazily, but Rian could see the pulse pounding in his throat, and there was sweat everywhere there wasn't leather. Belfast wasn't that hot in February, even here in the bowels of OTK. So the body language was a lie. Rian knew well when a man was near out of control, and that was precisely where this pure-sex-on-a-stick asshole was right now. "You and I don't need to worry about the door. Besides, we need some privacy."

"I was having exactly the privacy I wanted, before you barged in here." More than privacy, he'd been in the zone. Primed and ready, so close to the

17

sweet pain/pleasure he needed he had felt the tingle of it on his skin and the deep, visceral thrill of it in his sac. "And I don't quite understand why I'm not tying your nuts in a knot, now that I think on it."

The other man smirked. "That's your quality and good breeding showing."

Rian's lip curled in a snarl, even as he felt his nails cut into the palms of his hands. This *mac an striapaigh*, this son of a whore, had no way to know he'd been a foundling. "'*Sea*, my parents were good people. And my ma, at least, would be sore disappointed in me if she knew the joy I feel at the thought of sending you crawling out of here without your stones, to ask Feargal's pardon."

Part of Rian stood back, amazed, as anger fed anger, and the flames within him rose as high as those of any of the blazes he'd accidentally set, in the six months since his life had become a living hell complete with hell-fire. He still wanted this man, whoever he was, his cock was standing up like a feckin' flagpole and weeping for attention despite the interruption. Yet he growled, as viciously as any alley cur.

"*S'ocan*." The word sounded forced, reluctant, as if the speaker had wanted to say something else entirely. "That means 'peace,' as I'm sure you've forgotten by now."

"You might at least take the trouble to learn your Irish properly, asshole, it's *síochána*." Rian eased his way up onto the bench, trying to keep his gaze from traveling up and down the stranger's form, with a remarkable lack of success. A black leather harness hung with silver chains was the only thing that kept any part of an impossibly chiseled torso hidden from his view, and tight black leather trousers didn't do much more than that to hide a pair of thighs Rian would kill to have forcing his own apart. "And I've not forgotten it, it's just not a word I've much use for."

"Do tell, Highness."

Something snapped. Rian had his Irish from his Da, who had learned it shouted in defiance up and down the cruel corridors of the Maze, Long Kesh prison, and had passed on more than just the language to his only son. The only reason the son hadn't followed the father into the IRA was because the son considered the latter-day IRA unworthy of the name or the mission. And to mock a sworn enemy of the Crown with a royal title, when that sworn enemy was already pissed to the wide and looking for any good excuse? Very bad form.

His trouble had been keeping his curse at bay. Calling it up was no trouble at all. He surged to his feet, flame gloving his hand even before he formed a fist, and that fist was headed straight for the intruder's fecking smirk before the bastard could so much as twitch.

He'd been expecting the crunch of bones. He just hadn't expected them to be his own, as his fist smashed into an invisible wall inches from the other man's face.

"Not smart." The other man's pale green eyes rolled. "Although at least now I know for certain who you are."

Rian narrowed his eyes at the other man, as he licked the blood from his knuckles, and from the heavy gold ring on his fourth finger. Every now and then, his blood caught fire, and that was usually a bad thing. "Would you be after sharing that information?"

He hadn't meant to say that, but once it was out, he realized just how badly he wanted an answer. How badly he'd always wanted one, but especially since the curse had come on him. Even if the answer came from a fecking Loyalist ballroot who was, apparently, as bat-shite crazy as he himself was. And strangely familiar, come to think on it. No doubt from the kinds of dreams he woke from moaning.

The chains on the leather harness clinked as the fellow pushed himself away from the wall to stand toe to toe with Rian.

"You're the lost Prince Royal of the Demesne of Fire. Which makes you, by default, the ruler of all the Fae on this side of the Pattern. May the human gods help us all."

Chapter Two

Cuinn breathed a sigh of relief as Rian took a couple of hasty steps backward. He hadn't been able to breathe properly since he'd Faded into the dungeon. Though giving it that name dignified it more than it deserved. It didn't have a rack or a table or a cross or even the basic hardware for rope work. But its denizens obviously made do with what they had.

"You're madder than I am." Eyes of blue topaz glared at him, eyes that confirmed the male's identity as surely as did the Royal signet on the blazing hand the Prince Royal had just smashed into Cuinn's hasty shield. "Which is saying a great deal."

"It's possible." Cuinn took a slow, deep breath, and then another one. He was still shaking from the blast of testosterone that had nearly knocked him on his ass when he Faded in and saw the Fae Prince writhing with the pleasure of being fisted, and from the adrenalin jolt that had followed hard on its heels, as he realized why he had nearly murdered the human responsible on the spot.

Rian Aodán was his SoulShare.

Which was impossible. A Fae's soul was split in half when he went through the Pattern in order to let one half be reborn in a human. Because only a human could shield a Fae, to let him tap into the pure magickal power in the ley lines without getting fried like a bug in a zapper. Oh, and protect said Fae from the fuckery of the *Marfach*, the Fae race's exiled mortal and immortal enemy. Another Fae couldn't do any of that.

Yet he'd taken one look at the lust-crazed Prince, and instantly known that anyone other than himself who touched the younger male the way the balding bear was touching him was dead and simply didn't realize it yet. Which was absolutely fucking classic *scair-anam* behavior. That, and the fact that his cock was anxiously looking for a way out of his leathers. It didn't help that the Prince was sporting an impressive hard-on with no self-consciousness whatsoever.

"Just get the feck out of here." Shit, there were actually flames in the other Fae's eyes. Was his Royalty on display like this all the time? It couldn't be, the humans would have him locked up someplace. Or starring in his own reality show.

"How would you suggest I do that, with the door locked from the outside?" Cuinn's voice was actually hoarse, though Rian of course wouldn't know that.

"You had no trouble coming in when it was locked from the inside."

"True." Cuinn took a deep breath, trying to look like he wasn't taking a deep breath. Calm. Collected. When what he wanted to do was turn this male around, pin him to the wall, and finish what the Dom-for-rent had started, only with enough fireworks to make the Prince scream his name. "Name's Cuinn, by the way."

"Tell me, do I look like I give a shit?"

Most Irish thought the Belfast accent harsh. But even angry, Rian's voice was anything but harsh. Like silk. Silk wrapping itself around the increasingly urgent situation in his leathers. *Oh, fuck, listen to me. I'll be swooning next.* "If I go, how are you planning on getting out?"

The blue eyes narrowed. "I'll just call Feargal and have him come back and open the door."

"Which would be entirely reasonable, if you weren't standing here sporting a conspicuous lack of any place to be carrying a phone. Among other conspicuous things you're sporting."

The other Fae flushed at this. "Don't go flattering yourself, there's no cause."

Sure there isn't, scair-anam. *You're at least as ready to fuck or be fucked as I am.* "Suit yourself." He shrugged. "But you're not planning to call anyone, are you?"

"No idea what you mean, boyo."

Like hell you don't, you're sweating rivers. "I think you know perfectly well." Time to turn up the heat. "Let me see, you'd have turned 21 some time ago, yes? And chances are, a few strange things happened to you about that time. The Fire, for one." He nodded toward Rian's hand, still licked by a few lazy tongues of flame. "Though you could stand to learn some control."

Rian's already fair skin whitened by several shades. "You can be made to shut the feck up if you won't do it yourself."

"That already worked really well for you once, Highness." Cuinn shook his head, carefully ignoring the way Rian's teeth clenched at the honorific. "More to the immediate point, though, I'd imagine you disappeared at some point. Vanished from where you were, found yourself someplace else. Someplace you'd already been."

Cuinn would never have thought to imagine the sight of a Fae making the sign of the Cross, but this one was. With an unsteady hand, at that. "How do you know?" There was still nothing of trust in Rian's voice. But, then, he was Fae. Trust would be as alien a concept to him as to any other Fae.

How the hell are we supposed to Share? Something about that thought brought him up short. 'Supposed' was just the right word. 'Supposed,' as in intended. Which meant someone had intended it. Arranged it. His fellow Loremasters had *meant* for him to share the soul of another Fae. Not a human. Why?

No time for that. Bad enough he'd had a three-week time-slip coming back from his last trip to the Realm. Every minute he delayed was yet another minute the Realm decayed, and another minute in which the *Marfach* might figure out how to use the power Lochlann had been forced to give it. Of course, if it worked that out, it wouldn't matter if a little more of the Realm died in the interim, because it would *all* be dead as soon as the Fae's ancient enemy figured out how to reverse its own banishment.

"How? Same way I know why those busted knuckles of yours are already healing. Why you can take the kind of punishment your Neanderthal seems to like dishing out." *Time for a good guess.* "Why the Fire found you, and why it won't leave you alone." For any Fae, coming into the birthright of power around twenty-one years of age could be frightening.

And if there was no one to help them adjust to the new way of life created by free access to magick, and to guide them in their first use of that power? For a Royal, an elemental in Fae form? He'd never heard of one coming into the birthright alone. Royals were never alone. Unless they were being kidnapped.

"You're talking like it's alive." Almost no blue was visible around the darkness in the centers of Rian's eyes, and the flames within twisted as if in a wind.

"And you're talking like you wish it weren't."

"Son of a *bitch*." Rian swung around abruptly, his fist lashing out and smashing into the dungeon wall, this time. The truegold of his heavy ring skidded off the concrete and took no harm from it. In fact, it was the wall that ended up marked.

Once again, the other Fae licked away blood from his knuckles, and from the bits of white bone showing under the splits in the skin. His eyes glittered as they fixed on Cuinn's. "I actually prayed I'd gone mad, you know." Rian shook his hand, testing it, nodding as the cuts started to knit closed. "When it happened. It was the Twalf, do you know of it?"

Cuinn almost forgot to nod, he was so caught up in watching Rian. Fuck, the male was beautiful. Perfect. Thick, golden-blond hair worn short except for a long forelock, deep-set eyes, and full lips that absolutely begged to be wrapped around the erection Cuinn was fighting to subdue. Torso lean and hard, with the Prince's Pattern-mark in the form of a trail of stars, identical to those in a Royal's diadem of office, inked in silver-blue knotwork in a spiral that apparently started on one shoulder blade and ran around, under his arm, and down his abs, smaller and smaller until they disappeared into a dark-gold bush of hair. He yearned to take a razor to that bush, and discover whether the stars went all the way.

"Only a sick society marks hatred with its own holiday. The Glorious Twelfth, the triumph of William of Orange at the Battle of the Boyne, commemorated by the fecking Orange Order with kick-the-Pope bands and bonfires and gunfire and rioting amongst the Catholic neighborhoods every twelfth of July." Rian was still looking at Cuinn, but not seeing him. "Since I was old enough to walk, my da took me out, on the night of the Twalf, to throw my own wee stones at the sons of bitches when I was small, and to do more as I grew."

Cuinn nearly interrupted, but something in those faceted eyes told him it would be a very bad idea to do so. So he continued to look. To want.

"This last summer." Rian paused. His throat worked as he swallowed. "Da passed six years ago Christmas, they said it was his heart but it was his years in the Maze what did it. But even without him, I still went out, whenever I could but especially on the Twalf. And last summer..."

This silence went on so long, Cuinn felt it in his gut. "What happened?"

Rian shook his head. "The only thing what matters, that happened, was that I called down fire. That's what I thought happened, any road." The wide-eyed, staring expression was back, flames dancing in the depths of dark pools rimmed with blue. "At first I thought they'd built their fecking bonfire near explosives, or used petrol to make it burn hotter and the flame followed a trail back and exploded a canister. But that wasn't it at all. It was me."

"Oh fuck." Barely a breath.

"Fire everywhere, but none of it touched so much as a hair of my head. Five died, some further from the bonfire than I was. And me without a scratch, without a singe mark."

Cuinn nodded. "It's yours, it wouldn't harm you. But why did you do it?" Shit, if it had been truly spontaneous, nothing around the Prince Royal was safe. Including, possibly, himself.

The beautiful face shut down. Completely. "I've not even told my priest about that night, what the feck makes you think I'll tell you?" The voice was so cold, Cuinn was surprised he didn't see a rime of frost forming on the walls.

Since when does a Fae have a priest? Or a god? In the grip of an uncharacteristic spasm of good sense, Cuinn kept those questions to himself. This particular Fae had no idea what he was, after all. No doubt he had other human quirks of character, too. "Suit yourself. But I might be able to help."

"I'm not looking for help. Come to think on it, I wasn't looking at having my session with Feargal interrupted, either." The Fire in Rian's eyes had nothing whatsoever of warmth in it. "And for all you've promised me answers, all you seem to have are questions."

Cuinn opened his mouth to answer. Closed it again. For all Rian's youth, and the fact that he'd been raised a human and had no clue what a Fae was —nor any belief in the legitimacy of royalty, apparently — the fucking arrogance was every inch a Royal Fae.

And I thought Tiernan Guaire was a pain in the ass, and him just a Noble. Shit. "I don't recall *promising* you anything. I've already told you who and what you are. But if you're not interested in my help, then I'll be on my way, and good luck to you the next time that Fire gets away from you." *What am I, fucking insane? We need the smug son of a bitch in D.C.* Never mind what he himself needed, needed very much, in order to relieve his growing and deeply personal stress. But the Prince had gotten under his skin, and then some. "I'll keep an eye on the news to see what you blow up next."

Cuinn's Fade was stopped cold before it could properly start by Rian's hand gripping his bicep hard enough to bruise anyone but a Fae. There was no way he was going to find the inner equilibrium required to Fade, not when Rian was touching him. *I am so screwed.*

"Wait." The word sounded dragged out of the other Fae. "You were serious? You think I'm some sort of missing faery prince?" The last wisp of flame danced across the back of the hand that held on to Cuinn's arm, guttering out as they both stared at it.

"No, I don't think. I know." Shit, it felt as if live current was running through his arm. Elemental magick and pure magick didn't work and play well together, as Tiernan loved to complain; as a Noble, Tiernan preferred to channel elemental magick, the stuff of which Rian was made, but could handle the pure form in an emergency. Tiernan hated emergencies.

Cuinn was beginning to think that he hated them too. At least, he hated this one.

28

"Assuming I believe any of this, what do you want me to do?" Slowly, Rian let go of him and backed off a pace, his expression guarded.

"Why do you think I want you to do anything?" Was there a point to baiting the Royal? Hell, yes, there was. Those eyes were red hot fucking sexual when they flared in anger.

"If you're *not* wanting something after barging in on me as you did, then best you bend double and kiss your stones farewell." The tone was dry, but the eyes...

Cuinn swallowed hard as he realized just how badly he wanted the blue fury of those eyes taking in every inch of him. Preferably as Rian's head was twisted around to watch over his shoulder as Cuinn's cock pounded his ass until he screamed for mercy.

It was just too fucking bad that the fate of the world was going to have to take precedence over blowing his SoulShare's mind. For a little while, anyway. "Since I have things I'm planning on doing with those, you win, for now. You're right; I do have plans that involve you. You thought I was bullshitting you, I know, but that Flaming Fist of Death of yours ought to at least suggest to you that I'm right, and you aren't human."

"Let's pretend I'm not convinced yet." Rian's eyes gave nothing away. "Go on."

Cuinn shook his head. "You are one stubborn son of a suppurating bitch even for a Fae. Which is what you are. More than that, you're of Royal blood. Which makes you essentially a fire elemental. If you'd been raised in the Realm, you'd be the co-ruler of the Demesne of Fire, with your lovely mother the Queen." *Who would be skinning me alive and rolling me in salt if she knew what had happened to her son. Probably best to skip the 'how you got here' part of the story for now.* "As it is, you're the only Royal Fae in the human world. Which makes you the de facto ruler over all the Fae on this side of the Pattern."

"I know who my mother is." Rian spoke through clenched teeth. "She's been under the ground these past five months, and the best part of me went with her."

Cuinn stared in astonishment as a tear slid down Rian's face —a human tear, not a Fire Royal's flickering ember. *He has human tears, for someone who isn't related to him by blood, the* ceangail *ritual, or SoulSharing? This is one seriously fucked-up Fae. Just what we need.*

"If you don't mind, Highness, can we discuss that some other time? I'm under orders to bring you to meet your subjects. We're having a bit of a crisis at the moment."

Rian stared for so long, Cuinn was starting to wonder if he'd heard him. Then he shook himself, and the moment, whatever it was, was past. "Where are these supposed subjects of mine?"

Yeah, back to sitch normal. The other Fae's sarcasm was beginning to get to Cuinn. "All the ones I know of at the moment are in Washington, D.C."

"Not sure how I'll get there, I'm fresh out of fairy dust."

Mercurial moods and wiseass comments were all very well, Cuinn reflected. As long as they were his own. "Then keep your mouth shut and your eyes open, and let one of your elders do the heavy lifting."

"Elders?" Rian laughed shortly. "You're no older than I am."

30

"If you only had a clue."

"More mystery." Rian's voice dripped scorn.

"Allow me to clear some of that up for you, Highness." This was one of those moments when it would have been a good thing to have a god to pray to, in the hopes of having enough magick to pull this stunt off the only way he felt safe doing it. The thought of guiding a prickly Fire elemental through a Fade, to someplace said prickly elemental had never been before, just didn't appeal. *At least once this is done, maybe he'll shut the fuck up about not believing he's Fae.*

Cuinn grabbed the Prince by the elbow —*doesn't feel so much like a live wire this time, more like a really good vibrator* —and, before Rian could protest, reached within for magick and channeled a rift into the Realm.

"Oh, fuck me."

Cuinn was only slightly amused to hear Rian's voice echoing his own. No doubt the other Fae was stunned by his first glimpse in twenty-one years of the land of his birth. Cuinn, on the other hand, was stunned in a very different way. The rift opened into a gazebo, on an island in the middle of a large ornamental pond, the surface of which was covered with floating blooms the size of dinner plates, in a hundred different colors. A footpath wound past the pond. A footpath being walked by entirely too fucking many Fae.

A footpath that went straight to the single unhealthiest place in two worlds, for him at least. The Queen's Gate of the Royal Palace of the Demesne of Fire.

Rian's free hand sketched the sign of the Cross. "*Tá sé sin go hálainn.*"

Modern Irish sounded enough like *Faein* that Cuinn could guess that Rian was marveling at the beauty of what he saw. Cuinn didn't give a shit about the beauty, though; his mind was racing, weighing odds. Closing this rift and opening another would be a waste of magick, and replenishing once they were in the Realm would risk killing everything for a few hundred yards around. Using this rift, going through it, they'd be safe enough in the gazebo as long as they didn't move, the latticework of the sides would keep them hidden from anyone who wasn't actively looking for them. But he'd still have to absorb magick from his surroundings once they passed through if he was going to have enough to get the two of them safely back to D.C. and still be able to function once they got there. All of which would sure as hell attract attention. Not to mention the fact that opening a rift in the dead zone he'd create by drawing magick out of everything around him was undoubtedly a Very Bad Idea. So they'd have to move somewhere else. And Rian couldn't Fade anywhere in the Realm because he lacked the necessary personal knowledge of anywhere to Fade *to*.

All this passed through his mind in the space of a couple of heartbeats. Which still took too damned long. He could feel the magick flooding out of him, working to hold the rift open. "Shit." Gripping Rian's elbow more tightly, he shoved the younger Fae ahead of him through the rift, drawing it closed behind them so quickly he thought he left part of the heel of his shitkicker behind. *Could have been worse, I could have been barefoot.*

Rian was backed up against the elaborate scrollwork of the gazebo wall, trying to turn his head to see in every direction at once. "Don't move." Cuinn tried to keep his voice down to a hiss. It wasn't likely that there were any Air Fae around, not this close to the stronghold of Fire, but any Fae had hearing many times more acute than a human's. And the way his fucking luck was running, there would be an embassy visiting. Or a hostage exchange. "Don't move at all."

Rian looked pointedly down at Cuinn's hand on his arm. "I get the impression you're not all that welcome here."

"Got it in one, Sherlock. I'd call this an unfortunate accident, except I don't believe in accidents." Half his attention was turned inward, doing triage. The surge of magick within him was much weaker than it had been. Shit. This mode of travel wasn't designed for passengers, though he'd been forced to use it with Josh LaFontaine before. It was the only option he had left at this point. But it was expensive.

"Where are we?"

Cuinn decided to ignore the question. After all, anything he could say would sooner or later lead back to questions that would be even more awkward to answer. Instead, he concentrated on drawing magickal energy into himself, doing his best to pull it from the ground directly underneath his feet. If he could keep the rot, the death, that would follow after from taking over the whole island, they might make it out without being noticed.

Three things happened, more or less at once.

First, the wooden floor under their feet collapsed,

completely rotted away. Not so bad, the floor wasn't built up all that far off the ground, just enough to make the floor level.

The gazebo walls giving way and falling on them, though, topped off by the roof, that was a bitch.

Then, as the dust started to settle, Cuinn heard the shouts of startled Fae. And over that sound, the baying of hounds.

Chapter Three

Greenwich Village
New York City

"You are really boring the shit out of me, you know that?"

I told you before, this is necessary.

Janek rolled his one eye, before going back to staring at the floor. The same concrete floor the Marfach had been making him stare at for over an hour. No, asking him to stare at. It couldn't make him do jack any more, and it knew it. Which was sweet. And, at the same time, weirder than fuck.

Which pretty much described the last couple of days. Tiernan Guaire was still at the top of Janek O'Halloran's list of people whose throats he was looking forward to slitting, but the cocksucking twink Conall Dary was a close second. Being shredded down in the basement of the sex club he'd worked at while he was more alive had been bad enough, but what had happened to him in the boarded-up storefront, being sucked through a fucking straw —hearing in his head some priest from when he was a kid, droning on about "a camel through the eye of a needle" —and then

35

being blown back out of the straw into the master bathroom of Bryce Newhouse, prime grade A USDA approved asshole, had been worse, in a lot of ways. It had looked like Lochlann Doran doing it, pissed off after Janek had killed his pretty little dancer, but the *Marfach* told him there was no way Doran had that kind of power; it had to have been Dary somehow.

So Dary could die too. But Guaire was first. Even the *Marfach* had to accept that, if it wanted anything out of him. "You didn't tell me why."

He felt the female sigh. He irritated her. That was good. ***With Purgatory barred to us, we need a new source of power. Unless you would like to try your luck with the stairs again.***

Janek ground his teeth. "You don't want me doing that either. You squealed like a stuck pig." He actually knew what a stuck pig sounded like; he'd spent a summer on an uncle's farm in Iowa when he was a kid and listened to them butchering hogs, his idea of a good time even then. "This isn't going to do you any good. Whatever used to be here, it's stone cold dead now."

No deader than you are. Janek fucking hated the male voice. ***And you have what they call a vested interest in helping me find somewhere to plug in. Assuming you want what's left of your brain to keep working, and prefer not to rot. Doran may have pumped you up once, but it's not going to last indefinitely.***

"Fuck off." Janek looked up again, just to remind the motherfucker he could. The basement had been cleaned up after his rampage last summer, of course. Probably Newhouse. Although it could have been the dick on the second floor, the one with the Rottweiler he'd met the day after he and the *Marfach* had showed up here. He looked like another neat freak. Whatever. It was just another basement full of other people's shit.

The lines aren't dead, Meat. He didn't think the male knew how to talk without a load of bullshit coming along for the ride. Kind of like his late Uncle Art, who'd had his asshole-ish grin moved down to his throat and made permanent. He kind of wished he had that murder back, though. It had been his first, he'd been rushed, and he hadn't had time to enjoy it.

The male's voice jerked him out of pleasant memories. *They aren't dead. There's something between us and them, but underneath it, the lines are as strong as they ever were.*

"Something. Well, that's helpful as fuck."

The event we felt last summer was a powerful, uncontrolled magickal discharge. The female sounded like a college professor. Not that he'd ever been anywhere near a college. *I believe it altered this floor, and probably everything else between the floor and the lesser nexus. Not unlike what happens when lightning strikes sand and fuses the silica into glass.*

"If I wanted a lecture, I'd go dig up my old juvie probation officer and let you stick a piece of yourself in him." That was what the *Marfach* had done to enslave Bryce Newhouse. Well, 'enslave' wasn't the right word. Newhouse could make up his own mind about most things, even do pretty much whatever the fuck he wanted most of the time. But when the *Marfach* wanted him to do something, he did it. The dickhead was lucky the monster hadn't wanted much from him since then.

But now? Now Janek and his passenger had rent-free digs in Greenwich Village for as long as they were interested. Right on top of a power source that could keep him kind of alive indefinitely, except that Dary had fucked it up.

I am not interested in creating any other minions at the moment. The bitch sounded like she found the idea funny. *Although if you enjoyed carving a piece out of your face —*

"Don't get ideas." He still had the knife he'd used to cut living Stone, in a boot sheath. But the *Marfach* had told him what it was, a Fae dagger made specially to kill Fae, and now he was saving it for that. Not to mention that using it to cut a piece out of what was still kind of his own face had hurt like a son of a bitch.

As you wish. He could almost hear the female sniff. *It was not a pleasant experience for me either. And it should not be necessary.*

"You sound like you have a plan."

The beginning of one, now that I have had the opportunity to study the damage here.

Janek could feel the bitch lick her lips in anticipation. At least *his* tongue stayed where it was. Doran, or Dary, whichever it was, had done him a favor, at first, after the fun he'd had with Doran's little whore. The fucking Fae hadn't been able to heal the dancer without healing Janek too. Nothing could have made him any more alive than his passenger kept him, and he still looked like an extra from *The Walking Dead,* but he had the strength to fight back when it tried to take control of him. And his thoughts were his own. If the *Marfach* wanted anything out of him, it had to play nice.

"What's the plan? And how does it get me what I want?"

To say you have a one-track mind, Meat, would be stating the painfully obvious. After a pause, the female laughed.

Like trying to make a joke out of it is going to help you. "Maybe I do. Tough shit. Talk."

It was hard to tell which of them sighed. Maybe they all did. Well, the male and the female. No way did the obscenity sigh. He didn't think it breathed. It was the male who went on, though. *Maybe the bitch gave up.*

The cap over the lines here is the result of, well... call it a short circuit. Something interrupted the magick. The male laughed, and Janek got the impression that he was stroking a hard-on. Like that was anything new. *What do you suppose would happen if something similar happened down in the Fae orgy room under Purgatory?*

"Same thing, only a lot bigger." Janek shifted off his hands and knees, planting his ass on the cement floor. No more staring at the fucking floor. "I thought you needed that energy. It's not going to help either one of us if you can't get at it."

The male cackled. *Remember the power surge, when the nexus here was sealed?*

"No. I remember being down in the tunnel, with you bitching at me, and I remember waking up with my face in a puddle of piss. That's all I remember." He'd been going through the pockets of the security guard who had found him doing the *Marfach*'s dirty work in a subway maintenance tunnel, and who had pissed and shit himself after dying.

That was the shock wave from what happened here. The male groaned, in a pleasant, conversational way. ***Imagine what the shock wave from a short at Purgatory could do.***

"Probably kill me."

I would never let that happen, Meat. Oh, damn, the bitch was back. ***Remember, it was not pleasant for me, either. We will be far from any ley lines when I trigger the event.***

"But what's in it for you? And for me?"

At worst, it will merely render the Purgatory nexus inaccessible, just as this lesser one is. Which means the wards it powers will fall, and you will be free to hunt your prey.

"That's the worst? What's the best?"

The chill that ran through him told him the obscenity was out, even before its grating voice pierced his ears. ***The shock wave will shatter the barrier here. The living magick in your human body will convert the ley energy into more living magick, and I will feast.***

Then we will both hunt.

Chapter Four

The Realm
Outside the Queen's Gate, Palace of Fire

I really am barking mad.

Rian blinked blood out of his eyes and tried to push himself up to have a look around. The fancy scrollwork on the gazebo had looked flimsy enough, but apparently the verticals at the eight corners, not to mention the fecking roof, were made of sturdier stuff.

"Keep your head the fuck down," Cuinn hissed, yanking at the arm he still held.

"I hate to tell you this, but we're not exactly inconspicuous." Rian could see curious onlookers gathering around the edge of the pond.

"Doesn't mean we want them to see our faces." Cuinn moved experimentally, grimacing as beams failed to budge.

"You mean, you don't want them to see yours. I've never been here before."

"That's where you're wrong, Highness. And would you kindly put a sock in it while I work this out? We have exactly one shot at getting out of here before those hounds find us, and I don't dare spend magick to make it happen."

The baying he'd noticed in the background was growing louder. "I take it we don't want the dogs to find us?"

"Unless we want to be torn limb from limb by carnivorous hounds the size of stags who can follow our scents even when we Fade." There was a pause, as Cuinn tested the rubble again. "You might enjoy the experience, at that."

"I doubt it, 'twould be over too quickly. What exactly are you trying to do?"

"We have to get away from the dead zone I created when I drew magick out of the Realm. Recharged my batteries. Whatever. Which means getting out from under all this shit. And if I spend magick to clear it, I'll need to draw still more, I don't dare go home with less than a full supply."

"Is that all?" Rian laughed. He'd been told there was something wild about his laughter. Maybe it was because there was something not human about it. Any road, he'd had enough practice with his curse, or his madness, to do for the half-rotted ruins of the structure. He closed his eyes, focusing on the inhuman and implacable power that had wakened in him that twelfth of July. Coaxing it out, and setting it free to devour the remains of the gazebo.

"What the motherfornicating hell do you think you're doing, you crazy bastard?"

Rian opened his eyes. The fire was burning hot and fast, the embers were already beginning to crumble. But it burned only the wood, as that's what he'd created it to do. Cuinn was staring at him, wide-eyed, whites of his eyes showing all the way around widely dilated pupils.

He couldn't resist. "Don't be afraid, I'll not let it harm you, little one."

"Fuck you, Highness, and the horse you rode in on. Maybe *by* the horse you rode in on." Cuinn rose to his knees, drawing Rian up with him, bits of flaming wood falling away from them both —and froze. "Oh, shit."

Rian followed the line of his gaze, and felt his own blood turn to ice in his veins. Six dogs burst from a line of trees. Like Irish wolfhounds, only Cuinn's guess as to their size had been on the small side. These were the great hounds of Culainn, out of legend. On fecking steroids.

"Move your ass, Highness. And hold your breath, this time."

Cuinn's hand turned into the grip of a vise around his arm. Together, the two of them surged to their feet and made an ungraceful dive into the pond, Rian barely managing to fill his lungs first. He hated water. Always had.

A deeper darkness opened up in front of them, a tear in the cool darkness of the water. He thought he saw Cuinn gesture, and then the water seemed to come alive around the two of them. It wrapped around them, bound them together, and shoved them through the great fecking hole in the world.

***

Rian found himself sprawled on a black leather sofa, dripping wet, Cuinn on top of him. The lights were dim, but he could see other sofas, and lounges, and chairs, of the same sort, though there was a wavering barrier between himself and them. Most of the furniture was occupied, with couples and threesomes and more, twinks and bears and leather boys and drag queens and a few types he lacked the words for, men of every size and shape and age, far too busy with what they were doing to notice two Fae suddenly appearing in their midst.

Two Fae?

Well, maybe he'd try believing. For a while. It might turn out to be better than madness.

"Where the feck are we?"

Cuinn didn't answer, and Rian twisted his head around to see the sandy-haired Fae looking round intently, to all appearances ignoring him entirely. Finally, he nodded, and gestured, and the strange wall around them dissolved. Rian was immediately kicked in the gut by the sound of dubstep filling the air all around them. It was a *good* kick in the gut. Made even better by the erection he could feel pressing against the crack of his ass every time Cuinn shifted his weight.

Then the other man's whole weight was on him, as Cuinn leaned forward to put his lips next to Rian's ear. Even better. "We're in Purgatory."

"Not so sure about that." If he turned his head just a little, he could see a slight, dark-haired, heavily tattooed young man in a choke collar, on his knees going down on the guy who held his leash, a fellow who reminded him of Feargal, only with more hair on his head and slightly less on his chest. Rian had been something of a twink himself, back in the early days, and the sight warmed his heart. "It's about as close to

44

Heaven as I personally ever hope to get." He wriggled slightly under Cuinn, and hid a wicked smile as the other man groaned softly.

"The club Purgatory, your Royal Obtuseness." Rian felt Cuinn starting to push himself back up, but freezing the moment his hard-on ground deeper into the cleft between his, Rian's, buttocks. "I couldn't think of anywhere else on the spur of the moment where one male in leather and another in nothing but a fucking attitude problem would blend in."

"Are you certain that's the only reason you brought us here?" Jaysus, that leather covering Cuinn's groin felt good against his ass, and he arched his back concave and circled his hips to get himself some more of it.

"In your dreams." The voice so near his ear was tight, the breathing he could feel against his back rough. He could hear both, somehow, even over the pounding music.

"There hasn't been time for those yet, we've hardly met." *'Sea*, he was pissed at the Fae for interrupting his session, back in Belfast —wherever he was now, he was fecking sure it wasn't anywhere in Ireland, in the Six Counties or the Twenty-Six —but the best revenge wasn't to beat the other male bloody for it, or even to turn the fire loose on him.

Rian would make him burn.

"Don't flatter yourself, Highness, it's not becoming." For all the scorn in Cuinn's voice, he was slowly and deliberately settling his hips firmly against Rian's buttocks. Pumping in a steady rhythm, almost as if he were unaware of what he did.

It was a rush, to feel Cuinn's body taut and

trembling against his. More than a rush. Rian's heart raced with it, his cock pressed painfully into the leather sofa as it responded to the Fae's desire. There was something else, too, some sensation just out of reach, or as insubstantial as a ghost. Something that laughed, not with mockery, but with an unfamiliar joy.

Rian answered Cuinn's thrusts by rocking under him—the pond water slicking the leather, both above him and below, made the movement easier —and heard the hiss of an indrawn breath. He twisted around, glancing back over his shoulder at the Fae with the eyes of pale green jade. "Flattering myself, am I now?"

Cuinn's eyes narrowed. Wet hair fell forward, framing his face. High cheekbones, strong nose, pouting lips. Tongue tracing around those lips. "No answer?" Taking his weight on one elbow, Rian reached up and tangled his fingers in the chains hanging from the black leather harness Cuinn wore, drawing him down, until the other Fae's breath was hot against his lips. "I think you're fighting with yourself, boyo, to keep yourself from taking what you want. What you brought me here to take."

The sensual pout curled into a snarl. "When I decide to take what I want, *Highness*, you'll be the only one fighting—"

A blond head blocked out the overhead light.

"Not in the cock pit, Cuinn, I already have the Health Department on my ass and my insurance doesn't cover what an overstimulated Fire Royal can do to all this leather."

46

Chapter Five

"You are *so* fucking lucky I'm forbidden to kill a Fae." Cuinn could feel the magick thrumming in his hand as he brought it back down to his side, the magick he'd been about to use to stop the heart of whoever had interrupted him.

Tiernan, the bastard, didn't so much as twitch. "One of these days, I'm going to make you answer when I ask you just who has the balls to forbid you to do anything. But not right now." The blond wasn't really paying attention to Cuinn, his eyes were all for the naked Fae who moments earlier had been daring Cuinn to take what he wanted.

Daring him. Daring. *Him.*

Fuck, yes, he wanted Rian Aodán. Or whatever the hell the Prince Royal had been calling himself for the last 21 years. Wanted him badly enough he'd been ready to take him, give him exactly what he wanted without caring who saw. Though he'd paused, just for a heartbeat, as a shiver that wasn't cold, or even lust, ran through him. Delight. He shivered again, now, remembering it. Fucking addictive. He knew enough to know this was the *scair-anam* bond at work. Already. *Shit. I'm not ready.*

"You can quit staring now, your Lordship." *Or I can sandpaper your eyeballs*, he barely managed not to add. SoulShare jealousy. Which he needed right now like he needed a third testicle. In the middle of his forehead. "Lord Tiernan Guaire, of the Demesne of Earth, meet Rian Aodán, Prince Royal of the Demesne of Fire."

Rian's hand let go the chains dangling from Cuinn's harness. "What did you call me?" He was looking from Cuinn to Tiernan and back again, but mostly he was staring at Cuinn.

"Rian Aodán. As you haven't seen fit to introduce yourself yet, I used the name you were born with." Apparently, the Prince didn't give a shit how hard he was making it for Cuinn to hang on to even the tiniest shred of his self-control. Much less conceal the truth of things from Tiernan. Which it was important to do, for some reason, one which would presumably become clear in time.

"That's my name. Rian. But it's Rian Sheridan. Not Aodán." From the look of him, this correspondence ranked right up there with Cuinn tearing holes in the fabric of reality, when it came to persuading him of the truth.

Tiernan cocked a brow, the thin gold ring in it catching the track lighting. "If you weren't half blinding me with elemental light, Highness, I'd have a hard time believing you were Fae."

"Which would be fine with me. I'm not half convinced of it myself."

Rian's weight shifted under Cuinn, as if the Prince wanted to sit up. Cuinn weighed the distraction already being caused by the Royal's perfectly rounded ass against the distraction which would likely be occasioned by a clear view of his undoubtedly erect cock and his eight-pack, groaned softly, and moved to let him. "Oh, he's Fae. Trust me." Cuinn sucked in a breath as Rian's long legs swung down and all of him came into view, including the visible end of the trail of silver-blue stars slanting across his abs. *Motherfucker*.

"If you think you can convince me I should start trusting you now, I'm all ears."

"On second thought, you have enough bad habits already; I don't think I should be giving you another one."

Rian sat stone-still, only his eyes moving, his gaze flickering back and forth between Cuinn and Tiernan like a flame in the wind. Belatedly, Cuinn threw a silence back up around them —so far, the conversation had been quiet enough that only a Fae's keen hearing could have made it out over the pounding music, but there was no telling what the Royal who wasn't entirely convinced he even *was* a Fae might do next.

Is he feeling this too? Not just the arousal, but the jealousy, the SoulShare joy? The young Prince's face wasn't readable. Cuinn hoped his wasn't either, because his thoughts at present weren't any he could share with anyone.

Why did the Pattern pair me with another Fae, instead of a human? He didn't think his fellow Loremasters predetermined every pairing, but he also knew damned well they arranged some of them. No fucking way would they have left the Royal's SoulShare to chance.

Or mine. Cuinn tried to ignore that thought. It had

an uncomfortable End Times vibe. His own end. It was sure as shit no coincidence he'd been sent to fetch the Prince just as the grand endgame commenced, the endgame he'd been promised a part in. The Realm was dying, starved of magick. Somehow, he and Rian were part of the Pattern's response.

Which meant he wasn't going to do a fornicating thing about bonding with the Royal until he'd figured out what the fuck his fellow Loremasters were playing at. Even if that meant he was signing up for the worst case of blue balls in Fae or human history.

Tiernan's snicker snapped Cuinn out of his reverie. "You'd think you'd never seen a naked Fae before."

"Oh, was I staring? Pardon me." Hell, yes, he'd been staring. He'd have to be dead three days, *not* to stare at the Royal. The silver-blue trail of stars alone was like a fucking magnet. Cuinn could see himself, outlining each star with his tongue, as Rian writhed under him, begging. He could almost taste them.

He was doing one fucking lousy job of not getting any closer to Sharing with the cocky bastard.

"Don't stop, I like it." Rian's smirk made Cuinn's cock press against the zipper of his leathers with a whole new urgency.

Cuinn gritted his teeth and turned away. Tiernan, too, was smirking, but at least he could be sure the Noble wasn't bent on seduction. Not unless it involved Tiernan's own husband and SoulShare. "Don't encourage him, your Grace. He's not quite housebroken."

Tiernan, like Cuinn, ignored Rian's laughter. "He's *rachtanai*, that's what he is."

"Addicted?" Cuinn frowned. Human drugs generally did little or nothing for Fae, though he'd known Fae to use for a quick thrill; the only things that could be counted on to fuck up a Fae were alcohol and honey. "To what?"

"To the thrill of the cock-tease." Tiernan shook his head in response to Cuinn's wordless skepticism. "Remember the old stories, about how we used to toy with humans, drive them mad?"

"Not so old, I've started a few of those myself over the centuries."

Tiernan was perfectly happy to ignore him, too. "Turns out leading other Fae, or humans, around by the gonads gives some Fae a genuine rush. And that rush can be addictive if it's overindulged." He nodded toward Rian. "I think your boy there has about a three-BJ-a-day habit."

"He's not 'my' anything." *Which is a fucking lie.*

"Am I not?" There was a strange, hot glitter in Rian's brilliant blue eyes, but Cuinn only got a glimpse of it before that gaze went wandering around the cock pit. Purgatory was known for the best dance floor, and the hottest pole dancers, in Washington, D.C., and possibly on the entire Eastern seaboard, but it was also known for its sybaritic lounge, a sunken pit filled with leather furniture, which was usually itself filled with men doing just about everything two or more men might enjoy doing to one another. "Maybe I should be about sampling a bit of this intriguing night life, then." He started to rise from the sofa, his heated gaze already fixed on three heavily pierced young males lost in a passionate circle jerk.

"In your fucking dreams." Miraculously, Cuinn

kept his voice almost even. Only his magick betrayed his jealous fury, lashing out and freezing the Prince half-risen. In several senses.

"You might want to consider letting him breathe." Tiernan eyed the younger male speculatively.

"In a minute." Cuinn took a slow, deep breath of his own, fighting for calm. Fighting the impulse to blind everyone in the motherfucking room. "Is the vacant apartment upstairs ready for our Royal guest?"

"No, I've been sitting here with my thumb up my ass for the last two days. Of course it's ready." Tiernan's measuring gaze was on Cuinn, now. "What's going on?"

"Nothing." Cuinn felt his face heating. Apparently his poker face only worked while playing poker. "Our Prince just needs to learn a little maturity."

"And you're the perfect one to teach him."

"Are you that anxious to learn how long you can hold your breath?"

Tiernan scoffed. But at the same time, he took a step back. "Tell you what, you let him go and I'll take him upstairs. If he really is *rachtanai*, I'm pretty sure I'm immune to his charms."

No shit. The human undoubtedly waiting in Tiernan's bed was the perfect antidote to the kind of games Rian apparently liked to play. However, he was such solely for Tiernan. Kevin Almstead was Tiernan's *scair-anam* and husband, and anyone giving the dark-haired, dark-eyed human more than an appreciative glance would face the considerable wrath of a Noble Fae.

Not to mention the fact that ever since Cuinn had

followed the Pattern's directions and Faded into the makeshift dungeon under Belfast city, thoughts of anyone other than the infuriating Prince Royal did nothing for him. But the male he was bound to was addicted to making men lust after him. *If the other Loremasters planned it this way, n'anamacha do n-oí gan derea.* Their souls to the eternal fucking night in truth. Of course, they were most of the way there already.

"Yeah, you do that." Cuinn nodded at Tiernan and released the magick, without looking at Rian. He heard the Prince's gasps for air as he staggered the rest of the way to his feet, though. *Damn. I want him to sound like that because I've made him come so hard he can't breathe, not because I've had to put him in a time-out.*

"Give me just one good reason why I should go with him, instead of torching you where you stand."

Cuinn's head jerked around as if Rian had him by the hair. The scorching sexuality of the Prince Royal's anger left him feeling as if all the oxygen had been sucked out of the air around him. But apart from the heat of his gaze, Rian's expression was so cold it practically smoked.

Cuinn's mouth opened. For maybe the first time in his very long life, nothing came out.

"First you barge in on what I had every right to expect was an intensely private moment, with not so much as a 'pardon me,' and with not a thought as to the importance of what you were interrupting."

Shit, even from here he could see the flames in the younger male's eyes.

"Then you haul my arse half way round the

world, pausing only long enough to drop a fecking house on my head and half drown me. And then you suffocate me. *After* letting me know —and not even to my face —that I'm nothing to you."

"That wasn't what I—"Cuinn's voice stuck in his throat, to his utter astonishment. Turning the Elementals into the Fae's rulers might have been solely an exercise in keeping the bloodlines pure, but nobody had ever told the Royals that. And somewhere in the last twenty-three hundred years, they'd obviously started taking their role seriously. Seriously enough for it to have been bred into Rian Aodán's very bones. *Fuck me backwards.*

Rian's glare froze Cuinn where he stood. It also made him hard enough to carve granite. Not that the Royal apparently gave a shit about either. He faced Tiernan, with a slight turn of his shoulder that was more of a dismissal than Cuinn had ever received from anyone who had lived through the experience. "I'll go with you, then. Provided the accommodations are private." Somehow, his voice sent a needle straight between Cuinn's eyeballs, even though the words weren't directed at him. "And I'm hoping there's a chance of obtaining clothing, as I was taken too quickly to collect my own."

"You're close enough to my size, I think we can make something work." *Burned*, the look Tiernan shot Cuinn over the Prince's shoulder said. Yet it seemed there was something of sympathy in that gaze. In addition, of course, to the innocently malicious enjoyment to be had from watching the Loremaster get smacked down. "Come on, Highness, I'll get you settled in." Again the strange look at Cuinn, before he turned and started to make his way through the crowded pit.

Rian didn't even glance back. Just followed, with as much dignity as he'd have if he were clad in royal scarlet instead of naked as the day he was born.

Naked as the day I sieved him through the Pattern.

Cuinn sat down heavily, letting the silence he'd thrown up around the three of them fall and wincing as the bass beat pushed at his eardrums. *What the hell good does it do me to have a Fae as a* scair-anam? He tipped his head back against the back of the sofa, closed his eyes, and rested a forearm over them. *The whole point of having SoulShares in the first place was to shield the Fae from the motherhumping* Marfach. *Human nature is impervious to it, at least when the Sharing goes the way it's supposed to.* The flaw in Tiernan and Kevin's bonding had given the monster a foothold in the human's psyche, and had nearly destroyed both of them.

Every bonding was flawed in some way, too. Which gave him *so* much confidence in the Pattern's crack-brained scheme to pair him with another Fae. Tiernan and Kevin's flaw had been Tiernan's refusal to love. Josh and Conall's, Conall's loss of the ability to channel, and having that ability forced on Josh.

Lochlann and Garrett's, that one had been harder to figure out. He'd finally had to resort to picking Lochlann's brain —carefully, it would be all kinds of clusterfuck if any of the other Fae ever found out the extent to which they were all experimental subjects under observation. Fortunately, he'd regained most of his former friendship with the healer, any other Fae

55

would have told him and his questions to fuck off. The two of them eventually figured out the imbalance; it was nothing less than life itself. Lochlann had too much of it; he'd been the first Fae through the Pattern, and had wandered the human world until he'd lost his magick and the only thing keeping him alive was the Pattern's gift of immortality until SoulSharing. Garrett, Purgatory's star pole-dancer, had too much death. Not only was the dancer HIV-positive, but his virus had mutated just before he met Lochlann, into full-blown AIDS that resisted every combination of medications. He was certain the Pattern had had some hand in that, since Garrett's illness had forced Lochlann to risk his own life, interacting directly with the ley energy that had once fueled the Realm, and channel more magick than a Fae should ever have been able to handle —

Cuinn sat bolt upright, staring at nothing. What was it Aine had told him about Lochlann? He'd asked her, asked all of them, why it was so important for him to sit back and observe while his friend —the only real friend he'd ever had —risked death to save his SoulShare. He'd demanded to know why it was so important for the Loremasters in the Pattern to know how much magick Lochlann could channel, what his limits were, how far a Fae could be stretched before he broke. *Why the hell do you need to know that?*

And her reply?

WE DO NOT. YOU DO.

He was completely, epically, fucking screwed.

Chapter Six

"Look, just let me get my husband on the phone, will you?"

The detective sighed. "You don't need your lawyer; it's not that kind of visit."

Tiernan ignored the man, calling up Kevin's office number and hitting the button, wandering away and trying to make it look like he hadn't heard, and was checking the stock behind the bar. No way he was letting Vice into his office. "Come on, come on, pick up."

"What is it, *lanan?*"

The Fae groaned. His *scair-anam*'s tone was the near-whisper that told him he'd interrupted a meeting. *Shit.* "I need you here. Now."

"Can't. Conflict conference. I can't talk about it until the meeting's over."

"I love it when you talk dirty."

"What's going on?"

"Detective Harding is here. He says he's not here to cite the club, but after the night I had, I'm not sure I could deal with him if all he was doing was selling Girl Scout cookies." Dealing with a naked *rachtanai* Royal had turned out to be the least of his problems, the Prince had calmed down quickly enough once he was out of the club. Getting Cuinn down off the pole he'd found him clinging to when he got back downstairs, without resorting to some very unsubtle magick, had been another story. And he'd had to call Lochlann in to sober the bastard up enough to Fade home. *I am so fucking locking up every drop of Tennessee Honey in the bar.*

"I'm sorry. Really. I'd come if I could." His husband usually dealt with the D.C. cops on his behalf, or more precisely, on behalf of the club. You couldn't run a club like Purgatory without constantly riding the ragged edge of being busted, and Tiernan knew that if they had to rely on his diplomatic skills to stay open, well, there would be a lot of dancers and bartenders and rent-boys looking for work. Not to mention an undefended ley nexus under the basement floor.

"Yeah, I know you would. Wish me luck."

"You don't need it. Detective Harding might, though." A soft chuckle. "I'll call you when I'm done here, *lanan.*"

Tiernan stared at the phone in his gloved hand for a few seconds before sliding it into a hip pocket and walking back down the length of the bar to the lone occupied stool. Detective Russ Harding looked more like a cop from a strip show than a typical police detective, with his short reddish-brown hair, dimples, ready smile, linebacker shoulders, and what Tiernan freely admitted was a marvelous ass. But the human was most definitely all vice squad, and his smile camouflaged a relentless sense of duty; he'd come close to shutting Purgatory down three times in the nine months or so since Tiernan had taken it over.

Twice over drugs and once over an asshole trying to go into business for himself, using the bar as his base of operations to arrange hookups between customers and underage boys. Tiernan had actually stolen a march on Vice with respect to that particular piece of shit, and still wished the detective had left the business for him to finish. *Some things were simpler in the Realm.*

"Sorry about that." Tiernan put on the best smile he could muster. "What can I do for you?"

The human shook his head. "I told you, no need to call your lawyer." Reaching into the front of his coat, he pulled out a couple of folded sheets of paper stapled together and slid them across the bar. "I was just passing by, and saw this stuck on your front door. Thought I'd see if you were in yet."

Tiernan picked up the paper, turned it so it was right side up.

NOTICE OF HEALTH INSPECTION
WEEK OF MARCH 18, 2013

By the time he trusted himself to speak again, he'd mentally run through his alphabetical list of human deities all the way down to Ganesh, lingering over Beelzebub and Belial. "Son of a *bitch*, I thought we'd cleared this up."

"Mind my asking what's going on?" Detective Harding studied him, head tilted slightly. "You run a remarkably clean place, given all the shit I know goes on in here."

"You're far too kind." Tiernan glared at the papers, wishing his trace of Fire blood was enough to let him torch them with a look. *Damn. Less than two weeks.*

A raised brow was all the answer he got; the detective was in a very small class of humans who weren't impressed by his moods. He sighed, and chose his words as carefully as he could. "We've been having issues with customers passing out. Not many, and it's not alcohol, and it's not drugs, unless they're coming in the door drunk or high. But a few have complained, so now I have a health inspector riding my ass."

Detective Harding's mouth opened, closed again firmly.

"Good man." *Don't make me hurt a lawman. Though that would certainly be the crap icing on the shit cake.*

"Maybe I'll get to work before I get myself in trouble." The human slid off the barstool and headed for the heavy black glass double doors; stopped in the act of reaching for the handle, and turned back. "By the way, I'm ignoring the indignant phone call we got last night from a customer at the ATM across the street. She said there was a naked blond walking around outside. But I know you know better than to let the nudity hit the street. Cheers."

Tiernan cursed under his breath, *as 'Faein,* as the door swung shut. *Fucking Royal, making a point. Should have made one of my own.*

The sound of footsteps on the stairs faded, and as soon as they were gone, Tiernan hauled the phone out again, calling up a different number.

"Conall? Tiernan."

"I'm busy." The voice on the other end of the phone was breathless, and Tiernan heard low laughter in the background.

"No. Really? What was I thinking? After all, it's—"He checked the phone's display. "9:22 in the morning. Of course you're busy." Tiernan snorted, he couldn't help it. "And listen very carefully; this is the sound of me not giving a shit. Make your *scair-anam* untie you, I need your ass down here in Purgatory five minutes ago." He regretted his choice of words the instant he touched the phone off; if any Fae was capable of time travel, it was the master mage.

"How did you know he had me tied up?"

The voice came from behind him, and Tiernan turned, rolling his eyes at the still mostly-erect mage, in the act of belting an obviously hastily-donned silk robe. "Give me some credit, will you? You keep leaving your toys in the nexus chamber. Besides, you still have rope burns. But that's beside the point." He held out the folded papers to the other Fae. "I need to know what you've figured out about our little problem. Now would be excellent."

Conall glanced at the papers briefly before tossing them on the bar. "You want the short form first? My hunch was right."

Tiernan's brows shot up. "The one about magickal sensitivity?"

"Your powers of memory are really phenomenal. Do you do children's parties?" Conall perched on a bar stool, chafing his wrists and looking as out of place as usual. Purgatory was probably the only bar that didn't card the three-hundred-year-old Fae, and that was only because all the bartenders knew him and had seen the fake I.D proclaiming him to be twenty-two.

"Spare me. I have to keep the Health Department out of here, or we risk losing access to the nexus."

He'd lain awake too many mornings of late, running through disaster readiness scenarios in his head. "You and I and Lochlann could Fade in to get at the nexus even if they boarded the place up, but that doesn't get any of us very far without our *scair-anaim*."

"You're babbling." Conall propped his chin on his hand, making him look even younger than he'd looked a minute ago.

"I've thought about fuck-all else for the last week, it has to go somewhere." Tiernan drummed his gloved fingers on the bar.

"The Health Department really cares that much about a few people passing out on the club stairs?" Conall quirked one ginger brow. "You'd think they'd expect that to happen from time to time."

"They care when one of the fainting flowers is the barely legal son of a member of a diplomatic mission from one of those countries where the kid would be welcomed home into a prison cell or a pine box if word got out he'd been here." Tiernan grimaced. "Talk to me. What the hell is going on, and how do we stop it?"

"I noticed that everyone who was passing out did it in exactly the same place, five steps down from street level. That's where the inner ward intersects with the stairs, it's as small a sphere as can contain the nexus, the main door here, and Josh's tattoo studio upstairs."

Another freakish phenomenon associated with the nexus —Josh LaFontaine could channel magick on a subconscious level, at least while he was inking. And his ink tended to come alive in the presence of concentrations of magick. Good thing the piercings the

62

human did didn't behave the same way, Tiernan didn't want to think about what would happen to his Prince Albert every time he climaxed. "Please do continue, I have the entire fucking day to sit here and listen to you."

Conall, unperturbed, rearranged the folds of his robe, taking his time about it while Tiernan tried not to grind his teeth together. "Some humans, not many, have at least a rudimentary sensitivity to magick. Their bodies tend not to handle it well. Josh is an exception, at least up to a point, but as far as I can tell, that's because he has a Fae soul."

"They react when they pass through the ward."

"Brilliant, Watson."

"Nice accent. But you don't look anything like Benedict Cumberbatch, so don't even try." *I swear by the first thirteen gods on my list, I'm cancelling the dish subscription for this building.* "What do we do, then? We can't take down the ward; the *Marfach* will shuffle in here and use the nexus to blow the Pattern all to hell."

"Not to mention, its meat wagon will be carrying your head around by the hair," Conall supplied helpfully.

"Your confidence in my fighting skills is touching." Tiernan's gaze strayed to the black doors, as if he could see through them and up the stairs to that problematic fifth step from the top.

Conall, too, studied the door, but more cheerfully. "I think I know how to handle it. I'd been meaning to re-work the wards anyway. I've been thinking about the wards around the Pattern, back in the Realm, and I think I can replicate a few of them, turned outward instead of inward. Not to mention that I've done two different kinds of banishings now on the *Marfach* and its host. I know it, them, a lot better than I want to. I'm sure I can set up a ward specific to them."

Tiernan's initial rush of enthusiasm quickly self-smothered. "We have Newhouse to worry about, too, if you and Josh are right and he's under the influence."

"Shit." The red-haired mage didn't swear often, and when he did, Tiernan found his precision and vehemence funny. "I don't know him nearly as well. Though I've met him a few times. The bit of the *Marfach* in him ought to respond to the same warding pattern as the mother ship, though..." His voice trailed off; his faceted peridot eyes stared at nothing in particular as his long-fingered hands started sketching bits of patterns in the air.

"You make me twitch when you do that."

"I need to work out the channeling."

"Do you need to do it right here?"

"Fine." Conall shot him a glare. "I'll just go back upstairs. Where I won't get *any* work done."

"You are such a fucking horndog. And you have to let Josh open up the studio."

"I stopped denying that a while ago, I think. And I'm perfectly capable of walking down a flight of stairs." Slowly, Conall started to Fade. "Hopefully I'll have something worked out by close of business tonight. Try not to need my help until then."

"I'll do my best to keep things together without you." No way of knowing if the other Fae heard the snark, of course, as he was gone by the time Tiernan finished.

He shrugged, and started for his office, through

the cock pit. Which didn't really look all that much different in the light of day, since no light of day ever made it down this far. He ascended the few steps back up to floor level.

Frowned, at the light spilling out from under his door.

No one had asked him, last night, why he had come out of his office just as Cuinn and Rian arrived. Normally, a Noble saw mostly elemental magickal force, which meant that only a fraction of the awesome raw power of the ley lines that met almost directly under his office was visible to him. But last night...

Last night there had been a surge of pure proto-magickal energy like nothing he had ever seen in his tenure as the guardian of the nexus. A herald of the Royal arrival.

They'd thought the nexus was overwhelming before? The fucker was just waking up.

Chapter Seven

Rian groaned, turning his face to the mattress and groping about for a pillow to cover his head. Jet lag was a right sac-twister, and no mistake. If you could call it jet lag when there had been no aircraft involved, only an obscenely hot man who hauled you off into another world and turned the one you thought was your birthright on its head.

I'm no Fae. I know who I am. Who my people are. He didn't have to close his eyes to see his father, or at least his father as he'd been in years past, aged early by his years in Long Kesh prison and what he'd seen there, but still with a ready smile for the girl he'd loved beyond reason and the son he'd cherished. Or his mother, her heart broken from losing her husband, his body ravaged by the blanket protest and hunger strike from which he'd never fully recovered, and then losing her only child, bitter and vengeful, to the streets of Belfast. Small wonder she'd gone off to the convent in Ardoyne, and taken the veil. Perhaps if he'd been able to find the same solace in the cloth, a similar strength, his own life would have been something else entirely.

But there was no going back to those days of

simple faith and love of family. No wishful thinking, either. He'd known he was a foundling, his parents had told him as soon as he was old enough to take proper care of the ring they had found with him, tucked into his swaddling clothes. The knowing had frightened him at first; he'd had nightmares of shadowy figures coming to take him back, and of Ma and Da hauling him down the street by the arm, looking for the one who'd left him so they could give him back. He woke from those dreams sobbing, but always in the arms of his Ma, or his Da, or both, held and rocked and loved and reassured. *You're the child of our hearts*, Ma had sung, like a lullaby. Over and over, until the melody of the words had found its way into his own heart.

But he'd watched them both die, Da collapsed on the kitchen floor and Ma gone from the cancer, and now he was of no one's heart. He was not even human.

He gave up on trying to sleep, rolling onto his back and sprawling out in the great bed fit for a king. Or a Prince. *Shite*. He didn't want to be a fecking Royal. Whatever that meant. But if there was one thing he could say he'd learned in life, it was that what he wanted had fuck all to do with what happened to him.

Though ever since the Twalf, last summer, there was one thing he nearly always got, when he wanted it. The thrill. They'd thought to break him that night, and perhaps they had, but after the breaking he'd been made anew. Into a man who craved what the bastards sought to shame him with, and who used them, in the end, more cruelly than they had used him. After all, he could use them, and others like them, any time he liked.

Addicted? Hell, no. Victorious.

"Oh, shit."

Rian kept himself from jumping, but only just, and his eyes narrowed as he rolled to face Cuinn. The Fae was no longer in leather and chains —*pity, that* — but even in jeans and a Muse t-shirt his lazy sensuality reached from the doorway all the way across the room and grabbed Rian by the balls.

"And a pleasant good morning to you, too. Or is it afternoon?"

"Fuck if I know, Highness. Time does weird things when you can't sleep." Cuinn leaned against the doorjamb, one hip jutting out in a very 'do me' kind of way. "And I was trying for the living room."

"Is that an apology?" Rian stretched, slowly, thoroughly, then rolled to lie on his stomach, facing the Fae in the doorway, propped on his elbows. Cuinn's gaze met his, then swept on, over the stars on his shoulder blade, down his back, and couldn't he just feel those eyes sizing up his arse?

Cuinn shrugged, but the movement was tight, and Rian didn't bother trying to hide his grin. "If you think you need one. Damn, you're distracting."

"Am I, now? That's something of a change of tune from yesterday." Rian worked his hips against the mattress, needing to ease some tension of his own, as well as to cause more for Cuinn.

To his astonishment, Cuinn turned red. "I assume you're referring to my telling Tiernan you weren't mine. What I meant was that I don't control you."

"You could if you wanted to." Rian was practically purring, reveling in what he sensed from the other Fae. "If you like that sort of thing."

"Son of a *bitch*." Cuinn's hands clenched into fists, and though he didn't otherwise move a muscle, his sexy slouch was anything but lazy, it was movement just barely arrested. But whether that movement was to take him or flee from him, Rian had no idea.

He knew which he wanted it to be, though. He'd slept like the dead, the night and morning just past, but dreams like the ones he'd had of Cuinn lingered in the body as well as the mind, and he could no more forget them than forget his own name.

"Why are you fighting me?" Rian's voice was barely above a whisper, and hoarse with the intensity of a need he didn't fully understand. From the first sound of the Fae's voice, shattering all hope of attaining the fragile peace he'd been so close to finding at Feargal's hands, his anger at the cocky bastard had never cooled. Not even as he slept. But the anger was like petrol on a fire of another sort entirely, hotter than he'd ever known. "You don't want to fight me. I know you don't. So do you."

"Shut the fuck up, before I do something—"

"We'll both regret?" Rian's laughter was light, brittle. "You know better than that. I'll not regret it." Sweet Jesus, the heat in those pale green eyes. "I promise to make sure you don't either."

"You have no idea what you're playing with, Highness." Cuinn crossed his arms over his chest, as if trying to hold himself together. Or hold himself back.

"Please do explain." No man he'd ever teased had wanted him more, he was sure of it. Sure because he'd never wanted any man more, himself. There had been no point to looking at the others last night in Purgatory, no point at all to making them want him, except to fan Cuinn's flames higher.

Sweat beaded on Cuinn's upper lip and gleamed

69

on the muscles of his arms. "There's a power higher than either one of us. It's been using every Fae to come through the Pattern for over two thousand years, and now it's gaming us. Both of us." For all his square-jawed resolve, his eyes never stopped roaming Rian's body. "It wants me to do exactly what you're trying to make me do. And I don't know why."

Rian's eyes narrowed. "Well, fuck that." He could feel the hairs rising along his forearms, the way they did sometimes before the fire came. *Higher power, my arse. Anything comes between me and what I need, we'll see how well it burns.* "Do you want me, or do you not?"

"Oh, I want you." A muscle twitched in Cuinn's jaw. "But on my own terms. Not on theirs. And I don't know what theirs are yet."

Something twisted, heart-deep. There was something Cuinn wanted more than he wanted Rian. Jealousy was hotter than fire, and so was anger, and so was thwarted need. There were forms of pain he sought out, pain that satisfied a deep wordless craving in his soul. But not this kind of pain. The pain of not mattering.

Rian rolled and stood, reaching for the shirt Tiernan had left over a chair for him the night before. The fit was snug; he had an inch or two in height on the club owner and was slightly broader across the chest, but so much the better, for his purposes.

"Think you're going somewhere?" Cuinn didn't so much as twitch. But his gaze raked over the tight-fitting shirt, as if he could see through it. Maybe he could.

"'*Sea*, I do." Standing as he was, and faced with a male putting out sexuality he could all but feel against

70

his skin, Rian had a great need to adjust himself. So he did, and took his time about it. "You interrupted something yesterday, in case you've forgotten. Something I was enjoying a great deal. And all this talk of wanting and taking has me of a mind to finish what Feargal started. With someone who doesn't let some mysterious Higher Power lead him around by the balls."

"Sit back down." Cuinn's voice was low, even, quiet. Charged with hunger so raw, it was all Rian could do not to groan.

"I think not." Rian took a deep breath and started for the doorway. "You've chosen not to control me, so live with your choice."

Cuinn slammed Rian into the wall beside the door so hard there were white flashes at the edges of his vision. Before he could so much as shake his head to clear it, the Fae's hand was fisted in his shirt and he was being kissed. Kissed? Ravaged. The kiss was punishing, he could feel his lips swelling already. Cuinn snarled, his tongue forcing bruised lips apart; he stepped in, his hard-muscled thigh forcing Rian's apart, his body pinning Rian against the wall. Rian was taller, broader, and it didn't matter a damn.

A Mháthair Dé... Though the Mother of God was probably politely averting her eyes, as Her wayward child's knees threatened to buckle and his cock went instantly rigid. He gripped Cuinn's shoulders, as much to stay upright as to pull the Fae closer, and groaned wrenchingly into the kiss when his fingers barely dented the hard muscles.

Laughter, deep in his soul. Joy. A taste only, but so rich and pure, his eyes swam with tears of flame.

Cuinn shoved himself back, away from Rian, his

pale eyes wild. His chest heaved with each gasping breath, his hands trembled uncontrollably. "You're insane. And you're fucking contagious."

"*Cuinn—*"

Rian had no idea what he wanted to say, but that didn't matter, as he had no chance to speak. The Fae fixed him with a glare, nearly bringing him to completion on the instant.

"If you go down to Purgatory, I swear to you on my own beating heart that any man there who touches you will be dead by sunrise tomorrow."

Cuinn was gone, faded to a pale wash of himself in one instant and vanished utterly the next.

Insane. He continued to stare at the place where Cuinn had been, fingertips lightly touching his tender, swollen lips. *I am that. Or I soon will be.*

Rian stretched out once again on the bed, unfastening the borrowed jeans and groaning with relief as his tortured cock sprang free. He hardly ever needed to pleasure himself, he could always find someone willing to give him that, and in a manner more to his liking, edged with the sweetness of pain. But the memory of Cuinn's kiss would give him no rest. His hand flew, wringing his dark-veined shaft, and his hips bucked.

It was Cuinn's name he screamed, as white fire spurted in thick jets from his pulsing cock, sending up tendrils of smoke where it touched his borrowed shirt, but none from his flesh.

Blessed relief. Slowly, his hard-arched back relaxed, as the flames flickered and died.

Relief, but no joy. No laughter.

So in the end, it was naught, really.

Chapter Eight

Cuinn was only mildly amused to find himself taking form in his shower. *I don't need a cold shower, I need a fucking lobotomy.*

Had he really threatened to kill any male who laid a hand on the Mad Prince? Yes, he had. He'd meant every word, too, at the time. He stalked into his bedroom, crossing to the bedside table where he'd left his iPad, feeling the fumes of madness clearing from his head as he went. Maybe not quite madness, not in the diagnostic sense of the word. But Rian was most definitely addicted. *Rachtanai.* It figured, sometime in the last twenty-three hundred years, Fae had learned how to get hooked on driving others insane with lust. *How the hell did I miss that happening?*

More importantly, how did he stop it happening to him? He shared a soul with Rian, though how the merry hell *that* occurred was still an open question. One among many he intended to have answered. And judging from his reaction to the Prince Royal, at least some of Rian's addiction was communicable, probably through the SoulShare bond. *So here I sit, hard as iron and complaining about being addicted to sex. Karma is a bitch.*

Cuinn grabbed his iPad and touched it on, dropping to the bed with a groan. There was a down side to communicating with the Loremasters in the Pattern this way, instead of in one of his books, of course —the shapings didn't stay in the pad's memory. But, then, if he went back to a prior discussion captured on paper in order to make a point, his colleagues generally caused it to vanish in a fit of collective pique anyway.

The swirling grey surface of his contact interface of choice beckoned. Or maybe it threatened. How to get his fellow Loremasters' attention? They'd been known to leave him hanging fire for days, and he wasn't in the mood for that shit, to put it mildly.

The shaping he ended up tracing with a fingertip was a simple one. *D'aos'Faein* script had no letters; each phrase, each thought was a piece of knotwork, with its meaning conveyed in its elaborate loops and angles. Humans thought it looked Celtic, or sometimes tribal; Josh, the tattoo artist, complained that it kept changing from one to the other. This particular phrase, though, was less intricate than most, and in fact bore a striking resemblance to an upraised middle finger.

I QUIT.

The screen blinked. Blinked again. *IMPOSSIBLE.*

Cuinn rolled onto his stomach, grimacing as he caught himself grinding his hips into the mattress, exactly the way Rian had done. Probably for the same reason, too. He couldn't stop seeing the Prince Royal's eyes. Mouth. Extremely grabbable hair. Perfect ass. *Down, Cuinn. Bad Fae. IMPOSSIBLE? I'LL TELL YOU WHAT'S IMPOSSIBLE. EXPECTING ME TO PLAY ANY PART IN YOUR GRAND DESIGN WITH*

A CRAZY FAE FOR A SCAIR-ANAM. *THAT'S IMPOSSIBLE.* Each iteration of "impossible" was drawn with a heavier hand, until the silver-blue lines started to blur together.

More blinks. Cuinn pictured the disembodied souls of the Loremasters who had survived the last battle with the *Marfach*, reduced to brilliant lines of magick in the Pattern, arguing about what to say to their delinquent and pissed-off colleague. *RIAN AODÁN IS NOT INSANE. YET.*

YET. Cuinn traced sarcastically over the end of the Pattern's shaping. *I AM SO FUCKING FILLED WITH CONFIDENCE.*

The lines shifted again, this time into Aine's gentler configuration. *HAVE FAITH IN HIM, CUINN. HE IS STRONGER THAN YOU REALIZE.*

I already know how strong he is. Cuinn had heard the young Prince describe the terror of being reborn in Fire on what was surely the occasion of his coming into his birthright of power, alone and unguided and unaware of what he was. And he'd been stricken to his core, in Purgatory, when Rian had responded to his jealousy by wrapping all the anger and authority of a Royal around his nakedness like a cloak and smacking him down hard enough to leave him sleepless for a night. His colleagues in the Pattern had no need to know about any of that, though. *THAT'S NOT THE FRICKING ISSUE. HE'S A FAE. HOW THE HELL AM I SUPPOSED TO MAKE USE OF THE LEY ENERGY WITHOUT A HUMAN BUFFER?*

Instead of vanishing, his shaping wavered, as if seen through rippling water, and slowly dissolved. *They're playing for time.* No wonder. The energy in the ley lines wasn't magick, in the same way crude oil wasn't gasoline. If ley energy were to run directly through the body of an unprepared Fae, said Fae would, unless obscenely lucky, be smoked from the inside out, nothing left but a sparkling blot of grease. Protection from that sort of fate was what a *scair-anam* was for. Once a Fae and his human were Shared, half the Fae's soul was safely housed in a human body, insulating the Fae and letting him convert the ley energy into living magick.

Joy, bliss, laughter, love? Those were side effects of Sharing. Nothing more. What other use could they have?

Silver-blue lines sketched themselves slowly across the screen. *THIS FAE IS AS HUMAN AS WE COULD ARRANGE FOR HIM TO BE.*

Now it was Cuinn's turn to go still and silent and considerably less horny. He'd had his suspicions for a while on the subject of 'arranging'. He'd been allowed to believe, originally, that the mechanism by which a Fae's soul was divided, and half of it sent out into space and time to be reborn in a human, was wholly random. He'd seen the Sundering with his own eyes; he knew what the endgame of the battle against the *Marfach* had cost. It had taken almost everything the Fae Loremasters had, to divide the magickal Realm from the non-magickal world it had been part of from the beginning, defeat the *Marfach*, exile it to where it theoretically could do no harm and would hopefully starve its malevolent self to death without living magick to feed off of, establish the Pattern to bar its way back, and set up the system of *scair-anaim* to protect traveling Fae. There had been nothing left, or so he had been told, to enable any further fine-tuning of the process. No way to control a Fae's destination, or to influence the human who received the severed half of the Fae's soul.

Trouble was, that had been bullshit. He'd first suspected it when the Fae mage Conall Dary had been thrown, literally, at his human SoulShare's feet, during the Pride march in New York City last summer. The flaw in the Pattern caused by his absence from it had played a role in other aspects of that particular clusterfuck, too. But despite the flaw, the Pattern had managed to target Conall's arrival precisely.

Then there had been the matter of Garrett Templar, Lochlann Doran's human *scair-anam*. Garrett had been HIV-positive for years before meeting Lochlann, but it wasn't until just before he and Lochlann had met that the infection had gone wildfire. Which, in turn, had been what drove Lochlann to such insane lengths to get his magick back. His former colleagues had a certain amount of control even over a human, provided that human had a Fae soul.

Now, if he'd understood correctly, the Pattern had arranged for the infant Royal to be raised as human. In a loving family, from what little Rian had mentioned. Which would be little more than a touching moment on the Lifetime channel, if not for the fact that the humanity the Pattern begged, borrowed, or stole for Rian was eventually going to be the only thing standing between Cuinn and spending eternity as a stain on the floor of Purgatory's basement.

IT STILL DOESN'T MAKE SENSE. Another drawback to using the iPad to communicate was the lack of a stylus to chew on while he tried to get his thoughts in order. *I LOST HALF OF MY SOUL TWO THOUSAND YEARS AGO. THAT HALF WAS SUPPOSED TO GO TO MY SOULSHARE. BUT THE PRINCE WENT THROUGH THE PATTERN TOO. SO WAS HIS HALF DIVIDED IN HALF? WITH HALF COMING BACK TO ME?*

A bright flash cut him off, like a throat being cleared. *RIAN HAD NO SOUL WHEN YOU LEFT HIM ON THE PATTERN. HE RECEIVED HIS HALF OF YOUR SHARED SOUL WHEN HE TRANSITIONED.*

Cuinn took a deep breath and made himself forget, once again, what it had felt like to abandon an infant to the merciless mercies of the Pattern. *THAT'S BOGUS. I WAS AT HIS ENSOULING CEREMONY, THE MORNING BEFORE I KIDNAPPED HIM.*

BOGUS? The design rippled with quiet laughter. *YOU EXPAND MY VOCABULARY EVERY TIME WE SPEAK. THE TIME OF HIS CEREMONY REFLECTED CUSTOM AND CONVENIENCE. NOT THE ACTUAL HOUR OF HIS BIRTH OR THE TIME OF HIS ENSOULING.*

Well, butter my ass and call me the life of the party. WHY DIDN'T YOU TELL ME?

Another one of those long pauses. *YOU MIGHT HAVE DEDUCED THE CONNECTION BETWEEN YOU, IF WE HAD.*

Which, of course, completely justified lying to him. No Fae would give a second thought to that kind of deception.

No Fae but a SoulShare.

What else had they manipulated? *DID YOU ARRANGE FOR HIS ADDICTION?* Cuinn's hand was shaking, a little; it was hard to get the curves of the shaping right. No infant should have had to suffer what the Loremasters made him put Rian through. If they'd fucked with his head into the bargain, well, that was just one more reason to quit.

IT WAS NECESSARY. TO BE SURE YOU SHARED.

BULLSHIT.

TRUTH. Aine's hand, or whatever she was using to shape, was steadier than his own was. *WE KNOW THERE IS AN ATTRACTION BETWEEN FAE AND HUMAN SCAIR-ANAIM. BUT HUMANS ARE NORMALLY CAPABLE OF SUCH, AND MAYHAP THEY BRING ENOUGH ATTRACTION TO THE PAIRING FOR BOTH. PERHAPS YOU WOULD HAVE WANTED EACH OTHER WITHOUT THE ADDICTION. BUT TOO MUCH IS RIDING ON THIS FOR US TO TRUST TO 'PERHAPS'.*

Cuinn's lip curled in a half-hearted snarl. *DID IT EVER OCCUR TO YOU TO JUST ASK?*

TRUTHFULLY? NO. There was no trace of angularity to Aine's shaping now. *YOUR SHARING IS ONE PART OF WHAT YOU MUST DISCOVER ON YOUR OWN.*

There it was, the eight-hundred-pound gorilla in the middle of the room. Everything the Loremasters had been working toward since the worlds were sundered was riding on him and Rian, somehow. *TELL ME AGAIN WHY YOU CAN'T TELL ME WHAT IT IS I'M SUPPOSED TO DO.*

He could have sworn he heard the iPad sigh. *IF WE SIMPLY TOLD YOU TO PLAY YOUR PART, YOU WOULD RESIST. THAT IS YOUR NATURE. IT MUST BE YOUR OWN IDEA, YOUR OWN WILL.*

Cuinn blanked the screen, ready to shape an angry retort. He had been furious, over two thousand years ago, when the other Loremasters had told him their plans had been made, and that he was the only one of their number who would not become part of the Pattern. They'd needed him there, with them —the fact that his soul, his name, was missing from the Pattern had damaged every pairing of SoulShares, and for all he knew it had fucked up every Fae who came through the Pattern, before they ever had a chance to Share. Maybe killed some of them. But the others had been adamant. They'd told him his role was still ahead of him, and his task was to learn for himself what that role was.

His task. Like a schoolboy.

Like a good boy, he'd followed orders —mostly —for all the time between the battle and today. He'd helped or sent or shanghaied other Fae through the Pattern, sometimes observing them on the human side, refraining from assisting them even when it tore what passed for his heart out to watch what happened to them. All right, he'd really only given a shit what happened to a transitioned Fae once. But that was bad enough. And now they thought he was ready to throw it all away? In a fit of temper?

No. Not in a fit of temper.

I'M NOT DOING A FUCKING THING UNTIL I'M SURE MY SCAIR-ANAM *WON'T BE HARMED.*

There followed another long silence. On both ends of the conversation. Cuinn, for his part, was trying to figure out what he'd just said, and what he'd meant by it. *Am I ready to let two millennia of planning go to hell, risk letting the Realm itself die, all for the sake of a sex-crazed Prince? Who I haven't even Shared with yet?*

Maybe.

When the shaping resumed from the other side, Aine's graceful curves were nowhere in sight. *THE ROYAL MUST NOT BE HARMED. HIS STRENGTH IS ESSENTIAL TO WHAT YOU MUST DO.*

YOU'LL FORGIVE ME IF I RESERVE JUDGMENT AS TO YOUR INTENTIONS, I HOPE. Cuinn's fingers flew with minimal input from his brain; sarcasm was a well-honed reflex by now, and he had other things to be thinking about. Such as the first clue the other Loremasters had let slip in over two thousand years.

He needed Rian's strength in order to do whatever it was he was supposed to do. What kind of strength? Not physical, that didn't make sense. He hadn't been waiting twenty-three hundred years for someone to fetch and carry for him.

OUR FORGIVENESS HAS MEANT VERY LITTLE TO YOU, OVER THE CENTURIES. WHY SHOULD IT MATTER NOW?

Cuinn's mind raced.

YOU COULD STAND TO GET THE METAPHORICAL STICKS OUT OF YOUR METAPHORICAL ASSES. He sketched quickly, barely seeing what he shaped.

What strength did he need?

His *scair-anam* was his safety, in dealing with the ley energy. *Shit.*

YOU ARE HARDLY IN A POSITION TO BE CRITICAL OF US.

If Rian could function the same way a human

could, Cuinn could finally replenish his magick from the ley nexus. But it wasn't just *his* magick that needed replenishing. Memories of the blackened scar in the Realm, the rot he'd caused under the gazebo on the Fire island, reminded him of the stakes in the game he and the Pattern played. On the same side, though. He hoped.

WHAT'S THIS 'YOU' AND 'US'? I THOUGHT WE WERE ALL ONE BIG HAPPY FAMILY. Except without having the inconvenience of having to give an actual damn about one another, the way Fae family did.

Maybe this *wasn't* the first clue. What was it Aine had said to shut him down, when he'd wanted to help Lochlann rescue Garrett from the *Marfach?* Something about channeling —

The fucking computer queeped at him. *Low battery. Shit.* The other down side to this means of communication was that it was a total power suck.

The other Loremasters hadn't yet dignified his last retort with a reply. No doubt they were chattering among themselves, raising their virtual eyebrows at his attitude problem. Maybe he'd spoken truer than he realized. He'd called these Fae colleagues, a few thousand years ago. But apart from Aine, and a few others, his only contact with them in all that time had been receiving the marching orders they gave him.

Now they pulled the strings and expected him to dance.

Casting about in vain for a good parting shot, he settled for simply switching off the iPad. He tossed it aside and faceplanted on the soft pillow with a grimace.

Was he still a colleague? Or just one more tool?

Even if he was a tool, if he worked out what he was for, and if it made sense, his lack of choice in the matter wouldn't stop him from doing what had to be done to save the Realm. They'd been wrong about that.

But if they were fucking with Rian, or if what they planned would hurt him, their tool would turn in their hand. And it would cut deeply.

Chapter Nine

Greenwich Village
New York, New York

How long are you planning on torturing me with that vile mucus?

"How long do you have?" Janek grinned as he dug a spoon into the thimble-sized carton of yogurt. He still couldn't taste the shit, and probably never would be able to, but at least he could get the lids off the damned things and use utensils. So he had to hold the spoon like a knife and stab with it. Big hairy fucking deal. All the better to piss off his passenger.

Fascinating. The female sounded anything but fascinated. ***You manage to make me wish I still had direct control over that bloated appendage you call a hand.***

"On the rag today, Princess?" Janek licked the spoon, sticking his tongue out far enough that he could see the grey of it. Grey was not a good color for a tongue. But at least it wasn't rotting any more. It didn't really take much to make him what passed for happy, these days.

The *Marfach* fumed silently. Janek lurched to his

feet and made his way through the living room to the kitchen, where he pitched the mostly empty carton in the direction of the sink and yanked open the refrigerator door. Rows of Corona longnecks filled almost all the shelves. He could usually get the caps off those, and it hadn't taken Newhouse long to learn to keep the fridge stocked properly. Longnecks and those orange Jamaican meat pies that had fuck all to do with Jamaica, and if there was any meat in them it had either neighed or barked when it was alive, but he could almost taste something when he ate them, so it was all good. Newhouse's sushi shit had been gone five minutes after Janek had hauled his ass out of the shower, and his passenger made damn sure it never came back. Even a zombie had to have some standards.

Grabbing a bottle, he twisted the cap off, sucking down half the bottle as he watched the little cuts in his palm bleed. Whatever healing he'd gotten from Lochlann Doran was long gone by now. He was as close to healthy as a mostly dead person could be, but that was as good as it was going to get. Still, he supposed the Fae prick had done him a favor. There was a chance his brain was working better now than it had when he was alive. Maybe he'd thank Doran for that. After he killed him.

A key turned in one lock, then another, and finally the third. The front door to the apartment swung open, and in walked Bryce Newhouse, wearing a designer coat, two-thousand-dollar suit, and a shitload of attitude.

Newhouse glared, first at him, then at the bottle in his hand, and finally at the open refrigerator door. "Mind closing that, Stretch?" Janek's unusual appearance didn't faze the investment banker, because the *Marfach* continually told him he wasn't fucking fazed. Whatever the *Marfach* thought, the tiny sliver of it Janek had helped it bury in Newhouse's gut made sure Newhouse thought the same.

"Mind fucking yourself?" Janek gestured with the neck of the bottle.

The *Marfach* sighed. ***Every time you do that, I have to spend magick to make him forget about it.***

Maybe if he remembered it, he wouldn't be such an irritating little shit all the time. It took some effort, but Janek switched to commenting in his head. He'd finally figured out how to force his thoughts into the monster, and pissing it off by talking to it took a back seat to avoiding stupid-ass questions when Newhouse was around.

You might have a point, Meat. Janek felt the male part of the monster in his head giving its balls a good, thoughtful scratch as Newhouse's eyes unfocused. ***Some other time, though. Right now, I need to talk to you.***

You couldn't have done that while we were alone?

You were... eating.

Janek could feel the monster shudder, and he grinned. He had a shitload of payback to unload, and there wasn't anything the motherhumping *Marfach* could do about it. Not if it wanted him to take it where it needed to go, do what it needed done, kill who it wanted killed. *So talk.*

Bryce continued past him, into the living room. A paper bag rustled, and Janek craned his neck to look through the pass-through. Chinese take-out again.

Sometimes the bastard complained about all the take-out food he had to suck down. That was just more tough shit, of course. Janek needed the refrigerator kept full of beer and yogurt, and watching the prick try to cook from scratch was more annoyance than he needed.

I've been thinking. About how to reopen the lesser nexus in the basement. Janek wished to hell the male would quit scratching. *I keep running into one problem. And I think you and I need to negotiate.*

Janek growled and reached into the fridge for another Corona. *You might have better luck with begging.*

You might wish to be more civil. Ah, shit, the bitch was back. *Without me, you will be unable to obtain what you desire. Assuming you still want Guaire's head, that is.*

His upper lip curled. Probably showing off a mouthful of rotten teeth. Which he didn't care about either, now that he'd been healed, but his breath had been so foul before that he'd actually given himself away to a couple of his victims by the smell. Chasing them down had been a pain in the ass. *You know I do.*

Then listen.

Janek twisted the cap off his second beer and stifled a groan as the bitch shifted into lecture mode.

I believe I've deduced what happened to the lesser nexus in the basement of this building. The voice was smug, satisfied. Janek wished the monster had a face to stomp. Other than his own. *Tell me, when Guaire attacked you with his living Stone, was he sexually aroused?*

Janek snorted, not caring if Newhouse wondered what the fuck was going on. *Are you shitting me? He and Almstead had been up to something before I got there; I had to pull Almstead off him. But Guaire's dick was as limp as a wet rag, and it didn't turn him on to wake up to see me holding a knife on his sugar daddy.*

As I suspected. Janek wasn't sure, but he thought the bitch was smiling. He preferred smug. ***Even in the time before I was banished, a Fae's magick was strongest when he was aroused. Fae mages such as Conall Dary even channel accidentally when aroused. I believe direct contact with ley energy is harmful for a Fae, unless the Fae is aroused.***

Not that I want you to keep talking, but what the hell does that have to do with what happened to the nexus here? His beer was getting warm. Janek grimaced and slammed the rest down.

You test my patience, Meat. The female sniffed. ***The contact is harmful for the nexus as well. I felt a power surge just before Guaire attacked you, and rode the surge out of the ley lines and into the Stone Guaire created from it. I believe the nexus here was also disrupted by a Fae.***

Janek stopped in the act of reaching for the refrigerator door. *You think you can make it happen again. This time at the great nexus.*

Clever boy.

Good thing it couldn't control him anymore, it would probably be patting him on the head if it had the use of his hands. *You're going to somehow force a Fae who isn't sexed up to touch the great nexus? They've turned the fucking basement into an orgy room. And I don't think we're lucky enough that the wards will short out a second time to let us in there in the first place.*

This does pose certain logistical difficulties.

Janek didn't like the silence, it felt like the female was thinking. Since she was the smartest of the three that was usually bad news for him. *You seem to have become something of a strategist. You had no such aptitude before being healed.*

You think I planned for that to happen? If Janek could have sweated, he would. He needed the monster in his head in order to get what he wanted —the bleeding head of Tiernan Guaire —but he also hated it. Was at war with it. He wasn't going to forget a year of being forced to live while being allowed to rot, and being treated like shit while it was happening. But the monster had shown him what it had done to its enemies, back when it was free. And it only made sense it would do the same, or worse, to him, once it had gotten what it needed out of him, especially if he pissed it off enough. He had to stay on its good side, until he had what he wanted and could either kill it or die clean.

Hardly. The bitch was laughing now. *Even assuming you have the intelligence and foresight for that now, you certainly lacked them then. I am simply surprised.*

Janek could feel one bitch-kitty of a headache building up right between his eyes. He'd been pushing his thoughts on the monster too long already, and it wasn't any closer to telling him what it was thinking than it had been when Newhouse walked in. *Just keep talking. If you have anything to say. I'll just sit here and suck it all up.* He yanked open the refrigerator. Maybe another Corona would help the headache.

Poor Meat. The female's voice oozed like a festering sore. Which was something he knew way too fucking much about. *Very well. Your points are both*

89

good ones. It is probably impossible to force an unaroused Fae to touch the nexus. Our best weapons, the human SoulShares, are undoubtedly guarded by now from physical attack as well as from assault from within. We had only one chance to take them by surprise, and you wasted it.

I did my fucking part. Janek grunted at what felt like an ice pick between his eyeballs. *I got your Fae alone and I made him give you what you wanted.* The cap to this bottle wouldn't give. Snarling, he smashed the neck against the kitchen counter, then sucked down a few swallows of painkiller. The glass shards weren't anything to worry about. Not like they were going to kill him or something. *You were the one who lost control of him. Not me.*

"I'm not cleaning that up!" Newhouse sounded pissed. But he didn't sound like he was getting up or planning to do anything about anything, either.

"Ask me if I give a shit." It felt good to use his voice, and even better to bitch out Pencil Dick. Especially when the monster in his head shut the fucker down hard before he could reply.

You may regret forcing me to waste magick on him, someday.

I doubt that. Janek poured most of the rest of the beer down his throat. *You said you had a plan. Talk about it.*

After a pause, it was the male who came back, and Janek didn't bother hiding his grin. Getting under the bitch's stony skin was one of the few real pleasures he had. **We need another way to disrupt the great nexus. Cause a power surge that will come back up the ley lines and blow the cap off the lesser nexus in the**

basement. Janek felt phantom fingers on his scalp, the prick checking for head lice, or whatever the things were that crawled through his dreads when he was male. Good thing he wasn't checking for crabs. *Or it'll blow the hell out of the protective wards they have up.*

How are we going to do that? Janek wondered if zombies could get migraines.

The male laughed. *Killing a Fae while he's in contact with the nexus should do nicely.*

Holy shit.

Exactly. The murder of a Fae who has all the power of the great nexus running through him ought to be all the disruption we could ever wish for. Though how we're going to do that, when we can't get anywhere near the nexus, and all the Fae and their pet humans probably have Dary on speed dial, is something I haven't worked out yet.

Janek rubbed the spot between his eyes. So what do you need to negotiate with me?

I require your patience. A commodity which is in very short supply of late. The male wasn't laughing any more, he was as deadly serious as Janek had ever heard him. *If this plan succeeds fully, you will want to go straight to Purgatory, for Guaire's head. But if this nexus opens back up, you have to bring me here first, to let me feed.*

Janek's stomach twisted and he knew the obscenity was going to speak by the way he felt even colder inside than being dead made him.

You have one Fae to slaughter. I have a world of them.

Chapter Ten

Washington, D.C.

"Still no fecking knock?"

I need a god to swear to. Or at least one to curse for my fucking wretched luck and aim. It was almost totally dark in the bed- room, and even Fae eyes needed a moment to adapt to the faint glow that made it through the curtain sheers. Moonlight and garish lights from the shops across the street showed Cuinn a bedroom that hadn't changed much since he'd had the good sense to get the hell out. In fact, the only thing different was the Prince himself. Formerly sprawled on top of the four-poster in nothing but jeans and a scowl, he was now tangled in sweat-soaked sheets, and while the scowl was still intact, the jeans were nowhere in evidence.

Cuinn stood squarely between Rian and the window, no doubt a perfect silhouette. *Fuck me purple.* "My aim obviously sucks where you're concerned, Highness."

He caught a glimpse of twin pinpoints of light, tiny dancing flames in Rian's eyes glaring at him out of the deeper darkness. Only a glimpse, before the eyes closed and the blond head fell back onto a pillow as twisted as the sheets.

"If you're not wanting me, then why in the name of the Blessed Virgin have you come back? To torture me?" Rian spoke without opening his eyes, without moving. "That's not the sort of torture I fancy, surely you know that by now."

"I've never said I don't want you." Cuinn had to force the words out, through a throat gone tight. Hours of trying to figure out where the fuck his head was at, and he was no more able to say what had to be said than he'd been this afternoon. He'd give almost anything to be able to shrug, to put the Prince in his place with an arch remark. Keep him at a safe distance. But he couldn't. And the fact that he couldn't pissed him off. Royally, to use an apt phrase. "There are things I have to make you understand. Before I can even think of..."

Shit. Think of putting him back up against that wall and kicking his legs apart, twisting his arm back up and around to hear the soft keening sounds he just *knew* would follow, tasting the sweat running down Rian's temples. He could feel his cock throbbing as it rested in the cleft of those perfect buttocks, waiting to be driven home into darkness.

But that was what the Loremasters wanted, and fuck all if he was going to put his body, and Rian's, at their service before he knew why.

"Maybe I should make you understand a thing or two." Those amazing eyes were on him again, faceted blue with flame in their hearts. "You call me addicted, and maybe I am. But until you appeared out of nowhere, until you found me bare and bruised and needing and turned away from me, any man would do, to feed that addiction."

Rian pushed up on an elbow, and the sheet fell away, revealing the stars that trailed across his abs. "You've taken that from me. I don't understand, don't know how or why, but I need more than I ever did and you're the only one what can satisfy me." A film of sweat gleamed on Rian's forehead, his chest, in the moonlight. "And you refuse me."

Cuinn could only stare. Could only need. Could only curse. "I refuse the ones who are pulling our strings."

"Maybe you have strings to be pulled. I have none." Rian slid up the bed, until his back was propped against the headboard, and Cuinn's mouth went dry as the sheet slipped down his torso, caught and held in place only by the Prince's mostly-erect shaft. *Damn, those stars...*

"You're wrong, Highness. *Támid faoi ceangal ag a'slabra ceant.*" Cuinn had to look away. At the carved headboard of the bed, the soft-edged shapes on the wall made by the lights from the street below and the sky above, the moldings over the door. Anywhere but at the male who had no fucking idea what he was trying to compel Cuinn to do. "We are bound by the same chains, you and I."

"I don't understand."

"You and I share a soul." Rian's eyes narrowed, and Cuinn stifled a groan. "I'm sure you weren't raised to believe that's possible. But there's a hell of a lot else in your life of late you weren't raised to believe in, either, so you're just going to have to trust me on this."

Rian ran a splayed hand down his own torso, slowly, and watched raptly as each fingertip left a trail of faint auroral Fire. "I'm listening."

Big of you, Cuinn nearly snapped. But he didn't. There was too much at stake here for him to let his mouth derail everything. "The first time I crossed over into the human world from the Realm, my soul was torn in half. Half was supposed to go out into the human world ahead of me, to be born into a human. For me to find, and rejoin the two halves, and live happily ever after."

Rian said nothing, only watched. Cuinn's heart rate was speeding up, his breath likewise. *I shouldn't have looked at him.* "It didn't work that way, though. The other half of my soul stayed in the Pattern —the portal between the worlds —and waited. For you. You were too young when you went through to have one of your own, so you got the other half of mine." Shit, he was practically stammering. His gut was telling him, very firmly, that it would be an extremely bad idea for Rian to figure out, right now, who had been responsible for snatching him from his Royal birthright.

And I care what he thinks of me why? I don't have to be on his good side to shove him up against the wall. In fact, he'd probably like it better if I wasn't.

"So we're due to be rejoined, then?" One winglike brow quirked up. "Except, I forgot, you don't want to." An edge crept into Rian's words, sharp enough to cut and hot enough to cauterize. "You've perhaps lost your taste for the other half of your own soul?"

Cuinn closed his eyes, and took a long, slow

breath in through his nose. And was just as pissed off when he finished as he'd been when he started. *I'm beginning to understand why some people consider 'cock-tease' an insult.* He spoke without opening his eyes, to be safe. "You have no idea how much I want you. Or what you're going to unleash if you keep pushing me."

"Teach me, then."

Cuinn felt his nails cutting into the palms of his hands. Focusing on the tiny pain helped him think about things other than fisting the tantalizing lock of hair curling over one of Rian's eyes and using it to yank his head back, for a kiss the one this afternoon had only hinted at. "The Pattern *means* for us to be joined. Because it wants to use us for something. I told you before, we're being gamed. And I don't know about you, but I don't enjoy being used."

"Depends entirely upon who's doing the using." The smile Rian gave him should have been illegal. It probably was, in most places in the former Soviet Union and a couple of countries in Africa.

I have one more chance to try to salvage this before it all blows up in my face. Cuinn wasn't sure how he knew, but he knew. "It doesn't bother you at all that you want me because you've been forced? That it's not your choice?"

Rian's face went suddenly, utterly still. Even the flames in his eyes guttered. "I have never been forced. Never."

"Then what did I see, back in Belfast?" Cuinn's throat was suddenly dry.

"My choice. All of it." The Fire was back in Rian's eyes, roaring, orange-white hot like the sparks falling from an arc welder. "And you are my choice. Whatever you wish to do to me, is my choice."

Those eyes...

Rian slid the sheet from his body, and Cuinn's body responded, heart pounding, cock and nipples iron-hard, breath catching low in his chest and his abs heaving with it. The spiral of stars seemed to gather the moonlight and give back a silver-blue glow, leading the eye from strong shoulder to rippled abs to tall, curved, moist-tipped cock. *It's too late, for me. For us.*

The other Fae's voice dropped to a richly accented whisper. "If you speak true, then I was forced to this threshold. But no one can force me across it. I choose who takes me."

"And no one pushes me." Two steps took Cuinn to the bed. He barely paused to rip off his shirt and throw it aside. On all fours, like a great cat, he stalked his prey. His willing prey.

The Prince's breath was as rapid as his own, his eyes wide. He tried to wrench away as Cuinn closed with him, but Cuinn was faster than he was. He straddled Rian's muscular upper thighs, pinning him, leaning in and grinding his denim-clad groin into that magnificent cock. Finally —*finally* —grabbing that fucking insolent forelock and using it the way it begged to be used, to drag Rian's head back and present his mouth for a bruising kiss and his throat for hot kisses and bites that left marks.

He needs this. Cuinn could barely think, but that much was clear to him. He thrust his hips harder, his own cock in nearly as much pain from the confinement as Rian's was sure to be from chafing against the brass of the zipper and the rough fabric. Rian reached down, to free him. Cuinn grabbed the other Fae's wrist and forced it up over his head with one hand, leaning into his other arm without letting go of Rian's hair. "Not until I say, *Highness*." He punctuated the word with another jerk of his hips.

Rian's response might have been a snarl of his own, or a groan, or a plea. Tiny, nearly invisible flames rippled over his skin, more like heat rising from a concrete road on a scorching day, as he arched and fought Cuinn's grip. "More, damn you. *More*."

The muscles of Cuinn's arms bulged and shone with sweat as he strained to hold the Prince down, and fuck if his own thighs weren't aching already, from their struggle to pin the other Fae and the beating they were taking from the legs they held.

Use magick? Hells yes.

Power surged through him, intensified by his arousal, attacking Rian's wrists, clinging and drawing them up and binding them to the posts at the head of the bed. Cuinn's smile became predatory as he watched Rian realize that Cuinn wasn't the one holding his arms any more. Rian yanked, and yanked again, hard enough to slam the headboard into the wall, but the channeling held.

He needed to do something about the legs, too. But only for a moment, Cuinn was looking forward to struggling with Rian's magnificent thighs to get what he wanted. He had another craving to deal with first, though. He channeled, and Rian's legs shot out, shackled to the bedposts at the foot of the bed with the same invisible chains binding his arms.

"What the fuck are you —oh, God..."

Rian's voice faded to choked silence as Cuinn bent to him. The inked stars called, and the Loremaster answered, his tongue tracing every line, every curve, every angle, one star after another. Rian trembled under him, small broken sounds forcing their way out of his throat.

The Prince didn't thrash, didn't try to escape. But he watched. Fuck, yes, he watched, Cuinn glanced up from the second star to the last and lost his breath to the sight of the raging Fire circled with glowing faceted blue. Rian was rapt, straining to hold his head up, running his tongue unthinkingly around full lips.

Such a little thing pleases him so much? Cuinn held the Prince's gaze as his tongue wandered to the last star, as intricate as the first, though much smaller. The bottom point of this star was lost in blond curls, curls Cuinn stirred with the tip of his tongue. Rian's head fell back, and his cry was as much anguish as ecstasy.

He's a pain slut. When would he have ever asked anyone to do something like this for him?

It was hard to breathe. Something was grabbing his chest. *What the particular fuck?*

Sympathy. The thought that maybe no one had ever touched Rian gently... hurt.

"Cuinn. Please."

Cuinn's head jerked up. Rian wasn't looking at him, his head was tipped back. His chest muscles strained, his shoulders likewise, as he pulled at his invisible bonds. "What?"

The Prince's head came up again, fair hair darkened with sweat. "*That* isn't for me." The tight jerk of his chin toward the swirl of stars made it clear what 'that' meant. Tenderness. "You know what I need. You've seen it."

Be damned if I'm fisting you. Cuinn opened his mouth to say exactly that, but before he could speak he was slammed with a blast of pure need that nearly rocked him back on his heels. Even a Loremaster, it turned out, was helpless before the unalloyed hungers of a Royal Fae. Cuinn freed Rian's legs and forced one up toward Rian's head. He would have forced both, but one hand was occupied opening his jeans and working them down far enough to free himself, then gripping his throbbing length and bringing it to Rian's tight, puckered entrance. "You want pain, Highness? You're about to get it." Going in dry, as hard as he was? Hell, yes, it was going to hurt. Both of them, probably.

"Stop talking and fuck me."

Cuinn braced his knees against the mattress and his arm against Rian's leg. The Prince tensed —to fight him, he was sure. *Good. Very good.* He thrust hard, penetrating past resistance from Rian's tight ring that brought tears of pain to his eyes and stole his breath.

But the *fuck-yeah-this-is-heaven* hadn't even made it all the way from his cock to his brain before something else happened. Something as strange as sympathy. Joy. He'd felt its ghost this afternoon, as he pinned Rian to the wall for that first kiss. Then, he'd thought it some strange part of the other Fae's madness. This sensation, though, was all his own, no fucking ghost of anything.

He shook his head, hair tumbling into his eyes. He was still burning, as if his Fire Prince was doing something to boil the very blood in his veins; still groaning through clenched teeth, knuckles bone-white from his grip on Rian's thighs as he continued to hammer his way into the other Fae's tight dark hold. The pleasure from each thrust was blinding. But there was more. Each thrust was a taste of delight, each moan he wrung from Rian sent laughter racing down his every nerve. In a heartbeat, he'd gone from fucking a male who had pushed him beyond his endurance to pleasuring a lover. And he'd lost none of his own arousal in doing so. If anything, he was wilder. Greedier. Determined to give Rian everything he'd ever wanted. Pleasure the Prince, and his own pleasure would be volcanic.

Rian writhed under him, gasping for air, straining against his invisible bonds. Tears of flame licked at his cheeks; impulsively, Cuinn did the same, burying himself balls-deep at last and bending to stroke the flat of his tongue over Rian's rough cheeks. Flames danced on his tongue, they felt like champagne and tasted like sex.

Bowed down over Rian as he was, now, he could hear something he hadn't been able to before, lost as he had been —and still was —in lust and laughter. Rian wept. "*Ní hé seo an mianach*," the Prince whispered. "*Ní hé*."

The words were close enough to *Faen —né seo a'manach* —that Cuinn thought he understood. *This isn't for me.*

Son of a bitch. Rian was feeling it, too. The joy coursing through Cuinn, changing him. The difference was, Rian rejected it.

Not fucking acceptable. Releasing Rian's thighs,

Cuinn braced his arms to either side of the Prince's head and reared up over him, for better leverage. The sight of the other male's beautifully inked, sweat-drenched torso acted on his need like bellows on a blast furnace. Rian's own tortured hunger hammered him, wave after wave.

Cuinn, too, hammered. Everything from his shoulders to his toes worked to place every thrust, drive him into Rian's dark passage, hard enough the bed shook with it. The pleasure alone wasn't enough, though. Even moans so low he could feel them against his groin weren't enough. Not while Rian still rejected the rest of it.

Cuinn caught Rian's white-hot gaze, refusing to let the other Fae look away. Willing him to feel, to accept. Not to understand —Cuinn couldn't do that himself —but to let the joy in. "This is real." His balls slapped against the other Fae's perfect ass, again and again; he circled his hips, working himself deeper still, feeling the heat of a sphincter rubbed raw surrounding the base of his cock, gripping, pulsing. "This. Is. Yours."

Rian shook his head. But Cuinn wasn't having it. A thought released the magick binding one of Rian's wrists. "Touch yourself." His voice rasped, in a throat that only wanted to be screaming with pleasure or laughing for joy. "You're fucking well coming with me, *m'crocnath.*"

My completion? Really? This laugh escaped him, startling the Prince. *Hell, yes, he is.*

Rian bit down hard on his full lower lip as his palm encircled the base of his cock. Cuinn looked down, and swore vehemently at the sight of the plum-colored tip of the Royal cock, dripping thick, creamy Fire onto heaving abs. There was enough light in that Fire to let him catch glimpses of his own shaft, too, the base of it, emerging briefly only to plunge back in, harder each time. Shining with his own fluids, and slicked with blood.

Cuinn's hips slowed at this, but Rian's legs locked around them like bands of iron. "Almost there," the other Fae choked. "Harder. So close. *Harder*."

It wasn't quite joy Cuinn saw in his lover's face. But it was close. And when Rian clamped down hard around Cuinn's throbbing length, and caught his breath and arched his back, it was more than enough. Cuinn's balls drew up tight; he could feel his cock curving inside Rian's clasping hold, he couldn't breathe, couldn't move —

Someone was shouting, a hoarse, raw cry. Cuinn thought it might be him. Or maybe it was Rian. Maybe both. Hot splashes coated Cuinn's groin, heat pooled in Rian's curls, around the pulsing base of his own cock. But Cuinn could only tell any of this by the feel of the fiery jets, because his eyes were rolled back in his head far enough to ache.

Even if they hadn't been, he would have been blinded. Blinded by the pleasure, but also by the pure, staggering joy. Especially the joy. He was only dimly aware of the thick spurts jetting from him into Rian's clasping darkness, of his own body convulsing and trying in vain to breathe. The best part of him was swept away, lost in an emotion he hadn't let himself experience in over two thousand years.

Hell, he'd never let himself feel this. Ever. How many times had he taken someone, Fae, human, male, female, didn't matter? Used them, controlled them, taken everything he wanted and given fuck-all nothing. Exactly like any other Fae. Thousands of years of indulging his every desire. But the joy that had whispered to him in that first kiss, and threatened to overwhelm him at the first cry from Rian's throat, the first nearly tangible wave of the pleasure of his first real lover in all those centuries, wiped out even the memory of the rest of it.

Cuinn released the magick, gripped Rian's shoulders, and bent over him, using that grip to bury himself even deeper as he finished emptying himself. He moaned, burying his face in the hard sweaty curve of the Prince's shoulder, as Rian wrapped both arms around the small of his back and drew him into a fierce embrace. Rian's fiery seed slicked them both, and he could feel the other Fae's cock softening between their bodies.

I don't care if the Pattern did *fucking set us up.* Closing his eyes, Cuinn breathed deeply, filling himself with the scents of sweat and sex and, yes, smoke. The joy, the wonder, was a gift, however it had been intended. He was bound, his half of the Sharing complete. But he felt none of the anger, the panic he'd expected, when he'd vowed to wait to take this step. Hell, he was as close to being at peace as he'd ever been in his life. Which would probably freak him out once he'd had some time to think about it, but right this minute it was perfection.

Rian's chest rose and fell under his, unevenly. The grip around the small of Cuinn's back trembled, and it gradually dawned on him that it wasn't just the ferocity of the grip that caused the trembling. "What is it, *Elirei?*" No sarcastic 'Highness' this time, his *scair-*

anam was a Prince Royal and Cuinn was feeling just mellow enough to grant him the title. Suddenly remembering the blood, he eased himself from Rian's body, to let the Fae's naturally rapid healing begin.

"What the feck was that?"

Startled by Rian's tone, Cuinn raised his head, just enough to look down into the other Fae's eyes. Eyes that looked back at him with confusion, and more panic than joy, and not even a trace of mellow contentment. "That was *scair'ain'e*." He shifted his weight in the cradle of Rian's thighs. "Soulsharing."

Rian grimaced. "Was that why you wouldn't give me what I needed?"

Cuinn could only stare. "You'd rather have pain than..." There weren't any words to describe the wonder of the Sharing, at least no words he wouldn't feel like a total idiot for speaking aloud. *How could a sane male not want what I just felt?*

Is *this a sane male?*

"I need what I need." Rian's voice sounded as if there was a hand around his throat. Which Cuinn had seriously been considering at one point. "I need it rough. You know that."

"Why?" He blurted the question before he thought. Normally he wouldn't give a shit why anyone needed or wanted anything. But there was nothing normal about this, not any more. This was his *scair-anam*, trying to reject the idea of Sharing.

Rian frowned. "Strangely enough, I find myself wanting to tell you."

"So?"

The frown smoothed away. "So get the fuck out of my flat before I set your arse afire."

Chapter Eleven

"I don't like this, *d'orant*."

Conall looked up at his partner. Josh didn't often loom over him like this, he was usually more careful not to draw attention to the difference in their heights. Which meant that he meant what he said, and was willing to go to some lengths to prove he meant it.

"I understand, *dar'cion*." 'Brilliantly-colored,' his pet-name for Josh from the very beginning, back when he'd had no idea all humans didn't look like his magnificently-inked partner. "But I have to do it. And I might as well do it now, if only because we aren't going to be getting any sleep for a while."

Proof of his words came from the apartment next door, ardent moans and what sounded like the headboard of a bed slamming against a wall. Their Royal neighbor was, apparently, entertaining. Or being entertained.

Josh's well-muscled shoulders slumped. "I still don't like it. I don't care how right you are. Bryce is a shit, and with a piece of the *Marfach* in him he's a *dangerous* shit."

"I'll be careful." Conall pulled Josh's head down into a kiss, and made it a long one; he'd recovered from the pains of transition months ago, but he was still happiest when he was touching his *scair-anam*. "Besides, I've taken on the whole monster twice. I doubt a tiny piece of it will give me much trouble."

"I wish I could go with you."

Conall melted into his partner, as Josh's large hands slid down his back and cupped his ass, drawing him in close. He'd gone for more than three hundred years without being touched this way; to be gifted a *scair-anam* who ranked loving touch right beside air, water and food among the necessities of life was sheer bliss. "This won't take long. I promise."

Before Conall could give in to temptation yet again, he Faded. He took form again in deep shadow, under the stairs leading to the second floor of the brownstone. A homecoming, of sorts; Josh had brought him to the ground floor apartment in this building when he was newly transitioned. Better to remember that, than to remember the time he'd spent bodiless and trapped in the mirror in the basement after his ill-fated attempt to access the minor ley nexus he'd sensed there. Much better to remember Josh carrying him through the crowded New York streets. That first shower they'd shared. Josh putting him to bed, holding him.

Conall shook his head. It was time to get to work, not time to get lost in memories. Besides, he had the real thing waiting for him at home once he finished here. No light shone from under the door of the ground-floor apartment. Good. All he had to do was Fade into the living room, to avoid being noticed in the unhappy event Bryce Newhouse was a light sleeper. From there, he'd move on to the bedroom, and spend as much time as he could studying the odious prick-dribble, the better to craft a ward that could keep him out of Purgatory. No amount of studying would give him the same understanding of what made Bryce tick that he'd gained from taking his master the *Marfach* apart, one molecule at a time. However, every little bit helped.

Closing his eyes, he reached in and found his inner sense of the magick he'd left behind inside the apartment, and embraced it. All magick touched all other magick, in a way, and travel by Fading simply meant choosing a new place to manifest his own magick. In this case, the living room on the other side of the wall.

Sweet Mae West on a unicycle.

He wasn't alone. Bryce was restlessly asleep on the sofa, his feet hanging off one end; though for some reason it was natural to think of the investment banker as little, he was actually almost as tall as Josh. Conall froze, holding his breath as Bryce shifted, and letting it out again slowly as he settled.

Why is he sleeping out here? Conall couldn't help an unhealthy fascination with the tight knot of concentrated evil warping the air around one side of Bryce's abdomen. Though the magickal energy was distorted from passing through human flesh, it was unmistakably that of the *Marfach*. He hoped he never got any closer to seeing his race's deadliest enemy than this attenuated glimpse. The few moments he'd looked at the monster during timestop didn't count; what caused a Fae to go mad looking at the *Marfach* was the way it warped and twisted magick into a vile new reality. It didn't use magick for an evil purpose; it changed the essence of the magick itself to evil. So the old tales said, anyway. And the changing, the warping and the

108

twisting, required time to happen, so apparently it was safe to look at the monster when time was stopped. Safe, but not pleasant.

A loud snore came from the direction of the bedroom. Conall spun —

And froze, again. A filthy grey hoodie was draped over a chair. No, it was too stiff to drape. *How did I not smell that when I Faded in?* There was no way in hell the fastidious Bryce would touch a *shmatte* like that, much less throw it over one of his antique wingback chairs. Conall could practically hear the satin upholstery crying out in distress.

Or maybe that was his memory, crying out. He recognized that hoodie. Janek O'Halloran had been wearing it the terrible night he had kidnapped and tortured and murdered Garrett. The fact that the pole dancer's death had ultimately been reversed took nothing away from the horror of the memory; Fae didn't usually find death, even a gruesome death like a throat-slitting, terribly upsetting, and a human's death even less so than a Fae's, but Garrett was a SoulShare. The thought of a Fae, any Fae, losing a SoulShare was enough to make Conall think of Josh, and groan.

Focus. I have to focus.

Bryce was on the sofa, a familiar hoodie lay on the chair, and a sound like a duet between a banshee and a buzz saw was coming from the bedroom. The mathematics involved weren't exactly rocket science. But Conall had to be sure.

Between one heartbeat and the next, Conall Faded to insubstantiality, and started a slow drift toward the bedroom. In this state, his heart couldn't be racing, yet he felt it hammering. Sure, he'd beaten the *Marfach* before. Twice. But once, he'd been standing at the great nexus, close enough to tap into it directly, and the other time, Lochlann had been feeding him raw ley energy, tapped from a ley line in a way only Lochlann could manage. If he had to go head to head with the monster here, he'd be doing it with only his own magickal resources. Which at best meant his death, and at worst meant being seized, warped to harbor the *Marfach*'s malevolence, and turned into a weapon. Against his *scair-anam*, against all the others, against the Pattern itself.

The door to the bedroom was closed. No light came from underneath it. *One thing gone right, at least. Now, where is the damned mirror?* One look in a mirror while Faded this way, and he'd be trapped there. One experience like that was more than enough. Closing his eyes, more or less, he brought up the memory of lying in that bed, after Josh carried him home from the Pride march. His feet had been pointing almost directly at the door, and there had been a mirror on top of the small chest of drawers to the left of the door. He'd be safe upon entering.

Provided the *Marfach* wasn't lying there awake and waiting for him. Intellectually, Conall knew that the monstrosity couldn't see him when he was Faded like this. Intellect, however, had very little to do with the instinctive reaction of a Fae to his race's eternal enemy. Cold sweat, and a sac contracting hard enough to draw his balls up into his gut, those reactions were much more typical.

Enough. Conall forced his way through the door, trying to see in every direction at once. Ready for anything.

Almost anything. The sight of Janek O'Halloran sprawled naked on his back, faded ink covering about half his body, his cock semi-erect, the ravages of the year he'd spent slowly rotting before Lochlann arrested the process on full display, made him glad he wasn't corporeal. He hated vomiting.

The male obviously thought himself king of all he surveyed, or would if he were awake. It was obvious both in his splayed-out posture and the fact that it was Janek in the bedroom and the apartment's rightful tenant on the sofa. *And if Bryce is still on the sofa, when he could have run, it means he's either fine with the arrangement or being controlled.*

The thunderous snore —no doubt the product of half-rotted nasal passages —turned into incoherent mumbling, as Janek groped blindly at himself, scratched his crotch. Conall held his breath as the giant lurched and sat up, and turned his attention hastily away when the faintly glowing mass of red crystal that took up most of the right side of the human's head came into view. *Shit. Shit. Shit.*

"Oh, I'm sorry, your Majesty, did I interrupt your beauty sleep?"

What the hell?

Judging from the sounds, Janek scratched his groin again, and swung his legs over the side of the bed. "I'll drink as much as I like." The words were hard to make out. "And I'll fucking well take a piss if I want to." The bed creaked as Janek got out of it, and Conall was willing to swear he felt the floor shake as the behemoth plodded to the bathroom.

Fuck me purple, to borrow a phrase. The first time he'd fought the Janek-*Marfach* monstrosity, they'd been in the little room under Purgatory that housed the great nexus. Janek had forced his way in, with Kevin Almstead as a hostage. Conall knew — everyone knew —that Janek wanted Tiernan dead, but he hadn't attacked the Noble. He'd done only what the *Marfach* wanted; whether the monster got access to the nexus or to a living Fae hadn't really mattered at that point.

A sound like someone training a fire hose on the toilet came from the bathroom, along with a satisfied grunt Conall didn't need to hear. *The* Marfach *was running the show, that time. No question.* But in their second meeting, the hellish encounter over Garrett's battered body, he'd made a desperate attempt to sever the connection between passenger and host. With no way to be sure it had worked.

Apparently, it had. Sort of.

The toilet flushed, and Conall heard footsteps again. The footsteps weren't going back to bed, though, they were headed for the door.

Conall couldn't move fast enough in Faded form to get completely out of the way. The best he could do was to draw back enough to let Janek and the *Marfach* go by without any of the *Marfach*'s substance passing through him. Which meant sharing space with Janek, while he fumbled with the doorknob. Maybe being insubstantial *wasn't* going to be enough to save him from being violently ill.

"If I want another beer, I'm going to have another goddamned beer." At last, Janek managed the knob and pushed the door open, heading off down the narrow hallway toward the kitchen.

I am not *going back out into the living room.*

112

Reading Bryce had just become much less important than getting back to Josh, and to the others, with this news. The enemy was found, and the enemy was divided, or so it seemed.

Getting the hell out of here before the giant came back was also extremely important. The longer he stayed, the more he risked being caught. A Fae's presence, embodied or not, left behind a sort of magickal residue; it was this stray magick that let a Fae Fade to any place he'd been before, since Fading was usually a simple matter of traveling between magicks. If he stayed here long enough, sooner or later —and he had no idea how long either 'sooner' or 'later' might be —the *Marfach* might be able to see the traces he left behind.

It was impossible to travel by Fading while in a physically Faded state, though. He waited, his presently incorporeal heart hammering, until he heard the refrigerator door open, and let his physicality start to trickle back.

Janek cursed incoherently at something. Conall gritted his teeth. There was something bitterly amusing about being in a race for his life with a zombie trying to open a bottle of beer. Maybe sometime he'd figure out what it was.

Glass shattered. *Ah, a direct solution.*

With a sigh of relief, Conall Faded.

Chapter Twelve

Washington, D.C.

Cuinn's stunned expression slowly gave way to a grimly furrowed brow, and eyes glittering a pale green even in the diffuse moonlight from the curtained window. Rian fecking hated moonlight. Always had.

He wanted to throw Cuinn off him, get him the hell out of his bed, and preferably his life. Before he spilled the secret that for some reason was battering at the walls of his mind screaming to be let out. Screaming. *'Sea*, there was a hell of a lot of that going on in his head of late.

He had no idea what he'd just felt. Some sort of cousin to what he'd felt when Cuinn first touched him, and again when the Fae kissed him. But a very distant cousin it was, because whatever had seized him at the moment Cuinn's heat flooded him had been almost enough to light up the dark burning at his core.

Almost.

"You could try to set my ass on fire." Cuinn's voice was silken, soft, yet somehow it had an edge to it. "But you'd find I have a few thousand years of experience dealing with that kind of shit, and no

114

patience with it." The other Fae's grip on his shoulders had scarcely slackened, since they'd both had their pleasure, and now it tightened again, enough that Rian would probably have found it pleasurable in other circumstances. "I'll say it again. You and I share a soul. We're one, whether either one of us likes it or not. And I need to know what's made you this way. What makes you crave pain from me."

Rian rolled his shoulders, but that grip wasn't giving, not at all, and he growled. "You were glad enough to give it, so why should the reason matter?"

"It matters because you're ready to reject the rest of the Sharing because of it, whatever it is."

"There's more?" *Shite, no,* was his immediate reaction. Not another blast of that force which rocked him to his very foundations. Threatened to bring down the walls that kept at bay his own fear of what he was, what he'd become, that night in the shadows cast by the Orangemen's bonfire. Go through that again, all for the sake of letting a stranger in? *Never.*

"Did you think we were finished?" Cuinn's weight shifted on top of him, making him aware all over again of the hard-muscled hips forcing his thighs apart, the sweat-slick chest suspended over his own. "We're bound, whatever you choose to do —we were bound before I ever laid eyes on your fucking teasing ass —but you have to take your pleasure with me, to finish the circle. And at the moment, *dhó-súil,* your needs being what they are, I'm guessing there's not a chance in hell of that happening."

Fire-eyes? Not that he was going to let a pretty pillow-name distract him. "So I ask again, why does the 'why' of it matter? I need what I need." Rian

115

would have shrugged, but for the tight grip on his shoulders.

Strangely, Cuinn seemed to be more sad than anything else. Sad and bewildered. "I wasn't expecting to feel what I felt. I still think I'm being used. And you're being used. And that pisses me off more than I can tell you. But at the same time, I'd have to be an even bigger idiot than I am to keep insisting it wasn't the most fucking incredible thing I've ever experienced." Jaysus, Cuinn was kissing his forehead, though from his expression the other Fae thought the gesture near as daft as Rian himself did. "Everything I know about SoulSharing tells me you should have felt it too, not as strongly as I did, but that will come. But you're rejecting it. Because you need something different, you need the Sharing to hurt. If I understood why..." Fingertips that didn't feel at all accustomed to gentleness brushed Rian's forelock out of his eyes. "Maybe I could help."

"Why the fuck would you want to do that?"

"The answer 'beats the hell out of me' is just so damned tempting." A tic made a brief appearance in the corner of Cuinn's eye. "But the truth is..." Cuinn's head dropped, briefly, sending sweaty sandy hair tumbling over Rian's neck and shoulder. He could hear the other Fae draw a deep breath before looking up again. "I wasn't expecting this to be good. The SoulSharing, I mean, but it was. It is. And I want it to be good for you, too."

A harsh laugh died before it had a chance to get as far as Rian's lips. Cuinn was serious. "I really ought to pitch your arse out of this bed."

"You said that before. I don't think you mean it."

Rian tried to shove Cuinn off to one side. His hands, though, had their own ideas as to what they wanted to be about, and glided over curves of muscle and bone, learning the other Fae's body like a blind man discovering Michelangelo's David. *Shite.* He'd never had the slightest desire to be the one doing the touching, before today. "I don't know, maybe I don't. But that doesn't mean I want to tell you my life story."

"I don't need all of it." The tight grip on Rian's shoulders relaxed, into open-palmed caresses that sent a sharp shiver racing through Rian's body. "Just one part."

Rian's teeth ground together. The effort of trying to keep silent was painful. Not the good kind of pain, either. And Cuinn's eyes wouldn't fecking let him go.

"It was the Twalf. The twelfth July, just past." Sweet bleeding Christ, his throat felt sandpapered and salted. "I was out that night, me and my Da had always gone out to cause as much trouble as we could at the bonfires, and I continued on after he was gone."

"Your father's the King of the Demesne of Fire—"

"If you want to hear this you'll not open your mouth again, not to speak of something you know fuck-all about." Rian gripped the sheets to either side, to keep himself from stroking the body lying atop his own. "I've known I was a foundling near as long as I can remember. But my Ma and my Da are the ones who loved me as their own."

Cuinn opened his mouth, closed it again.

"Da was in the 'RA, back during the worst of the Troubles in the North of Ireland. He was in Long Kesh in '81, he knew Bobby Sands and Kieran Doherty and the other eight who died on hunger strike. And he raised me to carry on the good fight, even after the 'RA ceased to be worthy of their name." Deep breaths. *This isn't the story he wants, and he sure as hell doesn't need to know it. But I'll not hear him speaking against my Da.*

"You loved him." The other Fae shook his head, as if to clear it.

"And why ever would I not?"

"You don't —never mind. Go on." Again the unnerving caress of open hands.

"I'd visited two fires already that night, done my share of damage. But at the third, they were waiting for me." A chill wracked him, one Cuinn apparently felt, too, as he moved to cover him. This was a memory Rian only rarely revisited, and never on any pleasant errand. "Bastards came at me from behind, as I was scoping out the best vantage, kicked my kneecaps in and took me down and ground my face into the dirt till I tasted it at the back of my throat. But that was just the start."

His voice was a bare whisper now, he wasn't even sure Cuinn could hear him. "There were five of them. One to hold each arm, one to hold each leg. Fuckers needed them all, too."

"Oh, shit." Cuinn's whisper was almost as faint as his own.

"And one to have the denims off me and show me the worst humiliation their twisted minds could conjure, for a Papist prick." The words were practically falling over one another in their haste to be out of him. "Each in turn, and each worse than the last."

118

"*A'súile do na prachái̇n, a'gcroí do na gaoirn.*" Cuinn scarcely raised his voice, but this murmur was lethal. "*N-anamacha do n-oí gan derea.*"

The strangeness of the words brought Rian out of the dark, fire- shot memory, a brief respite before the worst of the tale. "Should I know what you're saying?"

"It's an oath." Pale-jade eyes glittered like gems. "Their eyes for the crows, their hearts for the wolves, their souls for the eternal night."

"If that's an offer to hunt them down, it's too late for that." Rian turned his head aside, blinking back angry tears. He didn't need, didn't want, the sympathy that fueled Cuinn's anger. "As you'll soon learn, if you let me go on."

A soft kiss fell on the line of Rian's jaw. "There's more?"

"I've scarce begun." Rian swallowed. "In the middle of it all I blacked out. And when I woke, to the light of the fire and the laughter of the audience we'd gained—"His voice caught, hard and painful. "It was then I first knew for certain that I was either utterly mad, or other than human."

"How?"

"I woke knowing how to defeat them. But it was nothing that would occur to a sane man. Fuck, it was nothing that would ever occur to a human being at all."

He closed his eyes, too late to stop tears from running down his temple to end in corkscrews of smoke on the pillow. "I changed myself. Embraced what they were doing to me, what they were still doing, what they'd been doing even while I was unconscious. Changed myself into one who craved what they did. Everything they did, what they thought was abuse and degradation, it was all for my pleasure."

Despite the pain of the memories, despite the shocked silence of the male who'd thought he wanted to know what lived in the cesspit that was Rian Sheridan's heart, he laughed. It was a short and bitter laugh, true enough, but a real one. "The Prod bastards were no more than whores for a Papist. Giving me everything I wanted. They knew it, too. Long before they were through with me, they knew."

"*Asiomú.*" Cuinn stared, his caressing hands stilled. "Reversal."

"Please, could you be more cryptic? I love it so." Sweet Jesus, he still wanted Cuinn. The arse-pounding he'd just taken should have been enough to hold him for a few days at least, but no, he wanted to start the tease all over again, leave the sensual Fae no choice but to fuck him bloody a second time. No doubt he was ready for more by now, he'd always healed quickly. Good for another round.

If Cuinn was aware of Rian's arousal, he gave no sign of it. "Vengeance has always been an art form, among the Fae. You'd know, if you'd been raised in the Realm. The only love we know is love of kin, and everyone else is fair game. You're describing a form of revenge, one that allows a captured Fae to turn his torture back on his torturers."

"It's fecking effective." Rian's hips started a slow, gentle rocking under Cuinn. Warm slick skin against skin felt so good, and soon it would feel even better. "The first time they had me, there was nothing of their needing about it, though they knew something was amiss. But after they'd finished, and were standing about mocking me..." '*Sea*, this memory was one to put a smile on his face. "All I had to do was look from one to the next, and one by one they groaned, and hardened, and couldn't keep their hands from themselves." The rage, the horror in their bloodshot eyes and the snarls accompanying their groans, as they'd found themselves lusting after their former victim, had been sweet then, and were sweet now.

"Oh, fuck." Cuinn's body was responding to him, Rian could feel his spent shaft stirring where it was pressed between their bodies and his lean, hard hips shifted in rhythm with Rian's own. "That's not *asiomú*. That's your addiction. That's where it started, I'd bet my left nut."

"Whatever it was, it worked too fecking well." The trouble with telling this story, Rian decided, was having to tell the end of it, to come face to face with the creature he'd become that night. Maybe that's why he'd never told the full story, until tonight.

"Motherfucker!"

Rian looked up. He was still where they'd thrown him, only he'd raised himself up to hands and knees after the last of them finished with him. Hadn't moved from there, though. Hadn't needed to, in order to send all five of them mad with lust. The short balding one who had spoken, he couldn't stop grunting and groaning long enough to get a whole word out, though he struggled mightily. He was also a mighty hand at the jacking off, and he couldn't take his eyes from Rian as he did it. That's it, boyo. You want to put that in me, don't you? *Rian smiled at the little man with the little dick, savoring his lust and confusion and fury.*

You're fantasizing about it as you look at me, you'd fight any man here for the chance to do it, and you're hating yourself every moment.

Shorty wasn't alone, either. All five of his attackers were occupied, getting themselves ready for their chance to beg for the honor of pleasuring him. He couldn't see them all, they were in a circle around him, but he could hear them all, clear as the Angelus bell. He could hear the onlookers, too, and the way their japes had gone from crude insults hurled at him to laughter at the predicament of his tormentors.

Rian's eyes closed for a moment, his head dropped. He needed to get his breath, gather his strength, the beating that had started his nightmare had been nearly as brutal as the rapes and there was blood drying on his skin in any number of places besides his arse and inner thighs. A couple of cracked ribs made it hard for him to get his breath properly, but those would soon mend. As would the rest of it.

A fist closed in his hair and hauled his head up. He was staring straight into the barrel of a gun, and at Shorty's beady eyes looking down the barrel at him. "You can suck on this instead, ye fecking pole-smoker." He shoved the barrel of the gun into Rian's mouth, his finger tightened on the trigger.

At first, Rian thought someone had thrown petrol, or some kind of explosive, on the bonfire. Fire blazed up all around him. It was all he could see. He could hear the roar of it, like a train. He could hear the screams of the men who surrounded him. Relieved beyond measure, he waited to die.

But he didn't.

The flames flickered, went out. The circle of

onlookers had fallen back while the fire raged, and a few of them were beating out smaller fires that had caught on their clothing or hair. All of them staring at him, still kneeling in the dirt, pale and naked and bleeding. Staring, too, at the five charred-black and smoking lumps of meat surrounding him.

Rian's lips moved, silently. A Naomh-Mhuire, a Mháthair Dé, guigh orainn na peacaigh, anois agus ar uair ár mbáis. *Holy Mary, Mother of God, pray for us sinners, now and at the hour of our death.*

Rian vanished.

And when he took form again, in the tiny room that had been his since his first memories, he was marked with a swarm of stars, inked into his flesh like silver-blue brands.

Slowly, Rian became aware of lips brushing his rough cheek. A heart beating against his chest. A clumsy hand stroking his hair. Tears trickled down his temples, burning like embers until they hissed into oblivion somewhere among the sheets.

The tears themselves, though, were awkward as fuck, and so was the ridiculous catch in his voice when he could finally speak. "You need to get the hell out of here."

"Like fuck I do, *m'anam-sciar*."

Rian rolled the other Fae off him, and flung himself to the other side, kept going until he stood beside the bed. Part of him wanted to keep standing there, just looking, studying the perfect body sprawled out in his bed. Finish stripping off the jeans that still stubbornly clung to legs he had yet to lay eyes on. Eventually find himself being taken again.

Again? Look where the first time had gotten him.

One good fuck, and he'd spilled every secret he had. Stripped himself more naked than naked. He'd put his inner madman on glorious display. Surely even the other half of his own stunted soul was revolted by what he was. "Unless you want to see if my control over the fire has improved since the Twalf, you need to go. Now."

Judging by Cuinn's expression, there was something he wanted very badly to say. Instead, to Rian's astonishment, he simply faded away, becoming a wash of faint color, and then nothing at all. Nothing but the pale green gaze that was the last thing to go, intense even when the rest of the Fae was nothing but a ghost image.

This isn't over. Shite. It's scarce begun.

Chapter Thirteen

Lochlann was startled from a light doze by the vibration of his phone on the table beside the bed. *How the hell did I fall asleep? Tonight of all nights?* Grimacing, he scrubbed at his eyes with the heel of one hand while he touched the phone on with the other.

Are you home? The text from Cuinn glowed at him.

Yes. The Loremaster had a gift for doing things at inconvenient times.

A pause, then: *Are you decent?*

Lochlann rolled his eyes. *Would it even slow you down if I said I wasn't?*

"Not particularly." The voice came from the sofa at the other end of the room.

Lochlann rose up on an elbow, shaking his head at the sight of the Fae lounging shirtless on the cream-on-cream brocade. "Please tell me you aren't trying to be seductive."

"Not a chance." Cuinn sat up, stretched his legs out in front of him, and took his time about crossing them at the ankles before looking back up at Lochlann. "Look, I need to know. Are we back on speaking terms?"

Lochlann frowned. "You saved my life. You and Conall." The Loremaster and the mage had thrown him a lifeline, when he'd nearly vanished into whatever afterlife awaited humans in pursuit of his *scair-anam.*

Cuinn shrugged, leaning back into the soft cushions. "True. But we're both Fae, so that and ten dollars will get me a lap dance."

"You need to hang out in higher-class strip clubs." The mention of dancing sent his thoughts straight back to Garrett, who had insisted on walking home from Purgatory alone tonight, for the first time since his kidnapping, torture, death, and resurrection.

You can't be my babysitter forever, his SoulShare had pointed out, even as his aura prickled with apprehension. *I need to do this. I need to get my life back. And Conall's just a phone call away, right?*

Brave words from a brave human. Imagining Garrett working the pole at Purgatory, as he no doubt was this very moment, Lochlann missed Cuinn's undoubtedly smart-assed reply. "Say again?"

Cuinn pushed himself up to a sitting position, rested his elbows on his knees, and fixed Lochlann with a level gaze. "I said, I need some answers. And I hope you have them, because if you don't, I'm screwed, Rian's screwed, and possibly a couple of worlds are screwed."

"You lost me." Lochlann hauled himself up to a sitting position. "Who's Rian? The Prince Royal you said you were going to try to find?" The Loremaster hadn't returned from the Realm for several weeks, after he nearly spent himself helping Conall bring him and Garrett back from wherever it was they'd gone.

And when he had come back, it had been for just long enough to tell Lochlann and Conall and Tiernan that he was off to find a lost Prince.

"Yeah." Cuinn's hands plowed through his hair, and his fingers interlaced at the back of his neck. "Rian Aodán. Or Rian Sheridan, this side of the Pattern. Prince Royal of the Demesne of Fire." Cuinn took a deep breath. "He's my *scair-anam*. And I'm not sure, but there's a good chance he's on his way out of his fucking mind."

Lochlann stared. "You are shitting me."

"I shit you not."

A Fae, with a Fae for a scair-anam? "You told me we need humans. To ground us and shield us."

"I thought I was telling the truth, for once." Cuinn turned and put his feet up on the sofa, apparently unable to sit still. "If you think you're surprised, trust me, it's nothing compared to what I'm feeling."

"This is a stupid conversation to be having across a room." Lochlann crossed the little suite and sank into the armchair beside the sofa. This close to the other Fae, the scent of sex was unmistakable. There was another scent, too. Lochlann was willing to swear it was smoke.

"Feel better now?" Nothing would ever keep Cuinn an Dearmad from being a smartass, but the edge was missing from most of his jibes. "No need to wrinkle your nose, I know what I smell like. And no, I'm not apologizing."

"As if I'd expect that. Besides, if you've bonded with your *scair-anam*, no apologies are needed."

Cuinn coughed. "We haven't, quite. Yet."

Lochlann would have given almost any body part

he wasn't going to be needing for the next few days, if the sacrifice would get his aura-reading ability working properly. It had been intermittent at best since his sojourn on the far side of death, but if he could goose it to life right now, Lochlann suspected he would be treated to the once-in-a-lifetime sight of evidence of Cuinn's embarrassment. "Haven't *quite*?"

Cuinn's upper lip curled in the suggestion of a snarl. "We haven't finished."

"You don't say."

The other Fae crossed his arms behind his head and rolled his eyes at the ceiling. "Look, can we just agree that you're entitled to score points off me until we both get bored with it, and move on? I really do need some answers."

After two thousand, three hundred and some-odd years of letting me stumble blindly around the human world, losing my magick and damn near forgetting I was a Fae? You bet your ass I'm entitled. "You're worried your *scair-anam* is unstable? Maybe you just need to finish the Sharing."

"Maybe. But I don't think it's that simple. There was something off about him from the moment I first saw him."

Cuinn was looking straight at Lochlann, but it was obvious those pale green eyes were staring at something else entirely. Something the other Fae found both strange and profoundly arousing.

"Have you ever heard of something called *rachtanai*?" Cuinn's voice was soft, intense. "It's an addiction Fae have discovered since the Sundering. An addiction to being lusted after. To teasing."

"I haven't. Not by that name, anyhow." His

memories of the Realm were, literally, ancient history, at least the way humans reckoned things, but something about what Cuinn described was familiar. "It sounds similar in some ways to what happened every once in a while, when we still lived among the humans, when a Fae would overdo the *rinc' daonna*." 'Human dance' was the nickname the Fae gave to the pastime, popular before the Sundering, of sexually toying with humans, teasing and tempting them, and as often as not overloading their ill-equipped nervous systems with overdoses of magickal sex. "Sometimes they had a hard time stopping."

"You're right." Both of Cuinn's eyebrows went up. "Not a problem I ever had myself, of course, but now that you mention it, I do remember a few marvelous debaucheries with Fae who had just been *rinc'ean*."

"I'm not exactly surprised." Lochlann shook his head. Fae were sexually dormant until physical maturity, but any Fae who claimed celibacy after that point was lying through his or her teeth. Lochlann's own past was as randy as any Fae's, but he had generally confined his attentions to Fae who weren't under the influence of some uncontrollable impulse. "But you told us before you left, this Prince was raised by humans almost from birth. How did he find out he could 'dance' with them?"

"I'm not at liberty to say."

Now it was Lochlann's turn to be startled. "The only time you've said that in recent memory is when the Loremasters have had your balls on a choke chain."

Cuinn massaged his forehead as if it pained him. "Look, *mo phan s'farr leat sa masa*, you're the only one besides me who knows the Loremasters are presently anything more than an extremely dull history lesson. Can we keep it that way, please?"

"When did I graduate to being your *favorite* pain in the ass?"

"The title was purely honorary until about three seconds ago."

Lochlann shook his head, laughing softly. "I doubt that. And I'm not as easily distracted as you seem to think, *chara*. What happened to your *scair-anam?*"

Cuinn didn't answer, for so long that Lochlann was reasonably sure he wasn't going to. "It's his story to tell, not mine. I don't think he even wanted me to know it." The sandy-haired Fae refused to meet Lochlann's gaze.

"I'm going to need to know more if I'm going to be able to help you. Or him."

"What makes you think either one of us needs your help?" Cuinn still stared at the crystal light fixture in the middle of the ceiling, as if he were scrying in it.

"I'm a good guesser." Lochlann shrugged. "The male you describe sounds in need of healing. And you did say you needed answers, too."

"Fuck, yes. But I don't think what's happened to him is anything you can heal." Finally, Cuinn managed to look at Lochlann again. "He was traumatized. Which really is all I can say about it. "

Lochlann stayed carefully expressionless. It would only add to Cuinn's distress if the other Fae knew how obvious his emotions were.

"From the way Rian told the story, I think it

130

happened just as he was coming into his birthright of power." Cuinn took a deep breath. "And to survive it, he somehow instinctively pulled off an *asiomú.*"

Reversal-vengeance. Whatever had happened to the Prince Royal, turning it back on its perpetrators had led to his becoming addicted to the energy rush created by unsatisfied lust. *It's not all that hard to figure out.* "I'm amazed you can sit there quietly and talk to me. I'd be out hunting down the bastard who did it and feeding him his own skin, a sliver at a time."

"Bastards, plural. But there's nothing left of them to hunt down." As grim as Cuinn's expression was, there was a spark of joy in his eyes. "Rian took care of that."

Lochlann completely understood the joy. "Pissing off a Royal probably wasn't the smartest choice they ever made." Dismissing the late unfortunate assholes from his thoughts, Lochlann sat back, frowning slightly. "At least *asiomú* is temporary. I'm not sure if there's anything I can do about the addiction. I can't heal magickal injury, if that's what it is. And I've never tried dealing with psychological issues."

Cuinn sat bolt upright. "*That's* what's wrong."

"Fill me in?"

The other Fae's hands clenched into fists. "The *asiomú.* It was supposed to end when the danger was past. That's what it does. But for him, it didn't."

"I'm surprised he was able to do it at all. Maybe it's not so strange that it didn't work the way it was supposed to." Any Fae was theoretically capable of an *asiomú,* but even in a culture in which vendetta was considered a high art, it was a form of vengeance only rarely attempted. Mostly because the reversal turned into an insult so profound, if the quarrel wasn't already deadly it became so. Forcing yourself to crave what another used as torture essentially turned the other into your whore, made them give you exactly what you wanted, everything you wanted, because you wanted it.

And if there was a deadlier insult than *fracun*, whore, in the Fae language, whoever had come up with it had undoubtedly taken it with him, or her, into his or her sudden and premature death. Not because there was anything wrong with the notion of promiscuity —that was a word he hadn't learned until he lived among humans, it wasn't even a Fae concept. No, the insult in *fracun* lay in the implication that the one so named only had use-worth. When the *Marfach* had called Garrett a *fracun*...

Lochlann cleared his throat. Those were memories he never revisited if he could help it. "So the Prince, your *scair-anam—*"

Cuinn startled, as if he had been off in his own tangled thoughts, as well. "He likes it rough. Needs it rough." He nodded, clearly unhappy.

"I wouldn't think that would be a problem for you." Even before the Sundering, Cuinn had a reputation; Lochlann had lost track of the numbers of floggers and precious searing-stones and *folabodain* his friend had received as Midsummer and soul's-day and courting gifts.

Cuinn cut him a sidewise glare. "It wouldn't, ordinarily. But there's a difference between what I like and what he craves, and I don't think I can go there. Not with my *scair-anam,* anyhow."

"You *have* changed."

"Think so?" Cuinn rolled his eyes. "Tell me

something, *lasihoir*. If Garrett begged you to fuck him until he bled, would you have an easy time of it?"

Lochlann felt himself go pale. "No. Of course not."

The other Fae nodded. "Rian goes way beyond needing it rough. He only wants to suffer. If he gets pleasure from it along the way, he's good with that. He is a Fae, after all. But what he's looking for, what he really wants, is pain. If he were anyone other than my *scair-anam*, I'd have no trouble with that."

Lochlann thought he was starting to understand. "The SoulShare bond is all about joy."

"Exactly." Cuinn shifted restlessly on the rich brocade. "I didn't go to him tonight intending to start the Sharing, but it happened. And the joy was there. I felt it, and I know he felt it. But he doesn't want it."

"Garrett rejected it at first, too." Even now, knowing how it had all come out, Lochlann winced as he remembered being pushed away.

"How did you stand it?" The Loremaster's voice was unsteady, his gaze reflecting what could only be remembered pain. "Your *scair-anam* not wanting to share that?"

"It wasn't that he didn't want it." Lochlann went a little pale, just at the thought. "He didn't trust it. He didn't think it could last. He didn't want to be tempted to hope." How could anyone not *want* what a SoulShare felt?

"Your point?" The pain was gone; the pale-green gaze holding Lochlann's was as sardonic as ever.

The pain hadn't gone far, though, Lochlann guessed. "Don't give up. Rian might just need some time."

"Time isn't something I have a lot of."

A change of subject might be a good idea. "If his needs are that specific, you may have a problem, when it comes to completing the Sharing."

"What do you mean?" Cuinn slouched against the back of the sofa, but nothing about him was lazy. Certainly not his keen, glittering gaze.

Lochlann cleared his throat. *On the other hand, maybe I shouldn't have brought this particular subject up right now.* "I've talked with Conall and Tiernan, about their Sharings. And I've noticed a pattern. The Sharing is never completed with just one act. There has to be a balance, with Fae and human each having a chance to focus on pleasuring, and being pleasured."

Cuinn nodded. "That was the way it was designed. Why is it a problem now?"

He must really still be my chara, even after everything that's happened. Because I have no idea why the hell else I'd be telling him all this. "I thought at first that the way it happened between me and Garrett was a coincidence. The result of his condition. He had no reason to believe me when I told him he couldn't give me HIV or AIDS. He wouldn't let me inside him, and he refused to take me. He was afraid he'd infect me. He wouldn't even do oral. It was hands or nothing, he insisted. And while you were still in the Realm, I had the idea of comparing notes with Conall. He told me that for him and Josh, it had been oral. Both ways."

"Oh, shit," Cuinn whispered.

"Two could still have been a coincidence, though. Tiernan told me to go fuck myself, at first, and he never did give me specifics, but he eventually told me that he and Kevin had both done the deed the same way." The Noble's choice of words had actually been considerably more colorful, but Cuinn didn't need *all* the details.

Cuinn wrapped his arms around himself, as if cold. "I really needed more complications in my life right now. Which reminds me of something else, actually."

Lochlann frowned. 'You're being unfocused, even for you."

"Thanks so much. I've been knocked ass over tip, these last twenty-four hours or so, excuse me for needing some time to tuck in my privates." The look Cuinn shot him was far from unfocused. "I have a job to do. And I think I need to know what it was like, when you went after Garrett. After he died."

"*Eiscréid.* You don't ask much." Lochlann's heart was kicking violently against his ribs, at the thought of pulling out those particular memories for examination. He knew why Cuinn was asking, though, or he thought he did; he would never forget the long hours of watching the last surviving Loremasters surrender their bodies to the Realm and their souls to the Pattern, or his *chara*'s frustration at not being allowed to join them, at being told his part would be played elsewhere. "You think you're going to have to go after Rian? —Wherever I was when I followed Garrett, I don't think it was any kind of Fae afterlife."

"I don't know yet what I'm meant to do. Not entirely." From Cuinn's guarded expression, Lochlann guessed the other Fae actually had more of an idea than he was comfortable with. "But what you did is important, somehow."

Lochlann sighed, more to delay having to answer than for any other reason. "What was it like? I was scared shitless." The understatement of a couple of millennia; he'd just seen his SoulShare's head nearly severed by Janek's rusty butcher knife, felt the heat of his male's blood pouring from him to pool on the floor. *Scared shitless* wasn't even a fair start. "I wasn't trying to follow him. I was just channeling pure magick into him, as much as I could. Drawing the raw stuff straight from the ley line, using my body to convert it to living magick, and filling him with it. I thought —I don't remember exactly what I thought, maybe I wasn't really thinking. But I know I had some idea that I would stop channeling, and start shaping the magick into healing, when I sensed he was full. Only I never sensed it. The magick poured out, as fast as I poured it in."

Lochlann was shuddering. He couldn't stop. "I realized nothing I was giving him was staying. Like pouring water into a barrel with the bottom missing. So I did the only thing I knew how to do, I channeled more. And I started to lose myself. It was like being swept away in a river, but being the river, at the same time."

"I saw you go." Cuinn was slumped back against the back of the sofa, staring across the elegant suite, out the window, at the moon framed between the partly-open sheers. "I could see the magick pouring through you, out of you. Taking you with it. Wearing you away." The gaze the other Fae turned on him was bleak. "Do you think there's a chance that you could have held on, if your *scair-anam* had still been alive to ground you?"

"If he'd been alive, I wouldn't have been doing something so incredibly fucking stupid and dangerous in the first place."

"I realize that. Humor me." Cuinn still hugged himself, but whatever warmth he was generating didn't seem to be touching him.

"I'm not sure." Lochlann closed his eyes. Going back to those memories without getting sucked into them was a trick he couldn't always manage. "Possibly. Garrett centers me. Strengthens me. If he'd been there for me to hold on to, or to hold on to me..." He shook his head, meeting Cuinn's gaze almost, but not quite, apologetically. "I can't be sure. I'm just guessing. How can that help you?"

Cuinn rubbed his eyes with the heels of both hands, taking his time about it before replying. "Remember when I told you I thought you were showing me where I'm supposed to go? I'd like to find some lesson I can take away from this that doesn't involve me following my *scair-anam* into death."

Hell, yes, I remember. "Once upon a time, you were angry when the other Loremasters refused to let you follow them into the Pattern. Into oblivion."

Cuinn's head dropped back against the sofa back. "You don't understand. I've known from the start that I was almost sure to lose myself, when it came time for me to help save the Realm." His eyes were fixed on the ceiling. "But if I'm meant to follow him into death, then logically that means he has to go first. And he's suffered enough."

Lochlann probably shouldn't have been stunned. SoulSharing changed a Fae. Profoundly. But this was Cuinn an Dearmad, and a prudent Fae would at this point be listening for the other three Horsemen of the Apocalypse. "You'd tell the Loremasters to fuck off, after two thousand years, for the sake of your *scair-anam*?"

"You have no idea." If jade could burn, it would be Cuinn's eyes.

"I think I do, *chara*." Lochlann glanced at the bed, where he'd nearly fallen asleep waiting for Garrett to finish his shift and his solitary journey home.

Cuinn came abruptly out of his lazy slouch and turned toward the door, gone as still as a startled animal. By the time the Loremaster started to become transparent, Lochlann could hear the footfalls in the plush carpet of the hotel hallway. He surged to his feet and took a step toward the door, then stopped, mid-stride, and turned back to his friend.

Pale-jade eyes were all that remained, and a whisper that lingered in the air as the eyes vanished and the doorknob turned.

"They can't make me send him on ahead. Not again."

Chapter Fourteen

Greenwich Village
New York City

I need to borrow your eye, Meat.

Janek yawned. He'd probably give the bitch what she, it, wanted, sooner or later. But right now he was bored shitless, and arguing with the *Marfach* was more entertaining than another scavenger hunt through the basement. "Your need matters about as much to me as my need to take a piss. Less, actually." To drive home his point, he started fumbling with the button of his jeans.

Not down here.

The lecturing voice was back. Janek ignored it, cursing his clumsy fingers. Why couldn't the fucking Fae have given him back feeling in his fingers, when he made them stop rotting off?

If there is a smell down here, the other tenant may decide to clean.

"Big hairy fucking deal." Janek continued to grope. Maybe smashing the mirror that had been down here hadn't been such a hot idea after all. At least it would have let him see what the hell he was doing.

And who gave a particular fuck what the asshole on the second floor did?

If there is anything down here useful to us, he may remove it. And unless you are willing to let me carve out another piece of myself from our shared face in order to control him the way I do Bryce, there is no way for me to prevent it.

Even with most of his nerve endings dead and decayed, the thought of taking Guaire's Fae knife to the living crystal in his head made Janek's atrophied balls try to crawl up into his gut and hide. "I could always just kill him."

You may get your chance. Later. For the moment, at least, I would rather not draw attention to this place.

"What the fuck ever." Janek was getting bored with pawing at himself, too. "So convince me there's something *I* need down here."

He felt at least one part of the monster in his head sigh. Maybe both of the parts of it that still thought they needed to breathe. *My senses may not be as directly effective as yours, but they are independent of your flesh-based means of detection. I am sure there is magick here. Magick that could be useful to both of us. But I need your eye to see it.*

Janek's lip curled in a silent snarl. He genuinely hated to let the monster living in his head have the use of any of his body parts. It reminded him too much of the bad old days, the days that had only ended a few weeks ago, when the *Marfach* had been able to take over his body at will. Hell, he'd only been conscious when the motherfucker allowed it, until the first time Dary had put him through the meat grinder. Being a passenger in his own body sucked balls. "Just the eye. That's all you get."

His vision wavered, shifted. All of a sudden, he could see colors he knew didn't exist. Colors that moved. Colors that human eyes couldn't see unless an alien monster made them do it. *I forgot how much this part sucks, too.*

Fortunately for his stomach, there wasn't much of the light to deal with. All of the crawling light he could see was being cast by his own body and the crystal mass in his head, and even that was watered down by the sunlight slanting in through the basement's one window. *Fucker had better not tell me to cover the window.*

Look around. Slowly. The female's voice was tight.

She's probably having to work like hell not to try to take over. Janek smirked as he did what she asked. Loving the fact that she had to ask. *She knows that if she pisses me off, she doesn't get what she wants. Ever.*

Of course, if she didn't get what she wanted, then Janek wouldn't get what *he* wanted, either. Guaire's head. He played a game of chicken with her, no more. Still, it felt damned good to make her squirm. The male, too, whenever he got a chance to dick with him.

Turning his head, Janek looked around the basement store- room. It hadn't changed much since he'd come after the twink mage here. Dary. *Fuck him with a rusty knife*. Twice now, the pansy-ass had given him enough pain to make him beg the *Marfach* to let him die. Dary was next on his death list, assuming he got past offing Guaire.

141

Janek had pretty much trashed the place, after Dary disappeared and somehow sealed up the nexus. It had been cleaned up —Newhouse had admitted to doing most of it, the son of a bitch was an anal retentive freak about neatness. Which was what made it so much fun to fuck with him now.

Pay attention, Meat. The bitch's cool voice jerked Janek back to the here-and-now. Walls lined with mismatched shelving units, piled with decades worth of shit from who knew how many ten- ants. The frame of the mirror he'd smashed and then stomped to slivers was gone, of course, no neat freak would have let it sit there.

Something on the set of shelves opposite where the mirror had been was glowing, though.

That's it. Janek thought he could hear both the female and the male voices. Which meant this was something fucking special. *Go get it, boy,* the male voice added, laughing.

"Fuck off, asshole, I don't fetch." Janek crossed his arms and leaned back against the stairs, turning his head away from the weird-ass light show.

Moron.

The bitch obviously wasn't talking to Janek, and he couldn't help laughing. Let the two of them fight. He had some entertainment coming to him, after the last year or so of living in hell.

Pay no attention to him. The female might not have a body, but she sure as hell sounded like she was talking through clenched teeth. *Please. Go see what causes the light.*

Oh, what the hell. Janek pushed off the wall and crossed the concrete floor. There was a jumble of stuff on a shelf, shit that had probably fallen out of a box or something. Most of it just sat there, but a few things glowed as Janek poked through them with a finger. A key ring, an old-fashioned mother-of-pearl lady's compact, a box of upholstery tacks. And, brighter than anything else, a faded black leather dog collar.

Janek cringed, wishing he couldn't hear the laughter suddenly echoing in his head. For some reason, the monster's laughter made him think of burning bones. His own, most likely.

Collect all of it, it may be useful later. But the collar is precisely what I need.

"Why?" Janek blurted without thinking, as he started gathering up the glowing objects. *Shit, the last thing I want is for the monster to get chatty.*

Fortunately, it was the female who answered. She never missed a chance to lecture him. ***Humans have stories about what they call 'sympathetic magic.' To some extent, the stories are true. These items must have been directly exposed to the blast, when this nexus was triggered. They have retained some of the essence of the ley energy, and some of the essence of the Fae mage who caused the accident.***

"But I can't use any of that shit. And neither can you." The keys, the pocket mirror, and the small, heavy cardboard box went into Janek's pockets. He couldn't resist running the collar between his fingers, though. It wasn't soft, or expensive; an old, worn piece of leather that had probably gone around the neck of the fucking cannibal Rottweiler on the second floor. Whatever fucked-up mojo his passenger gave off, it apparently didn't impress dogs.

But there was something about the collar. The

143

kind of magickal light it gave off. It looked dangerous, somehow. Unstable. Afterimages stained his fingertips, throbbing and shifting. The light made him smile. Not so much the light itself, the colors still made his eye feel like it had been etched with acid. But the promise of chaos, hell, yeah, that felt good.

His passenger shared his happiness. *The ley energy and the essence of an unShared mage are not supposed to be able to coexist. But a collar is meant to restrain things. This binding should be impossible, but sympathetic magick makes it possible.*

"So how does that do anything for us?" Giving his passenger shit was second nature by now, but his heart wasn't really in it. He slapped the leather gently against his fingers, imagining he could feel the tingle on impact.

The trapped pairing of essences is highly volatile. He could hear the bitch smiling. *Once this collar is brought anywhere near the great nexus, the first time it flares up, as we have seen it do when a Fae is tapped into it, the resulting magickal detonation will certainly destroy the nexus. And, most likely, any Fae in contact with it.*

"I'd rather see the real thing. Bring the whole fucking place down." The thought of Guaire's asshole-buddies pancaked under slabs of concrete, bleeding out and suffocating in darkness was almost enough to give him a hard-on. *I just hope it's Dary who sets it off. It won't be as much fun to take Guaire's head if it's smashed.*

You may well get your wish, Meat. The male cackled. *There's no way to be sure until it happens.*

"How do we get it there, though?" It was hard to

force his mind away from its new set of happy pictures, but Janek tried. "I can't get us in there, not with the fucking ward up. And no one's going to fall for a UPS package marked *Please Put This Behind The Bar*."

I have that all worked out. The male's giggle sounded insane even to Janek. ***Let's go upstairs, shall we, and wait for our roommate to get home from work?***

Chapter Fifteen

Washington, D.C.

Rian rested his elbows on the chipped laminate table, staring at his half-full cup of coffee, turning the heavy gold ring on his finger round and round. Not that he was seeing either the coffee or the ring. No, he was seeing eyes, of a green so pale they could almost have been the fecking moonlight.

Shite, how he hated moonlight.

He'd been so close to getting what he needed. So close. Fire and blood and pain. The kind of pain that reached into him, offered him... what? A key. Something within himself, to be set free. But what? Something as beautiful and as terrible as the fire had been?

If there was anything left in him of such magnitude, it could fecking well stay locked up. Except he needed to let it out, because he was being burned from within. And how much longer could he stand the burning?

He snatched up the paper cup, barely noticing the splash of hot liquid against his skin as his hand shook. Cuinn had almost given him what he needed; he'd come closer than any man since the night of the coming of the fire. But then it had all gone arse-end-up, the very moment the Fae had drilled into him.

Rian covered his eyes with a hand, in case the tears stinging his eyes were flame. He had little control over that, and such would surely attract notice in a run-down coffee shop. Notice he could ill afford.

He'd never felt a joy like what seized him in that moment. Never in his life. It had rocked him to his core, jarred loose secrets he'd sworn to go to his grave clutching to himself. All told to the Fae with the beautiful eyes, the punishing cock, and the gentle kiss.

Whatever it was between himself and Cuinn had, of course, ended there. All of it. No way was he going to go beyond those minutes of pure nakedness. What more did he have in him to give, any road? The coffee scalded on its way down, and he fought down a cough.

Maybe those memories of love, the ones he oughtn't to have. *The only love we know is love of kin*, wasn't that what Cuinn had said? A foundling had no kin in this world. His Ma and his Da, as dearly as they'd loved him, and he them, they weren't 'kin.' Not the way Cuinn meant.

Well, fuck that.

Rian kneaded his forehead, rested his head on the heel of his hand, and groaned softly. A pretty *cailin* at the next table looked up, eyes wide and startled; he shook his head, and waved her off gently, until she returned her attention to the battered paperback she clutched in one hand, and he returned his to the depths of his coffee cup.

Rian darted a glance across the street, up and down the block. *Big Boy Massage*, one sign said, its fresh paint looking a hell of a lot better than the rest of the place, with its papered-over front window. Next came Raging Art-On, a tattoo and piercing parlor whose window was as neat and inviting as the massage parlor's was leprous.

He could barely see the black glass door closing off the entrance into Purgatory, at the bottom of the stairs, no doubt locked at this ungodly early hour of the early afternoon. But the street level doors stood open, and the strange swirling light was awake, alive, foaming up the stairs and settling back down, into the cement and concrete. Mesmerizing, it was.

So much so that he nearly didn't notice the other door opening, the one that led upstairs to the apartment he'd only quit an hour ago.

"Aww, feck."

Cuinn closed the door behind him and emerged onto the side- walk. Walking sex, the male was, as he shrugged a heavy brown bomber jacket into place across his perfectly muscled shoulders and looked up and down the street.

Rian pulled up the collar of his own jacket, denim lined with sheepskin, as best he could, and slouched down in the rickety wooden chair. Hoping not to be seen, even as something within him laughed at the futility of it. Of course Cuinn would find him.

He didn't even look up as the door to the shop opened and closed. Just swirled the coffee around in its cup, watching the fluorescent light glint off his ring, with its deep-cut design that looked sometimes like dancing flames, and sometimes like a heart. And always like something he'd lost.

He waited for Cuinn to take the seat opposite

him. Cuinn didn't. Instead, hands fell on Rian's shoulders from behind. Gentle, but as heavy as mortal sin, a weight nothing could dislodge.

"I wish I could hide, too, *dhó-súil.* You have no fucking idea how much."

"Then do it." Jesus, Mary, and Joseph, he needed to get a grip, his hand holding the coffee cup was shaking uncontrollably. He set the cup down firmly, hoping the other Fae hadn't noticed. "Get the hell away from me. I'll not chase you down."

"I think you would." Cuinn bent over him, half surrounding him, and fuck if the sandy-haired Fae's presence didn't make the rest of the place disappear like frost on the window behind a candle. "Just like I would, if you ran. As much as the thought pisses me off."

Rian couldn't keep back a short, harsh laugh. He tipped his head back, and instantly wished he hadn't, because those impossible jade eyes were there looking right back at him, and what the hell was a man supposed to do about those? "Why don't you let me try?"

"Would you grow the fuck up?" Cuinn's voice was tightly controlled. The grip on Rian's shoulders enough to bruise even through denim and sheepskin. "There's more at stake here than you can imagine."

"If this is where the wise old councillor reminds the brash young prince of his duties, you can save your breath." To keep himself from looking into those eyes, he fixed his gaze once more on the ring. Reminder of his unwanted heritage it might be, but the reminder beat the shit out of seducing the Fae again. Which is what he would do in another heartbeat, if given the chance, for all his fine resolve.

149

"And just what should I be saving it for, Highness?"

Fuck. That's done it. The honeyed edge to Cuinn's voice might as well have reached into his denims and palmed his Volunteer to attention. He didn't will his dark gift out, it just went, reaching for the other Fae and taking him into an intangible embrace. He didn't even have to turn, he could feel Cuinn go rigid against his back. "Moaning my name, might be a start."

"Damn you." Cuinn barely whispered, but Rian could hear his tension. "This isn't what I want. Not this time."

Again the grip on his shoulders tightened, and Rian winced, a thrill running through him despite his reluctance. Surely he could push Cuinn harder this time. Hard enough. "Are you sure?" He tipped his head back, and his heart missed a beat or two at sight of the heat in the gaze Cuinn leveled at him.

"I suppose I should thank you for making this so easy."

As Rian opened his mouth to ask what the feck Cuinn was on about, the other Fae gestured, a rotating movement of one hand. A lattice of light grew up from the floor, in a circle around them, icy bluish-silver lines that arched up over the two of them, and the little table, until they met somewhere over their heads. The light flared brightly, then faded to near invisibility.

"A Fae always channels magick more easily when he's aroused." The hand that had brought the lines into being now cupped Rian's jaw, with a tenderness he suspected was as strange to Cuinn as it was to him. "Right now, I think I could vanish Mr. Lincoln from his great stone chair without breaking a sweat."

"That's lovely for you, but—"

Cuinn caught at Rian's arm and hauled him to his feet, turning him around. Rian stumbled against the chair he'd been sitting in, knocking it aside; Cuinn grabbed him, steadying him, and looked up at him. Rian had a good six inches on the shorter Fae, but somehow that didn't seem to matter a damn. Cuinn held him transfixed.

"Has anyone ever been gentle with you? Even once?"

The question was a stunner. Rian blinked down at the other Fae, wondering which sense was going to play him false next. "You're not serious."

"I am."

"Then you're daft." Rian tried to twist away, but Cuinn's grip was relentless.

"And you're avoiding. Which is a total shock."

The scent of leather and sweat and Cuinn hit Rian all at once. *Damn it to hell, I'm not supposed to be the one whose fecking knees are giving way!* He tried to focus, to picture Cuinn losing all interest in his awkward questions and setting about groping himself like the sons of bitches around the fire on the Twalf.

No fucking luck whatsoever. Oh, Cuinn wanted him. He could scent the other Fae's arousal, right along with the leather and what he was pretty sure was Versace Pour Homme. But he wasn't doing anything about the wanting, wasn't even paying the condition of his cock any mind, from the look of him. No, he was waiting for an answer to his question. The question that made his, Rian's, head hurt like a very motherfucker.

"No. *Now* will you let go of me?"

The only answer he got was a hand around the

back of his neck, drawing his head down. He resisted. Or he tried to. Cuinn's mouth was on his, Cuinn's tongue was teasing at his lips, slipping into his mouth. Cuinn's body was against his, lean and hard and as hot as the air outside was chill and dank.

The kiss? The kiss was heaven.

And there was no heaven, not for him.

"Oh, no, you fucking don't." Cuinn held Rian firmly, one hand around the back of his neck and one arm around his waist, preventing him from turning away, or even looking away. "Relax, no one can see us. Or hear us. Not till I lower that shield. Which, in case you're wondering, isn't happening for a while yet."

Rian stopped trying to twist out of Cuinn's arms. For now. "Mind telling me what you're doing? Apart from going barking mad?" Hopefully, the light tone would hide the way his heart was pounding. *It's just a kiss. It's not what I need. Not even close.*

"If I knew for sure, you'd be the second to know." Cuinn's mouth was warm on his throat, in the hollow of it left bare by his shirt. "Look, would you mind sitting? Bad enough you being a Royal, did you have to be so fucking tall?"

"You could always kneel." One last attempt to turn this clusterfuck into something that might get him what he craved.

"Not yet."

Before he could protest, Cuinn had turned him, hooked the chair back over toward them both with a booted foot, and gently urged him to sit.

"Much better." Cuinn swung a leg over to straddle Rian's lap, then settled in, his forearms resting on Rian's shoulders.

This has to stop. Now. "Look, you can either figure out what the fuck you're playing at, and tell me, or you can find out what happens when your head goes through this pretty shield of yours. Your choice. Me, I'm good either way." The words would have sounded more convincing with an edge to them, but for some reason Rian's head insisted on dropping back, and his eyes on trying to close, and it was too damned hard to put an edge on a threat when he kept catching himself holding his breath waiting for the next time that mouth touched his throat. *What the god-damned hell is he doing to me?*

Cuinn leaned closer; sandy hair brushed Rian's cheek, dark- blond lashes smudged the other Fae's cheekbones as his eyes drifted closed. "I don't know where to start. It's clear in my head, but when I try to explain it to anyone else —myself included —it makes no fucking sense at all."

"Welcome to my life." Rian laughed, a sharp staccato sound. "There are exactly two things that have made sense to me since I charred those motherfuckers last summer. And in case you're curious, you going sweet on me isn't one of them."

Cuinn straightened. "What are they?"

"Shite." The pain was like a knife between his eyes; he scarcely noticed as Cuinn's hand slid up to cup the back of his head, and drew him in. *I just had to go and run my mouth.* "One, the fuckers gave me the key to a door, when they savaged me. And two..."

Cuinn said nothing, only waited, stroking the back of his head with an unsteady hand.

Rian couldn't get his breath. He'd never been one to confide in anyone. The Sacrament of Confession

153

could have been a torture designed expressly for him. Secrets were a part of his soul, and not to be given away.

But he's part of my soul. Maybe that's why I can't but tell him. He looked up, for once not caring if someone else saw the truth of his feelings in his eyes. "Two. I don't know where the door is, or what's behind it. But I need it. It's my death if I don't find it."

"I'll help you."

Cuinn's voice was soft. Nothing like the snarl Rian remembered so fondly from the night before. The other Fae's breath was warm in his ear, threatening to calm him.

His head jerked up as if pulled by a string. He could only bear Cuinn's regard for a moment, before he laughed again, this time through clenched teeth, and turned his head away. "Why the feck should you want to do that?"

He was looking out through the light-lattice at the coffee shop window, now, and through it out to the street. Somehow the world was going on quite nicely by itself, all oblivious to how strange this small corner of it had become.

"I told you, I don't know." Cuinn's laugh didn't sound all that different from his own. Just as bewildered, and almost as frustrated. Saner, though. Maybe. "All I know is that what I felt last night —you felt it too, don't bother to deny it —I've never felt anything like it in my life. Which life has been going on long enough that I really did think there was nothing new left. Until I realized how badly I need you."

Reluctantly, Rian turned back to Cuinn, drawn by

the force of those words, the effort that went into them. "You don't want to need me."

"Hell, no." Cuinn shifted on top of him, and all the scents and sensations of arousal flooded over him anew. "One thing you'll learn soon, if you don't know it already, no Fae ever wants to *need* anything. Especially not from another Fae."

Rian understood, or thought he did. "If you need something, whoever has what you need has power over you."

"Congratulations, you're a Fae."

For all the bitterness in Cuinn's voice, there was a longing in his beautiful eyes, one Rian wanted to be able to ignore. Unfortunately, he was shit-out-of-luck in that regard.

"And you're my SoulShare." Cuinn's hand cupped Rian's jaw, a thumb stroked his cheek. "I want you to share what I felt. Need you to. That alone is enough to make me wonder if I've lost my mind."

"Cuinn..." The touch on Rian's cheek tingled, burned. Drove out the pain in his head, and made it worse at the same time.

Cuinn didn't appear to hear him. "But you don't want the joy. You don't want any part of it. And it bugs the shit out of me that it bugs the shit out of me to know that."

"I'm sorry." To his mighty astonishment, Rian believed what he said. It would be good, to see Cuinn smile, to be able to give him what he needed. He wished he could do it. But it wasn't in him, not if he was honest about who and what he was. "There's no joy to sex, no wonder. It's not about making someone happy, or being happy myself. It's about getting what I need."

"You don't need wonder?"

Rian started to shake his head, but was stopped, dead, by a kiss. Not one like last night's, not the first move of a duel. A gentle, lips-parted kiss, an exchange of breath. Closed eyes, the soft touch of a tongue. A shiver, arrowing down his spine.

"You're so fucking wrong," Cuinn whispered, before taking Rian's mouth for fair.

Shite. Cuinn's kisses were even hotter than his body, which was at the moment rocking slowly, teasing, promising, hardening. But his kisses demanded nothing. Took nothing. Cuinn's insistent tongue stroked his own, tasting somehow of honey and an excellent single malt.

This has to stop. Rian's hands weren't listening, they were hauling Cuinn's t-shirt out of his jeans and sliding open-palmed up his back, feeling muscles shift as Cuinn took his face between his hands, the better to cover it with slow, sensual kisses. *Any minute now.*

He felt a shiver run through Cuinn, heard and felt and tasted the other Fae's soft moan. All he felt, though, was a pang of envy, which was made worse when Cuinn pulled back and looked questioningly into his eyes. He shook his head slightly, surprised at the depth of his disappointment.

"Could you possibly be any more obstinate?" The words were murmured against his lips like an endearment. Maybe they were; they were followed by a gentle nip at his lower lip, a swipe of the tongue. "You felt it last time." Cuinn's kisses traveled along his jaw, slowly down his throat. "Unclench and let me in, you stubborn Fae son of a bitch."

Rian couldn't help laughing.

That was when he felt it. A faint, unfamiliar ripple, starting where Cuinn's mouth searched his skin and spreading until every inch of him tingled. He flinched, or he tried to; there was no way to pull away from himself.

He could feel Cuinn's lips curve into a smile against his throat. "Got you."

Rian would have protested, except that Cuinn immediately started giving him too many other things to be thinking about; hands inside his shirt, pushing it up to let Cuinn bend to lick his nipples, then one hand moving down to tease at the curve of proud flesh trying to push its way out of his denims before setting to work at the button. And every touch gave him that strange sensation, that gentle wash of joy.

"Damn." Rian closed his eyes and let his head fall back. It felt so good he didn't want to think about anything else. But the pain in his head was relentless now, throbbing in rhythm with his aching erection. Cuinn's mouth, sweet bleeding *Christ*, working its way down his abs as the other Fae slid from his arms to kneel on the floor in front of him.

Rian gripped the seat of the chair, white-knuckled, trying to get control of his breathing. Cuinn opened his denims, slid his hands around to the sides, stroking Rian's hips with his thumbs before working his fingers into the waistband.

"Raise up for me, *dhó-súil.*" Cuinn's breath was hot against the tight blond curls and brick-red flesh visible in the vee formed by the open zipper; Rian's hips jerked with the too-brief caress of Cuinn's tongue.

"You're going to fecking kill me." Rian could barely understand his own words.

"Only if you don't rise up and let me get the fucking jeans off you."

He sounds serious. Rian took his weight on his hands and arched up, just enough to let Cuinn start working the slightly-too-tight denims down. As he was bared, he took a quick look around. The latticework of the shell Cuinn had put up around the two of them was barely visible, but it had to be working, because no one was paying any mind whatsoever to either of the Fae. Not the girl perusing her battered paperback, not the barista engrossed in some game on her phone, not the gent outside checking the part in his hair and the set of his collar, using the store front as a mirror. No one could see Cuinn easing his trousers down to pool around his ankles, moving to kneel between his spread thighs.

I hope to God no one can hear us, either, because I believe he means to make me scream if he can. The intent was obvious, from the way the other Fae was kissing, licking, nipping the soft skin at the very tops of his thighs, while completely ignoring the cock that speared upward in front of his face. Wavy hair tickled the insides of Rian's parted legs, and his fingers twitched with the desire to be buried in that softness. Not to mention, use that softness to put Cuinn's mouth where he was beginning to be desperate about wanting it.

"Jaysus." Rian stared, wide-eyed and beginning to sweat, as Cuinn stroked first one ball and then the other, slowly, lavishly, with the flat of his velvet tongue. Moaned in the back of his throat, watching Cuinn take one of the heavy globes into his mouth, gently suckle it, his eyes slowly closing as he slid his hands round Rian and interlaced fingers in the small of his back.

Has anyone ever been gentle with you? Even once? The question still echoed in his head, deep down in the little corner left for thought amid the throbbing pain and the crazy need and the fever that always seemed to lick at the ragged inflamed edges of his sanity.

Cuinn started a nice, slow lollipop. All the way down at his taint —and didn't that make him bite his lip near through? —the flat of the Fae's tongue gliding up the underside of Rian's cock. No hands; Cuinn's palms were splayed out over his lower back, now, and there was nothing to control Rian's twitching shaft except Cuinn's mouth. Beads of clear flame welled up at the tip, one after another, trickling down over the crown or being scattered by the random jerks of his aching organ.

"Do you feel it, Highness?" The tiny flames trickled down Cuinn's cheek, against which Rian's cock leaned to allow the Fae to use his mouth for something other than driving Rian fucking insane. He felt Cuinn's hot breath against the base of his shaft, stirring the dusting of hair on his balls. "Still not interested in wonder? Joy?"

"Feck off." Rian's lips moved soundlessly, and his hips came up off the chair to make liars of the silent words. *'Sea*, the sweetness still ghosted over him, soft seductive ripples spreading from each touch of Cuinn's mouth, each stroke of fingertips in the small of his back. But if he thought about it too much, the pounding of his head rose up to drown it out. Better to just focus on the warmth, the softness of Cuinn's ministrations, the searching mouth once again making its way up his deeply-veined shaft.

A quick tongue-tip flirtation with the sweet spot under his flared crown, and then Rian's eyes tried to roll back in his head at the sensation of Cuinn's mouth engulfing the head of his cock, all at once, taking him in all the way to the back of the other Fae's throat. Rian's legs jerked, he choked on a gasp and whispered a stream of curses *as Gaeilge* at the sensation of being swallowed.

Oh fuck it all Cuinn's finger sliding into him, crooking ---

Rian's back spasmed, twisted, arched. Cuinn followed his every move, sucking hard, his lips rimmed with flickering white flames as he took in and swallowed gout after gout of fire from Rian's pulsing cock.

And for one exquisite, blinding instant, bliss.

"Rian? *Dhó-súil?*"

He was being shaken. His head sounded and felt like a bodhran being beaten with a claw-foot hammer for a tipper. "I'm here. Jesus, keep your voice down, my head's dinnlin'."

"Well, shit." Cuinn staggered to his feet and reached out to help Rian up. "At least you felt it, that's something. Even if this wasn't what it took to finish the Sharing." The other Fae flashed him a quick, hesitant smile.

Rian's eyes burned with tears, as Cuinn helped him set his clothing to rights and dropped the shield around them. Tears he'd never allow to fall. He didn't know much yet, about being Fae. But he suspected that the race into which he'd been born seldom wept for what they'd lost.

Chapter Sixteen

"Hey, Red." Terry looked up from where he sat hunched over his drawing board, behind the cash register in the little front room of Raging Art-On. "Josh is back in his studio, he just finished up with a client, so he's probably still cleaning up."

Nodding, Conall crossed to the register and craned his neck over the counter to look at the design Terry was sketching out and carefully painting, a design to be inked later. A wolf, not quite at Josh's level of skill but still beautiful. "Someone's going to be very lucky to get that." The Fae was still unaccustomed to having friends, and having his *scair-anam*'s former lover as one of them was an experience bordering on the surreal. But Terry had been good to Josh, and kind to Conall himself, when Conall was in a bad way after arriving from the Realm. Besides, one never knew when being good at small talk with humans might come in handy.

Terry blushed, his already olive complexion going several shades duskier. "I hope so. Josh wants me to put it on him. Why, I have no idea, he could do it himself just as easily and a lot better."

But if he did, it would come alive every time he

and I make love. Which could be a problem. The hawk and the dragon were bad enough.

The door to Josh's studio opened, and Conall looked up from his perusal of Terry's art with a smile that probably told his SoulShare exactly what his errand was. "May I borrow you, *dar'cion?* I don't think it will take more than a few minutes."

"Go ahead," Terry piped up, without looking up from his work. "The next appointment we have booked isn't for twenty minutes, and it's for a piercing, so I can handle it."

Josh leaned over the counter beside Conall, close enough that Conall's skin tingled with the nearness of him, in a way that he suspected was never going to get old. Josh waited for Terry to notice he was there, and to look up from his work; once he had Terry's attention, Josh's brows knit together into a stern line. "You're my partner, Terrence. If you couldn't handle anything and everything that walks in through that door, I wouldn't have taken you on. *Capisce?*"

Terry's blush darkened. Conall understood the embarrassment, or thought he did. It would have been impossible for a Fae in Terry's position, thrown out of his home by the male he'd broken up with Josh to take up with, to turn to Josh when he had nowhere else to go. But Terry had trusted, and Josh's utterly big, utterly un-Fae heart had done the rest.

"*Capisco.*" Terry flashed Josh a smile, then looked back down at his work, the smile lingering.

Some kinds of magick, only humans can work. Conall slipped his hand into Josh's and smiled up at his partner. "I'll try not to keep you too long."

"I kind of hope you do, *d'orant.*" Josh's

answering smile was wicked, and Conall suddenly felt warm all the way to his toes.

The pair emerged from Raging Art-On, and disappeared immediately down the light-swallowing staircase leading to Purgatory. Light-swallowing except for the magickal light that spilled up the stairs. *Damn, the nexus is active today*, Conall thought. It had been ever since Cuinn had arrived with the Fire Royal, come to think of it.

Conall felt the protective ward whisper against his skin as he made his way down the stairs, and made a face. *It was sloppy work putting that up. Just give me five minutes, I'll do better.*

Lucien the bouncer was waiting for them at the bottom of the steps, as they pushed their way through the heavy black glass doors. The bouncer was as close to a human bulldog as Conall had ever seen, and when it was necessary, he showed the temperament to match; he'd never been any less than cordial to Conall, though, and today was no exception. "Afternoon, gentlemen, always a pleasure." Bald head topped massive shoulders over a bear's gut and wrestler's legs. It was a good thing, Conall had always thought, humans had gods to pray to for divine intervention should one of them piss off Lucien.

"Are you ready to fix the ward?" Josh spoke softly, since it wasn't so early that the bar was empty of customers; Mac, the amputee Vietnam veteran, was pouring for a cluster of men in business suits, and Conall thought he recognized the man at the end of the bar, a young Japanese who transformed into a striking drag queen most Thursday and Friday nights. Now, though, he was nursing a bottle of Kirin Ichiban, bereft

163

of makeup and with his bleached hair pulled back with a mesh band.

"I think so." Just to be safe, Conall channeled a screen to keep the sight of the door opening onto the secure stairwell hidden from the humans, for as long as it took for him and Josh to skirt around the far end of the bar, and for him to channel the lock open and let them both down into the semi-darkness. Semi-darkness in the visible spectrum. In magickal light, it looked more like the fireworks display Josh had taken him to, not long after their Sharing. "I had to play with the channeling parameters for a while in my head. I've never tried to do anything like this."

Josh waited outside the second door, the one to the nexus chamber proper, while Conall tapped in the entry code. And even Josh blinked as the inner door swung wide. SoulShared humans were moderately sensitive to magick —the result of having a Fae soul in a human body —and Josh was more so than most, since at least part of Conall's own freakish channeling ability was housed in his body. "Damn." His beautifully inked *scair-anam* pinched the bridge of his nose as he sat down on the black leather chaise in the middle of the room. "It feels like that time I had a fever of a hundred and five when I was a kid, except I don't feel sick."

"Never having had a fever, I'll have to take your word for it." Conall swung a leg over and knelt astride his partner, arms wrapped loosely around his neck. "The nexus is being incredibly hyper. Do you need me to do something about it for you?"

Josh shook his head, blinked hard a couple of times, and smiled up at Conall. "I can manage. If it gets too bad, I can always close my eyes and work by touch. I know how you like that."

Conall couldn't help purring, just a little. "True. Or I could make you wear a blindfold, for a change."

"That's new, you proposing to make me do something." The laughter in his human lover's dark eyes took most of the edge off his words, leaving just enough to send a delicious shiver skittering down Conall's spine to take up residence in his sac. Josh stripped off Conall's shirt and let it fall to the floor; one arm wrapped around Conall's waist, holding him as Josh bent to work at the mage's throat, gently, with his teeth.

"You might like it." Conall tilted his head to give Josh better access. Even a glance from his *scair-anam* was enough to make his cock rise; this kind of attention was, needless to say, even better.

"I'm sure I would." Tongue soothed where teeth had nearly pierced. "Why do the wards need to be fixed in the first place? —not that I mind taking a break from work for a good cause, mind you."

"The Health Department's liable to shut Tiernan down if I don't." Conall got off Josh's lap and stretched out on the chaise, raising his arms over his head and offering his hands for the shack- les attached at the corners. "It turns out that some humans react badly to a non-specific ward, and they get dizzy and pass out when they cross one. Tiernan's gotten two citations already, and one more incident could get the club locked down."

Josh paused, frowning thoughtfully, in the act of closing one of the padded cuffs around Conall's wrist. "I've had issues with a few clients doing the same,

165

when they come into my studio. But you expect a certain amount of that when your art involves needles, skin, and usually bleeding."

"That makes sense." Conall nodded. "I made sure the ward encompassed your machine, once we found out you channel magick when you use it." He caught his lower lip briefly between his teeth as Josh finished locking the shackle. "The new ward will be tuned to Janek and the *Marfach*, so it shouldn't cause those problems. And because it's specific, I can make it bigger, and more powerful, and still use less magick. I can shield the whole building, including our apartment and the massage parlor." Lochlann had just signed a lease on the long-vacant massage parlor next to Raging Art-On, with plans to offer actual therapeutic massage himself, in addition to hiring a staff to offer the kind of services Big Boy Massage's clientele had apparently come to expect over the years.

"So, a happy accident." Josh was on his hands and knees atop Conall, and dark eyes glinted wicked amusement as he tugged Conall's shirt out of the waistband of his jeans with his teeth. "Will it be enough to keep Newhouse out, too? —since you were interrupted last night?"

"I hope so. He has the *Marfach* in him somehow, and that should be enough to —damn it, *dar'cion*, if you want me to be able to talk, you need to keep your tongue out of my jeans."

He felt Josh's hard body shaking against his own with suppressed laughter. "I'd say I'm sorry, but you wouldn't believe me." Strong fingers opened Conall's jeans, soft warm lips closed around the head of his erection and then mouthed down his length while Josh worked his jeans down his hips. "What do you need this time, *d'orant*?"

Conall couldn't answer for a moment. All he could do was marvel at the love in the deep brown eyes with laughter in their depths. "I need you to take me right to the edge, and keep me there. Don't let me release." Arousal was what let him tap into the nexus safely, and while some channelings were quickly done, the one he needed to do in order to put up the kind of ward he had in mind was going to take him several minutes. Several minutes of trying to concentrate on the technicalities of channeling while his lover pleasured him blind. *I have such a difficult life...*

Josh's answer was a long, slow swipe of the tongue, one that started with a tease at Conall's entrance and didn't stop until the human groaned with pleasure at the taste of the effervescent drops he licked from Conall's crown. Conall sucked in a breath between clenched teeth, and sweat prickled on his forehead as he felt the leather band Josh had tattooed around the base of his cock and balls spring to sweetly constricting life at the inrush of magick.

Thoughtfully, Josh stroked the leather with two fingertips, played with the little buckle. "Not a bad job. I think I'll leave it on you a while."

Though this was exactly what Conall wanted to hear, his arms still jerked, making his chains clank softly as he reflexively tried to reach for the already-strained leather. "Are you sure it isn't too tight?"

His *scair-anam* chuckled. "Looks just fine to me." He put two fingers into his mouth, sucked on them just long enough to give Conall a good look at what he was doing, and then slipped them into his tight

167

puckered entrance, hooking and spreading them. "How does this feel?"

Conall told Josh exactly how it felt, *as'Faein*. A Fae of the Demesne of Air could understand any language the air brought to his ears, but Conall had never heard anyone use the words he needed in English, not even during an orgy in Purgatory's cock pit on a Saturday night.

Josh only understood the Fae language when the two of them were dreamwalking, but he obviously caught the spirit of Conall's curses. The smile he flashed Conall before he applied his free hand and his mouth to Conall's rapidly-purpling shaft was damned near enough to bring the Fae off all by itself. "Maybe you'd better start, *d'orant*. That ring might be a little small, at that."

"Oh, fuck." Sweat beaded on Conall's upper lip, now, and trickled down his temples, darkening his red-gold hair to auburn. He closed his eyes once more, savoring the heat of his lover's mouth playing over stretched-tight skin.

Then, with a groan, he reached within for his magick, for the channeling he had so carefully constructed. Once released, and fed with the faintest trickle from the endless stream of power underneath them, the channeling would open out like a Hoberman sphere, with a shell tuned to the life energy of Janek O'Halloran, such as it was, and of his malevolent passenger. Any contact between the ward and its subject would, in theory, annihilate the would-be intruder.

First, though, he had to get the damned thing up. Magick was surging through him in waves, each a little stronger than the one before it, building in intensity as Josh skillfully worked him. Carefully, or as carefully as he could under the circumstances, he released the channeling. The act felt like shaking out a length of gossamer silk. In a windstorm that had tornado -like ambitions.

Josh caught his breath. "I can feel that."

"So can *Scáthacru.*" Bronze-wing, Josh's tattooed dragon, had come to life at the touch of Conall's magick, and was raising his head from the human's forearm in a lazily interested sort of way. Sometimes Conall wondered if the ancient legends were true, and dragons and cats were actually cousins. They both certainly acted like it.

"Down, boy." Josh laughed softly.

"I hope to hell you're talking to the dragon." Conall's laughter was breathless and light. It felt as if it floated on the magick, and maybe it did. "Nothing else is going down."

"I'm not so sure about that." Josh's lips sealed around his crown, his tongue played over the smoothness and continued to lash as Conall slowly arched his back.

Little whimpering sounds welled up in the back of Conall's throat, like beads of fluid at the tip of his cock. The channeling surrounded him in a caul, slowly inflating as magick coursed through him. The nexus was restive, its energy wilder than Conall had ever felt it, and using his body to tame it was exhilarating. Almost too much so. Easy to let himself be carried off, swept away. But the pleasure kept him present in the here and now. And the joy kept him bound to his partner. His lover.

Conall could feel the ring growing tighter; the combination of the hot heaviness of his cock and the tracings of Josh's tongue sent magick coursing through the ward-channeling. And damn near shorted out his brain, too, an enjoyable side effect. It was cool in the basement, but he was sweating, his skin peeling away from the black leather every time his back arched up.

Josh took him deep, and as he did, Conall released the channeling. Not dramatically, no *fly free!* moment. More like letting a soap bubble go, if it was possible to do that from inside it. He could feel it as it moved away from him, a charge that was almost electricity, prickling the hair on his forearms and legs. If he chose to, he could see it, an intricate silver-blue patterning, there and not there, like most magick. A pattern tuned precisely to the life energy of the unholy composite being that was the *Marfach.*

Josh's hand wrapped most of the way around Conall's swollen testicles, and he groaned, yanking yet again at his chains. Now all he had to do was lie back, succumb to Josh's ministrations, and try like hell to hold out for the fifteen minutes or so it would take for the slowly-expanding ward to fully envelop the building.

The sacrifices I make for my art...

Chapter Seventeen

The Realm

The first branch, the one he'd called the Great Stair, as a boy dreaming of palaces, was almost exactly where it had been, the day he decided he was too old to climb trees. Fortunately for Cuinn, trees didn't grow in the Realm the way they did in the human world. Didn't age and die, either.

He swung himself up onto the lowest branch, then dug his toe into the deeply ridged bark and started climbing. About halfway up the ancient oak, a three-way fork in a branch formed a natural seat, one he'd spent many hours in as a child. Hopefully it remained. It had been over twenty-five hundred years, and the Realm wasn't immune from storms.

Spending the magick to come back here, with the Realm in the state it was in, was probably insane. But he had to talk to Aine, and he couldn't go back to his Greenwich Village flat. Purgatory was likewise out of the question, with the nexus in flux. Hell, moving Rian in right on top of it had probably been an act of idiocy, too. Though the torrent of magick had yet to make it much past street level, even at its most restive, and certainly not up to the second floor. Yet.

What he needed was a place that was quiet, and private, and fed his soul. What there was of it. Someplace he could go to contemplate the very real possibility that his life was about to end.

The fork wasn't as high as he remembered it. It was also considerably narrower. Cuinn settled into it as best he could, then dug in his pocket for the little notebook and stylus he'd brought with him. Hopefully, Aine would be willing to tell him if his guesses were right. It was past time to stop dicking around.

He flipped open the leather-bound book, and wasn't entirely surprised to see the shaping on the first page. *HAIL, YOUNGEST BROTHER.*

Cuinn grimaced. *Sweet talk already? I must be right.* I NEED TO TALK TO YOU, AINE. ONLY YOU. GOT THAT? The last shaping nearly put the stylus through the paper.

There was a pause, a hesitation, before the next shaping appeared. *WE ARE ALONE. THOUGH THIS IS NOT EASY.*

You think you've got problems? I THINK I KNOW WHAT YOU EXPECT OF ME.

An even longer pause. *TELL ME.* Then, strangely, the image erased itself, was replaced by a hastily-sketched *WAIT.*

Wait for what?

Cuinn startled as an enormous rainbow-winged dragon-fly touched down on a branch that drooped just over his head. Staring at the slowly shifting wings, he almost missed the *d'aos'Faein* shaping in the book propped on his knee.

THIS MESSENGER CAN LISTEN FOR ME,

THOUGH HE CANNOT SPEAK.

"What the particular fuck?"

BE CAREFUL, DO NOT STARTLE HIM. MY CONTROL OVER HIM IS NOT GOOD.

"How the hell are you doing this?"

OUR ABILITY TO MANIFEST PHYSICALLY IS TRAPPED HERE, ALONG WITH OUR SOULS. BUT WITH CARE, OUR SENSES CAN BE ANYWHERE MAGICK IS FOUND.

Cuinn supposed that made sense, since the souls and physical potential of each of the Loremasters was embedded in a sympathetic representation of all the magick to be found anywhere in the Realm. But still... "I've never even heard of a channeling like that."

WE HAVE LEARNED A FEW NEW THINGS, IN OVER TWO THOUSAND YEARS. Somehow, Cuinn sensed a smile in the shaping. *LIFE WOULD BE UNBEARABLE, ELSE. BUT SPEAK, TIME IS SHORT.*

"No shit." Cuinn took a deep breath and leaned his head back against the tree, watching the dragon-fly with his eyes half closed. Dragon-flies in the Realm were more dragon than fly, though the iridescent wings were similar. Unblinking gemmed eyes stared back at him. "I've had most of the pieces for a while, I just didn't know what to do with them. The last one, though, I didn't have until this latest cockup with the M- with the enemy." Yeah, letting the sound of the *Marfach*'s name in with all the names and essences of the Loremasters who were the Realm's last —only, really —line of defense against it probably wasn't a good idea.

He didn't bother looking down at the book in his

hand. He didn't really give a shit what Aine might have to say at this point, anyhow. "Tiernan showed me how the SoulShare works. How it lets a Fae touch the nexus safely, turn ley energy, wild magick, to living magick. Conall showed me the kind of power a Shared Fae can handle. And Lochlann showed me..."

His voice trailed off, as once again in memory he saw his friend, his *chara*, wild with a grief he himself was only now starting to understand, surrendering to a torrent of magick and being swept away by it. A torrent that was no more than a trickle, beside the maelstrom of the nexus. "Lochlann showed me what I'm going to have to do."

Now, he glanced down. *YES.* The shaping was simple, powerful.

"I'm the conduit for the ley energy. To send it back to the Realm."

YOU ARE. THE SPACE WAS LEFT FOR YOU IN THE PATTERN. WHEN YOU FILL THAT SPACE, YOU WILL LET THE LEY ENERGY SAFELY INTO THE REALM, TO BECOME LIVING MAGICK. TO BECOME LIFE, AS IT WAS BEFORE.

Cuinn looked up, past the dragon-fly, out through the canopy of leaves. The sky was bluer than any sky in the human world, the sunlight that dappled his skin through the impossibly green leaves more golden, the air scented with flowers and as intoxicating as wine.

And as clearly as any of that, he saw jewel-cut blue eyes. A male, the other half of his own soul, discovering joy in a world where he once thought he only wanted pain.

"I don't want to go," he whispered.

YOU WILL SAVE THIS WORLD, YOUNGEST

BROTHER.

"Which was all I cared about, once."

YOU WILL NOT FAIL US.

A sudden, terrible thought sent ice sleeting down his spine. "Are you planning for us what you planned for Lochlann and Garrett?"

WHAT DO YOU MEAN?

"You know perfectly fucking well what I mean." His free hand clenched into a fist so tight his nails cut bloody, stinging crescents in his palm. "Lochlann wouldn't have done what he did if he hadn't been out of his fucking mind over his human. If you in all your omniscient glory hadn't gotten his SoulShare killed."

The dragon-fly launched itself into the air, with a spit of flame and a whir of wings. *NO. NO. NO.* The single curve shaped itself over and over. *YOUR PRINCE WILL LIVE. HE MUST. HE IS YOUR PROTECTION.*

"Yeah, I was—"Cuinn grimaced as he remembered Aine's eyes-and-ears had just left, and turned to a clean page in the book, gripping the stylus white-knuckled. *I WAS MEANING TO ASK YOU ABOUT THAT. JUST HOW SURE ARE YOU THAT THIS IS GOING TO WORK?*

AS SURE AS WE CAN BE WITHOUT FORESEEING. The shaping wobbled, then firmed. As if Aine was struggling to keep this private link open. *WE DARED NOT INTERFERE, NOT EVEN TO WATCH, AS HE GREW TO MANHOOD. ANY TOUCH FROM US MIGHT HAVE BEEN TOO MUCH, MIGHT HAVE CAUSED HIM TO DOUBT HIS HUMANITY.*

Cuinn thought about that, remembering Rian's

haunted eyes as he recounted driving his rapists insane, before burning them to death. His *scair-anam* was a *rachtanai* Fae prince, instinctively capable of *asiomú* but now stuck in his reversal and unable or unwilling to find his way back. A Fae who loved humans who were in no way blood kin to him.

Was Rian's borrowed humanity going to be enough to let him do what he had to do?

Did he want it to be?

YOU HAVE A PROBLEM. He sketched quickly, lightly.

ONLY ONE?

Was that a joke? Cuinn shook his head, wondering. At himself, at Rian, at the ancient mages who had steered a whole world through more than two thousand years of history with- out the slightest understanding of what they were playing with. *SOULSHARING WORKS. AND YOU'RE ASKING ME TO WALK AWAY FROM THE OTHER HALF OF MY SOUL WHEN I"VE ONLY JUST FOUND HIM.*

I AM... The shaping paused. *SORRY.*

Cuinn's jaw dropped slightly. He would have had to pick up the stylus and shape if he wanted to ask what the current temperature was in hell, rendering it somewhat easier to curb his wiseass tendencies. A Loremaster, apologizing? Noticing someone else's pain?

Not to mention the fact that another Loremaster was feeling pain to start with.

BUT YOU ARE AS STRONG AS ANY OF US. The shaping started to wobble again, to race. *YOU WILL BE ABLE TO COMPLETE THE PATTERN. I HAVE FAI*

The shaping stopped.

Fuck me oblivious.

Sighing, Cuinn swung his legs out of the fork in the branches, wrapped an arm around the trunk of the old oak, and started to climb down. He was going to have to replenish his magick before opening a rift to go back, and he didn't want to permanently siphon the life out of a branch he was still sitting on. Come to think of it, before he gave the land his kiss of death, he wanted to be a long way from anything that had ever meant anything to him.

Which was kind of fitting, really. Seeing as that was exactly how he was going to spend eternity.

Chapter Eighteen

Washington, D.C.

I can do this.

Rian concentrated, biting his lower lip to keep focused as he stared at the sheer curtains. It would take just the right kind of Fire to make them burn without being consumed. And if he could do that, then he was the master of the fecking Fire, wasn't he? And not it, the master of him?

The smell of smoke hung in the air around him, despite the open window, mocking him. He ignored it. He'd only scorched a couple of chairs. Well, three. And the towels had been unfortunate. But it had worked. A few times. He'd make it work again.

Even when his control had failed, the fires had helped. Shite, his life had been easier when he thought he was naught but a fecking pyromaniac. There was something in him, a pressure, a need, which only the fires relieved. Backburning, he supposed it was, setting limits about his own inner fire to keep it from consuming him.

Only it wasn't working, any more. Not since two days ago. No wildfire, no controlled burn eased what

Cuinn awakened in him. Rian groaned, let go his focus on the drapes, and rolled to bury his face in the pillow. Their sexual collision last night had promised relief, in a strange way, but it hadn't delivered on the promise. And then, this afternoon...

Groaning again, Rian pulled a pillow over his head. How could something as good as what Cuinn did to him have made an even bigger balls-up of his life than it had been before? The only pleasure he'd ever known had come from pain. Before the night of the bonfire, he'd been something of a joke among his friends, the beautiful boy who'd never been kissed, not that he gave a fuck. It never mattered to him. On the Twalf, he'd embraced the pain. At first for the sweetness of the vengeance, a vengeance and a sweetness he'd known even then couldn't be anything human. But there was more, beyond the pain, beyond the pleasure that followed on its heels. Each time he indulged his dark craving, there was a delicious terror, as something buried in him came closer to stirring to life. Something he feared, but something he needed. And whatever it was, since yesterday it was barreling down on him like a lorry with failed brakes.

The treatment Cuinn had given him in the coffee shop had done nothing for any of his needs. Not a fecking thing. *Has anyone ever been gentle with you?* the other Fae asked. Hell no, for he'd never wanted that.

Why was it so good, to get what he didn't want, didn't need, and couldn't use?

"Dhó-súil."

Shite. Apparently thinking of the male was enough to make him appear. Although, to be honest, if

179

that were the case, Cuinn would have been here several hours and a dozen small fires ago. "I don't suppose you'd feck off if I asked."

The answering silence went on for so long that Rian finally hauled the pillow off and turned his head toward the voice.

Oh, Jaysus. Never had he seen a man so beautiful; the sight stopped his heart. Beauty had never been a concern of his, only what a man was willing to do to him, to bring him closer to what he needed. But there was little of desire in the way the Fae looked at him. Nothing like what he'd grown accustomed to, through the use of his gift, making men want him whether they willed it or no.

"I wouldn't." There was exhaustion in Cuinn's voice, as if he'd spent the time since their coffeehouse tryst at some heavy labor. "Though I would, if I had any sense of self-preservation."

There was a sobering, and unsettling, sense of finality to the other Fae's words. "I'm not after destroying you." Not that he hadn't wanted to, a time or two. But the taste of joy he'd had in the coffeehouse had changed all that.

Cuinn shook his head. "It's not your doing." He seemed about to say something else, but stopped, and sniffed, brows arching as he glanced around the bedroom. "I realize everyone needs a hobby, but arson? Really?"

Rian pushed himself up to sit against the headboard, with a sense of *deja vu.* Had it only been the middle of last night, when Cuinn appeared to him, determined to resist him but doomed to fail? "It helps. A little."

"Helps what?" Cuinn crossed to sit on the edge of the four-poster bed, fingering the scorch marks marring the quilt.

"Beats hell out of me." Rian tipped his head back to rest against the carved wood, and stared at the ceiling. "I need something. There's a great hole in me, and I've no notion of what might fill it." *'Sea*, best to look at the ceiling, and not at the Fae who was most likely the cause and the solution of all his troubles. "And at the same time something stirring in me, needing to be free. Something waiting at the bottom of that hole." *Something that frightens me*.

"Look at me."

I don't dare. He swallowed hard, his throat gone tight enough to hurt. Pain was his friend, but fear was his bitter foe.

"I said, look at me, Highness." Fingers touched Rian's chin, forced his head around.

Íosa, Muire, agus Ióseph. He wanted to look away, but he couldn't. *Those eyes*. Pinning him to the headboard, searching him right down to his soul. His half a soul. Compelling, and as beautiful as the strong cheekbones, the sensual mouth, the dark-blond hair that fell in waves almost to the other Fae's jawline.

He couldn't look away. He couldn't make himself want to. More than that, he needed to make the Fae react to him. Had to compel him. He teased along the line of Cuinn's jaw with his fingertips, stroked around the curve of his ear, even as he stared into the beautiful cut-jade eyes. *Shite, I really* am *addicted*. But addicted to the tease? Or to Cuinn?

Cuinn grabbed his hand and forced it down. "We have to finish the Sharing. You need it."

181

Rian didn't bother to question how Cuinn knew. No doubt his madness was writ into every line of his face by now. "How do we accomplish that, then?" The fingertips of his free hand danced along Cuinn's hard bicep; the hairs rose on the other Fae's forearm, and a smile spread itself over Rian's face, even as his heartbeat roared in his ears.

"We start by you keeping your addiction the fuck to yourself," Cuinn growled. "In order to complete the SoulShare, you have to do unto me as was done unto you. Which will be a hell of a lot easier to accomplish if you don't drive me to the point of needing to slam you into a wall and fuck you senseless."

Rian laughed. He couldn't help it. He was capable of no such self-restraint, of course, and the relief of knowing he'd not be forced to confront whatever it was that sought to be free in him, or risk filling the emptiness, was damn near too much for him.

In just those few breaths of laughter, the earlier pain that had driven him to set the fires was all but forgotten. More madness. He welcomed it. He ran his hand up Cuinn's arm, skimmed his cheek, and worked his fingers into thick wavy hair.

"Shit." Cuinn's whisper was almost too soft to hear. "How the fuck am I going to do this?"

"Let go." Rian pulled Cuinn closer, brushed his lips against dark-blond stubble, teased with the tip of his tongue. "Don't do anything. Except want." He laughed, the heat of his breath stirring the lock of hair that curled in front of Cuinn's ear. "Wanting would be good." His gift was stirring again, his curse, and he set it free, wrapping it round Cuinn like a cord of silk.

"Oh, no, you don't." Cuinn's voice was low, dangerous; he caught Rian's wrist and forced his other hand down. "Maybe it always had to happen this way. But I would have chosen differently, if you'd given me a choice, *dhó-súil*."

"What the feck do you—"

There was a new fire in him. And not one of his own kindling. Suddenly he was trembling, with a kind of need he'd never known. A need, not to be taken, but to take. Hard.

Pale green eyes glinted at him, alight with a hard-edged desperation. He could hear Cuinn's breathing, harsh in his throat, could even hear his heartbeat. The other Fae's tongue darted out, licking parted lips gone abruptly dry.

"You want it now, don't you?" Cuinn's whisper was like velvet, with flecks of broken glass embedded in the softness. "Take what you want; I'm not going to stop you."

"*Asiomú*." Rian's lips barely moved. "You fecking bastard. It's vengeance on me you want?" A reversal of his own dark gift, forcing him to drink of the cup he forced on others. Jesus, his cock hurt. He'd soon remedy that, no fear, but with the new fire there was a new hurt, and he suspected no brutality he could devise would ease it. *Vengeance is an art, among the Fae... torturing the torturer.* "You son of a bitch."

"No." Cuinn shook his head, slowly, his gaze never leaving Rian's. "But right now, *asiomú* is the only language you speak."

"You can stop talking, now." Rian flowed to his feet, grabbed Cuinn's shoulder, and threw him onto his stomach, his torso sprawled across the bed and his

183

booted feet still on the gleaming hardwood floor. Christ, what an amazing arse, and be damned if the Fae tease wasn't arching his back to show it off. "Denims off."

When Cuinn was slow to respond, Rian leaned forward, fisted his hand in the other Fae's hair, and drew his head up and back. Brushing his lips across Cuinn's rough cheek in a mockery of tenderness, he murmured, "I want you to bare yourself for me. Are we clear?"

Before Cuinn could answer, Rian kissed him, a bruising, punishing kiss. Exactly the sort he himself had reveled in receiving, the night before. Cuinn struggled briefly, fought the kiss, fought Rian's grip. But then the hard body against his relaxed, the other Fae groaned and fumbled at the button and the zipper of his trousers, and Rian laughed into the kiss. *Call me mad, for wanting what I want. We'll see how mad you think I am once you've drunk deep from the same cup.*

Cuinn's denims dropped to pool around his ankles, and even through his own clothing Rian felt heat grinding back against him.

"Please."

Rian breathed in the word, and it seemed he could taste the reluctance of it, as well as the hunger. "I should make you beg." He nipped at Cuinn's lower lip, tugged at it with his teeth.

"That *was* begging." Cuinn was glaring, but at the same time there was an almost feral pleasure in his eyes, the set of his jaw, the way he held himself.

Rian was looking in a mirror, he realized. *This is what* rachtanai *looks like.* Hunger that was magnet and mockery and surrender, all at once.

184

And knowing what it was gave him no immunity against it.

I'm going to take him. First time for everything.

"What are you waiting for, Highness? I'm not in a position to be giving you an engraved invitation." Cuinn rocked back against him; the bed was high, and the Fae's firm arse pressed warm and hard against an erection that threatened to burst the button on Rian's borrowed denims. "You've wanted into me since I first caught you *in flagrante delicious.*"

A quicksilver ripple of laughter skated across the surface of Rian's fierce arousal, startling him. Snarling, he took Cuinn's mouth again, tongue forcing its way into the Fae's mouth to smother and swallow his moans. Laughter threatened to clear his mind, and he needed his madness.

Rian fumbled wrong-handed at his waist, his left hand being occupied in keeping Cuinn where he wanted him, until his straining cock fell free. Already streaked with pearly fire, it landed in the cleft between Cuinn's criminally perfect arse cheeks.

The other Fae hissed in a breath. "Shit, that's hot," he mumbled, before Rian took his ability to speak away from him again, biting at his lips in between kisses that fucked Cuinn's permanently pouting mouth.

Rian's hips swayed, rocked, sliding his shaft along the track Cuinn made for it, the flared head staining the t-shirt neither of them could be bothered to remove with droplets of liquid fire. Zipper teeth caught golden hairs and pinched the soft loose skin of his sac, giving him the barest hint of the sweet hot bite of pain he needed.

Something else threatened as well, as sharp-edged as the pain. It was the joy he'd felt, and fought, each time before. *You're being tricked, boyo,* a wicked voice whispered in the back of his mind. *This isn't for you, not happiness, not fecking laughter and sweetness and light and joy. Your part is the dark, and the fire that tries in vain to drive it away.*

"Do it." Cuinn's plea was almost too faint to be heard. But the longing in it was plain. "Please. I've never..." The blond head dropped, until Rian's hand tangled in his hair stopped it. "I need this, too." Cuinn tried to twist his head around. "As much as you do."

"Do you really?" Rian's lips brushed Cuinn's rough cheek as he whispered. "Have you burned your entire life, never knowing what you needed or why you needed it? Have you watched the life you thought you knew go up in a Hell of fire that devoured everyone around you and left you whole?" He pulled back, and felt the fire-slicked head of his shaft probing Cuinn's clenched-tight entrance. "Do you have no idea who the fucking hell you are, and are you left with only pain and surrender as your guiding stars to bring you home?"

Jaysus, the mocking voice whispered. *You've a silver tongue in you, and no mistake. Even if your whole life till now has been a lie.*

"It doesn't matter what I've been." Hair shrouded Cuinn's gaze, but fever-gleam still shone through, a light of its own in the gathering dusk. "I'm not going to be whole until you do this. Neither are you."

Strange fire blazed up in him again, and from the other Fae's breathy laughter Rian knew it was him had caused it, again. His lips curled back in a silent snarl as

186

he straightened enough to get a grip on the base of his cock and shove it to Cuinn's entrance.

He still hadn't let go of the long dark-blond hair, and Cuinn's back bowed as his head was hauled up and back. He cursed under his breath and struggled to get his arms braced under him, to take his weight. Rian caught just a glimpse of rock-hard straining biceps, heard the rasp of Cuinn's breath.

But his attention was all for what he was about. He didn't think his shaft could get any harder than it already was, but he was so wrong. It lengthened and hardened and throbbed as he looked at it, the head near piercing Cuinn's tight puckered entrance.

The rasping stopped. Cuinn was holding his breath, his whole body wrenched round to see. The bed itself trembled, with the shaking of the other Fae's arms as he strained to brace himself.

You heard him, boyo. Again the mockery. *He wants to know what it's like, for you. Show him. Show him the truth.* No joy, no wonder. Only the pain.

Rian clenched his teeth, and drove in hard. As hard as any man had ever taken him.

He couldn't breathe. He couldn't fecking get his breath. Pleasure hit him like a padded sledgehammer, he staggered with it, nearly fell onto Cuinn. Who, himself, was crying out, a sound like a wild creature at rut.

A low, animal sound rose up from deep in Rian's gut. Down where his trail of stars disappeared into Cuinn's incredible arse —the stars that had appeared that awful night, along with the fire, branding him, marking him. The sound filled him, echoed in him.

Something else was trying to fill him, too. Joy. He could feel it, wave on wave.

He fought it.

Rian drove forward again and again, his hands braced to either side of Cuinn's taut, tanned arse, grunting each time he seated himself deep. Cuinn clutched the sheets with white-knuckled hands; his head hung slack, between his shoulders, and he worked his hips against the bedclothes, his earlier cries given way to a soft steady moan that made the short hairs prickle on Rian's forearms. Sweat dripped from the long forelock that hung down as Rian bent over Cuinn's straining body, sweat that was sparks and sparks that fell to burn tiny holes in Cuinn's shirt before extinguishing themselves.

Pleasure. He'd never felt aught like this, blinding, deafening. Sucking him in, filling him. All there was, was the pleasure, his body moving, Cuinn working his length like a fist in a velvet glove. Cuinn's moans.

"Harder. Damn you. *Harder.*" Cuinn's voice was ragged; he lurched forward, as if his arms were about to give out.

Rian slammed into him, circled, rammed home again, sending the bed sliding across the hardwood, staggering after it. Leaned forward, covered the shorter male. Buried his face in that glorious hair.

Screamed, with the abrupt fiery rush of his release, his body jerking, its rhythm gone, painting Cuinn's dark hold with light, with thick gouts of fire. No pain had ever given him pleasure like this. *Nothing* had ever given him pleasure like this.

But the joy, the fucking sneaky bastard, it flooded into him along with the pleasure, and he was defenseless. He heard Cuinn's moans crescendo, felt the other Fae's body stiffen under his, and as Cuinn joined him in release, the joy doubled. More than doubled. And the pleasure along with it.

Cuinn was sprawled on the bed, and Rian on top of him, six-four and sixteen stone of utterly boneless weight. *Fuck, I'm his and he's mine,* was Rian's first barely coherent thought.

Then a wave of dizziness threatened to draw him under. The crushing pressure was gone. But in its place was a clarity almost too much to bear, and a sight awful and beautiful enough to stop a heart. Behind his closed eyelids, Rian saw the hole in his own being, unobstructed now by thoughts of pain or fire. A hole that went so deep, there was no seeing the bottom of it, only a faint silver-blue glow.

The rape, it taught me to embrace the pain, and turn the lust back on them what hurt me. The turning it back gave me the addiction to the power my Fae self has over men. And the pain... it calls to that hole within me, and what's at the bottom of it. Something what's kin to it.

The pain won't let me rest, not until what's at the bottom is brought up into the light.

Chapter Nineteen

Greenwich Village,
New York City

"Fucker picks a hell of a time to work for a living."
Janek's bulk took up most of the sofa; he'd already
kicked over the oh-so-precious lamp on the table at
one end, not that he gave a shit. It was starting to get
dark, and his passenger was impatient to put its plan
into action. So naturally, Bryce Porn-'Stache had to
pick tonight to be late getting home.

For once, I agree with you. The female would
have been drumming Janek's ragged fingernails on
whatever was handy, if she'd still had control. ***I am
anxious to see our courier off.***

"About that whole 'off' shit." Janek raised his
remaining eyebrow, grinning inwardly as he felt the
bitch fuming. She hated it when he questioned her. She
hated it even more when he had a point, and wasn't
just doing it to yank her chain. She was going to
seriously hate the next few minutes. "How are you
planning to get the little pissant to do the suicide
bomber thing?"

We'll persuade him. This was the male, jovial as

usual, no doubt playing the skin flute in his mind. Sitch normal. *We might even let you help, now that we know about your special talents.*

"Don't try to suck up to me. You're no fucking good at it. We both know if I go to work on him, he's not going to be able to do anything but cry like a girl and bleed like a pig." The way the dance-whore Garrett did. At least he'd gotten to see that before Dary sucked him out of reality. Again. "How do you plan on making him stay persuaded, once he's on the train?" They'd experimented, shortly after their arrival; the piece of itself the *Marfach* had carved out of the living Stone in Janek's head and stuck in Bryce Newhouse's gut was enough to let the monster fuck with the mewling little asswipe's head if they were in the same room, and talk to him if they were within about a city block of each other. Anything else took a hell of a lot of effort and concentration—Janek still wanted to yark whenever he thought about the *Marfach* trying to make Newhouse make a phone call, while he'd been in D.C. and Newhouse had been here.

The male laughed. Not a good sign. *I've been giving that some thought. You might not like what I...*—

A key started turning in the first of the locks on the front door, and the monster cut off mid-sentence. *If I don't like it, it doesn't get done.* Back to forcing his thoughts on his passenger, otherwise Newhouse got confused trying to tell who Janek was talking to.

Meat ain't happy, ain't nobody happy. More shit-assed laughter. *Maybe we should get that on a shirt.*

Maybe you can shove it up your —

191

The door swung open and the light switched on, chasing off the growing gloom neither Janek nor his passenger gave a particular fuck about. "Oh." Newhouse's voice was flat. He turned and shut the door, re-locked it slowly and methodically. "I thought maybe you'd be off wherever it is you go, doing whatever it is you do."

Janek smirked. Or he tried to, the half of his face he needed in order to do that was partly gone and what was left didn't feel very much. "It's your lucky night. I have a job for you." He'd go along with the *Marfach*'s plan, the way they'd rehearsed it. For a while. Until he found out what he wasn't going to like.

"You? Or your squatter?"

Moments like those, Janek could almost like the annoying piece of shit. "I'm just the go-between, this time."

Newhouse shrugged out of his coat and hung it on the brass tree next to the door. He didn't pay any attention to the ruined lamp, because the *Marfach* had been making sure he didn't since he walked in the door. "I suppose it doesn't matter all that much." He started for the kitchen. "Do I have time to eat something first? I didn't get dinner at work." From his tone, that was pretty close to the end of the world for an investment banker.

"No." He could feel the *Marfach* doing something —killing the poor sonofabitch's hunger for him, probably. "You're going to be on the train to D.C. soon enough, you can get something to eat then." Janek wondered why the fuck the male was laughing in his head.

"Whatever." Newhouse glanced at the broken

lamp, sighed, hit the wall switch, and looked around for somewhere to sit.

Move your partially decomposed ass, Meat. There was a wink in the male's tone. ***No need to hog the whole sofa. Besides, we need him close.***

Janek grimaced, but swung his legs off the sofa. Newhouse dropped onto the velvet next to him with a put-upon sigh. "All right, I'm listening. What do you need me to do?"

"Just go clubbing for a few nights. In Washington, D.C."

"A few nights?" The dickhead had the nerve to look outraged. "I can't just walk away from work, I'm in the middle of a—"

Newhouse twitched and fell silent. Janek wondered if he'd looked like that, back in the day when the *Marfach* had been able to zap him when he got out of line. Probably not. What the investment banker was getting were sloppy wet kisses compared to what the monster had shot through Janek.

"You're leaving tonight. There's a gay club in D.C. called Purgatory. I can't get into it, because the fucking Fae twink Conall Dary put up a ward that keeps me out. It won't stop you, though." If he gave a shit, Janek would feel bad about not warning Newhouse about the possibility that the ward would fuck him up royally.

"Dary." Newhouse's eyes rolled dramatically. "Humoring Terrence by letting him have his ex stay here for Pride week was one thing. But LaFontaine bringing his pickups back here—"

"Shut the fuck up." Janek wasn't interested in hearing the old grudge rehashed again. The *Marfach* had made Newhouse throw Josh LaFontaine's former fuck-buddy out not long after the cockup under Purgatory, and Newhouse apparently never got tired of running his mouth about it. "What I need you to do is to take something into Purgatory. Every night until it does what it's supposed to do." He couldn't figure out how to get any closer to explaining what the *Marfach* figured was actually going to happen without coming right out and saying that Newhouse would probably be blown to pieces along with most of the fucking club.

Naturally, the dickhead couldn't just let it be. "What is it? And how am I supposed to know when it's done whatever the hell it is?"

You want to take it from here?

Go get the collar, Meat.

"Wait here." Grumbling, Janek lurched to his feet and back to the bedroom, where the Rottweiler's old collar lay on top of the dresser. It took him a few tries to grab it, his fingertips being mostly numb, but he finally managed to snag it. He curled his fist around it, and brought it back out to the living room, where Newhouse looked as bored as ever.

He sat up a little straighter, though, when he saw what Janek was carrying. "That's not what it looks like, is it?"

"Does it look like a dog collar?" Janek dropped back down onto the sofa. He heard wood creak, and saw Newhouse wince, and grinned, one-sided. "You're going to wear it in, and no one's going to give a shit."

"Like hell I'm going to wear a collar into a sex club. You think I want every amateur Dom in the place coming down on my ass?" Janek swore he could hear the *Marfach* yawning, as Newhouse twitched again.

194

Like either one of them was worried about whether Newhouse would run into trouble. Other than the magickal kind, anyway.

"Just stay away from the cock pit. Sit at the bar." Janek did his best to sound helpful. Of course, the closer the dickhead was to the storeroom under the bar where the nexus was, the better the odds in favor of the kind of explosion both he and the monster were hoping for. "The ones most likely to give you shit are probably going to be down there."

Newhouse stroked his mustache with two fingers, a habit that made Janek want to break his fingers. "So, you expect me to deck myself out in leather finery, take the train to our nation's capital, walk into a skin club, and wait for something to happen. What, exactly?"

I will tell him. The abomination's grating bone-on-bone voice made Janek shudder.

Be my guest. Janek wished he could get out of his own mind. The thought of sitting through this conversation made his throat dry up and his balls shrivel, but he didn't have anywhere else to go.

I am going to destroy the club Purgatory. The voice wasn't quite as bad when it was talking to someone else, but that was kind of like the difference between a red-hot spike shoved in your ear and a room temperature one. *The collar you will wear is my means of doing so.*

Janek could almost hear gears grinding in Newhouse's head, and smell smoke.

"Fuck that shit."

Newhouse surged to his feet. Janek caught his wrist barely in time, and yanked him back down so hard there was a cracking sound when he landed and one corner of the sofa sagged. Not to mention, from the way the bastard's shoulder deformed, it was probably dislocated.

Boo fucking hoo. The monster was obviously doing damage control, going by the way Newhouse wasn't struggling much. Although that might have been the pain, too. But his eyes were practically bugging out of his head, and Janek wasn't sure, but he thought the little dick-sucker had just pissed himself.

Maybe the monster shouldn't have been quite so blunt, but Janek sure as hell wasn't going to be the one to tell it so. Just like he wasn't going to be the one to ask if it had any bright ideas about what to do next.

Here comes the part you're going to hate, Meat. The male voice sniggered. ***The Fae twink cut the cord between you and me, but he didn't do anything to the young and lovely Bryce, here. I can still control him. But in order to force him to do something against his will, using only the little piece of myself tucked in his gut to do it, and at a distance, there needs to be magick in him.*** More laughter. ***Like there is in you.***

Why am I going to hate —oh, fuck. It didn't take a rocket scientist to figure out where the male was heading. Especially not a male with a perpetual hard-on. *Hell no.*

You have to ask yourself, how badly do you want a shot at Guaire? The male wasn't laughing any more. If this piece of dung follows directions, you'll get it. ***Or, second best, you'll know he's dead. And with Fae healing powers, it'll take him a long time to die. Chew on that.***

Janek was silent. Thinking. Which was a lot

harder than it used to be, and even harder when the thought of a dead Tiernan Guaire was being dangled in front of him like bait. How badly did he really want to kill Guaire?

Incredibly stupid fucking question.

Do I have to fuck him? Janek ignored the stupid shit trying to get free again, except that he clamped down harder on his wrist. *You know it's just about impossible for me to get it up.*

I knew you'd see reason. And I don't want to set you a task beyond your limited means. You can either have him blow you, or open a vein for him. The laugh was back. ***Your choice, Meat.***

The way his stomach tried to turn itself inside out made Janek glad he hadn't eaten recently. He had no doubt the *Marfach* would keep Newhouse sucking until his cock —which was just as mostly dead as the rest of him —responded, but he wasn't volunteering for hours of a living hell worse than the one he usually lived in, not unless there was no other way. *You realize I may never heal if I cut myself?*

You disappoint me, Meat. Oh, shit, the female was back. Janek wasn't sure if the thought of her riding him during a BJ made him feel more or less sick than the thought of the male doing the same. ***But I am sure we can find you a needle and thread. Or a hot iron rod.***

"Big of you." He didn't realize he'd spoken aloud until Newhouse jerked out of the trance or whatever it was he'd gone into and stared at him. Janek laughed harshly and reached down, into the top of his boot, for his special fancy-ass Fae-killing knife. Sure, he kept it so he could deal with Fae who needed to die, but that didn't mean he couldn't use it for other things in the meantime.

"What the hell are you doing?"

Janek ignored him. He cut into the wrist of the hand he was using to hold Newhouse in place. His blood was brown, and flowed like sludge as he re-sheathed the knife. The bitch was laughing inside his head. Janek rolled his eyes as he remembered, too late, her lust for blood. *Choke on it*, he shot at her, as he grabbed Newhouse by the back of the neck and forced his wrist into his mouth.

Newhouse gagged on the blood, tried to vomit. Fought, too, apparently his passenger was getting off on watching their victim struggle too much to do anything about it. Hard to blame it for that, but it made his job a pain in the ass. Janek kept his wrist shoved into Newhouse's mouth, deeper every time the sorry bastard tried to gasp for breath. The porn 'stache was caked with blood the color and texture of mud by the time Newhouse quit struggling.

Just a taste, Meat?

Fuck you, I'm not tasting my own blood. He let Newhouse fall against the back of the sofa and lurched to his feet, a hand clamped around his wrist. *You talk to him. I need to go find something to stop the bleeding.*

The female sniffed. ***Very well***.

As he shuffled off toward the kitchen, he sensed the conversation starting. If you could call it a conversation when one side wasn't talking, and the other side was lolling against the back of the sofa, his breath sounding like a pig rutting in mud, blood like chocolate syrup dribbling from the corner of his mouth.

198

To answer your question, human, you will know your task is complete when the great nexus below Purgatory is tapped by a Fae working magick, the ley energy touches the collar, the collar explodes, and what remains of your head parts company with your body...

Chapter Twenty

Washington, D.C.

Cuinn didn't want to move. Rian was collapsed on top of him, still buried in him, his chest rising and falling with his deep, gasping breaths. Breaths he could feel against his shoulder, his neck. Intimate warmth, weight, the occasional soft, involuntary groan. It couldn't be any more perfect.

His tangled hair was nuzzled away from the back of his neck. Soft lips caressed him.

So I was wrong.

He'd figured things would change if he could provoke Rian into finishing the SoulShare. A little. There wasn't anything left to happen to him, now that he'd finished his own part. Right?

Damn.

"Feck." Rian tried to push himself up, gave up, and fell back. "Cuinn?" His *scair-anam*'s thickly-accented voice was unsteady, breathless. "What just happened?"

"Rise up, will you?" Cuinn waited for Rian's weight to shift, then rolled under him, and somehow managed to wrestle the two of them up to where they could lie entangled on the bed.

Once he got them there, though, he was right back to his initial problem. He didn't want to move. Not for anything. He was wrapped around the lean, hard, inked body of a Fae Prince, his nose buried in hair that smelled of smoke and a charred hole in the sheets where a wet spot would have been after any other encounter like this one. Except that there had never been an encounter like this one.

Never.

And never would be again.

Rian's mouth sought Cuinn's, found it. The kiss was fucking amazing, tender in a way suggesting that the Prince was as unsure of what was going on as he himself was. As unaccustomed to kissing just for the pleasure of it.

"Why did you do it?" Rian's voice was choked, as if his throat was trying to close around the words, yet for all that the kiss resumed as if he hadn't spoken at all. "The reversal. Vengeance, you called it. An art. Torture turned back." The Prince's breath was hot against Cuinn's mouth, and uneven. "Because the only love known to our kind is love of kin, and the devil take all else."

Oh, shit. Cuinn pulled back, enough to look Rian in the eyes. He brushed back the lock of hair that hung over the Prince's forehead, and found himself kissing the forehead before he could go on. "Yes, that's what it usually is. Torture. That's what you used it for, the first time, without even knowing what you were doing." His fingers felt clumsy, as he ran them through Rian's sweaty hair. His digits weren't used to being put to such a gentle purpose. "But I didn't want to torture you. I swear I didn't. I needed you to finish the SoulShare.

201

And I knew that it would be hard for you. Maybe impossible. So I did the only thing I could think of to make it possible." Shit, there was a tear flickering on Rian's cheek, almost invisible flame. Gently, he kissed it away, feeling the slight flare of heat against his lips. "I'm no good at apologizing, because I don't think I've ever done it before. But I'm sorry."

How strange, that he was holding his breath, waiting for Rian to answer. With the SoulShare completed, there was nothing standing between himself and his appointment with the nexus. But the fact that he was about to die, or at least to cease to exist in any way he understood, didn't matter at all, not compared to the next words out of Rian's mouth.

"Why do I give a damn, whether or no you're sorry?" Rian didn't pull away from him, but his gaze dropped, his lids lowered. "Why does it tear the heart out of me, to think you meant to hurt me?"

Cuinn gathered the Prince close. He'd never needed to hold anyone before. Not like this. "We're bonded." The word felt strange on his lips. "SoulShared." Slowly, he breathed in, filling himself with Rian's smoky scent. "Everything's different."

For as long as I have left. Which isn't long. The images of the dead zone he'd created in the Realm after he grabbed Lochlann by the scruff of the neck and dragged him and his Garrett back from the far side of death, and the creeping rot that had spread from his touch before this latest return, sprang into his mind as if pushed there.

Rian shook his head against Cuinn's shoulder. "No. I mean, *'sea*, it's changed, all of it." Cuinn felt him tense, as if the thought brought more fear than pleasure. "Everything I am. But this, it hurt before we finished sharing. While I was still my own man."

Fae don't love. Although Cuinn was considering calling bullshit on that tried and true maxim, at least where SoulShares were concerned. "I'm sorry. I am." Turning his head, he kissed an awkward trail along Rian's blond-stubbled jaw. "I'd never hurt you deliberately. Not any way you didn't ask of me."

You pathetic liar. What he was about to do was going to devastate his SoulShare. Assuming Rian felt about him the way he was nearly willing to admit he felt about Rian.

Cuinn groaned softly as Rian kissed him. The kiss was tentative at first, but then the other Fae's arms tightened around him, and he was rolled onto his back. Rian's thighs pushed his apart, and the sweet weight of the other male's body left his, as Rian's back curved up into a hard arch under his hands. If he opened his eyes, if he looked down the length of his own body toward where his legs were slowly stirring to wrap around the other male's, Cuinn knew what he would see —a trail of stars, the Pattern's claiming mark on a Royal, gleaming silver-blue along the torso of...

Of the male he loved.

Fuck. I have to stop this. Before I can't.

"I have to get up, *dhó-súil.*" Yet he made no move to, and the only thing the proclamation earned him was an arched brow. "Seriously. You do, too. And we need to dress. And I need to figure out where the fuck my phone went."

Still neither of them moved, and Cuinn's gaze played up and down Rian's perfectly chiseled body, lingering on the strange and beautiful Pattern-mark.

"Why?" Rian's voice didn't seem to be working all that well either. "I'd as soon stay right here."

"So would I." As strange as that felt. "You deserve more than one taste of gentleness." Steeling himself, Cuinn rolled Rian onto his side and eased himself out of bed. "But there's a world we need to save, and we don't have much time to do it."

***

It took some effort, which was to say, more cajoling and pleading and sarcasm than Cuinn had time for, to get all the Fae of what Tiernan had once half-jokingly dubbed the Demesne of Purgatory, and all their human SoulShares, into one room. Which was, actually, a good thing. That much busy-work left him less time to think about other things.

Such as the likely reaction of the other Fae to his news.

Such as the fact that if his *scair-anam* ever felt a gentle touch again, it wasn't going to be his.

I need to just shut the fuck up. Cuinn glanced over at Rian, who was where he'd been since their guests started arriving, in a corner of the living room talking quietly with Lochlann, and fought down a hot stab of jealousy. SoulShare jealousy. All the jokes he'd ever made about that particular phenomenon were undoubtedly about to come back and bite him hard in the ass.

Lochlann had been the first to arrive; he'd been downstairs at the massage parlor he was about to take over. Josh had been next, he'd had to call his business partner in early to mind the tattoo parlor. Followed shortly by Tiernan, who had complained bitterly about leaving his club supervised only by humans. Until he'd gotten a look at Cuinn's face, anyway. *Is it that fucking obvious?*

Yeah, it probably was, given the way all the other Fae were looking at him.

Get a grip. Fae don't get maudlin. Maybe that was another myth.

One by one, the other Fae Faded in, the other humans made their way up the stairs, and knocked, and were admitted. Kevin Almstead was the last to arrive; he'd had to talk his way out of a late meeting and then find a taxi.

The dark-haired human kissed his husband, tossed his expensive suit jacket over a chair, and dropped down on the sofa beside Tiernan, and the room started to go quiet. Lochlann and Rian broke off their conversation, and Rian crossed to the armchair next to Cuinn; as he lowered himself into it, silence fell. Too abruptly for Cuinn's tastes. Everyone was looking at him. He felt naked, and not in a good way.

Reaching down, he rested a hand on Rian's shoulder. It seemed to help. Of course, now every Fae in the room was giving him one of those I-know-what-*you*-just-did looks. Which *didn't* help.

"Yes. We're Shared." Cuinn's grip tightened on Rian's shoulder as he looked from one face to another, from gem-faceted eyes to human. The number of Fae and men in the room sorely tasked its capacity for hospitality; Rian was in the lone armchair, beside him, and past the Prince, Tiernan and Kevin crowded into a loveseat that was probably never meant for two such well-muscled male physiques. Kevin had the good grace not to be amused at Cuinn's expense, or if he was, he didn't let it show. The male was far too kind-hearted to be a hotshot lawyer. His husband generally labored under no such restrictions —Tiernan was probably the only Fae capable of being a bigger wiseass than Cuinn himself, on his better days —but, strangely, apart from that knowing gleam, there was little of mockery in his bright-blue eyes.

Puzzled, Cuinn turned to the other side of the slightly claustrophobic living room —the two apartments over Purgatory were definitely not large — and saw the same reaction repeated, four times over. Conall and Josh and Garrett shared the sofa, Twinklebritches and Josh holding hands and presently sharing a smile that shut the rest of the room out, and Garrett leaning a little bit into Lochlann, who perched with one thigh resting on the sofa arm, hovering protectively. Hard to blame the Fae healer, considering how recently his *scair-anam* had been snatched back from the far side of death's door.

Cuinn's eyes narrowed. No one was mocking him. Not a situation he was used to, at least not when he'd done as much to earn a bit of mockery as he had with most of the males in the room. Not so much as a *dúrt me lath mars'n*, and if anyone in two worlds had earned the right to say 'I told you so,' it was this group of males.

And you're stalling. Asshole. There's no time for that.

To hell with small talk. "Welcome to the beginning of the end. And no, that's not me being a drama queen."

He took a deep breath, one that caught in his throat as Rian rested a hand over his. *Damn.* He hadn't had a chance to tell his *scair-anam* what was about to happen. No, fuck that, he'd had the chance, he just hadn't taken it. He'd let Rian chat up Lochlann, while he made himself busy calling in the troops, so he wouldn't have to look his male in the eyes and tell him the truth.

He looked down, now. Rian's chair looked like something that had been stolen from a church, all carved wood and high-backed red velvet. Maybe Tiernan *had* stolen it from a church. Or maybe he'd just gone to a lot of trouble to find something right for a Prince.

And a Prince his *scair-anam* most surely was. What should have been a nervous youth, looking back at him, or a sexually sated one, or a bitingly sarcastic one, was a male whose concern was all for him. The touch of the hand overlaying his was reassuring, for fuck's sake.

Cuinn closed his eyes. He had to. "The whole reason the Pattern exists, the whole reason SoulShares exist, it's all coming to a head right now. And all of it, everything that's happened in the last two thousand, three hundred and twenty-seven years, everything all of you have been through—"

Oh, now, *that* got some attention. Not exactly angry attention, but Lochlann and Garrett's stares were nearly enough to make Cuinn break a sweat, and no one else looked as if forgiveness was high on their list of things to do, either.

The Loremaster squared his shoulders. *Yeah, they're going to be pissed. That's legit.* "It's all happened in order to make it possible for me to do what I have to do in a few minutes."

"And that would be?" Lochlann's gaze was locked with Cuinn's, but his hand was finding Garrett's.

"Complete the Pattern. Save the Realm." Cuinn turned his hand under Rian's, gripped it tightly. "And probably die."

Chapter Twenty-one

There was a moment of perfect silence after Cuinn's pronouncement.

"How the fuck *dare* you?" Rian's voice cracked like a whip. He surged to his feet, turning to glare at Cuinn, as smoke began to rise from the shorter male's clothing, a mad Royal's fury made manifest.

"Shit!" Cuinn closed his eyes, and Rian watched the light bend around him, swirling like wind, like water, until the haze dissipated.

Rian averted his gaze. The last thing he wanted to do was look into those pale-jade eyes, when they opened again, and to read the betrayal written there. *I trusted him. I opened myself to him, I fecking* gave *myself to him.*

"Dhó-súil."

He shook off the hand resting on his shoulder, turning away. A mistake, perhaps, for now it was Tiernan's regard he had to face. He flinched, anticipating the mockery awaiting him there. And flinched again, and dropped his gaze in confusion, when he saw sympathy instead.

"Tell us, Loremaster." Tiernan spoke softly, and was answered by an even softer murmur of agreement, running round the room. "Tell us what was done to us, and what you're to do."

The silence stretched out. Rian refused to turn back. He'd hoped the emptiness at his core might be filled at last, the pain deeper and older than the sweet pain he sought in sex might find what it sought and leave him in what passed for peace. *Hope is for the easily deluded.*

Cuinn grimaced. "The whole story would take too long." His voice was even, tightly controlled. "But I'll give you what I can. First, the Pattern, the portal to the human world, is alive. It's the names, the souls, of all the Loremasters who survived the last battle with the *Marfach*. Except me."

Conall and Tiernan both cursed. Rian, for his part, set himself to ignore the schooling Cuinn was patently aiming at him.

Cuinn barely paused for any of it. "Oh, it gets better, believe me. There was a space left in the Pattern for me. Because the Loremasters' work isn't done yet. I have to finish it."

At last, Rian had to turn and look, though he tried to keep his sense of betrayal from showing. That was for Cuinn alone, not for an audience.

This time, Cuinn was the one who flinched, even as he continued speaking. "The space became a flaw in the Pattern. Which led to something going wrong with every single fucking transit through it. I'm not going to tell you how many Fae died trying to make that transit. But we had no choice. We had to leave a way back through the Pattern, one there was no way for the *Marfach* to breach and use to return to the Realm."

Conall frowned. "Why leave a way back, at such

a cost, if none of us can use it?" The redhead was perched on the edge of the sofa, now, his posture and his keen gaze that of a hawk, or a falcon.

"Because the ley energy sealed away in the human world at the time of the Sundering is the only source of living magick, and we knew the Realm couldn't survive forever without it." Cuinn took a deep breath, straightened as if shouldering a great weight. "Time's up. The Realm's store of magick is used up. The ley energy has to go back, or the Realm will die. All of it."

Lochlann was the first to find his voice, to break the silence that fell. "*Magarl lobadh.* You're to be the conduit."

Cuinn nodded, his face pale and grim. "And they gave me a Royal SoulShare, as human as they could arrange for him to be, with the power to shield me long enough for me to open the way, and to keep the way back to the Realm safe, after—"

He didn't finish. Didn't need to. Couldn't, from the look of him. Which left his words space and time in plenty to echo through the dry, hot, barren place within Rian.

I'm a fool. His vision swam with the heat of his tears. *Fool to think this was ever about me.* His gaze swept the room, taking in one by one three stricken Fae, and their human partners distressed for them. His golden ring, his birthright, his Royal signet, was heavy on his finger, weighing down his hand. *I'm their fecking Prince, their dying Realm is my land.*

Then there was Cuinn. Insufferable. Arrogant. Beloved.

His SoulShare stood impassive, arms crossed, giving

away nothing. *He's to give his life. What's my happiness, the poor rags of my sanity, beside that?* "I'm sorry, *mo chroí*." He gripped Cuinn's arm, his hand closing around the curve of muscle that had held the other Fae braced to receive him such a short time ago, light glinting off the ring. "I'll do whatever you need of me."

Rian hadn't realized how much pain showed in his lover's eyes until it was replaced by relief. "*Dhósúil—*"

"No disrespect intended, Highness, but fuck that shit."

Cuinn seemed as startled as Rian by Tiernan's gruff pronouncement. "Since when do you respect Royalty, Noble?" The Loremaster's attempted jest was weak, and sorted ill with his astonished expression.

"Since I found a Royal worth my respect." Tiernan inclined his head to Rian. His gaze then took in the other Fae around the room. "Conall, can you eaves-ward this place airtight? —If the other fucking Loremasters are still alive, I'm assuming they can hear us?" He cocked a brow at Cuinn.

Cuinn nodded curtly. "When they want to."

A muscle jumped in Conall's jaw. He glanced at Josh, and rested a hand on the human's hard-muscled thigh; without a word, Josh bent his head and kissed a slow trail from Conall's shoulder up to the red-blond hair feathering around his ear. Conall sighed deeply, and as the breath left him, so did a lattice of light, wicked sharp and dangerous, forming a sphere that expanded until it disappeared through the walls of the apartment.

"That should hold long enough." Conall cupped Josh's strong jaw in one hand and drew him into a brief, but extremely thorough, kiss. "*G'ra ma agadh, dar'cion.*" Then, to Tiernan, "What are you thinking? —Although I can probably guess."

"All in favor of throwing one giant motherfucking monkey wrench into the Pattern's plans, signify by saying 'aye'." Tiernan's smile had an edge to it, one that only sharpened at the chorus of agreement that came back to him.

Cuinn was paler, now, if anything. "Are you completely out of your mind?" His voice and his hands were both unsteady. Rian had seen it happen, a time or two, back in the days when he and Da had kept company with Volunteers worthy of the name. When a man was set on going to his death, but was drawn back from the brink, the fear could be even greater. Fear of what probably still lay ahead, and fear of not being able to go to meet it bravely a second time. "This isn't something that was forced on me. The other Loremasters gave up everything to form the Pattern, everything but their souls and their wills, and I've always known I was going to be called on someday to do the same. And today is someday."

Lochlann shook his head. "The game's changed, *chara.*" The dark-haired Fae had mentioned, during their brief conversation, that he was a few years older than Cuinn, and had been formed in the same crucible, the battle with the *Marfach* and its terrible aftermath. "You're one of us now. You and Rian, both. You're *scair-anaim.*" Lochlann leaned against the wall, his stance casual but his eyes near glowing, an intense shade of aquamarine, and his fingers interlaced with those of his partner —Garrett, the dancer. "We know what it's like to Share."

"But that doesn't—"

Tiernan cut Cuinn off. "We know what we're willing to give up for our *scair-anaim*. Fae and humans, both." Tiernan's arm had gone around Kevin, at some point when Rian wasn't looking. In fact, Rian was coming to realize that it was very strange to see a Fae *not* touching his SoulShare, if the two were in company.

Tiernan seemed to sense Rian watching him, and quirked a pierced eyebrow at him. "I got off lightly." He raised his left hand, and Rian gaped at the slight wave from fingers of what looked like pure crystal but moved like flesh and bone. "I only gave up a hand." His arm tightened around his husband, as if in apology for the 'only'. "Josh, there, opened himself up to a flow of magick that really should have killed him — can't understand to this day why it didn't, no offense, Josh."

"None taken."

Rian got the impression that when and if Josh ever *did* take offense at something, a prudent man would find himself somewhere else to be until the mood passed.

"Really should have killed him," Tiernan continued, "because channeling magick was the only way to help Conall get his body back. And Lochlann went over to the far side of death, to get Garrett back after the motherhumping *Marfach* and his zombie killed him."

I'm hoping to hell I don't have to understand any of this. Rian gritted his teeth as his thoughts began to skip about again, like swallows with no place to land. Apparently, neither the Sharing nor the shock of

Cuinn's news had been enough to completely heal the brokenness of his mind. The siren call of some ancient pain would lure him back to madness eventually.

Now Tiernan's attention was on Cuinn again. "I'm not sure any of us really want to see what happens when a Fire Royal decides he can't bear to be separated from his *scair-anam*. Or when a Loremaster sees what happens to his *scair-anam* when the Loremaster's life starts washing away in a flood of magick."

"Enlightened self-interest on your part, then." Cuinn's smile tried to be a smirk, but missed the mark.

"Hell yes. To a point." Tiernan gathered in the rest of the room again, with his clear blue gaze. For the first time since meeting the Fae, down in the cock pit in Purgatory, Rian truly saw the nobility in him —a nobility even the most reluctant royalist, such as himself, had to respect. The others in the room, Fae and human alike, were ready to follow him. Not without dispute, not without sarcasm, but they would follow. "We're not going to let the Realm die. But we're going to work out a way to save it that doesn't cost your life, or the Prince's."

Shite. The others followed Tiernan. But Tiernan followed *him*.

Cuinn stared, as if Tiernan's words were sound without sense. "A plan a century in the making and more than two millennia in the execution, and you're going to come up with a replacement on the fly?"

"Do you want to die so badly that you won't let us try?" Conall smiled in quiet satisfaction as Cuinn shook his head. "I thought not."

"But that doesn't mean you've suddenly become miracle workers."

Conall rolled his eyes. "Quit running your mouth and let me think." He plowed a hand through his spiky hair. "I may already have the beginning of a plan. But it needs some work."

The mage paused, looking Rian up and down; the redhead appeared to be younger than Rian himself was, but there was something about the measurement in his spring-green gaze that made it clear he was many times older. Wiser, too, no doubt. "Highness, you don't look well."

Cuinn stepped between Rian and Conall. "Thank you, Doctor Twinklebritches, but I'll..." His voice trailed off, and a frown line appeared between his brows as he studied Rian. "Fuck me senseless. Did something go wrong with the Sharing?"

Jesus, Mary, Joseph and Patrick. Could everyone see his madness, now? "It's just me. I'm no different than I was."

Lochlann pushed off from the wall, took a step closer; stopped, closed his eyes, and kneaded the bridge of his nose. "Fucking aural vision, comes and goes like a sun-sprite on crack." He regarded Rian thoughtfully. "But I could have sworn I saw the aura of a transition dream, just for a second."

"A what, of a what?"

Conall put up a brow, but at Cuinn, not at Rian. "Loremaster, why don't you go into the other room and see to your *scair-anam*, while the rest of us figure out our next move?" The redhead's tone was cool; Rian suspected it had something to do with 'Twinklebritches.'

Tiernan didn't so much stand as flow to his feet. Was the Fae a martial artist? "You don't think the rest of the Loremasters can still eavesdrop on us through him, do you? Even after the ward you channeled?"

Cuinn's eyes widened, then narrowed. "At least one of them has some interesting talents along those lines. It's probably best if we get out of earshot." He caught at Rian's arm, his hand sliding down to interlace fingers. "And take my advice, if you see any bugs, kill the little bastards."

Rian liked the touch. It calmed him. A little.

"Let's leave them to their plotting, *dhó-súil*. And you and I can talk about transition dreams."

Chapter Twenty-two

Bryce Newhouse's feet felt so heavy it was hard to drag them up the stairs from the bowels of the Metro station. He still had a couple of blocks to walk, too. Too bad taking a cab was out of the question since if he did that, he just might puke his guts out all over the upholstery.

That was just wishful thinking, of course. The thing nestled in his intestines wasn't going to let him get rid of the sludge he'd been forced to drink back at the brownstone. It was probably mixed with his own blood by now anyway, just like in one of those shitty vampire movies.

Bryce winced. Apparently a touch of gutter language came with the blood.

Can this just be over?

One thing he'd learned, on the train from New York, death was going to beat the hell out of living like this. Although the monster's influence wasn't quite as strong here. It was kind of like the difference between being crushed to death by a whole collapsing building, or by just one wall, but hey, it was a difference.

A gust of wind hit him as he reached the street

corner, and he shivered all the way down to his gut. Of course, his parasite didn't give a damn about the cold. *It* wasn't the one flouncing around the nation's capital in a too-small leather harness, tight leather shorts, and a fucking dog collar.

Well, all right, he wasn't flouncing. Not even close.

The trouble was, he didn't want to be doing what he was doing. He didn't necessarily mind blowing up Tiernan Guaire's nightclub, the guy was a total asshole, to the extent that it hadn't really been a surprise to find out he wasn't even human. The club could go. Guaire could go with it, for all the fuck he gave. He just didn't care to go with them.

Not that he was being left a choice. Try to drag his clumsy feet as he might, the monster still had enough control over him to keep him moving toward his certain doom.

Great. Melodrama, now. Although he wasn't sure why that bothered him so much. He'd given up anything remotely resembling dignity the moment he boarded the train in these shorts.

Bryce looked up after crossing the street, and he could just make out the low-key sign for Purgatory, a little past the middle of the block. Not much farther. The monster was trying to make him hurry, but he resisted until he was almost to the massage parlor two doors down from the club.

Then he caught fire, from the inside.

He could feel the blood trying to boil in his veins, in his heart. Every heartbeat was agony, and lasted forever. The monster wasn't letting him scream, or even grimace. It kept him trying to walk forward like a mime walking into the wind, except there wasn't any wind. A barrier of some kind that was boiling his blood.

No, not his blood. Janek's. The fucking vampire golem. Jesus, he wanted to scream. But he inched forward. Forward.

The parasite in his gut hit the barrier.

He got a glimpse of something hideous, like a legless scorpion with serrated teeth where its eyes should be. Then his passenger started thrashing. And chewing.

Bryce's whole body jerked, like a seizure. The involuntary movement did what no amount of force could have done; he fell through the barrier and lay panting on the sidewalk on the far side of it.

No one seemed to notice him, on his hands and knees, shuddering and gulping in air. Maybe that sort of thing wasn't such an uncommon sight, on the street housing Purgatory. The piece of crystal inside him was quiet again. He hoped he'd imagined the chewing, though his hand stole up to palpate the area around his scar. Just to be sure.

The monster didn't let Bryce rest long. It urged him to his feet and sent him lurching forward. Past the dark windows of the massage parlor, past the display window of the tattoo parlor next door to it. *Raging Art-On*, the sign said. *Shit, that's LaFontaine's place.* He still had vivid memories of being humiliated by the freakishly inked son of a bitch. He could get blown up too, that would be good.

Terry always loved him more.

The thought of Terry actually gave him a twinge. *I can still feel something. Who knew?* He'd taken

Terry away from LaFontaine, back in the day. All it had taken was a shitload of money. Which was pretty much the only thing he had going for him, but it had been enough. Not enough to win Terry's heart, but he wouldn't have known what to do with that if he'd gotten it. He was only pissed that it still seemed to belong to Josh LaFontaine.

That had all ended after the vampire zombie put the piece of the monster in him, though. The creature hadn't wanted anyone observing what Bryce did, just in case it wanted him to do anything. He'd let it talk him into throwing Terry out. Things had been getting boring, anyway. Time for something new.

Maybe that was a bad idea.

Too fucking late now. The recessed entryway sheltering the stairs down to Purgatory gaped in front of him. A few men walked past him, coming up the stairs; more passed him going the other way, shouldering past him and hurrying down.

Bryce held on to the brass railing, white-knuckled. This was another line to cross. Maybe the last one.

A flash of light came from his right, someone opening the door to the tattoo parlor. As if it didn't want him being seen, the monster gave him a shove in the small of his back. Felt like a boot. He nearly fell down the fucking stairs. *So much for a last stand.*

He regained control before he reached the bottom of the stairs, though. He would be damned if he walked in staggering like he should already be leaving. There were doors of frosted black glass at the bottom of the stairs; he pushed one aside and walked in.

Up to that point, the doors had done a pretty good

job of keeping the sound in. Now he could feel it hitting him in waves, with a bass line that made his guts quiver. He hoped it bugged the shit out of his passenger.

"Can I help you, sir?"

The voice made Bryce think of gravel. He turned, and looked down at the bouncer. Had to be the bouncer, even though every other club he'd ever been in hired them tall and ripped, and this guy didn't even come up to his shoulder. But with his bald head, craggy brow, shoulders a yard and a half across stretching a plain black shirt with the club's logo on it to its limits, and hands the size of hams, there really wasn't much else he could be.

"Uh, no, I'm good." It didn't really matter that his voice was unsteady, there was no way anyone was going to be able to hear him over the dubstep. His head swiveled around until he finally spotted the bar. His final destination. Ever.

Unless nothing happened tonight downstairs in the magic room. *It fucking well better.* His bowels felt loose at the thought of going back through that barrier. Maybe it wouldn't try to keep him in, the way it had tried to keep him out, but then he'd have to come back tomorrow night —

"Come here, Pet." A finger hooked through Bryce's collar and yanked; he almost fell into a fresh-faced boy in black leather, holding a riding crop and a leash in the hand that wasn't busy strangling him. Behind the kid was a dimly illuminated pit, full of sofas and chairs and lounges. And mostly-naked men. Purgatory's famous cock pit. Exactly where there was no way in hell he was going to go. Not as a sub to a barely-legal twit of a wannabe Dom.

222

"I'm not *your* pet," he snarled, thinking at the last instant to lean on the 'your'. Let the stupid prick think he belonged to someone else. Someone with muscles like the bouncer's, who would beat the shit out of anyone messing with his property.

"Your Master needs to teach you manners." It was hard for the kid to look properly disdainful and shout at the same time.

"What. The fuck. Ever." Bryce turned on his heel and stalked over to the bar, wishing he could hear the little prick spluttering. His grand exit was spoiled a little by the fact that there didn't seem to be any room at the bar, but he finally managed to work his way in to rest one ass cheek on a bar stool and lean against the wall at the end of the bar.

The bar itself was one of the strangest he had ever seen, and he'd seen more than his share. The top was clear glass, and light played beneath it, all the colors of fire, orange and dull red and yellow and an occasional flash of blue. But if he looked straight down into it, there was no way to see where the light was coming from, the damned thing looked bottomless. If his mind weren't quite so firmly fixed on his own impending demise, he might have tried to figure out how they managed to get the effect.

"Is someone ordering for you?"

"Hells no."

The bartender, a good-looking guy who could have been anywhere from thirty-five, by his body, to sixty, by his gray brush cut, didn't seem particularly put out. But bartenders were paid to not be put out. "Sorry, it's always best to check, when a guy's collared. Can I get you something?"

223

The noise was a little less punishing here, some trick of the architecture, maybe. "Yeah, I'll have—"He peered at the array of bottles against the back wall, red-lit so as not to compete with the light show inside the bar. "Give me a double Belvedere, straight up."

"Good eye you've got."

As the bartender went back and reached for the top shelf, Bryce noticed his prosthetic leg. *If I had any conscience at all, I'd tell him to get the hell out of here.*

That wasn't a problem, needless to say.

The glass that appeared on the bar in front of him caught the light from below, clear liquid in clear glass. He turned the glass around a few times, admiring the patterns of light.

"You paying for that now, or do you want to run a tab?"

"I'll run a tab, I may be here a while."

Bryce had a credit card, wedged into the waistband of his shorts. After all, he'd thought at the beginning he might need to get a hotel room here. So if it came to that, he'd be good for his bar tab.

Of course, with any fucking luck at all, he'd be dead before last call.

Chapter Twenty-three

Here we are again.

Rian winced as the door closed behind Cuinn. He'd never been one to suffer claustrophobia from being in closed rooms —cars and lorries and trains were an entirely different story, of course —but he'd spent a hell of a lot of time of late in this cramped space.

Not that some of that time hadn't been bliss.

"Would you mind leaving that?" Cuinn had been about to open the curtains, to let in the streetlight and the lights of the shops across the way. And the moonlight. "I fecking hate moonlight."

The flush on Cuinn's cheeks was dusky in the dim light. But Rian's eyesight had always been phenomenal, a trait he suspected was another part of his Fae heritage, and he knew a blush when he saw one.

"D'you want the light on, then?"

Rian shook his head and sat down on the edge of the bed. "Naah, I can see fine without." He cocked his head, studying his *scair-anam*. He could feel a pull toward the shorter male, rather like he suspected gravity would feel to a planet, and he actually sighed with relief when Cuinn sat down beside him on the bed.

The other Fae didn't stay sitting for long, though. Bounced up like a fecking rubber ball, he did. Went to the window, stood there with his head down, as if he was looking out through the opaque curtain.

"I'm so fucking sorry." Rian almost couldn't make out the words, so thick the voice was.

"For what?" Something about the other Fae was radiating don't-touch-me, so Rian stayed where he was. Though he wanted to go to Cuinn, touch him, comfort him. Which was a laugh, because when had his touch ever calmed anyone?

"Your need for pain. Your craving." Cuinn parted the curtains with a finger, stared down at the street below. "I know what's at the heart of it."

"Tell me, then." Rian went still, inward and outward. *Calm before the storm?*

Cuinn's shoulder blades twitched. Rian wanted to place a kiss between them. Sweet bleeding Jesus, he really *was* sick.

"It's as old as you are, isn't it?" Again the twitch, as if the male couldn't keep still. "You can't remember a time when you didn't have at least the memory of pain. Though it became worse —became a craving, started consuming you —on your twenty-first Soul's Day. The night of the Twalf."

A chill rippled down Rian's spine. "The night of the fire. '*Sea.*"

"When you came into your magick." Cuinn turned, just a little, and Rian thought he caught a glimpse of pale green gleaming through sandy blond hair. "Tell me, if you can —did your human parents ever tell you that you were a difficult baby?"

Rian nodded. "I was, for the first month or so

226

after they found me. Though they didn't tell me so until years later, well after they'd told me I was a foundling. Ma said I was the happiest baby she'd ever seen, except when I slept."

"And then you screamed." It wasn't a question. "You screamed because your baby dreams were of being sliced soul from body, as you passed through the Pattern from the Fae Realm to the human world." Cuinn's hands clenched into fists at his sides, clenched so hard they shook. "Transition dreams. We all have them. They help us process the unimaginable pain, get rid of it. But you were too young. You were only two weeks old when you went through. The dreams didn't work the way they were supposed to."

Finally, Cuinn turned back, so pale that even his eyes seemed dark against his face. "The pain that's been at the center of your being for your whole life is my fault. I'm the one who stole you away from your parents and sent you through the Pattern."

In the silence, Rian heard the pounding of his own heart, a drumbeat in his ears. He heard cars, passing on the street below. He heard murmurs from the other room, soft urgent voices. But of his own thoughts he heard nothing, for there was nothing to be heard. Not yet. But something stirred, in the pain-shot darkness of his mind.

"I had no idea what they intended—"

Heat flared behind Rian's eyes, spoke with his voice. "Did you not? You had no thought of what would happen here, tonight? No notion that I'd be forced to come to you, when the time was right, forced to give myself to you?"

Cuinn's mouth dropped open. "You're implying

that I put you through hell, solely for the sake of fucking and being fucked?"

"Implying, hell." Part of Rian stood back, like a spectator, horrified at the words spilling out between his lips. But part of him was fire and fever and pain, and wanted only to burn himself and everything else along with him, the way it should have happened the night of the Twalf. "It wasn't out of any fecking concern for my welfare. You've said yourself Fae don't love. So I'm thinking, either you wanted me bound to you, or you lacked the balls to say no when you were told to put an infant to torture."

Rian didn't see the fist coming. The explosion of white light as the fist connected with his left cheekbone and eye, *that* he saw. And something he thought was probably the ceiling, once his vision cleared.

His vision wasn't the only thing that was clear, though.

"Oh, shit —Rian, *dhó-súil—*"The bed rocked as Cuinn knelt beside him; a hand cradled his head, and he looked up at his lover's face gone stark white with fear. "I should be whipped and brined—"

Rian held up a hand, weakly, and when that failed to halt the stream of what almost sounded like good Irish curses streaming from Cuinn, he tried to shake his head. "Stop. Cuinn. Stop and listen to me." He blinked, with the one eyelid that felt like following instructions at the moment. "It's good. The pain is good. Clears my head."

"Son of a bitch," Cuinn whispered. "Did you push me to do that on purpose?"

"I don't think so." Rian felt gingerly around his eye with his fingertips, and winced. "But it's all good."

228

"Strange fucking definition you have of 'good'," Cuinn muttered, brushing Rian's forelock back from his face.

"Look, I've no idea how long I'm going to be in what passes for my right mind, so let's not waste time." All he had to do was focus on the pain, and try *not* to let himself heal for a change. "Whatever's gone wrong with me, it kicked up a notch when I met you, and now we've gone and Shared, I've no control over it at all." He shook his head, and winced. "But I'm seeing something clearly, maybe for the first time in my life. And you may be the only person who can make sense of it for me."

"I have a fucking lousy track record when it comes to things only I can do, in case you haven't noticed." Cuinn shifted his weight to stretch out beside Rian, his fingertips tracing awkwardly round what was probably the beginning of a spectacular bruise.

Rian caught Cuinn's hand, held it tightly. "You spoke of pain, beyond imagining. Pain my dreams were supposed to process for me, but they didn't."

He closed his eyes, searching for the emptiness in himself, the hole he'd hoped the Sharing might fill, the hole with pain at the bottom. The sudden clarity Cuinn's fist had delivered gave him the opportunity to see his twin curses, pain and fire, in a way he'd never thought to look at them before, through the eyes of a Fae.

Rian spoke without opening his eyes. "That pain has been slumbering in me all my life, I think, with no place to go. The night of the Twalf, it woke up." He took a deep breath. "I think I need to try this *asiomú*, the reversal, on the pain. Before it finishes the job of driving me mad."

229

When he finally opened his eyes again, it was to the sight of Cuinn staring.

Dear God, his eyes are beautiful.

"You need to accept the pain. Embrace it." Cuinn's tone said he understood, but his face added that he wished he didn't.

"I do. I think that's what I've been trying to do, all along, in small ways. Pain is all bound up with sex, for me, because of what was done to me. I think that must be why I seek the pain that way, and I suppose I should thank the good Lord the bastards didn't shoot me or knife me. But nothing anyone has ever been able to do to me has been enough."

"I can't imagine what *would* be enough." Rian felt a shudder ripple through Cuinn, where the other Fae lay close against him. "No Fae remembers exactly what it felt like to go through the Pattern. I don't think it's possible to hold that much pain in memory." Cuinn's gaze dropped, his eyes closed. "You're right, by the way. I did lack the balls to tell the other Loremasters to go fuck themselves the way I should have."

"What's done is done. And it was necessary, from what you—"Rian sucked in a breath through clenched teeth as a wave of heat swept him, igniting a fever having nothing to do with his temperature. "I think you're going to have to hit me again. It's back."

No need to explain what 'it' was.

Cuinn nodded tightly, and tensed. Instead of another blow, though, he delivered a kiss, one of such ferocity that Rian's lips bruised and bled even before the Loremaster bit.

Rian groaned, in pain, in bliss, and in frustration,

looking up at the stains of his blood on Cuinn's lips. Stains dancing with the fire that slept uneasily in his blood. The fever-madness wanted him to taunt Cuinn into taking him again, and even his saner self was having a hard time finding fault with the idea. "I think... I need a little more than that."

"Oh, shit." Cuinn grimaced, then reached down and gripped Rian's crotch, tightly enough that white fireworks started going off at random behind Rian's eyelids even as his hips arched up to ask for more.

More was, alas, not forthcoming. "*Please* tell me that's enough." Cuinn's face was flushed as he let go his grip, and Rian wasn't sure how, but he got the impression that his own addiction was at work again, against his will for a change.

"For a few minutes." Rian had a hard time finding his lower register. Had a hard time breathing, for that matter. Or focusing.

When his eyes finally stopped tracking separately, Cuinn was looking at him oddly. "I think I might have the answer to your problem." If he did, it was an answer that was making him very uncomfortable, from the look of him, and more so as the silence drew out.

Rian's tongue swept blood off his lip. "Ordinarily, I'd appreciate the dramatic pause, but I don't have long and if you clear my head the same way twice my problem may have a more permanent solution than either one of us would like."

It seemed Cuinn couldn't figure out what to do with his hand, now that it was done with being a vise; it hovered over Rian's arm, his side, looked like it might go around to hold him, but finally ended up cupping his jaw. "It's called *ceangail*."

231

The word might be Fae, but it was also good Irish, and Rian frowned. "Ties? Bonds?" He shook his head. "I've tried bondage before, every kind you can imagine, and it doesn't get me anything close to what I need."

"No, it's not bondage. Though I'd imagine some Royals would dispute that." Cuinn smiled faintly. "It's a ceremony Royals go through before they produce an heir. It creates the only kind of permanent pair-bonding Fae in the Realm know. So they can be sure the bloodline is pure."

"And it's painful?"

"Not when it's between two Royals. Fae genetics don't work quite the same as human do, but it's still important for Royals who pair-bond not to be too closely related." Cuinn paused, evidently at a loss for words. "The only genuine love Fae know is love of kin. And while it's hard to channel magick to sort for genetic compatibility, it *is* possible to channel it to react to the love between two Fae."

Cuinn was a fascinating shade of red. Rian couldn't keep back a smile at the sight. "If there's love between the two, the mating shouldn't happen, then?"

"Spot on." Cuinn cleared his throat. "If the *ceangail* is painful, the participants know it's not supposed to happen, and they can stop it."

Rian had never been much for maths in school, but even he could add up what the handsome, sensual, completely maddening Fae was trying to tell him. "This has to be the fecking strangest way to say 'I love you desperately and will you marry me?' I've ever heard."

"How many ways have you heard it?"

"Not all that many, now you mention it." His attempt to feign cool disinterest lasted all of two or three seconds. *Jesus Christ, boyo, wipe the fecking grin off your face before he decides you've gone raving mad and gives it to you in the nuts again!* But he couldn't help it. Couldn't hold back the joy, close cousin to the quicksilver blaze he'd felt during their lovemaking. Well, sexual collisions, really. So far. *Give it time. Let us get this ceangail thing over with and me back in my right mind, and then, who knows? —maybe I'll let him show me what it feels like to make love.*

The joy made no sense, really. Cuinn had just promised him the consuming pain he'd yearned for ever since the bonfire. And in a way that more or less put the passport stamp on his visa to Hell, come to think of it. But Mother Church had told him he was bound for eternal fire from the day he'd blown up his first lorry, under Da's watchful eye, at the age of eleven.

Maybe Mother Church was right. After all, his future surely held fire, any way you looked at it. And he would take his joy where he found it. "Yes, I'll bond with you. *Ceangail.* Whatever the feck you want to call it."

Cuinn's answering grin was only half wicked, and the other half carefully concealed delight. He leaned in to kiss Rian —

And Rian snarled, pushing Cuinn over onto his back, slipping a thigh between his legs to work his groin and kissing him hard as a blast of intense heat left him sweating, drops of fire falling down onto the other Fae. *Oh, feckitall, not this again! Not now!*

Startled, Cuinn grabbed Rian's hair, the forelock

hanging long over his forehead, and yanked his head up and back, bringing tears of pain to Rian's eyes and sweet relief to the rest of him.

"Thank you. For doing that, and for *not* doing the other thing."

"My pleasure—"

There was a staccato knock on the bedroom door. Before either of them could react, the door swung open, revealing Garrett.

"What the bloody fecking *hell* do you want?" and "Were you planning on ending your days as a scorch mark on the floor?" rang out in near-unison.

Garrett didn't look particularly fazed. "I drew the short straw. Got the privilege of being the one to come interrupt two recently Shared Fae." The curly-haired blond's slight drawl —Rian thought it was southern, but then what did he know about American accents? —was soothing, in a way. "Tiernan says to haul your asses back out into the living room, we have a plan." He peered at Rian in the dim light, and frowned. "What happened to your eye?"

Rian ignored the question. He rolled off Cuinn before trying to get up, so as not to further complicate their budding relationship with an accidental knee to the groin, and then gave the shorter Fae a hand up from the bed. He saw Garrett's gaze stray to the rumpled surface, and he couldn't help a mischievous smile. "No, we weren't knockin' wellies."

Garrett turned red. "Whatever you were doing, you need to be ready to do a lot more of it. For the plan to have any chance to work, we have to stir up the nexus as much as we can. And Conall says it's been going apeshit since just after you two came in here."

Rian and Cuinn traded glances as they followed Garrett back toward the living room, Rian's a frowning one. *I'm not so sure I like that talk of 'any chance.'*

Cuinn shook his head, almost imperceptibly. "Not to worry, Garrett. Everybody better fasten their seat belts." His hand crept back and found Rian's. "This is going to be a ride to remember."

Chapter Twenty-four

He'd put the idea out there. Cuinn had picked it up, from the moment he and Rian emerged. *Let them make it work, now.*

Conall slumped back, leaning against Josh, as the conversation went on around him. He had other things he needed to be doing. Closing his eyes, he send his magickal sense out, letting it expand until it encountered the ward he'd set up. It encircled this apartment, and part of the tattoo parlor below. If this plan was to stand a chance, though, it needed to extend all the way down to the nexus chamber.

"Josh?"

"Need help again, *d'orant*?"

"If you wouldn't mind." Months it had been, and he still smiled at his partner's pillow name for him. 'Impossible,' Josh had dubbed him, and not in the way most humans would consider most Fae impossible. No, his human considered him impossible because there was no way he believed that he, Josh LaFontaine, could ever have deserved a male like Conall Dary.

And how sweet it was, to have a partner in magick, one who knew his needs without him having to say a word. Small channelings, he could manage alone. He didn't even truly *need* a partner for greater workings. He'd never had one in the Realm. But alone, the great channelings exhausted him, drained him.

Josh shifted his weight on the sofa, tightened the arm he'd laid across Conall's shoulders, and brushed his lips gently across Conall's. "Tell me when to stop," he whispered.

Conall's laugh was a little breathless. "You are, as always, out of your mind." He caught Josh's lower lip between his teeth, nibbling lightly, running his tongue over the spot. "I never *want* you to stop."

Focus, Conall. That, of course, was the down side of magick with a partner. There were worse problems to have, though. At least he didn't have to worry about what the others thought. Not every Fae favored public sensuality, but no one thought the ones who did at all unusual.

Besides, everyone knew a mage's needs. Cuinn loved to rag on him about what a horny bastard he was, unable to keep his hands, or other body parts, off his beautifully inked human. But Conall knew better, and so did Josh. Conall had spent the first three centuries of his life untouched, prisoner of his immense capacity to channel magick. He'd never dared to risk becoming aroused, to put his own powers to the ultimate test, for fear of destroying everything around him. Not to mention the fact that anyone who got close to him invariably did so because they wanted him to do something for them. Another good reason to flee intimacy. Three lonely —no, three *fucking* lonely centuries had ended when the Pattern had thrown him at Josh's feet. The last nine months hadn't even started making up for those barren years, but he and his human were certainly doing their best.

So everyone knew Conall was making up lost time, and the Fae were —mostly —willing to cut him some slack. He closed his eyes, tipped his head back to rest against the sofa, and let Josh's gentle touches in just the right places draw him into the place within himself where the magick was strongest.

From there, he could see with his inner eye the ward he'd put up, gleaming with the bluish sheen of a freshly-sharpened blade. Turned outward, of course, against any force that might try to enter and spy out the plans of this little band of exiles.

Conall wasn't sure how he felt about Cuinn's first bombshell. From almost the moment he came into his birthright of power, he'd been compared to the Loremasters. *The greatest mage since the Loremasters.* So few true mages —non-Royal or Noble channelers of pure magick —had been born in the centuries between the Sundering and the present, hardly enough to hand down lore from one generation to the next. But the ancients' shadowy figures had always been there, to be envied or to act as spurs to his own powers.

They were shadowy no longer. And it wasn't going to be long before he would be measuring himself not against one of them, the way he'd done with Cuinn an Dearmad, but against what remained of all of them. *Son of a bitch.*

Josh took him into a quick embrace, before going back to his soft stroking. *I'm here*, his human said, without having to say a word.

Conall smiled, and set about making his eaves-ward larger. The Loremasters had numbers on their side, true. But he had Josh.

It wasn't even going to be fair.

***

Conall hung back a little, watching the others start to make their way out the door. Paired up, all of them. He was no different, himself; Josh had started to follow, but as soon as he noticed Conall staying behind, he stepped back to wait with him, his smile a warm reminder of his help in channeling.

"Something bothering you?" Josh bent so he could murmur; most of the others were deep in conversation, but that didn't mean they weren't multitasking, and eavesdropping was something Fae, especially, were very good at.

Conall laughed, but the sound was flat, and Josh winced. "Only this whole plan."

"The way you and Cuinn explained the channeling, it sounds to me like it should work. But I'm hardly the expert. If you don't think it feels right, maybe we should wait. Try to come up with something better." Josh rested a hand on Conall's shoulder. "There's no need to do it tonight."

"Yes, there is. There are at least two very good reasons." Conall was glad of the touch. His earlier optimism had been forced to yield to some hard truths, once he'd expanded the ward and rejoined the conversation. "You can't see it, none of the humans can, but the nexus is —well, I've never seen it like this." He stole one last glance, with his magickal sense, before whispering the words of the quick channeling that would dim his inner sight enough to enable him to get close to the great nexus without being blinded. The only known juncture of ley lines carrying the additional magickal energies of all four elements was glowing like a blast furnace, and sending out pulses of raw energy that reminded him of solar flares. "It's been getting more and more active ever since the Prince arrived. It almost looks unstable." He turned away, blinking away afterimages.

Of the original group, only Cuinn and Rian were left, and they were on their way out. Josh watched them for a second, then turned back to Conall. "I take it he's the other reason?"

Josh didn't need to specify which 'he' he meant. Conall merely nodded. He didn't have much experience with elemental magick, having not a drop of Royal blood in his veins that he was aware of, but he could see it. There had been something wrong about the young Prince's magick from the first time Conall laid eyes on him, something unsettled. Whatever it was, the nexus had responded to it, growing restive itself. After Cuinn and Rian had Shared, the disturbance was even greater. To the point where even the humans were starting to sense something off. Maybe he'd ask Lochlann if his aural sense had anything to add.

Rian and Cuinn left, Cuinn with an are-you-coming? glance back at the last two *scair-anaim* as he shepherded Rian out the door. *I wonder if he realizes what's happened to him.* During their hasty planning session, the Loremaster had been every inch his usual insufferable self, as easy for other Fae to be around as a porcupine orgy in a canoe. Except when Rian spoke. Or when Cuinn was speaking about Rian, or to him. *Do I look like that, around my* dar'cion?

Conall laughed softly and followed Josh out of

the apartment, murmuring a word of warding as he closed the door behind them. *Of course I do.* Every one of them knew what it was like to be awakened, however fearfully or reluctantly, to the SoulShare bond.

Which was probably why he'd been so determined to come up with some way to cheat the Pattern. He followed the others down the stairs, their cobbled-together plan on constant playback in his head. 'Cobbled-together' hadn't been Tiernan's word for it, needless to say —yet even he had muted his sarcasm and foregone snide commentary when Cuinn and Rian had emerged from the bedroom. Even a Fae who respected nothing else, of which Tiernan was a shining example, respected that bond.

They weren't going to let anything, or anyone, take either Fae away from his *scair-anam*. Even if one of them *was* the most purely irritating male in two worlds.

Even with his diminished sensitivity, Conall could make out the ley energy flowing up the last few stairs as they descended to Purgatory, spilling out as they pushed the doors open and were met by the punishing wall of sound. It reminded Conall of the smoke that came off dry ice, the way it acted as if it had weight.

The sound was certainly acting as if it had mass, too. Conall thought he felt his kidneys shuddering as he followed Josh through the crowd. It was a good thing his *scair-anam* was so tall and broad; Conall himself had stopped physically aging somewhere in his late teens or early twenties, younger than normal for a Fae, and was correspondingly more slightly built.

241

He overheard "twink" a lot. And Twinklebritches. *Don't go there, Conall, you're supposed to be practicing the empathy thing.*

They clustered around the end of the bar nearest the door to the nexus chamber, the Fae in the middle. Josh's arm was warm and solid around Conall's shoulders, and he leaned into his SoulShare, just for a second, before turning to wink at him. "See you in a few minutes, *dar'cion.*"

With that, he Faded to the basement, just outside the door to the nexus chamber. The glow coming from under the door pulsed like a heartbeat, and Conall knew a moment of uncertainty. As many times as he and Josh had been down here, he'd never felt anything like the kind of energy emanating from the nexus right now, and it was only going to get more intense. That much power would destroy an unShared Fae between one heartbeat and the next, snuff out his life as thoroughly as if he had never existed. A fate he'd barely avoided himself, even at the much smaller Greenwich Village nexus.

Damn. I didn't think about the dormant nexus. What's going to happen to it, once we start fucking around with this one?

Lochlann Faded in, interrupting his thoughts. They'd decided to send most of the Fae in separately, over the course of a few minutes, with the humans providing cover for their disappearance, and then the humans would come down together, bringing the young Prince with them. No one wanted to chance Rian Fading to the nexus chamber, least of all Rian himself, both because he'd never been there before and because he still wasn't completely in control of his magick. He'd apparently accepted his Fae nature, but his skeptical expression whenever anyone addressed him as 'Prince' or 'Highness' spoke of a ways to go before he believed himself Royal.

Just think, only yesterday I would have considered an un-housebroken Royal enough of a magickal emergency to keep me busy for a week.

The dark-haired Fae whistled under his breath, staring at the crack at the bottom of the door, through which raw ley energy spilled as if under pressure.

"What are you thinking?" Conall, too, was watching the river of not-quite-light.

Lochlann glanced up. "I'm thinking that it's a damned good thing I'm going to have my *scair-anam* as an anchor, when I try this stunt. And thinking about what I'm going to do if anything happens to him."

The second sentiment was voiced differently than the first, but Conall could hear the growl in it. "I understand. We're all at risk here."

"I know—"

This time Tiernan was the interruption. He put up a pierced brow as he studied the door. Even a Noble, who worked mostly with elemental magick, had to be able to see the power boiling out of the nexus chamber. "I wonder what the fucking Health Department would have to say about a nuke in the basement."

"Here's hoping they never find out."

Cuinn appeared, uncharacteristically silent and staring up the stairs. His tension was contagious; it felt like an hour before the door finally opened.

Kevin led the way down, followed by Garrett. The dancer and Josh had Rian between them, almost like a bodyguard as they came down the narrow stairs. Cuinn was like a hound straining against a leash, though he tried not to look any more anxious than the rest of them as the pairings reasserted themselves.

"Everything all right upstairs?" Tiernan slid an arm around Kevin's waist as he asked.

"Fine. Mac was helping someone down at the other end of the bar when we came down, so he didn't see us."

Conall keyed in the code to unlock the door to the nexus chamber, then placed his palm on the lock and whispered his key to the channeling. A Fae of the Demesne of Air used words as a key. Tiernan, from the Demesne of Earth, used the living Stone of his own left hand. Lochlann, of Water, usually used his own blood. Rian... well, the Fire Royal was going to be a challenge. And Cuinn? They'd never had to come up with a key for him; he'd never been free to come down here, before he and Rian Shared —

Conall stared, mute, as Cuinn and Rian edged past him into the nexus chamber. White showed all around the blue topaz of the Prince's eyes, and Cuinn was murmuring softly to him. But there was sweat beading on Cuinn's forehead, and his face was pale. *We've all been taking it for granted, that two Fae who have Shared will both be protected, that a Sharing with a Fae who's* almost *human will work as well as one with a human.*

What if it doesn't?

Chapter Twenty-five

Tiernan's hands, one gloved, one not, glided smoothly, possessively down Kevin's bare back. His husband had left his dress shirt downstairs for Josh to wear during the channeling to come, before the two of them had come back upstairs. The last thing anyone down there needed was *Scáthacru,* Josh's dragon, flying around setting things afire. Or *Aréan,* the hawk tattooed on his chest, sinking its talons into someone at an inopportune moment. No, better to have the tattoo artist cover up, which usually kept his ink quiet during a channeling. Besides, the lack of a shirt made Tiernan's present view so much better.

"Aren't you supposed to be keeping an eye on the basement door?" Kevin's quiet amusement was just what Tiernan needed. Calming, but at the same time sexy as hell. Which could come in handy if he had to channel in a hurry.

"I am. This amazing set of pecs just keeps getting in my way." Tiernan couldn't resist leaning in for a nibble. Especially knowing what was going on downstairs. It was asking a lot to keep himself to himself. Three pairs of *scair-anaim*, all getting ready for the channeling of a lifetime. The configuration they'd argued out in the last hectic hour sorely tried the available space in the former storeroom; Cuinn and Rian needed the chaise for their *ceangail* ritual, Lochlann and Garrett had to be far enough away from them that Lochlann would be able to draw energy off the nexus without getting sucked into it once they kicked it in the teeth, and Conall and Josh —soon to be just Josh, at least to the eye —needed to be close enough to Lochlann for Josh to be able to take Lochlann's hand, but close enough to the nuptial couple to be able to do their part when the time came. "Kind of like the bottom of a basket of kittens."

"I beg your pardon?" Kevin rocked his hips slightly, where he knelt straddling the Fae. They were taking up space in the cock pit, that leather garden of delights, and they needed to at least look as if they were doing something if they wanted to avoid drawing attention to themselves.

"The rest of the Demesne downstairs. Like the bottom of a sack of randy kittens." Tiernan couldn't help closing his eyes for a second, as his P.A. caught on the zipper of his jeans.

Kevin laughed, but quickly sobered. Bracing his hands on the back of the black leather loveseat, he leaned in. They were in one of the comparatively quiet spots in the pit, acoustic abnormalities allowing for almost-normal conversation even when the bass beat from the dance floor was more visceral than audible. "Do you suppose they've started yet?"

"Hard for me to tell." Not for the first time, Tiernan cursed his comparative blindness when it came to the pure form of the ley energy; his SoulShare, human but with a Fae soul, could probably see it almost as well as he could. Earth energy he could see, being a Noble of that House, and one of the lines meeting under Purgatory carried some of it. The nexus energy itself, though, would probably only be visible to him up here in the club if something went really, really wrong. By which time it probably wouldn't matter.

"Kevin? Tiernan?"

Kevin started and sat up; they turned to see Terry Miller, Josh's business partner. "What is it?" Tiernan had no time for or interest in pleasantries, he was too preoccupied, and he seriously needed to feel Kevin grinding into him again.

Terry shook his head, mutely apologizing. "Probably nothing. But I stuck my head out of Raging Art-On, a while ago, looking for a late client, and I saw Bryce Newhouse come in here. In one of my old clubbing outfits I had to leave behind when he threw me out, no less."

Tiernan stiffened. "What the particular fuck is that piece of dogshit doing in my club?"

"I seriously doubt it is coincidence." Kevin's hand slipped from the back of the loveseat to grip Tiernan's shoulder.

Coincidence, that one of the *Marfach's* tools had turned up here just as they were about to open a path back to the Realm? *Not fucking likely*.

Tiernan surged to his feet, as Kevin got gracefully out of his way. "Where is he, Terry?"

Terry nodded toward the opposite end of the bar from the door to the basement. "He's probably been there for about an hour."

While we were sitting around making plans. Shit.

247

"Get back upstairs. Shut the door. Someone will let you know when to come out."

Terry's mouth fell open slightly. But Tiernan gave him no time or space for argument, simply caught Kevin by the arm and started for the far end of the bar.

Kevin didn't need to be drawn for long, though. He matched strides with Tiernan, and by the time the pissed-off Fae and the former college wrestler turned lawyer reached the last bar stool, it would have been entirely reasonable if Bryce had assumed the wrath of God had arrived.

Except Bryce wasn't assuming much of anything, given that his eyes could barely focus. His hand was wrapped tightly around an old-fashioned glass, as if the heavy glass was in some way anchoring him to the bar. He sure as shit needed the anchor, too.

Tiernan didn't want to get too close, not after the suspicions Conall had reported about the Wall Street prick. *He carries the* Marfach *in him, somehow, I'm sure of it. But not in any way that shows, except for a scar.*

Tiernan looked up, just as Mac stepped up to the other side of the bar. "What the fuck, Mac? How did he get this wasted, if he only got here an hour ago?"

Mac shook his head. "I've only given him two drinks, and he hasn't even finished the second one."

"Guaire?" Bryce struggled to raise his head, struggled to sneer. "Lee'me the fuggalone."

"Like hell." Tiernan stared as Bryce's torso came into view, only partly obscured by the too-small leather harness he wore. A small, dark scar on the left side seemed to crawl, and glowed with a light that was actually darkness. Which made no sense, yet there it was.

Tiernan forced himself to look away. Something about his expression as he did so made Kevin turn a dark glare on a nearly oblivious Bryce. "Conall was right about him?"

Tiernan had no secrets from his *scair-anam,* not since the first one had nearly proved lethal to both of them. "Looks that way."

"May I suggest, then, that we get him out of here?" Kevin's dark gaze flickered to the door to the basement.

"You read my mind." Tiernan went around Bryce to the human's right, as far from the scar and its strange warped light as he could get. "Would you mind getting that side?"

"My pleasure."

As soon as their arms linked through Bryce's, the sodden lump suddenly started thrashing, nearly throwing them both off before they reasserted their grips. The collared human's lips were curled back from his teeth in a vicious, but silent, snarl. He kept fighting, even with his arms pinned, overturning the bar stool he'd been sitting on and damned near neutering Kevin in the process. Which earned him one of Tiernan's forearms across his collared throat and a knee in his kidneys.

"Jesus." Kevin was remarkably calm, all things considered.

Tiernan managed a shrug. "I took that personally."

"I —have to —stay here." Bryce's words were more gurgle than speech, and he continued to thrash as if he were in contact with a live wire. Or maybe an electric chair. Kevin motioned other club-goers back, but it wasn't really necessary. No one appeared anxious to be found in the path of one of Bryce's feet or to risk getting grabbed.

"Yeah, well, that's tough shit, because I need your ass out of here." Not for the first time, Tiernan wished for even a little Air magick. Using Earth on Janek had been more than enough of a lesson in what a bad idea the offensive use of his own element could become, but it would feel so fucking good to stop the air in Bryce's lungs. "And since I could choke you with just a little more pressure, I win."

Kevin, who was gracefully avoiding Bryce's legs, raised an eyebrow at this, but said nothing.

"Fucking moron." Bryce's voice, such as it was, was different. Squeezed, and hushed, as if he were trying not to be overheard. "*It won't let me die.*"

Magairl a'Ridiabhal. Tiernan suspected the whites of his eyes were showing all the way around his ice-blue irises as he met Kevin's gaze. Satan's balls, indeed. "We have to get this son of a bitch out of here. Right fucking now."

"Need help, boss?" Lucien's gravelly voice sounded from behind them; Tiernan couldn't spare more than a glance over his shoulder, but that was enough to show him the bouncer was wearing his special smile, the one he reserved for the most interesting possibilities for mayhem. It made Tiernan feel better.

"Thanks, I think we're good." Kevin spoke up before Tiernan had a chance to reply, then lunged in and managed to get his arms around both of Bryce's flailing legs at once. "But could you get the door?" His grim nod to Tiernan indicated he'd heard Bryce.

Tiernan blessed his husband's cool head as the two of them, with their ever more violent burden, followed Lucien to the thick black glass doors. Best not to involve normal humans in the fucked-up mess this was all but certain to turn into.

Their luck held as they emerged onto the stairs up to street level; no one was coming down to make things any more awkward than they already were. Kevin was doing a good job of controlling Bryce's lower half, but it took most of Tiernan's greater-than-human strength to deal with the upper. "What the fuck is going on with you, asshat?"

Tiernan didn't expect an answer, and he didn't get one; Bryce just continued to try to break away from them and get back downstairs, with a frantic intensity that surprised both SoulShares. "Where are we taking him?" Kevin grunted as he took a knee to the gut. "I don't think leaving him on the sidewalk is an option."

"Hells to the no." Tiernan looked around as he cleared the stairwell. "The massage parlor. No one's in there."

Getting into Big Boy Massage was both simple and complicated. Simple because Tiernan, being the landlord, had the key. Complicated because he had to do his share of holding on to Bryce while he looked for the damned thing. It cost him a bruised jaw, but he finally found it, and got the three of them inside before anyone showed up to start asking annoying questions.

Kicking the door closed, he spared just enough attention to channel Stone around its edges to seal it shut, then switched on the light with an elbow. No need to worry about being seen; the nature of the business being what it was, the windows were all covered. The three of them crashed against one of the massage tables, which was as good a place as any to put the asshole down.

Of course, there was then the issue of keeping him there. "What are we going to do with him?" Kevin was panting, and favoring one side, where a bruise was already starting to purple.

Tiernan growled at the sight. "It ought to be safe to leave the body here until they're done downstairs."

"Oh, no, you don't." Bryce's thrashing took on a new and understandable vigor, and Kevin was forced to break off to help Tiernan subdue him before he could continue. "I'm not running interference for you with Homicide. Vice is more than bad enough."

Tiernan rolled his eyes. "Any other suggestions?"

Oddly enough, the shabbily collared financier wasn't screaming, or calling for help, or doing anything else that involved making noise. He *was* biting, though.

Which was the proverbial last straw. Pinning the asshole down on the table with his right hand, Tiernan quickly stripped the glove from his left with his teeth, dropped the glove on the floor, and made a fist.

"What are you —oh." Kevin shrugged as Tiernan channeled magick, pouring it into his hand of living Stone and temporarily transforming it into the non-living kind. It made a very good blunt instrument, and Bryce went limp on the table, blood trickling into his glossy dark hair.

Brownish blood. Just like Janek's.

"Fuck me oblivious," Tiernan whispered.

Chapter Twenty-six

It's almost over.

Rian wasn't entirely sure why the thought gave him chills. It should be joyous, the notion of repairing what had gone wrong with him right from the start of his life.

Have I always been mad? Will I even know myself, sane?

He shook his head. Surely he hadn't always wandered the outskirts of madness, a flame looking for tinder. He remembered a childhood like any other, with its share of joys and sorrows and childish scapegracery and forgiveness for it. Normal. Yet haunted.

It's always been there, at the bottom of my mind. Like the bottom of the infernal Pit, the lowest place I could fall.

If he dared to turn his gaze inward now, he could see it, a silver-blue glow that had always promised him pain.

Now it's time to force it to make good that promise, and set me free.

"You're shaking." Cuinn's voice was soft, probably so as not to disturb the others' preparations.

Their own part, his and Cuinn's, the *ceangail* ritual, wanted preparation as well, but Cuinn had thought it might be better to wait until the others were nearly ready.

'*The nexus responds to you,*' he'd said. '*Like a horse to the whip.*' Best to lay the whip aside until there was need of it.

"Am I, now?" Rian tried to laugh, but it was a poor thing and hardly worth the effort.

Cuinn's hand rested on his thigh, lightly, demanding nothing. Hesitantly, Rian laid his own over it, then gripped it as a hot wind swept through his mind, searing places already raw.

He didn't realize he'd cried out with it until he saw that everyone had stopped what they were doing, and that every eye in the room was on him. "Sorry," he muttered, feeling the color rising in his cheeks.

"No, Highness." Conall was in the circle of his Josh's arms, leaning against him. "Don't be sorry. Just try to hold out a little longer. We're not going to have a second chance at this. It has to be perfect the first time." The redhead watched intently, looking from Rian to Cuinn and back again. Even after Rian's tight nod, he waited a moment longer before turning back to his partner and resuming the heated kiss Rian's cry had interrupted.

That kiss. *Jaysus.* Full body contact, hands stroking and grasping, soft and hungry and needing sounds. Lochlann and Garrett as well, Garrett had Lochlann backed up against the wall and was wrapped round him like the dark-haired Fae was a pole.

Under any other circumstances, Rian would have been tempted to call this an orgy, he'd enough experience of those to know one when he saw one. But this was nothing of the sort. The two couples were both just one fevered moment short of undressing one another and fucking each other senseless, true. But each was so wrapped up in his own other, they needed reminders the rest of the world existed.

The sight struck Rian heart-deep, like a spear, even through his madness. He'd not seen any two people so lost in each other since his Ma and his Da would look at each other. He'd never felt so alone.

Until Cuinn's hand shifted on his thigh, and he remembered that he wasn't. Rian held that hand more tightly, and used it as a sea anchor while he fought for self-control. When the worst was past, he took a deep breath, let it out a little shakily, and turned to Cuinn.

The expression on the other Fae's face was very like what he suspected his own must have been, moments before. Naked fear. Quickly covered over, but it had been there, he was certain.

"What is it? —I'm all right, or I will be." He stumbled over the words, as unsure about offering comfort as he was about comfort being offered to him.

Cuinn was pale, and though his hand in Rian's was cold, there was a sheen of sweat on his forehead. "Bad case of last-minute nerves. I'll be all right."

"Tell him, you idiot." Conall's voice was muffled by the other things he was doing with his mouth at the moment, but Rian made the words out without difficulty.

"Tell me what?"

Cuinn shot Conall a glare, which the redhead didn't even seem to notice. "Thanks ever so fucking much, Twinklebritches."

Even as anxious for an answer as he was, Rian had a hard time of it, keeping back a smile. "Don't distract him. Tell me what?"

Cuinn sighed. Even in the space of that breath, Rian felt, or imagined he felt, a kind of pressure increasing throughout the room. "This could still turn into a giant clusterfuck in a hurry. There's no way to tell until we try, though."

"How?" With all the arguing upstairs, Rian had thought everything worked out, every chance accounted for.

"Something I forgot. Tried to wish away, more like." Cuinn's gaze caught his, held it. "If there's danger, it's more to me than to you. You're going to be channeling the elemental energy, but you're an elemental yourself, you should be fine. Though the air, earth, and water energy will be the source of some of the pain you need." The hand on Rian's thigh squeezed, encouragement and apology. "But I'm going to be drawing in the pure ley energy, to fuel my half of the *ceangail* and then to open the way for Conall. And the point of a soul-sharing, before the two of us, was to give the Fae a human shield against the raw power of the ley lines." Cuinn cleared his throat. "They —we — saw the love as kind of a side effect, because what the fuck did we know about it?"

More than any of you think, I suspect. But Rian simply raised a brow, not wanting to interrupt. Needing to know what danger his SoulShare was in, his own fear all but forgotten.

"The other Loremasters told me you're as close to human as they could arrange for you to be. By which I think they meant, raised as a human, by a loving

256

family. Growing up believing you were human. Never knowing you weren't supposed to be able to love anyone but blood kin." Cuinn's face went from stark white to flushed, and he shifted uncomfortably on the chaise. "Plus, you're a Royal, so in theory you shouldn't even be touched by the pure form of the energy, no matter what. You don't just use Fire, you *are* Fire. I think my colleagues saw the potential that you might be an even stronger shield for me than a human would be."

"If it works, you mean." *If I'm Fire, then why do I feel so fecking cold?*

"It should work." Cuinn's arm slipped around Rian's waist; it wasn't as if the other Fae could draw him any closer than he already was, but the arm felt good. And perhaps Cuinn needed the support as well. "I didn't dare so much as stand on the stairs to this room, before you and I Shared. Couldn't be that close to the nexus. Now here I sit, trying to hatch the damned thing like an egg, and so far no magickal reaming out."

"Yet you're still afraid." A soft groan caught Rian's attention, and his gaze strayed briefly to the other two couples. Conall was oddly insubstantial, almost like a watercolor of himself, his wrists crossed and hands held together behind his back by one of Josh's large hands. Garrett's head had fallen back, and his throat was working in time with the same pulses of pleasure that drove his hips rhythmically into Lochlann's.

Cuinn was watching them, too. "Fuck, yes, I'm afraid," he whispered. "The Loremasters didn't expect me to survive, the way it was originally supposed to go, any more than they 'survived' themselves. And I don't know if our plan makes my chances better or worse."

Rian fought down the near-irresistible impulse to laugh. The impulse was born of the madness, and feck if he'd give in to it now, though the effort it took left him wracked. "If it's my task to keep you safe, then safe you'll be."

Cuinn sat in silence for the space of a few breaths, leaning into Rian. "It's not so much the thought of dying I mind." He spoke quietly, almost absently. "Though there was a time I thought I'd mind the hell out of it."

Josh cleared his throat. "I think we're ready for you two." It was Josh's voice, yet not, his baritone cut with a hint of Conall's tenor, and the copper-top was nowhere to be seen. Lochlann was braced against the wall, with Garrett wrapped around him for more support. All three males Rian could see looked to Cuinn, and then to him. Garrett nodded, and Lochlann and the Fae-human that was Josh and Conall bowed. Just a hint of movement, but each bowed to their Prince.

"Shit." Cuinn took a deep breath.

Yes, I have to know. "What *do* you mind, if not the thought of dying?"

Cuinn's faceted gaze met Rian's, and for maybe the first time, Rian truly understood how old the other Fae was. His face showed none of it, he looked not much older than Rian himself. No, it was all in those eyes.

"Leaving a great fucking hole in your life, where I used to be." There was pain in his gaze, and surprise at the pain. "No, I can't even say it's where I used to be, because I haven't had time to be there yet."

Rian's mouth dropped open. Before he could find words to answer, Cuinn had him by the shoulders, and was kissing him. Kissing him till his head spun, and his breath caught, and his heart hammered against the wall of his chest like it wanted out.

And the air caught fire.

Not in the literal sense, thanks be to God. But it was alive, alive with power, in a way that put Rian in mind of the firestorm he'd made of the bonfire, last twelfth July. The fine blond hairs rose on his forearms, and prickled on the back of his neck.

"Catch the elements." Cuinn's tense whisper was hot against his lips, so close Rian felt the movement as well as the breath. "Like we told you. Weave the binding."

As well tell a blind man how to tat lace, had been Rian's thought at the time. But it had to be done, and he had to do it. The beginning of the *ceangail*, and the first step toward facing the pain. Accepting it. Turning it back on itself, and on what had created it.

Oh, and binding himself for life to the male who held the other half of his soul. And hopefully not killing him in the process.

Use your inner eyes, Conall had urged. Rian closed his eyes, and was surrounded by a skein of phantom colors, swirling on waves of power invisible to him. Red was drawn to him, danced around him, made patterns on his skin, passed through him, leaving tingling wakes through his flesh. The others, the blue and green and white, less visible, avoided him.

He needed them all, they'd said. Every color.

Conall had suggested he use the elemental energy to form a net, one that would bind him to Cuinn. Rian tried. Sweat trickled down his temples, his neck, as he struggled. Shaping the will-o'-the-wisps into a net was like trying to coax fish to weave themselves together in the water, or leaves to blow themselves into a pattern in the teeth of a gale.

"It's no good." He choked on the words. Somehow, Cuinn's hands had ended up clasping his, and he held them tight, the gold of his heavy signet ring blazing with a light of its own. "The net's no good."

"Fuck the net, then." Josh/Conall's voice was crisp, clipped, though Rian suspected the speaker was less calm than his/their voice sounded. "Use something you know, Highness. The power will respond to you."

What do I know of binding?

The answer, when it came, was obvious. The shards of color started to shape themselves into the links of a chain almost before the image was finished forming in his mind, joining one to another to another. The colors jostled together, as if they weren't happy to be in such intimate contact, but the chain was solid. And *oh feck*, it just kept getting longer. There were always more sprites of power to link one to another, more pouring out from the invisible fountain beneath him. He tried to imagine what might happen, if all the space in the little chamber were filled with a chain formed of raw elemental power. Then he tried to stop imagining it.

"I think it's ready." Rian risked opening his eyes, at last, to lock gazes with Cuinn. "I think *I'm* ready."

Cuinn nodded, almost imperceptibly. The first words of the *ceangail* ritual, and the last, were to be his. "Brace yourself, *dhó-súil*. This is going to be all the pain you ever dreamed of."

"Thank you." *Truly, it's almost over.* He steeled himself, and waited.

Cuinn leaned in to steal one last kiss. One more bit of arousal, to fuel the magick he was about to work. Or was it more than that?

"I'll keep you safe, *scair-anam*," Rian whispered. "On my life, I swear it."

Cuinn's hands tightened around his. "If you don't, I'm coming back to kick that magnificent ass of yours all the way back to Belfast."

Rian tilted his head forward, until his forehead rested against Cuinn's. He could feel the other Fae shaking.

"Oh, fuck this." Cuinn tensed, setting himself as if to receive a blow. "Two fires, burning in the same hearth, become one."

God, Cuinn's eyes were beautiful. How had he not seen that from the start? From those first moments, in the dank cellar of OTK?

Sweat beaded on Cuinn's forehead and upper lip, trickled down into his eyes. "And so, two souls, bound, burn as one."

My cue. Rian closed his eyes, and breathed a sigh of relief to see the shimmering chain unchanged, except that it was even longer. At his silent command, it coiled about the two of them. Another command, and it tightened.

And the entire fecking world went up in Fire and magick and pain .

Chapter Twenty-seven

"Please don't tell me we have another Janek O'Halloran on our hands." Kevin stared in dismay at the trickle of brownish-red blood running into Bryce's hair. "One is more than enough."

"I don't think so." Tiernan frowned; touching his fingertips to the bloodstain, he waved them under his nose and grimaced. "No, he's not dead. Or even partly dead, whatever the fuck Janek is at this point. The scent's wrong." Tiernan bent over the unconscious man and breathed in deeply. "He smells alive. Like an asshole, but alive."

"So glad you're the one with the enhanced senses and not me. There are some things even a lawyer won't do." Kevin watched his husband channel magick again, bringing his crystal hand back to life. "I didn't know you could do that."

"May I always be able to surprise you." Tiernan's sexy smirk was unchanged by their present circumstances. Unfortunately, it didn't last long, because the Fae returned his attention to the approximately two hundred pounds of gently snoring dickhead on the table, looking him up and down.

"If he's not dead, though, then why does his

blood look like that?" Contrary to his weaselish reputation, and the impression Kevin had gotten during their brief acquaintance so far, Bryce was quite tall, at least as far as Kevin could tell while he was lying down, and well-built. Which made Terry's much-too-small leather harness a strange wardrobe choice. Had the guy really come all the way from New York in it? And what the hell was going on with the collar? A beat-up old thing that wasn't even the same color as the harness, and which barely closed around Bryce's throat.

Tiernan didn't appear to have heard him. He was studying a small knot in the skin of Bryce's abdomen, as best he could without being able to look directly at it. "Fuck. Come here and look at this for me, will you?"

Kevin skirted the table and bent for a closer look. "It's a scar."

"Yes, it is. And even with my sensitivity to magick damped down to the point where it's next to useless, so the fireworks downstairs don't blind me once they start, I can't stand to look directly at it. Which means it has something to do with the *Marfach*."

Kevin shuddered. A little over a year ago, the *Marfach* had been able to get into his mind, thanks to a flaw in his and Tiernan's Sharing. He'd been made to believe he was being eaten alive, from the inside, as part of the creature's attempt to possess Tiernan. Later, he'd arrived on the scene moments after the monster's first murder when its human pawn had damn near beheaded a blackmailing partner at Kevin's law firm. And then he'd been held hostage, a knife at his throat,

263

by that same human pawn, with the *Marfach* lodged in a mass of crystal in the hulking bastard's head, while Conall tried to repair the protective wards around Purgatory. He'd had about enough of direct contact with the *Marfach* to last him a couple of lifetimes. "Any idea what that something might be?"

"Actually, yes. Except that I can't look closely enough to be sure."

"All right." One last glance to be sure Bryce was still in Dreamland, and Kevin bent to study the scar. It was an ugly thing, even for a scar, an angry shade of blackish-purple. "What am I looking for?"

"Any sign that whatever left that scar might be a blade, not more than a half inch or so across and sharp on both edges."

Kevin twisted around to shoot a questioning look at Tiernan. "Problem, *lanan*?" The overhead light glinted off the ring in Tiernan's eyebrow.

"Dammit, Jim, I'm a lawyer, not a forensic pathologist." Kevin shook his head and returned his attention to the little scar. It was twisted, knotlike, and the very center of it was puckered hard and nearly black. However, he thought he could make out thin straight lines, on either side of the center, more cleanly healed than the rest of the scar. "It might have been. That's about all I can say."

"Good enough for me," Tiernan muttered. "The fact I can't even look at the scar is really all the proof I personally need, but that settles it. I think the scar was left by my knife, the one Janek stole from you. And since the enchantment on that blade means that it will cut through pretty much anything, including magickal Stone, I'm guessing there's a piece of the *Marfach*

264

itself riding around in this sorry son of a bitch's gut."

"Holy shit." Kevin's own gut wrenched in unwilling sympathy; his body was always going to remember the illusion the monster had created to break him. And then it wrenched again, as an even less welcome thought suggested itself. "It's pretty obvious it's controlling him. Do you think it's spying on us?"

"If I had to guess, I'd guess no. It had to fight to control Janek, when it came after Conall and took you hostage, and it had its full mass of Stone to work with then." Kevin loved the way Tiernan's eyes flashed pure murder at even the passing reference to their most recent showdown with the monster. "I don't feel like playing guessing games, though."

"Agreed. So what do we do?"

"You're *sure* killing Bryce isn't an option?" Tiernan sounded almost wistful.

"If it doesn't kill the piece of the *Marfach*, too, it's not going to solve our problem."

"Point taken." Tiernan sighed. "Not to mention that I'd probably have to use magick to get rid of the body, which would be a very bad idea with even a tiny piece of the *Marfach* involved."

"I hate to be the bearer of bad tidings, but Sleeping Beauty is starting to wake up." Not quite true, but Bryce was moving, a little.

"Well, fuck." The look Tiernan shot Bryce telegraphed a clear desire to hit him again, at least until the Fae's better nature gained at least temporary control. "Let me think."

Kevin's gaze strayed back to the unconscious body on the table. It was hard *not* to look at the scar, now that he knew what it was, but he tried. It really was amazing how Bryce managed to give the impression of being scrawny and undernourished, when the guy was obviously —probably fastidiously —cut and buffed. The collar he wore barely fastened at the last notch, and probably the only reason Terry's harness was staying on him was because Terry, in addition to being a tattoo and piercing whiz second only to Josh, was a ballet dancer who could probably hold Kevin over his head one-handed with no trouble at all.

He's just hollow. Miserable soulless bastard.

"I've got it." Tiernan's voice cut into Kevin's thoughts. "But I don't think you're going to like it."

"I'll try not to be too picky." Kevin loved his husband and *scair-anam*. Passionately. But his smirk was marginally less endearing than the rest of him.

Tiernan bent over, and when he straightened there was a knife in his hand, the one he carried in his boot. It was Fae manufacture, not magick-imbued truesilver like the one Janek had stolen, but still a fine blade, even to Kevin's untutored eye. A gift from the Realm, from Cuinn, when the Loremaster had been in one of his rare not-being-a-total-pain-in-the-ass moods. Tiernan hefted it in his hand, weighing it, studying Bryce as best he could.

Kevin groaned. "You're going to cut it out, aren't you?"

Tiernan's eyes were the same clear, compelling blue topaz that had stolen his heart, their first night at Purgatory. "No. You are. I have to build a fucking cage for it."

Kevin opened his mouth, a fervent *hell no* on the brink of utterance. Then closed it, reasonably sure his face was a delicate shade of green. "You can't look at it."

"Precisely." Tiernan offered him the knife, hilt first. "And you can't do the channeling."

Kevin's fingers felt numb as they closed around the hilt. He was fine with the concept of self-defense, and given the right incentive, he was sure he could use a knife like this to attack an enemy. But cutting into an unconscious tool, who was probably going to bleed hypo-oxygenated brown all over him, trying to dig out a chip of pure evil?

"If I could do it myself, I wouldn't ask you, *lanan*."

Kevin looked up from the polished blade, into unexpectedly compassionate eyes. "I know. I'll do it."

"Wait till I get the cage built, and I'll try to make it a little easier for you."

Tiernan faced the far side of the table, and braced his feet shoulders' width apart. Rolling his shoulders as if he anticipated some great physical stress, he settled himself and extended his hands, thumbs touching, palms facing outward. He closed his eyes, and bowed his head.

Kevin forgot all about the knife, and Bryce, and the *Marfach*, and watched in wonder as the air on the far side of the table started to shimmer. What formed, slowly, from the bottom up, looked like a crystalline soap bubble, shimmering and fragile and translucent. There was one difference between the sphere and a soap bubble, though. Even though the sphere looked perfectly transparent, Kevin couldn't see through it.

Finally, Tiernan lowered his hands, with a deep, unsteady sigh. Kevin moved to his side, wrapped an arm around him, and drew him in to lean against him. "I should have prepped you for that, sorry."

Tiernan shook his head. "No time for that. Here, give me back the knife for a second."

Kevin obliged, still staring at the floating bubble. "What is it?"

"The inside is an absolutely perfect spherical mirror. Reflects all energy that strikes it —light, heat, whatever. They're children's toys, in the Realm, only this one's a hell of a lot stronger. I hope." Tiernan straightened and balanced the blade across his palms, one flesh, one living crystal. "I suck at channeling pure magick, as you know, but I don't have a choice. And that's the one channeling I know that stands any chance of containing even a small piece of the *Marfach*."

"Why can't I see through it?"

"Because all there is to it is the inside. It doesn't really have an outside to see, or to see through." Tiernan curled his fingers carefully around the blade. "If you drop the piece of Stone into it, it'll pass right through and then stay where you drop it. Just don't let your finger go with it, I'm not sure it would come back out."

Kevin blanched. "Roger wilco." The not-bubble hung silently in mid-air, a dangerous puzzle he didn't have time to solve right now. "What happens once we have the piece of Stone in there?"

Tiernan's shrug was anything but casual. "Once they're done downstairs, I can probably get Conall to come dispose of it."

Assuming they live through what they're doing down there. Of course, if they don't, chances are we won't either. Cuinn and Conall hadn't been very specific about the potential backlash if things went south while they were all engaged with the ley nexus. They hadn't needed to be.

Kevin felt a low hum reverberate through Tiernan's body, and tiptoed to nibble at Tiernan's earlobe, to help with whatever lesser channeling he was doing.

The Fae's smile was like a touch. A very distracting touch. The air vibrated with power along the blade of the knife, until the blade sang like a tuning fork, and the power quickly faded away. Tiernan handed the knife back to Kevin. "There. I made Conall teach me a lesser Finding. It's not enough magick to feed the *Marfach*, but the channeling should attract the piece of it to the blade, if you get anywhere near it."

Damn. I'm actually going to have to do this. "You might want to hold him down. This is probably going to wake him up."

"I could always hit him again."

"Probably not the best idea."

"You're a real wet blanket, anyone ever told you that?" Tiernan moved around to stand by the head of the bed, looked down at the still-sleeping Bryce, and frowned. "That's strange."

"I know. It's odd when you realize he isn't really scrawny." Kevin stepped to the side of the table and rested his hand lightly on Bryce's abs. *If someone had told me a little over a year ago that I'd be in a massage parlor tonight, with my husband, about to vivisect an investment banker in order to put a monster that tried to kill me into a magickal cage —*

"That's not it." Tiernan pinched the bridge of his nose. "I think his fucking collar is magickal."

Bryce picked that moment to moan, piteously.

No time. The knife went in, dead center on the scar.

Kevin wasn't sure what he'd expected. More

resistance and less blood, probably. And more screaming. But the knife went in like the double-edged scalpel-sharp blade it was, brown blood poured out until he couldn't see a goddamned thing, and Tiernan's hand over Bryce's mouth pretty much took care of the noise situation. Bryce thrashing and twisting didn't help, though, and for one awful moment, Kevin was sure the son of a bitch was going to impale himself on the Fae-blade right down to the gold-chased silver leaf at the end of the hilt. But at least he wasn't trying to grab the knife. Possibly because Tiernan had just channeled living Stone to pin his hands to the table.

"Do you have it? —*magarl lobadh*, the stupid shit bites!"

"How would I know if I did?" Answering his own question, Kevin yanked out the blade. *That channeling had better have worked, I don't want to have to go digging in there!*

Clinging to the point of the knife was a shard of crystal that burned like a diseased limb set afire. There couldn't be any doubt as to what it was. Kevin wanted, no, needed to hurl, looking at it. He remembered, too well, what it had been like to have the obscenity that lived in it digging through the deepest recesses of his mind. Fucking with his head, telling him Tiernan didn't love him, could never love him, he might as well give up.

"*Kevin!* Damn it, *lanan!* Get rid of it!"

Tiernan's voice startled him, as did the realization that he'd been hearing it for a while. Skirting the far end of the table, Kevin approached the non-bubble, holding the knife out in front of him. Tiernan's face was turned resolutely away, but he still struggled

270

blindly with Bryce, who didn't seem to much care he'd been relieved of his parasite and was trying to rock the table.

Swallowing hard, Kevin plucked the crystal shard from the tip of the knife, holding it between two fingers, with his little finger sticking out and looking ridiculous, like the piece of *Marfach* was a teacup and he was a prissy dowager. The shard glowed its bilious shade of red, pulsing, throbbing.

"Alpha. Mike. Foxtrot." Kevin's whisper was hoarse, almost inaudible over the thumping of the table legs on the floor. He dropped the piece of living Stone into the cage Tiernan had channeled for it; it fell into the bubble, and vanished.

"What does that —son of a *bitch!*" Tiernan barely got out of the way as the table lurched and fell onto its side, with Bryce kicking mightily and spraying blood everywhere.

Shouting, too, now that his mouth was uncovered. "This is assault, you assholes. This is fucking aggravated assault with a deadly weapon!"

"Oh, for fuck's sake." Tiernan sounded more tired than anything else. He dropped to his knees beside Bryce's head, and started doing something with his hands; Kevin leaned over the toppled table, and saw his husband's hands on Bryce's neck and Bryce's face going an interesting shade of dark brownish-red.

As Kevin watched, Bryce's head fell forward, his eyes closed, and his body sagged against the Stone restraints in what looked like an incredibly uncomfortable position. Tiernan looked up, the blue of his eyes as innocent as a springtime sky. "I didn't feel like giving him time to enjoy it."

271

Kevin felt himself blushing. Well, he enjoyed breath play, and Fae were natural teases, all of them, and his husband more than most. "To answer your question, the Alpha-Mike-Foxtrot is something my dad used to say when he had something to get off his chest but Mom was within earshot. Military alphabet. Adios Mother Fucker."

Tiernan glanced up at the floating prison he'd created. "Let us fervently hope so."

It looks so harmless. Jesus, how does Conall deal with the whole Marfach? *And what's in Janek is just the smallest part of what it used to be, from what the Fae say.*

"What the hell is this?" Tiernan sat back on his heels, Bryce's battered collar in his hand. "I can barely see magick right now, but even I can see there's magick bound into this. The *Marfach* can't channel—"

Tiernan broke off, raising his forearm to shield his eyes. Kevin didn't see light, but for an instant it looked as if Tiernan was casting a shadow on the wall behind him that hadn't been there before.

"Holy shit," Kevin breathed. "Was that the nexus?"

Tiernan nodded tightly. "Looks like they've started." Crystal fingers closed into a fist around the leather strap. "Come sit with me, *lanan*. Just in case."

Chapter Twenty-eight

Breathe. In. Out. In. Out.

Focusing on something as simple, as basic as breathing didn't really keep the pain away. Cuinn suspected that nothing would do that. Except, possibly, fucking up what came next.

"Rian? *Dhó-súil?*"

"Here." The single word was hoarse. Rian had fallen against him, in the shock of that first moment, and the tension he felt in the male's body would probably have killed a human. "Give me a moment, thanks most kindly."

Pain surged through Cuinn all over again, following after Rian's words, a wash of fire that started at his core and flooded all the way out to his skin. He had to force his eyes open, just to be sure he wasn't really flayed and bleeding. *Still intact. Good. Still alive. Even better.*

Once he was sure all body parts were answering hails, he turned his head just a little, and his breath caught at the sight of his *scair-anam*'s face. Perfectly beautiful, and perfectly expressionless. Only the single tear of flame trickling down his cheek betrayed his inner struggle, that and the quiver like a plucked harp-string that ran through his whole body.

Cuinn reached up to cup the back of Rian's head in his hand, draw it to his shoulder. As soft blond hair tickled his palm, another wave of pain hit, worse than the ones before. As if everything inside him was battling to be outside. He fought it down, somehow managing to be gentle as he urged Rian to rest on him.

It's love. Shit. The pain was made worse by the one emotion the *ceangail* bond rejected. The one he almost hadn't recognized, and couldn't help feeling.

The one that fucking near killed him when Rian turned a gasp into a brush of the lips against his cheek, and whispered, "I'm ready. Hold on as tight as you need."

Might those be the last words he ever heard? *Oh, fuck it.* His arms tightened around his *scair-anam. Stop acting like a drama queen and start acting like a Loremaster.*

Cuinn allowed his magickal sense to venture out of his body. Down toward the floor, where the seething glow of ley energy was nearly blinding even with that aspect of his vision blinkered.

The energy leaped across the few inches separating them and slammed into him like the ground hitting a luckless parachutist. Rian's arms around him, and his around Rian, were the only anchor he had as he struggled to breathe, to make his heart beat. The energy filled him, became him. Burned him, too. The pain of the binding had only been a beginning.

O Mary, when our eyes close in our last sleep and open to behold Thy Son, the Just Judge, and the Angel opens the Book, and the Enemy accuses us; in that terrible hour, come to our aid...

Cuinn would have blinked, if he could move.

Those aren't my thoughts!

Nor mine. Somehow, Cuinn could sense Rian trying to smile. *Saint Lomman, nephew of Saint Patrick. It seemed apt.* Rian moaned softly, and the sound drew a near-perfect echo from Cuinn. *Jesus, are we both feeling everything twice? Everything the other feels?*

That would explain a lot. Maybe it was why he was still alive; two were strong enough to bear what one never could, even if they *were* both Fae. *Let's quit looking a gift horse in the ass, and get on with it. The others are waiting, and I don't think even Twinklebritches can stay horny forever.*

He felt the Prince nod. *My turn next.*

At first, all Cuinn heard was a soft, choked-off groan. The sound of a scream being held back. Then a gasp. Then silence, during which Cuinn wanted to rip something's motherfucking heart out so Rian could stop hurting.

"Earth, my cousin, I bid you to the binding, to be its strength."

It was strange to hear the ritual words in English, as strange as it had been to speak them, but with Rian's thick Belfast accent they almost sounded *Faen*. The chains Rian's magick had woven tightened, drawing the two males even closer.

"Air, my cousin, I bid you to the binding, to be its force."

Even tighter. On top of the pain, Cuinn was starting to see little flashes of white light, everywhere he looked, like exploding gnats.

"Water, my cousin, I bid you to the binding, to be its lock and its key, never to part and never to set us

275

free."

To the pain of the magick was now added the fresh agony of the binding. Cuinn didn't want to breathe —every time he exhaled, the chains pulled themselves tighter, and it was harder to inhale. There was no way they could be bound any more closely to one another, no place left for the chains to go. Except where they were going to be going next.

"Fire. My brother. I bid you to the binding, to be bound with us."

Cuinn didn't know if Rian screamed. He couldn't hear anything over the sound that ripped its way out of him as the chains tightened one last time and sank into their bodies. The pain had almost stopped being pain, overloaded nerves couldn't even call it that any more. It was like being trapped inside thunder, being pounded on with the fist of a seriously pissed-off god. Again. Again...

Oh, sweet Jesus, I feel it. Rian's thought was like a breath, a prayer. *It's coming. It's rising. It knows its own.*

The storm that went with the thunder was building around them both. They were as tightly bound as ever, though the chains were now on the inside. "Lochlann, Conall... time to save the world."

It wants me. Rian's whisper in his mind was audible even over the whirlwind of the magick. *I need it.*

Not yet. The power of Rian's surrender to the pain would open the rift between the worlds, wide enough to let them try to force their own plan for the ley energy on the Loremasters. And his *asiomú*, the reversal of that pain back onto its source, would focus the ley energy like a laser, directly on that source.

276

That was the theory.

I know. The whisper was even softer. *Hurry.*

Cuinn took one more glance around the room. Conall needed all the living magick he could channel, to keep the rift open and to open the conduit. But he couldn't tap into the nexus directly, because Cuinn and Rian needed to be where they were, sitting right on top of the thing, in order to do the *ceangail.* So Lochlann was going to draw the ley energy out —he was the only Fae with the ability to call the ley energy to him wherever he was —and give it back to Conall as living magick. Lochlann had been washed away once, in a flood of magick. But his SoulShare hadn't been alive, then, to keep him anchored. This time, it would work. It would. It fucking had to.

There were times Cuinn wished Fae had gods, because it would be nice to pray to one, for luck if nothing else. This was one of those times. But the closest thing the Fae had to a god was the very Pattern whose wrath they were about to incur.

Well, hell. Cuinn shot a blast of pure living magick into the nexus. Not everything he had, no, he was going to have to keep this up for as long as it took, and open the world-rift besides. He had to hold something in reserve. But enough to make the joinder of the ley lines go up like a fucking nova.

Lochlann cursed, short and sharp. Cuinn opened his eyes, just in time for the torrent of energy the dark Fae drew from the nexus to sear itself across his retinas, even with his magickal vision blinkered. He saw Lochlann stagger, nearly fall. Garrett clung to him, strained to hold him upright.

"Give it to me before you overload." Josh reached

a hand toward Lochlann. His voice, in Conall's tone, managed to convey eagerness, worry, and a case of performance anxiety like neither of their worlds had never seen. Cuinn supposed he understood. All his life, Conall had been measured against the ancient Loremasters. Now, here he was, having to face down all of them at once, and fuck up their entire twenty-three-hundred-year-old plan to save the Realm. And possibly be responsible for the destruction of the Realm, if Fate, or whatever Fae used for Fate when the Loremasters weren't fucking with their lives and their destinies, went against them.

And he's doing it because he doesn't want to see his Prince deprived of his scair-anam. *Or me reduced to nothing but a conduit for magick. The way I was supposed to be.* Cuinn closed his eyes. *Damn.*

"Cuinn, we need you. Now." Lochlann's words were almost unintelligible; his haggard expression reflected the strain of trying to hold in the magickal flow Cuinn had started.

He had one more thing to do, first. Bracing himself for the rush of pain he knew would follow, Cuinn buried his face in the curve formed where Rian's neck met his shoulder. He let himself feel the warmth of it, the solidness. Breathed in deeply, filling himself once again with the scents of sweat and sex and smoke. Worth waiting two thousand years for? *Hell yes. And fuck me if I'm letting go of it now.*

A tremor ran through the hard muscle of Rian's neck and shoulder. Cuinn could feel the unimaginable pain wracking Rian's body as if it were his own. Yet, incredibly, Rian laughed. A short, harsh laugh, but a laugh. *I heard that. And as mad as I must be to say it, I love you too. Now do this thing, please.*

Cuinn blinked, surprised his eyes were burning. A thought, and a tear opened in the air behind the chaise, darkness amid the brilliance of the magick.

He turned to the mage, in the body of the ink artist. "Now, Conall —open it wide."

Josh/Conall nodded, and whispered a word. Even Cuinn could feel the power of the word as it flew, and the edges of the rift parted before it. One hand outflung, the mage poured all the magick Lochlann sent him into the tear in reality, holding it open.

Through the rift, Cuinn saw the Pattern chamber, flooded with moonlight. The hard gloss that protected the soul-sundering blades of the Pattern was gone, and starlight shone between the silver-blue wires.

And the ghost of a lovely red-haired Fae female, with a mother's face and form, stood balanced on the killing edges, a sword in her hand and the tracks of tears on her cheeks.

"Aine," Cuinn whispered.

Chapter Twenty-nine

Rian heard Cuinn greeting someone. Presumably someone on the far side of the hole Cuinn and Conall had just torn in the world. He didn't turn to look, though, for two reasons. One, because he would have had to lean away from Cuinn to turn his head to do it, and Cuinn was about all that was holding him together at the moment. Two, because he had all he could do to keep himself balanced on the knife's-edge of pain, between struggle and surrender. Too much resistance, and he would conquer the pain and lose his only hope of healing his soul-deep wounds. Too little, and his surrender would come too soon to be the weapon they needed.

The pain was consuming. It was exquisite.

"Cuinn. Little brother." A woman's voice, kindly, yet sorrowing. "This is what we feared you were planning, when you cut us off. Why have you chosen to come to us in violence?"

"It doesn't have to be violence, Aine. But I won't do anything that will harm my *scair-anam*."

With some sense he couldn't define, Rian heard a low roar, like a wind-whipped fire, and knew it for the power of the energy beneath him and the magick around him. All his ears heard, though, was the strained, harsh breathing of all the others in the little room.

All but Cuinn. So calm, he sounded, as if he were taking his ease, and not shot through with the same agony Rian was experiencing. Or a worse one, since he, Rian, was accustomed to the pain, had spent all these long months since the bonfire seeking it out in the form in which it had first come to him. The first time he remembered, any road.

"There will be no harm to him, if you take your place in the Pattern. I promise you both."

Rian heard the woman, in his mind, speaking English, though the woman had a lilt to her voice that reminded him of home. But his ears were hearing something else again, a tongue that might almost have been Irish.

"That's a promise you can't keep, Aine. I told you before, SoulSharing works. I've been expecting to follow whatever your plan was for more than two thousand years. But everything's different now."

"Nothing has changed. Except the arrival of the moment we have all dreaded."

Cuinn shook his head. "The act that made it possible for me to take my place in the Pattern made it impossible at the same time. If I follow your plan — become nothing more than the gateway for the ley energy to return to the Realm —it probably won't be so bad, for me. Chances are I'll never know what's happened to me. But Rian will." The catch, the break in Cuinn's voice added a whole new pain to the agony bathing Rian. "I know how I'd feel, if I lost him. Even if he left me of his own free will." Cuinn paused, and Rian felt him take a deep breath. "I will not do that to

281

him, Aine. You can fucking well kill me first. Or you can put down that mage-blade, get out of my way, and let us solve this problem our way."

Feck the pain, Rian had to look. He pulled away, his hand finding Cuinn's and lacing fingers through fingers in silent apology, and turned.

Through a rent in the brilliance the height of a man, or a Fae, he saw darkness. A woman, a Fae, tall, red-haired, and more regal in bearing than he himself could ever hope to be, dressed in elegant robes and armed with a sword of pure silver. He could see through her, sword and robes and Fae alike, though something about the blade said it made no difference whether it were solid or no, it would do for him, or anyone, just the same. The moon was there, too, the fecking moonlight, shining full through a round window set into a wall of stone.

The moonlight would have been enough alone to set his heart pounding, but what it shone on made him doubt what precious little remained of his own sanity. Under the Fae's feet, etched in intricate lines of silver-blue, was the source of the pain in the depths of his own mind and heart. He was looking at the brand that had burned the stars onto his flesh and the madness into his soul.

In a panic, he looked up, into the eyes of the Fae who stood in the center of the Pattern.

"*Elirei.*" She nodded to him. "*Bual g'mai, aris.*"

Prince Royal, Cuinn's mind supplied. *Well met, once again.*

The blade in the woman's hand flashed, and Rian saw himself reflected in it. Overcome with dizziness, he fell into his reflection, fell without moving.

He was small. He was wet. He was wrapped in a blanket, and breathless from screaming. He was lying on a cold floor, with the moon shining on him through a window. So bright. A male towered over him, the male who had just put him on the floor. A male with sandy blond hair and pale green eyes. It was cold. Too cold. All he'd ever known was warmth. He struggled against the blankets, shivering. The male watched him. Suddenly hopeful, he raised his arms. The male had picked him up, once before. Had taken him. He would take him again, he wouldn't leave him here. Wouldn't leave him alone.

The male vanished.

"Damn you, Aine, let go of him!"

Was he weeping? He was, streams of fire licking down his cheeks. Cuinn held him close, turning his face away from the hole between worlds.

"*Dhó-súil*. Forgive me. Please." Cuinn whispered the words over and over, like a broken mantra, or a spell, the way Rian had once thought magick worked. Or, perhaps, a prayer. Not to any god, though, for he'd said Fae had none. To what, then?

To love?

"If the Prince will let you go, little brother, will you take your place with us in peace?"

A cold fury, colder than the chill of that remembered wind, swept through Rian. Shaking off Cuinn's attempt at restraint, he turned to glare at the Fae in the Pattern. "If you think to force me to give up what my heart is set on, I invite you to try again. I promise, there's no decision in your life you'll regret more."

The Fae matron stared. So, for that matter, did Cuinn. Slowly, the Loremaster lowered her sword. The hand not holding the sword gathered up the skirts of her jade-green robes, and she dropped a deep curtsy. "Your words are foreign, my Prince, but your meaning is clear. Forgive me." Her lips curved in a faint smile. "We wrought better than we knew, when we made the Royals."

"I could have told you that." Cuinn still sounded shaken. "Now, get out of our way."

"Do you mean to destroy us?" The female's smile vanished, her grip tightened on the hilt of her sword. "This semblance I wear is not real, but it carries all my power and I will oppose you to the last of it. And others will rise to carry on, once I fall." She seemed more sad than angry.

Cuinn looked around the small chamber at the others, and Rian did likewise. Lochlann's eyes were closed; he leaned against the wall, and Garrett held him tightly. His hand was stretched out to Josh, who gripped it white-knuckled. The tattoo artist's other hand was extended toward the rift; his borrowed shirt was soaked in sweat, and it seemed as if he was straining to keep himself anchored to Lochlann.

Shit, we need to hurry. Cuinn shook his head as he shared the thought. "Hell, no, Aine. The Realm needs the ley energy, and you're going to get it. There's already a gap in the Pattern, where my name ought to be. We're going to send the ley energy back through that gap, and make the connection between the nexus and the Pattern permanent."

Aine's eyes narrowed, but in calculation rather than anger. "If you do that, you will no longer be able to use the gap yourself, to go back and forth. The way here will be barred to you forever."

"I'd guessed." One of Cuinn's arms was still

around Rian, and Rian felt a hand stroke slowly down his side, along the trail of stars inked, or branded, into his skin. "A small price."

"There may be other prices."

Rian thought he recognized the look in Aine's eyes. He'd had a friend, Declan, back in his grammar school days, and Declan had been a certified genius at maths. He could get lost in some world of calculations inside his own head, and sometimes not find his way out for hours. Aine's face wore that same look of abstract rapture.

"We've thought about that—"

Aine waved Cuinn to silence, still caught up in her reckoning. Or, perhaps, a vision. Maybe when it came to magick, there was no difference between the two. "Any damage to the Pattern is certain to have consequences, but whatever they are, I am blind to them."

"We're not turning back now. Whatever the fallout is, we'll deal with it." Cuinn's grip on Rian tightened; Rian could feel the stars tingling, burning, perhaps in response to having the Pattern that created them so near.

The power of the ley nexus was agitated, leaping and flaring and then guttering, like flame in a chancy wind. Rian's pain surged and ebbed and flowed along with it. *I don't know how much longer I can hold on.*

A few more seconds. "We're out of time, Aine. If you can't bring yourself to help us, then at least get out of our way."

Silently, Aine stepped back from the center of the circle.

Not even his thought-sharing with Cuinn let Rian understand Josh/Conall's whispering, but it was impossible to miss the power building around his outstretched hand. At the heart of the growing orb of power, a silver chain gleamed on the artist's wrist, one Rian could have sworn hadn't been there when they began. *What is he —what are they —saying?*

Conall's of the Demesne of Air. Words help him focus. Fuck if I know what he's saying, though, there's something about the channeling he's doing that protects itself.

Magickal light lanced from Josh's hand in a solid beam, visible light curling up from the edges of it like smoke, and hit the Pattern dead center, in the one space not marked out by intricate loops of wire.

Is the tear supposed to be closing? Rian blinked away the burning sweat that threatened to blur his vision, but he still saw the same thing when he was done, the edges of the rift between the worlds drawing together.

Oh, fuck me oblivious, he can't hold it and open the passage at the same time. Keeping one arm tightly around Rian, Cuinn raised his other hand. Rian felt power humming through Cuinn's hard body, already quivering with their shared pain. Then the air itself began to hum, as a one-handed spreading gesture from Cuinn stopped the slow sealing of the rift and started it widening again.

I'm sorry, dhó-súil. The sandy-haired Fae was outwardly calm, but his inner voice was strained and breathless. *As long as I have to do this, I can't help you.*

No need to remind him of what he was about to need help with, the echo of the Pattern in the emptiness of his soul was all the reminder he required. *You're here. That's help enough.*

Light flared, on the far side of the rift. Josh/Conall's cry was jubilant. "We're through!"

Jubilation, though, quickly gave way to unease. The tattoo artist leaned back, looking like a man playing at tug-of-war. "I don't know what's... oh, *shit*." Josh turned back to Lochlann, whose hand he still held. "I need more. As much as you can draw."

"What's wrong?" Cuinn spared as much of a glance as he could before he had to return his attention to the gap between worlds.

"It's drawing the magick out of me. Faster than I can channel it."

Cuinn snarled. "Aine, make them stop—"

"No. Not the Pattern." Josh staggered; Lochlann's hand locked around his forearm and steadied him. "The Realm itself. It's parched. Dying."

The ley energy was like barely tamed lightning, arcing from the nexus to Lochlann, who glowed with it as his body transmuted it to living magick and fed it to Josh, and Conall within Josh. Yet with all that outpouring of power, the nexus was undiminished, seething like the heart of a furnace.

A furnace, I can handle. "Hold on another minute. All of you. That's all I need."

Without waiting for an answer, Rian closed his eyes. He needed to focus inward, for this, the way he'd done on the Twalf. He didn't need his eyes to see the ley energy now, any road. Nor yet to see the chains that bound him to Cuinn.

He'd not forgotten the pain, he'd only put it to one side, as he'd learned to do, and now he invited it back. It flowed into him from all sides, and from inside. Fucking with his mind as it came, as well, bringing alive every memory of every pain he'd suffered, these last long months, as he sought, without

287

knowing what he did, to uncover the pain of coming into this world. Feargal was there, and Corry before him, and Turk, giving him what he'd thought he needed, each in his own way. Their part of the burning, at least, was sweet, and Jaysus he was hard, aching with it. But that was all to the good, the arousal would make his job easier in the end.

If he made it as far as the end. Feargal and the rest gave way, in an eyeblink, to five faceless men and the roaring, skin-tightening heat of a bonfire, and in the time it took him to draw a breath, he was gagging on dirt and fighting once again to surrender to a pain that went far beyond the physical.

That, too, was swept away, and he hung suspended over the gaping hole that had always been at the heart of him. He'd fled from the memory that was the source of his pain, leaving this great emptiness at his core. Some instinct wakened at the bonfire had told him to seek the source, but he'd never dared abandon himself to the seeking.

Now, he was past daring. The bottom of the hole was rushing up to meet him, or he was plummeting to meet it, the beautiful deadly silver-blue he'd glimpsed through the rift to the Realm. The pain of the binding had finally cleared the way, and left him no choice.

Holy Mary, Mother of God, pray for us sinners, now and at the hour of our death. The wind of his falling blew his hair back from his eyes. Like a hand, one unaccustomed to being gentle, brushing his forehead. Pale green eyes, kiss-bruised lips.

Cuinn —

Rian didn't scream, as he plummeted into the Pattern. But he heard a scream, an infant's high-pitched anguished wail. The memory of a spider's web of blades keen enough to slice soul from body, or soul from soul, wrapped him round and held him in an embrace formed from hell itself.

Focus, damn it. Stop fighting. That was the hardest part, not fighting back. He'd always fought back, one of his first memories was pitching a stone at a PSNI officer when he was something like four years old. But he needed to surrender. *Like I did on the Twalf. I can't reverse it, else. And I can't be healed. Not until I crave the pain.* Sweet bleeding Christ, it was like being sandblasted from within. Like holding on for very life to a high-voltage wire, hanging over an abyss. Like dying, except he couldn't. Didn't dare.

But in the end, it was the memory of the bonfire that saved him. His salvation was just as simple as it had been, then, and just as terrible. Opening to the pain, and seeking more. More. Becoming the pain. Forgetting he'd ever been aught else. Accepting it, until it was everything. Until it was free within him.

Until it wasn't enough, and he needed more.

How strange, when he opened his eyes, to see everything just as it had been, Cuinn still fighting to hold the way to the Realm open, Josh/Conall braced and straining so as not to be pulled in, Lochlann and his Garrett glowing like a little sun, and the walls still echoing with a baby's cry.

The tear still hung in space, dark against the brilliance, Aine hovering on the far side of the hole Conall's magick had blasted in the Pattern. She stared, ghostly lower lip caught between her teeth, looking from the hole to Josh/Conall and back again.

Under Aine's feet, the Pattern shimmered. There

it was. The reality of what had lived in the bottom of his mind, for his entire life, the source of his madness. The true source of the pain he'd finally freed. *More. Give me more. You started this, you bastards, now give me the power to end it.*

All it took to reach into the other world on the far side of the rift was a thought, and another thought started to draw magick from the Pattern. It was the endgame of the reversal, demanding more of what the Pattern-dwellers had thought to force on him, and turning it to his own ends.

Aine stared, horrified, at the lines in the floor beneath her feet. They twisted, sparked, flared, and dimmed. "Prince, no —if you weaken the Pattern, you leave us defenseless!"

"Conall, can you get free now?" Rian hoped he didn't sound as desperate to the others as he did to himself. A Prince had to inspire, after all, and even if he wasn't fecking much of a Prince in any other way, surely he could manage that much.

"If I do, the passage for the ley energy will close—"

"I have it. Just do it. Get out of there. *Now.*"

Josh/Conall strained, Kevin's dress shirt sweated through 'til near transparent, showing the vivid ink underneath. Rian kept up the draw, trying not to wonder if it was possible to draw more than he could safely hold, and what would happen if he did.

Brilliant light, magickal and otherwise, flared, and Josh/Conall fell backward, colliding with the wall hard enough to stagger even a man Josh's size.

Rian couldn't spare more than a glance, though. He wasn't sure how to do what he needed to do next. Hopefully the wanting would be enough.

The nexus reacted to him, the others had said. Well, it sure as shit was doing so now; between his pain and the energy from the Pattern, the nexus seethed, light made solid but twisting like wind-whipped wildfire. He pictured the ley energy gathering around him, and it obeyed. The other Fae stared —*I wonder what they see* —as the power whirled around him, tugging at his hair, buffeting him like a physical wind. This was no true wind, though, and he could shape it. The ley energy was a tornado of fire, and himself the cloud spawning it. The hungry funnel plunged through the rift, arrowing straight for the hole Conall's magick had forced, and plunged into it.

When it made contact the flare was even brighter than the first had been, and as it blazed up Rian sagged. As he lay slumped against Cuinn, trying to remember how to breathe, he could feel the power on his skin, leaping from the nexus to the Pattern along the new connection.

"What the *fuck*?" Cuinn leaned forward as far as he could without losing hold of Rian, peering through the rift.

Not what I wanted to hear. With a groan, Rian hauled himself upright again, and forced his eyes to focus. Where the tip of the vortex of ley energy touched the Pattern, the blackness around the knotwork glowed a deep cherry red. The stream of energy itself was starting to bulge, next to the point of contact, a swelling that grew larger as Rian watched.

The ghostly Aine, too, studied the vortex. "The passage is too narrow," she murmured, almost to herself. "It has been more than two thousand years

291

since this land was fed from this spring, and it thirsts. It tries to take what it needs."

The nexus, too, seemed more than eager. The magickal glow was intense, even muted as it was by the channeling Conall had done for each of them before they started, and expanding ——¬¬¬¬¬¬¬it already nearly filled the chamber, and the flares had no doubt made their way up into Purgatory.

"I don't see any way to slow it down from this end." Josh's voice sounded even more like Conall than before. "The connection's becoming a new ley line. It's out of our hands."

"Shit." Cuinn's eyes went wide. "Anyone have any idea what happens when a ley line is clogged?"

Josh/Conall shook his head. "No, but I have a feeling it'll eventually make what happened when I fried the lesser nexus look like a Fourth of July sparkler."

A cool flash of light from the other side of the rift caught Rian's eye; Aine, carefully tracing something on the floor with the tip of her ethereal sword. "I will deal with this." She looked up, her gray-blue gaze going from Cuinn to Rian and back again. "Be ready to close the way, little brother, and seal it."

"What are you going to do?" Rian could feel a new tension in his *scair-anam* and hear it in the edge his strained voice acquired.

"Only what is necessary." Aine laughed softly. "I may not have been the best student, Cuinn an Dearmad, but I believe I have finally learned something about humanity. There is no power greater than a willing sacrifice for love's sake."

"*Aine...*"

"My place in the Pattern has always been next to yours. When I am gone—"

"No!"

"— the ley energy will flow freely."

Jaysus, she's Fading. Rian's hands clenched into white-knuckled fists. "Aine, don't, there has to be another way."

"You would try to stop me, Prince, after what I did to you?" Aine curtsied, becoming even fainter as she did so. "One last lesson in being human. I thank you."

"*Damn* it, Aine..." The helpless note in Cuinn's voice tore at Rian, wounding him near as sore as anything the Pattern had done. "I should be the one. Like we planned."

Aine shook her head. "Two thousand years here have been enough. Though it has been good to see the world properly again, for a little while." It was almost impossible to see her now; a faint wash of red hair, the sketch of an outline, moonlight on mageblade were all that remained. "Besides, you have your Prince, and he has you. You must stay—"

A startled gasp, and the last of Aine was caught up in the flow of energy, disappearing feet-first into the torrent.

Cuinn was silent, but Rian heard his cry in their shared thoughts, and held him tightly.

Lochlann and Garrett came over to the chaise, the dancer mostly supporting the much taller, and clearly exhausted, Fae. "It's working." Lochlann's voice was unsteady, and Rian couldn't but wonder what the last few minutes had cost him. The dark-haired Fae was right, though. The bruised, inflamed redness around the contact point was gone, the dangerous-looking bulge in the stream was visibly shrinking.

Cuinn still stared bleakly into the silent, moonlit darkness, the hand through which he channeled the magick needed to keep the tear open trembling. "Damn," he whispered. "Just... damn."

I'm sorry. Rian rested his head on Cuinn's shoulder. The strange angle made the position awkward, but did he give a shit?

Cuinn took a deep breath, and let it out in a sigh. *Fae aren't good at having things taken away from them.*

There was more, unsaid and unthought, and Rian couldn't help hearing it. *She did it for you. For us. If you want to honor her, take the gift.*

Cuinn turned, favoring Rian with an utterly unreadable look. *If I ever hear you denying you're a Prince again, I'm going to switch your ass until you can't sit for a week.*

That's supposed to put me off? Rian laughed softly.

"I don't think we're finished here." Josh/Conall had come to join everyone else, watching the ley energy stream through the rift and disappear into the Pattern. "Is it going to be enough for you to just let go of whatever you're doing to hold the way open?"

I'll deal with you later. Cuinn flashed Rian a quick smile, with just a hint of the wickedness Rian remembered from before their Sharing, before twisting to look back at the other Fae over his shoulder. "No. It's getting harder to hold the damned thing open, but if I just let it close, it will always be like a door with something propped in it to keep it from closing all the way."

"Which means the *Marfach* could find a way through it." Garrett was, apparently, the only one in the room who could bring himself to speak the name of the Fae's ancient enemy.

"Exactly." Cuinn grimaced. "Unless the Boy Wonder has any objections, I think what it needs is one more shot of magick, as I let the edges of the rift go."

"You don't quit, do you?" Josh/Conall's eyes rolled. "No objections here. But I think it's going to take all three forms of power at once to seal it —pure magick, elemental magick, and the ley energy."

Rian tried not to groan. "How the feck are we going to do that?"

Cuinn's smile cut through the pain of the binding and made Rian's toes curl. "You and I have some unfinished business that should take care of it quite nicely, *dhó-súil*."

"Unfinished?"

Do you remember the rest of the binding ritual?

Oh, shite. Rian felt himself turning red. How the hell had he forgotten? *May as well ink 'eejit' on my forehead, to save folk the trouble of having to find out for themselves.*

Mother of God, how he loved Cuinn's laughter. *Test the bonds, Highness. Do they still hold?*

Rian didn't want to pull away, but he tried, just enough to feel the tug, and the pain, telling him the magickal links had survived his descent into the abyss and were still sound. *They do.*

Then let's finish this, so we can start our honeymoon.

This time, Rian returned Cuinn's toe-curling

smile. "The binding of magick is temporary; the binding of hearts is for all of this life. And beyond," he added. Fae might have no gods, and no afterlife, but he had both, and be damned if he was letting go of Cuinn after just one lifetime.

Cuinn quirked an eyebrow at the change, but his smile was pleased. "The chains now binding us are phantoms of magick, without substance. Yet we are bound, one to the other, heart to heart and soul to soul, of our own wills and no other."

Before they spoke the words together to end the ritual, a shudder swept through Rian, icy fingers running down his spine. *Why fear? Why now?*

"May it ever be thus."

The chains shattered, the magick of the four elements bound into them exploding outward. Cuinn, with one last longing look through the portal, let it close, and added the living magick to the fire-blossom. And the nexus, responding once again to Rian's touch like petrol to a spark, roared to life with a brilliance closed eyes did nothing against.

For an instant, even with his eyes screwed closed, Rian could see the new ley line, one end of it in the nexus, and the other nowhere at all in this world. The air around him was so charged with magick, it was hard to breathe. Then the light of the line's creation and the implosion of the rift overwhelmed him, and the fireball the magick made was the last thing he saw before everything went dark.

Chapter Thirty

"Do you ever wish you hadn't met me, *Ianan*?"

"Let me do the lawyer thing, and answer a question with a question." Kevin turned to look at Tiernan, which was a slight disappointment to the Fae, as burying his nose in his husband's hair had been a reasonably effective way to keep himself from staring at the ley nexus. "Are you out of your mind?"

"No more so than usual." Tiernan shrugged. "It just occurred to me that most humans would have a hard time taking this in stride." He gestured with the hand holding the collar, the movement taking in the whole room: peeling paint, linoleum floor in a checkerboard pattern Tiernan hadn't seen since 1954, two massage tables, one of which was overturned and had a male in not nearly enough leather manacled to it, half hanging over and half lying in a pool of his own brownish blood and snoring softly. And a shimmering soap bubble caging a piece of a monster hovering in the air just the other side of the overturned table. "If you'd turned me down, that first night, you might not be looking at that agg assault charge Leather Boy here threatened you with."

"You'll talk him out of it, I have faith in you."

297

Kevin's smile flared, faded. "You know I wouldn't trade any of my life with you for anything. What brought this on?"

"That." Tiernan nodded in the direction of the nexus. As if on cue, the not-quite-light flared up again, for the third time since Tiernan had started watching it. Or was it the fourth? "This is fucking insane. No way should I be able to see the nexus from here. No fucking way. But I *can* see it, through two floors and an odd number of walls. With no way to know what might happen if they lose control of it."

"And yet you're still sitting here."

"Call me certifiable." Tiernan sighed, shifting the arm he'd draped across Kevin's shoulders to relieve the prickling in his crystal hand. "Actually, Cuinn told me once that I'm the designated guardian of the nexus. You'd think that would be our newly arrived Prince, but apparently not." Tiernan dropped the collar in his lap and scrubbed his face with the heel of his hand, then tilted his head to look at Kevin. "You, on the other hand, should probably get the fuck out of here."

"Hell no." The flat tone of his husband's voice brooked no argument. "You stay, I stay."

"You're as stubborn as a —holy *shit*." Tiernan shielded his eyes with his hand, blinking away the searing afterimages left on whatever passed for his magickal sense's retinas. "That had to have hit most of Purgatory. I hope there aren't any of those magick-sensitive humans down there, all I need is the Health Department crawling up my ass."

Bryce coughed violently, his body jerking with the wracking spasms, rocking the massage table until the legs thudded against the worn linoleum. "Jesus fucking Christ, Guaire!" The captive male hawked and spat, narrowly missing Tiernan's leg. "You, too, whoever the hell you are, with the knife." He raised his head as best he could to glare across Tiernan at Kevin.

Tiernan backhanded Bryce, nodding in satisfaction at the sound of dickhead head hitting floor. "You can say whatever you want to me, but watch how you talk to my husband."

"And you can kiss my ass—"

Another slap left the human's upper lip split and bleeding into his porn-star mustache. "Did I say you could say whatever you wanted to me? I must have been lying."

"Tiernan..." The Fae didn't have to look to know that Kevin was trying not to grin.

This time, Bryce took some care to spit blood in a different direction. He hung, panting, from his awkward restraints, gingerly licking blood from his lip. When he finally hauled his head up again, there was less of arrogance about his expression, and much more nervousness. At least, Tiernan thought nerves were behind the banker's pale skin and sudden sheen of sweat. Maybe it was a concussion. *What the hell, I have to find something to smile about.*

"Get the fucking collar off me, will you?" Bryce coughed again, groaned. "Now that I'm not being forced, I've decided I don't hate you enough to want to die with you."

The Fae and his husband traded *what-the-fuck* looks, before Tiernan picked up the collar from his lap and held it out so Bryce could see it. "You mean this?"

"Unless I'm wearing another one, yes." Bryce

was trying to edge away from the piece of leather, his legs sliding over the linoleum, trying to gain purchase.

Tiernan ignored him, staring instead at the cracked, faded leather strip in his hand. He could feel something tickling his palm, some energy, but with Conall's magickal blinders on, he couldn't tell what it was. "This is supposed to kill someone?"

"Ideally." The dickhead had trouble smirking with a puffed-up lip, but he somehow managed to pull it off. "The monster said there's two kinds of magick in it, it's unstable as hell, and all it will take is one shot from something you have in the basement to pancake this whole building. I'm a little short on details, though, I was busy trying to vomit zombie blood while the freak was explaining it."

"Jesus," Kevin whispered fervently. "We have to get that thing out of here."

Every hair on Tiernan's body stood up at once. The air was thick, and tingled in his lungs.

"No fucking time." Pivoting where he sat, he whipped the collar back past his ear and flung it straight at the shimmering *laród-scatha* with a strength and an accuracy born of panic. *If the trap doesn't hold it, we're all dead.*

The subterranean explosion of ley energy was so intense as to leave Tiernan magickally blind and cast shadows of visible light, bright enough to leave Kevin and Bryce blinking.

We're still here. Tiernan rubbed his eyes to clear away the afterimages. *Please don't tell me that little shit saved our lives.*

"Is the trap supposed to be doing that, *lanan*?" Kevin nudged him from behind, extending a hand over

300

Tiernan's shoulder to point at the one-sided sphere. The translucent orb was darkening, its not-surface rippling like tarnished quicksilver. In the time it took to draw a breath, it went completely black, its shining surface starting to go matte.

"*Get down!*" Tiernan grabbed Kevin and all but threw him into the poor shelter of the overturned table and Bryce's body, then dove to cover him.

The *laród-scatha* heaved. Darkness and silence exploded.

***

"Over here!"

Tiernan heard footsteps, and sensed light through his closed eyelids, a harsh white light that made him want to keep his eyes closed. He lay on his side on the floor, his back against a wall. His back hurt like a son of a bitch, and trying to take a breath convinced him he had at least a couple of cracked ribs. The arm he wasn't lying on was around Kevin. His husband was mostly under him, and *oh fuck* he wasn't moving.

"Are they both under there?" Cuinn's voice. "Get that light down there, Twinklebritches, there's a dear child."

"Nice to see *ceangail* left you all your original tact and charm." The light brightened. "I see *three* pairs of feet."

"Three? Fuck."

"And none of them are moving."

Tiernan tried to move a foot. All it got him was a shooting pain up his back. Which made him groan. Or try to. The attempt made him cough. His ribs hated him for that.

301

"Let's get that table out of the way." Lochlann's voice. "I need to be able to get at them."

A few seconds later, the light got a lot brighter as a heavy weight was moved off both Tiernan and Kevin. "Newhouse? What the hell is he doing here?"

Against his will, Tiernan opened one eye. Josh had just rocked and dragged the table back, and he and Conall were staring at the unconscious leather-clad male hanging from the Stone manacles. Conall gestured, and the bindings vanished.

Any other time, the sound of Bryce's head hitting the floor would have made Tiernan smile. Now, though, he had other concerns. Big ones. "It's a long story." He didn't dare force his voice much louder than a whisper, the last thing he wanted was to start coughing again. "Lochlann, would you get the hell over here and see to Kevin?"

"Way ahead of you." Lochlann shoved back the other massage table and knelt beside Kevin, in a pile of what Tiernan could now see was drywall, plaster, and splintered wood. One of the healer's hands rested lightly on the back of Kevin's head, the other on his shoulder. "Shit." He went ash-pale under his day's growth of beard, and Tiernan stopped breathing. "His neck. It's broken. And he's concussed."

"Fix it." No asking if it was possible, no pleading.

"What about you?"

"Touch me before I hear my *scair-anam*'s voice and I'll be wearing your balls for earrings."

Tiernan sensed the others gathering around — Conall and Josh, Cuinn and Rian, Garrett —everything else forgotten, they watched in apprehensive silence. Especially Garrett, and small wonder, since the dancer

302

had crossed the line into death himself, not long ago. And had been brought back, by the same hands that now felt gently over Kevin's body, finding the broken places.

Kevin was so still. Tiernan's arm tightened around him. His eyes burned; he blinked, and coolness slid down his cheeks. Fae of the Demesne of Earth wept diamonds.

Lochlann closed his eyes. Tiernan whispered the word that stripped Conall's magickal blinders from his own eyes, just in time for him to watch the faint ripple that was all he could see of living magick, streaming from Lochlann into Kevin.

Tiernan leaned forward, ignoring the screaming of his back, burying his face in Kevin's thick dark hair. Fighting mindless SoulShare jealousy as he felt Lochlann's hand curved round the back of Kevin's neck. *I swear to you,* Ianan, *the* Marfach *is dead. I don't care how long it takes, or what it costs me, it's dead.*

"Talk to him." Lochlann's brows were drawn together in concentration; he didn't even look at Tiernan as he spoke. "He's just barely unconscious, and the closer he is to aware, the easier this is to do properly. And he'll respond better to your voice than he would to mine."

Tiernan made a face. None of the things he wanted to tell his husband were meant for anyone's ears but his, and with this many Fae around — especially one of the Demesne of Air —there was no such thing as a private whisper. "Stay with me, *Ianan.* It won't be long now. Just focus on my voice." He winced. *So fucking lame...*

"Tell us what happened." Rian went down on one knee, looking over the overturned table from which Bryce had fallen, to study the healing, and Cuinn rested a hand on his shoulder. "Tell us what did this to him."

Tiernan thought he could see flames, in the depths of the young Prince's eyes. *If we had to be saddled with a Royal, I'm glad it was this one.* "Newhouse was sent here to blow up the nexus, and the club along with it. He had a piece of the *Marfach* in his gut, driving him, and I'm not sure, but I think he was forced to drink Janek's blood. Probably to make him easier to control." He took a deep breath, and brushed his lips against Kevin's hair while he was about it. "Kevin got the chip of Stone out of him, and I built a *laród-scatha* to contain it—"

"Dangerously close to intelligent, Noble," Conall cut in dryly.

"I love you, too. I figured you'd be able to clean up after me when you were done downstairs. But it turned out our friend was wearing a dog collar with magick in it. He said it was two kinds of magick. Unstable as fuck, and if the ley energy got at it, it would, quite literally, bring the house down. We found him sitting down at the bar, incidentally, getting shitfaced and waiting for his head to get blown off."

"He's damned lucky it didn't." Cuinn dug a finger in his ear, as if it was still ringing. "I was wondering why there was such intense feedback when I closed the rift. I think I get it now."

Lochlann eased back onto his heels, frowning. "I've repaired all the damage I could find. But brain matter's a funny thing. It's safest to let him wake up on his own." Garrett moved to stand behind Lochlann, working the Fae's neck and shoulders.

We all do that. Tiernan's gaze roamed the room, taking in Conall and Josh, Rian and Cuinn, Lochlann and Garrett. Josh was glowering at Bryce, his expression promising mayhem. Yet his arms were around Conall, cradling him from behind, his cheek was against the mage's shock of red hair, and Conall's hand rested gently on Josh's muscular arm. *We get our strength from our humans.*

He looked back down at Kevin, his vision blurring; bent his head, and let his husband's hair take up the tears that turned to brilliant stones. *I don't want to hear about 'safest,' I want you awake.* "Newhouse warned us about the collar, but it was too late to get it out of range before you all finished your business downstairs. So I threw it into the *laród-scatha.* "

Conall put up one fine straight brow. "Another good thought."

"Must you sound so surprised?" Tiernan shook his head, and gritted his teeth at the lances of pain the movement sent down his back. "The ley energy got into the trap, of course —those things aren't meant to keep anything *out* —and I think the trap held in most of the explosion. We only felt what it couldn't contain."

Cuinn whistled under his breath. "You destroyed the piece of the *Marfach,* too, without Twinklebritches' help. Nice work."

"None of that happens to matter a damn to me at the moment." Tiernan couldn't keep the snarl from his voice entirely, but he tried to mute it as he turned his attention back to Kevin. "*Lanan,* please. Don't—"He

305

swallowed, hard, around a lump in his throat. "Don't go where I can't follow."

"Hell no." More a groan than words, but the groan was Kevin's.

For an instant, Tiernan was blinded by pure SoulShare joy. And then by pain, as he tried to roll his husband over to have the hell kissed out of him, but instead seriously fucked over his back. Before he could say or do anything to protest, Garrett was helping Kevin and Lochlann was giving him the same kind of scoping out he'd given Kevin.

Lochlann shook his head. "Do yourself a favor, Noble. The next time you feel the urge to use your back as a wrecking ball, resist."

"Surely you exaggerate."

"You cracked the plaster on the wall. And four ribs, and possibly a couple of vertebrae. Lie still."

"Fuck that." He struggled up onto one elbow, teeth gritted nearly to doing some cracking of their own.

Until he was urged back down by hands he knew, and that knew him. "Let him work, *lanan*." Kevin's smile was possibly the most beautiful thing Tiernan had ever seen. "You and I can still play doctor later."

Tiernan snorted, and interrupted himself with a groan of undisguised relief as Lochlann's healing magick invaded his body. It had been a hell of a long time since he'd been touched by a true Fae healer, and *damn* it felt good. Almost as good as the feel of his husband's hand in his.

"Where the *hell* is Newhouse?"

Josh's exclamation jerked Tiernan out of his reverie. There was no sign of the fucker, but the door

306

standing ajar was a clue it didn't take Sherlock to follow.

Kevin rose and offered Tiernan a hand. One Tiernan accepted, grabbing the glove he'd dropped as he rose. Grimacing, as newly healed ribs bitched him out for moving before Lochlann was done with them.

Everyone else was out the door by the time the two of them got there, past the Raging Art-On storefront and pounding down the stairs into Purgatory. Tiernan worked the glove back onto his crystal hand as he followed, cursing under his breath.

Lucien stepped back as the Fae/human posse burst through the black glass doors at the bottom of the stairs. Tiernan's gaze swept the space near the door, and when he came up empty he broadened the search. The asscravat wasn't at the bar, though he checked both ends just to be sure, the one by the door to the nexus chamber and the one where he and Kevin had found the sodden little shit in the first place. Not in the cock pit. Not on the dance floor.

He isn't here. An owl with icy talons gripped Tiernan's gut. *He could be anywhere. An asshole with a grudge, who knows about Fae and SoulShares and the* Marfach.

Kevin was down in the cock pit, making a quick tour. Probably wanted to be sure none of the naked heaving bodies was Bryce. More than anything else, Tiernan wanted to be down there with him. Working the last soreness out of his own body by worshipping his husband's.

You owe me for this, Newhouse.

Chapter Thirty-one

Bald Head Island,
North Carolina

There is something you're not telling me, Meat.

No shit, Janek nearly replied. But he didn't. And he wasn't going to, not until he figured out how he was going to play this. For now, he just shrugged, and looked out over the ocean. The monster didn't like large bodies of water, either. *Maybe I'll find us a beach house somewhere.*

Why are there holes in my memory? And what are we doing here?

'Here' was Cape Fear, North Carolina, and if Janek had felt like talking, he would have reminded the parasite that it had picked the spot off a map, because it liked the name, and because no fucking ley lines ran under it. The perfect place to wait for Armageddon.

Except, Armageddon hadn't happened.

Something sure as hell had, though. He'd been walking along the beach, a couple of hours ago, not really listening to the monster talking amongst itselves about the sweet shit that was going to go down when the nexus blew up. Then, all of a sudden, he was lying on his back, getting sand in his ass, and at least two of the *Marfach*'s three voices were yelling his fucking head off. He'd covered his head with his arms and waited for the shouts to die down.

And once things got quiet again, and he started asking questions like *what the fuck just happened?* He'd learned something really interesting. The *Marfach* had no memory at all of Bryce Newhouse, or anything involving him. It was like Janek had never stuck a piece of the monster into the shit with the 'stache. The last thing it remembered before screaming on the beach was killing the little whore dancer, Garrett, and then getting ripped apart by Dary. Again.

Dary must have sent us here.

You go right on thinking that. "Yeah, that's probably it." Janek stared out over the water again, and could almost feel the thing inside him shuddering.

No fucking way am I telling it what happened. The slash across his wrist was still dribbling dark blood, around the stitches and the red puckered places he'd tried to take a heated pair of scissors to it. Just one of the makeshift pokers he'd been forced to leave behind in D.C. would have been nice. He had a feeling the blood was going to be trickling for a long time. The last thing he wanted was the *Marfach* remembering that trick. It might decide it wanted a whole army of zombie slaves, and bleed him dry to get them.

Worst of all, it might decide one of them made a better meat wagon than Janek O'Halloran.

Even if the force that had knocked him down was exactly the explosion the *Marfach* had hoped for, and the minor ley nexus under the Greenwich Village brownstone was alive and well, he wasn't going back there. Maybe *especially* not then. Once the monster could suck up to a big glowing tit in the ground for magick, it would start trying to figure out how to do without him.

You're very quiet, Meat.

The female voice was trying to soothe him, and probably play him. *Whatever, bitch.* "It's late. Even a zombie has to sleep sometimes."

He felt the monster sigh. **It was so much simpler when I could turn your brain off when it wasn't needed.**

It was even simpler when my head still all belonged to me.

The trouble was, Janek couldn't really remember what that had felt like.

Not that it mattered. He didn't need a whole brain to kill Guaire. Just his hands, and the fucking Fae's own knife.

***

On the Acela
Somewhere between Washington, D.C. and New York City

Bryce moved his hand away from his side, gingerly, like pulling off a Band-Aid, just far enough to let him look down at the hole in his side. It looked like the bleeding had stopped, which was a relief, since it meant his internal organs were probably planning to stay internal. And the brown blood was freaking him out.

310

He let his head fall back against the seat back. He didn't bother turning his head to look out the train window. Nothing to see, not at crap-forty-five in the morning.

What the *hell* had he been doing in Washington? And how the hell was it March? He'd still been pretty much out of it when he staggered into the Amtrak station, and he'd assumed the date display on the big digital clock on the platform was broken. But the last thing he remembered before waking up... wherever it was he'd been... was coming back from the gym, maybe a week after the Pride march, to shower before a lunch meeting. But it certainly hadn't been July out on the streets he'd wandered until he happened on the train station.

Of course, the egg-sized lump on his head was probably behind the memory loss. He felt carefully around the edges of it, pretty sure it had gotten bigger since the last time he checked it.

Good thing I had a credit card in my shorts. But why did I go to Washington in nothing but leather shorts and Terry's leather harness? He shook his head, letting his hand drop to his side. *I hope he isn't pissed I borrowed it. I'm not in any shape to fight with him about it.*

But Terry wouldn't be pissed. He wasn't built that way. It was funny how things worked out sometimes. He'd met Terry something like seven years ago at a Paul Taylor Dance Company performance. He'd felt a physical connection right away —he'd always been partial to dancers —but Terry had been taken, partnered. Wooing him away from Josh LaFontaine had been an entertaining challenge. He'd

311

figured the attraction would fade once he got what he wanted. It always did, and there was no reason to think Terrence Miller would be any different from any of the others who had passed through his Greenwich Village brownstone over the years.

That had been six years ago. Terry, Bryce realized with a start, had been with him longer than all his other lovers put together. *Probably because he's the only one who's willing to put up with my shit.*

The thought didn't particularly bother him. Being the kind of person who was easy to be around wasn't high on his list of priorities. Hadn't been since he was twelve, when his grandfather greeted the news that he had a gay grandson with an offer to pay to have him institutionalized. And the best dear old Dad had been able to come up with in response was *Don't worry, we don't have faggot genes in our family. It's just a phase. He'll get over it.* All this right in front of him like he hadn't even been there.

Fuck them all. The only thing he'd gotten over was giving a damn what anyone else thought of him.

Still, it was going to be good to get home.

Chapter Thirty-two

"What the *fuck?*"

I was never supposed to see you this way, half undressed —

Cuinn groped for the phone, trying not to open his eyes and find out how much of the day was gone already.

Pretty pictures don't hide the scars, just make me want to touch, lick that hot ink —

Found it right next to his head on the pillow, where he'd left it. "Josh, you'd better be telling me you found him."

"He found us." Josh chuckled, but somehow he didn't sound amused. "He called Terry at five this morning, from New York, wondering where the hell he was."

"Bryce was in New York, but he didn't know where he was?" Cuinn rubbed his eyes, one at a time, with the heel of the hand not holding the phone.

This laugh sounded more genuine. For a human, Josh had a very sexy laugh. "Bryce didn't know where Terry was. You must need coffee."

"Or more sleep. Sleep would be good." Cuinn checked the time on his phone. 9:10 in the morning.

Which meant he'd been asleep for, let's see, not quite four hours now. In the hours between Bryce's disappearance and his own unconsciousness, those who had magick had been frantically using it to try to find the wayward dickhead, while those who didn't had alternated between helping their respective Fae channel and trying more mundane search methods, like the Internet. *Fucker couldn't have checked in on FourSquare or something. Shit.*

"Sorry to wake you. I thought you'd want to know."

"Hell, yes, I want to know." He hadn't wanted to give up the search at all, but a couple of days without sleep had caught up with him while Conall was trying, unsuccessfully, to do a Finding using the blood Bryce had left behind in the massage parlor, and he and Rian had both been ordered to bed. Ordered. Fuck Guaire's attitude. A little.

Cuinn pushed himself up on an elbow, the better to see the male sprawled out on the other side of the bed. Rian was, apparently, one of those fortunate few who could sleep through pretty much anything. He snored softly, a sound like a huge cat purring, his head pillowed on one arm. Peaceful.

No transition dreams, for either one of us. Fae usually had them, for a while, after finding their *scair-anaim*. Echoes, afterimages of the lightning that had just struck them. But, then, he and Rian had both more or less relived Rian's transition during Rian's *asiomú*. No need for dreams.

Josh's voice jolted him out of contemplation. "Terry says Bryce doesn't remember anything that's happened since late last June. Which means he doesn't remember throwing Terry out of the apartment."

"Or anything he ever heard or saw about Fae, magick, or the *Marfach*." Cuinn frowned with a sudden thought. "Speaking of our bitter foe, how do we know it isn't going to start this whole exercise over again? Or that it hasn't already?"

"We're one step ahead of you. Conall was with me when Terry told me about it, and he's done a reconnaissance. There's nothing left there that's the *Marfach*'s or Janek's except a fridge full of Corona, yogurt, and Jamaican meat pies, and we can probably let Bryce puzzle over that. He put up a ward there, too, covering pretty much the whole building, including the basement and the third floor apartment. Oh, and he said to let you know, the lesser nexus in the basement is still dormant, but it's livelier than it was."

"Tell Twinklebritches he did good."

"Only if you're keen for another invisible ball gag. Word to the wise, that's what he's planning the next time you call him that."

Cuinn smirked. "He can try. And I'll talk to you later. I have some good news to share." He touched off the phone, and for good measure switched off the ringer and lobbed the phone overhand into the chair in the corner, before rolling back to Rian.

He reached for the sleeping Prince, but his hand stopped short, then fell to his side. *When was the last time I woke up with someone?* The question was rhetorical and the answer simple: never.

As first times went, this was fucking spectacular. Rian's unruly forelock fell nearly over his closed eyes; golden lashes were smudges against high, chiseled cheekbones. The Prince hadn't shaved in a couple of days, and the stubble on his cheeks was a few shades darker than the hair tumbling into his eyes. Full, sensual lips were barely parted; even sound asleep, the male was begging to be kissed. He slept pillowed on one well-muscled arm; the other lay on top of the sheets that covered him from the waist down. His ink...

Cuinn groaned softly. That wasn't ink, of course, any more than the silver-blue whorls that decorated his own left calf were. Those were the Pattern's brand, in Rian's unique case invisible until he had come into his birthright of magick. Now they traced their tantalizing spiral path from behind the younger male's right shoulder, under his arm, slanting smaller and smaller down across his ribs, and disappearing under the sheet.

Cuinn knew where the trail ended now. He needed to see it again. *Damn. Even in his sleep he seduces me.*

He reached out, again, but before he could touch Rian's shoulder, the other Fae blinked sleepily and looked up at him. In an instant, though, all trace of sleep was gone, as he pushed himself to sit up. "Bryce? Have they found him?"

"Shh." Cuinn urged him back down, and couldn't resist running his hand over the smooth hard shoulder he gripped. "He's been found. All's well."

Slowly, Rian smiled, and the smile made Cuinn instantly hard. "Then the day is ours?"

"It is." He shivered as fingertips traced lightly over his abs. "And you're giving me some very definite ideas about what to do with it." He leaned in for an open-mouthed kiss, tongues fencing, teeth clashing, and groaned with sweet hot anticipation.

I wish I knew how to ask him to be gentle. The thought was in his head, but in Rian's unmistakable

Belfast tones. *I've never made love... but, then, maybe I'm not meant for such.*

Cuinn froze. *What the fuck do you mean, 'not meant for such'?*

Rian's eyes went wide, letting Cuinn see the flames in their depths. *You heard me?*

I did. Just as we heard each other during the ceangail *ritual.*

Cuinn drew back, eyes narrowing as he looked down at his newly-bonded mate. They could figure out later if this was some strange kind of honeymoon, or something more permanent. For right now, he had a message to get across. *And if anyone else had told me you weren't meant to be made love to, I'd be carving him a new asshole with a diamond-tipped drill bit.*

I didn't mean... well, maybe I did. Rian's gaze slid away from Cuinn's, his eyes half closed. *I only know pain. Except the once, with you, in the coffee shop. Not that I haven't tried. But it's never worked.* A muscle twitched in the Prince's jaw. *I always provoke them. No matter how hard I try not to.*

It's different now. You're different now. Cuinn laid a palm along Rian's whiskered jaw, stroked his cheek with his thumb. It felt awkward as hell, but he couldn't imagine *not* doing it. Couldn't imagine not trying to replace the sad resignation he saw with the joy that was supposed to be in a SoulShare's eyes. *I'm probably the last Fae in two worlds who should be teaching anyone anything about being gentle. But let me try.*

Cuinn held his breath.

Rian nodded.

Let's start this way. The kiss was as soft as Cuinn

could make it, lips brushing lips, the tip of his tongue tracing the soft fullness of Rian's lower lip, swollen from their earlier kiss. He felt Rian's breathing quicken, and breathed it into himself before deepening the kiss, and moving to cover the Prince's body with his own.

He felt Rian tugging the sheet out from between their bodies, and slid a thigh between Rian's. Not forcing them apart, but applying a gentle pressure, something for the other Fae to work against. Which Rian did, his back arching, his hips circling, his cock hardening. Cuinn could feel it stirring against his abs, and bit his lip to keep from groaning. *Damn, that's sexy.*

What is? —oh. Cuinn could feel a slow smile in Rian's mind, right about the same time he felt Rian's fingers working into his hair, drawing him into a longer, more thorough kiss. *So far, so good.*

Let's try for better than good.

***

What are you going to —oh, Jesus, Mary, Joseph, Patrick, and Bridget... Rian fecking near bit through his lip, as Cuinn's mouth traveled down his throat, the other Fae taking his time and savoring every inch of his progress. Not quite kissing, not quite biting, just enough tongue, and a low, satisfied growl that made Rian's balls ache.

Legs around me, dhó-súil. *Hold me.* The growl didn't stop with the words, but it did deepen to a thrumming purr Rian could feel against his cock and his balls and his thighs, and more or less everything from his waist to his parted knees as he complied.

Rian watched as the sandy-haired Fae worked his way down, from throat to chest to ribs, and caught his breath at sight of Cuinn's tongue tracing the intricate knotwork of one star, and then the next, and the next. Until this moment, his ink had been simply one more thing to set him apart from human folk, not because of the way the stars looked, but because of the way they'd come.

Now? Now they pleased his partner. His bonded mate. *Holy fuck.*

Tip up —your hips —rock them —ohh, yeah. Perfect. For an instant, the purr in his mind and the purr against his body were one and the same, and Rian's eyes closed in an excess of bliss. *Just the feel of you against me could finish me off if I let it.*

Then let it. Rian's tongue flicked out, circling his lips, teasing. His hips pulsed up against Cuinn's beautifully cut body, his cock rubbing against the other Fae's chiseled pecs. *I'll bring you there again. And again. Anything you want.*

Cuinn looked up, pale green eyes gleaming from under his brows. "*S'ocan*," he murmured aloud. *Peace*, his mind supplied. *Believe me, you don't have to taunt me to make me want you.*

Rian felt his cheeks flame. *I'm doing it again.*

Just trust me. Though I can't quite believe I'm saying that.

Rian had a sudden urge to wrap himself up in the sound of Cuinn's laughter, to let it feed the tiny pure flame of joy deep within him.

I've promised you this, and I've promised myself I'm going to give it to you. I'm not about to let you stop me. Or rush me, for that matter.

319

One of Cuinn's hands slipped between Rian's buttocks, and Rian instantly clenched tight. Cuinn shook his head, his mouth never leaving off what it was doing. *Let me in.*

Rian swallowed hard and did as he was bid. And a moment later, he was certain he'd died and gone to Heaven, against all expectations, as two long, strong fingers slid inside him, a gentle but insistent thumb stroked the taint between sac and sphincter, and Cuinn's warm mouth engulfed the head of his cock, lips sealing tight and sliding down his length. Cuinn's free hand stroked his chest, easing him, gentling him.

Cuinn... oh, damn... It was hard to breathe, and getting harder, and Rian truly didn't give a flying fuck. As long as it stayed this good, he'd figure out how to do without breathing.

Cuinn's answering laughter was all in his mind, and pure delight. *I forgot, last time I tried being gentle with you was no-hands.* Cuinn's hot velvet tongue played over his aching cock, and Rian cursed ecstatically as hooked fingers stroked his sweet spot.

You're going to fecking kill me. Even the mental words were almost unintelligible, lost in a groan of pure pleasure.

Not yet. To Rian's great consternation, Cuinn released him, and gathered his legs under himself to sit back on his heels. Not that Rian minded merely looking, or minded the sight of his bond-mate's mighty shaft straining upward, curving back toward washboard abs, a thin intermittent trickle issuing from the moist brick-red tip. No, he just craved something on him, or in him, a hand, a mouth, a cock, anything Cuinn might care to give him.

Cuinn held out a hand, palm up; there was a swirl of air, and a crystal bottle sat on his palm. He removed the stopper, inhaled the scent of whatever was in the bottle, and nodded with a smile. *Hold still.*

Rian near bit through his lip again as warm scented oil poured over his balls, and down into his tight and needy entrance, into it and past it. His body jerked at the touch of Cuinn's fingers, penetrating and working the oil deeper. *That's not needed.* Even his mind's voice sounded breathless.

Oh, yes, it is. With maddening slowness, Cuinn poured oil into his palm; vanishing the bottle with a thought, he stroked and anointed his own shaft, gasping softly with the pleasure of it as his palm moved up and down.

Rian's vision blurred, his body curled up from the bed in the grip of a wave of raw need that stole his breath. *You're going to need more than just a few drops of oil, if you think to take what you want this time.* Fire flared in his eyes, flickered against Cuinn's tanned skin, before his lids half-lowered and his lips curved in a smirk. He edged back, propping himself on an elbow and reaching down to grip and wring his own cock. *I've no business being treated this way, I'm made to be used and used hard, and it's time he learned that.* He tried to hide that thought, and the sorrow and regret that rode it, under the hunger filling him like another living thing sharing his skin.

No, you fucking don't.

Before Rian could move, Cuinn was on top of him, pinning him to the bed. Cuinn's hand caught the back of his neck, gripped tightly; Cuinn loomed over him, the difference in their heights mattering nothing when they were like this. "You want this." Rian could feel Cuinn's lips moving against his own as the other male whispered. "You think I don't know? You think you can hide it?" Cuinn's lips brushed lightly over his. "I'm inside your head now, *buchal dana*, and you can't hide from me. Any more than you can force me to force you."

Rian swallowed, hard, but the lump in his throat wasn't going anywhere. "Cuinn—"

One more thing. Cuinn stopped whispering, in favor of small nibbling kisses along the line of Rian's jaw, lips rasping in the soft stubble there. *Fae don't have gods, but I'm perfectly happy to swear to yours. And the next time you tell me you don't deserve to be made love to...*

Cuinn closed his eyes. Opened them, and it was as if Rian was falling up, to drown in deep black pools rimmed with faceted jade.

...I swear I'll let you taste what it's been like to feel that way for more than two thousand years.

The utter truth of Cuinn's words, his whole unimaginably long life, was in his eyes. How was he, Rian Sheridan, Rian Aodán, Belfast corner boy, freelance Volunteer, pain slut and maybe Prince Royal of a lost realm and a band of exiles, supposed to be the answer to all that?

By fecking starting.

God, this kiss tasted good. And his arms going round Cuinn, while their tongues sorted out which was doing what, felt even better. He ran his hands down Cuinn's back, feeling the muscles play as lean hard hips pulsed into his, the other Fae's oiled cock gliding hot against his groin and abs.

Please. Rian couldn't remember a single time he'd ever asked for pleasure. Pain, yes. Asked, pleaded, begged. But he'd never asked for pleasure. Which made Cuinn his first. *Jaysus, Cuinn, please, I need you in me.*

Cuinn didn't answer. Rian got the impression he couldn't. Instead, he raised himself up, just enough to work a hand between the two of them, and grip himself, and position his slick moist head at Rian's entrance. All the while, he continued to devour Rian's mouth, his soft groans hardening Rian until he gasped into the kiss with the sweet pain of it.

One hard thrust, and Cuinn was seated almost all the way inside, raking over Rian's sweet spot as he went and making Rian see stars. *Shite, I can't breathe.*

Then don't. Cuinn's laugh made Rian's cock twitch, scattering a few droplets of clear Fire over his abs. *Just kiss me.*

As if you had to tell me to do that. There was laughter around Rian's words, as well, though of a sort to which he was unaccustomed. Sarcasm, mocking, even the light musical tones he now knew for a Fae tease, those kinds of laughter he knew well. But he'd never laughed with delight into a kiss before, and it struck him as a fine thing to keep on doing.

Until he lost his breath again, and wrenched his hips up in a desperate attempt to take Cuinn even deeper, when Cuinn's hand closed round his shaft and gripped him tight. *Jesus, will you just finish me?*

I think you have me confused with someone else. Cuinn ran his tongue down the side of Rian's throat, and down his chest, to lick his nipple and tease it with tiny bites. *And no, I'm not going to finish you yet. One thing you need to learn is that once the bottom's done, everyone's done.* Cuinn held the hard nub between his teeth and flicked his tongue rapidly over the tip. *And I am so incredibly not done with you.*

Rian groaned between clenched teeth as Cuinn's hand clamped down almost as hard as a cock ring, and Cuinn's hot ivory-hard cock glided in and out of his hold, the oil making the sensation pure bliss. *This much pleasure could kill a person. Or a Fae.*

Not going to let that happen. Cuinn's answering smile was wicked.

Yet under the wickedness, Rian saw something else. Heard something else. *I'll let you taste what it's been like to feel that way for more than two thousand years.* Feel like he had no right to let someone make love to him.

Rian waited for Cuinn to withdraw, then tilted his pelvis to let the male slip out of him. Cuinn didn't have time for more than an indignant yelp before Rian caught him round the waist with his legs, surged up from the bed, and not-quite-neatly flipped him onto his back.

"What the *fuck—*"

Rian laid a finger across Cuinn's lips, and grinned when Cuinn tried to bite it. "Hush, now, boyo." Bending, he replaced his finger with his mouth, and kissed Cuinn slow and hot and tender. *I can't promise when this mood will be on me again. I'm as wild as ever I was, though God willing no longer mad, and as much a tease and a torment as I've ever been. But right now, in this moment, there are two thousand years of your feeling unworthy I need to be doing something about.*

But —

I said hush. Rian knew what he wanted to do, but he'd never done it before and so had no fecking clue how to do it. He felt around, working his hands under Cuinn's strong shoulders and gripping from behind and underneath to anchor himself. Tucking his elbows under himself, he raised up, just enough to look down into Cuinn's eyes.

Just enough to come completely fucking undone, from the way Cuinn was looking back at him. Exhaling on a soft groan, he kissed Cuinn's bow-shaped mouth, gently and then deeply and then gently again. Cuinn's legs parted under him, tangling with his own as if Cuinn, too, felt awkward and uncertain, but finally making a place for him to lie, wrapping warm and hard around his thighs. Hands smoothed down his back, cupped his arse, traced where the stars slanted across his shoulder blade.

He didn't need to move much, to make it perfect. A gentle rocking, that was all it took. Oiled bodies rubbing together, rigid shafts lightly brushing, soft hungry sounds of kisses and tongues and gasps each time something small and perfect happened. *God, yes, exactly like this.* Not thinking. Not trying. Just being.

Needing, soon enough. Reluctantly, Rian made enough space between them to let him position himself at Cuinn's entrance. He stared in fascination for a moment at the droplets of liquid fire welling from him and coating the tight sphincter.

It's very pretty, Cuinn grumbled. The light in his eyes, though, was as far from grumbling as could be imagined. *Would you mind putting it where it belongs?*

Together they laughed, and together they groaned

as Rian slid deep and Cuinn gripped him along his whole length. Rian tried to keep their sweet slow rhythm going, but Cuinn was far too good at what he was doing; it wasn't long before Rian was braced over him, arms locked, sweat stinging in his eyes, panting softly. Still trying to go slow, though, because Cuinn's eyes drifting closed and head tipping back told him that each stroke was bringing his bondmate a little closer to heaven. Trying to go slow, but failing, Jaysus it felt so good, the twin weights below his cock swinging and smacking warm and solid into Cuinn's tipped-up and eagerly presented ass.

Oh, fuck. Cuinn's hand went to his cock. *Remember what I said about the bottom?* He stroked swiftly, spiraling up his considerable length and back down. *I think you have about ten seconds, tops.*

Rian wanted to laugh. He *did* laugh. But he also braced his knees and locked his arms tight and dropped his head. And took his mate. Hard. Sweat dripping down in sparks, splashing bright on Cuinn's chest. Driving in harder. Faster. Again. Oh God oh God oh *fuck* oh *Cuinn* —

He felt Cuinn clamp down hard around his whole length an instant before everything vanished in a firestorm of pleasure and joy and thick liquid Fire jetting into tight clasping darkness and the sensation of legs gripping him tightly. And while he was still lost, Cuinn cried out and bucked up against him, and the scent of his release damn near had Rian coming again before he was fairly through.

Rian's arms were trembling like an old man's. Slowly, carefully, he lowered himself, covering Cuinn's body with his own, the sticky cooling pool on

Cuinn's abs one of the most intimate things he'd ever felt. Cuinn grabbed him roughly and drew his head down, cupping the back of his head. He could hear Cuinn's breath rasping in his chest, and his own doing much the same.

Was it good? Cuinn's inner voice was tentative. *Was it what you need?*

Rian didn't need Cuinn to explain what he meant. *I still enjoy the pain, I think. And the tease. My dreams, before I woke, holy* fuck *they were intense.* Cuinn's arms tightened as a shudder skittered through Rian. *But the pain? I don't think I need it.*

It would be all right, if you did. If you do. Rian felt a kiss land haphazardly on his cheek. *But the only thing I need is you.*

Rian smiled, he couldn't help it. *I thought you said Fae didn't need.*

I said we don't want to.

Rian hadn't been expecting the sudden, painful lump in his throat. *Do you not want to need me, then?*

Come here and let me show you exactly how much I don't want to need you.

Epilogue

The power bound for so long in the human world now rushes back into the Realm, flowing in a torrent, racing like a lover too long parted from the beloved. The magick-parched Realm takes it in, embraces it, and transmutes it to living magick, the land's healing, its substance, and its life's blood.

But the essence of living magick is wild —even the words, as'Faein, are nearly the same, fiánn and fiáin. Water always finds its level, they say, and magick always finds its freedom. The Pattern, the barrier between the worlds, is damaged, flawed, strained.

Would it be so strange, if magick eventually found a way, or ways, back to its source, a gift for a gift?

It was spring, on the shore of the loch, one spring out of hundreds the ancient oak had witnessed. It stood sentinel, sheltered among the hills that held the loch as if in the cup of a hand, and had stood thus far longer than any of the living memories that came and went around it. The wheel of the year turned around the old tree, each round the same.

Except this one. Something was feeding the oak's

roots, rising through trunk and branches and twigs, and the new leaves unfurling were a shade of green almost too rich for the human eye to take in, had there been any such for miles around.

A stonechat fluttered to a landing in the branches, just as dawn lit the crown of the venerable tree. The light turned the plain black and russet of the little bird's feathers to sable and copper; it ruffled its feathers, and piped its clear trilling call.

sUN uP sUN uP sUN uP sUN uP

Startled, it fluttered, then settled and preened.

nEW dAY nEW dAY nEW dAY nEW dAY

This dawn, this spring, was different.

Sneak Peek: Blowing Smoke
Prologue

Greenwich Village,
New York City

March 8, 2013
Fucking-dark-forty-five a.m.

Holy Christ, what crawled in here and died?

Bryce had thought it would be good to get home. Or at least that it would be better than sitting on the Acela from Washington, D.C. wearing nothing but a leather harness and shorts and dried brown glop he kind of remembered having been blood.

He'd been wrong.

The stench in the apartment he shared with Terry was so bad, he had to stand out in the little foyer of the brownstone and let the place air out before entering. It really did smell like something large had died, quite a while ago.

Shit, I hope it wasn't Terry.

Something cold gripped his gut. Something else twinged, right where the cold clamped down. He'd had a stab wound in his abdomen when he wandered the streets of D.C. Or he thought he had. There wasn't any sign of it now.

Where the hell was Terry?

Bryce reached around the doorjamb, flipped on the light, took a deep breath, and entered. *Jesus, what a mess!* His Louis Quinze sofa was sagging at one corner, covered with blotches and dried pools of the same brown shit that streaked his body. It stank, but the worst of the smell was coming from the narrow hallway leading to the bedroom.

Shit. Shit. Shit.

He tiptoed down the hall, not sure why he was tiptoeing except that it seemed like the thing to do under the circumstances. The bedroom door was closed, and no light came from under the crack at the bottom.

What am I going to do if he's dead in there?

Scream like a girl and faint, probably. I'm ever so fucking useful in a crisis.

Bryce's lips narrowed to a thin line. Anyone else would have been concerned with Terry first. Him? What a laugh. He had a giant hole where his heart ought to be. But at least he was an equal opportunity hater. He detested himself at least as much as he disdained everyone else. Grimacing, he gripped the cast-iron knob, twisted, pushed.

The light from the hallway slanted across an empty bed. The comforter had apparently fallen off it at some point, and someone had done a half-assed job of pulling it back up, but there was obviously no one under it. Bryce switched on the light with an unsteady hand. It didn't look any more inviting in full light; the comforter and the sheets were stained with something that didn't look like blood. Didn't look like any bodily fluid he had ever seen, actually, and he thought he knew them all.

But where was the smell coming from? The door to the bathroom was ajar; cautiously, he pushed it all the way open.

Bryce gagged. There was a pile of clothing on the floor, next to the open and nearly overflowing toilet. The clothes —a huge T-shirt and jeans, he thought, though they were so grey, stained, and ragged it was hard to be sure —smelled worse than the toilet, and were so crusty they couldn't lie flat. And he thought he saw something crawling in them, though there was no way in hell he was going to get close enough to figure out if he was right, or if it was just his eyes swimming with tears. From the smell, of course.

Going by the size, the clothes weren't Terry's. Which was a relief, but it still left him with a mystery.

One that started clearing itself up, somewhat, as he looked around the bedroom. Both closets stood open, his and Terry's. His held the suits and shirts and ties he wore for work. Terry's was empty, except for a heavy lambskin coat that had been hanging in the same place for so long it had dust on the shoulders.

Same story with the chests of drawers. His held socks, shirts, jeans, loose change, condoms, lube, toys. Terry's was empty.

Bryce sat down hard on the bed, ignoring the stains on the sheets. Terry was gone. Had been gone for a long time. He wished the hole in his chest would hurt. Would do something. But Terry didn't mean anything to him. Never had. He was familiar, that was all. Somewhere along the line, he'd decided that it was better to wake up to one face in the morning than a parade of them.

Besides, Terry would have moved on eventually. Everyone did. It was bizarre, really, Terry being around for this long. Things were just back to sitch normal.

A normal person would feel empty. Bryce *wanted* to feel empty.

Why couldn't he?

Glossary

The following is a glossary of the *Faen* words and phrases found in *Hard as Stone, Gale Force, Deep Plunge,* and *Firestorm.* The reader should be advised that, as in the Celtic languages descended from it, spelling in *Faen* is as highly eccentric as the one doing the spelling.

(A few quick pronunciation rules —bearing in mind that most Fae detest rules —single vowels are generally 'pure', as in ah, ey, ee, oh, oo for a, e, i, o, u. An accent over a vowel means that vowel is held a little longer than its unaccented cousins. "ao" is generally "ee", but otherwise dipthongs are pretty much what you'd expect. Consonants are a pain. "ch" is hard, as in the modern Scottish "loch". "S", if preceded by "I" or "a", is usually "sh". "F" is usually silent, unless it's the first letter in a word, and if the word starts with "fh", then the "f" and the "h" are *both* silent. "Th" is likewise usually silent, as is "dh", although if "dh" is at the beginning of a word, it tries to choke on itself and ends up sounding something like a "strangled" French "r". Oh, and "mh" is "v", "bh" is "w", "c" is always hard, and don't forget to roll your "r"s!)

ach   but

a'gár'doltas   vendetta (lit. "smiling-murder")

agean   ocean

amad'n   fool, idiot

anam   soul

m'anam   my soul. Fae endearment.

n'anamacha   their souls

aon-arc   unicorn

asiomú   'reversal-vengeance'. The act of making oneself crave whatever is being done to one as a punishment, thereby turning one's punisher into one's procurer.

asling   dream

batagar   arrow

beag   little, slight

bod   penis (vulgar)

bodlag   limp dick (much greater insult than a human might suppose)

bragan   toy (see phrase)

briste   broken

buchal alann   beautiful boy

ca'fuil?   Where?

ceangal   (1)   chains

ceangal (2) Royal soul-bonding ceremony in the Realm (common alt. spelling *ceangail*)

cein fa? Why?

céle general way of referring to two people

le céle together

a céle one another, each other

chara friend

cho'halan so beautiful

coladh sleep

cónai live

crocnath completion

m'crocnath my completion. One of Cuinn's pillow-names for Rian

croí heart

Croí na Dóthan *Heart of Flame*, the signet of the Royal house of the Demesne of Fire

Cruan'ba The Drowner. Name given to the *Marfach* by the Fae of the Demesne of Water.

cugat to you

d'aos'Faen   Old Faen, the old form of the Fae language. Currently survives only inwritten form.

dar'cion   brilliantly colored. Conall's pillow-name for Josh.

dearmad   forgotten

deich   ten

deich meloi   ten thousand

derea   end

desúcan   fix, repair

dhó-súil   fire-eyes. One of Cuinn's pillow-names for Rian.

dóchais   hope (n.) (alt. spelling dócas)

dolmain   hollow hill, a place of refuge

doran   stranger, exile

d'orant   impossible. Josh's pillow-name for Conall.

draoctagh   magick

Spiraod n'Draoctagh   Spirit of Magick. Ancient Fae oath. Or expletive. Sometimes both.

dre'fiur   beloved sister

dre'thair   beloved brother

dubh   black, dark

dúrt me   I said

eiscréid   shit

Elirei   Prince Royal

fada   long (can reference time or distance)

Faen   the Fae language. *Laurm Faen*—I speak Fae.

as'Faein   in the Fae language. *Laur lom as'Faein*—I speak in the Fae language.

fan   wait (imp.)

fiáin   wild

fiánn   living magick

fíor   true

flua   wet

fola   wounded, injured

folabodan   ae sex toy. Derived from *fola,* injured, and *bod*, penis

folath   bleed

fonn   keen, sharp

fracun   whore
Comes from an ancient Fae word meaning "use-value"—in other words, a person whose value is measured solely by what others can get, or take, from him or her.

galtanas   promise

gan   general negative —no, not, without, less

gan derea   without end, eternal

gaoirn   wolves

g'demin   true, real

g'féalaidh   may you (pl.) live (see phrases)

g'fua   hate (v.)

g'mall   slowly

grafain   wild love, wild one. Lochlann's pillow name for Garrett.

halan   beautiful

impi   I beg

lae   day

lámagh   shot (v., p.t.)

lanan   lover. Tiernan's pillow name for Kevin, and vice versa

lanh   son

laród-scatha   mirror-trap. Essentially a magickal ball with no exterior, only a mirrored interior. And the sweet revenge of all of us who failed solid geometry in high school.

lasihoir   healer

laurha   spoken (see phrases)

related words—*laurm*, I speak; *laur lom*, I am speaking, I speak (in) a language

lobadh   decayed, rotten

lofa   rotten

magarl   testicles (alt. spelling *magairl)*

Marfach, the   the Slow Death. Deadliest foe of the Fae race.

marú   kill

Mastragna   Master of Wisdom. Ancient Fae title for the Loremasters.

milat   feel, sense

minn   oath

mo mhinn   my oath

misnach   courage

nach   general negative; not, never

né   not, is not

n-oí   night

ollúnta   solemn

onfatath   infected

orm   at me

pian   pain

pracháin   crows

rachtanai   addicted (specifically, to sexual teasing)

Ridiabhal   lit. "king of the devils", Satan. A borrowed word, as Fae have neither gods nor devils.

rinc-daonna   "human dance", a game of teasing and sexually overloading humans

rochar   harm (n.)

savac-dui   black-headed hawk, Conall's House-guardian

scair'anam   SoulShare (pl. *scair-anaim*)

m'anam-sciar   my SoulShare

scair'aine'e   the act of SoulSharing

scair'ainm'en   SoulShared (adj.)

scian   knife

scian-damsai   knife-dances. An extremely lethal type of formalized combat.

scílim   I think, I believe

sibh   you (pl.)

slántai   health, tranquillity

slántai a'váil   "Peace go with you". A mournful farewell.

s'ocan   peace, be at peace

spára   spare

spára'se   spare him

spiraod   spirit

343

súil   eyes

sule-d'ainmi   lit. "animal-eyes", dark brown eyes

sus   up

s'vra lom   I love (lit. "I have love on me")

ta'sair   I'm free (exclam.)

thar   come (imp.)

Thar lom.   Come with me.

tón   ass (not the long-eared animal)

torq   boar

tre   three

Tre… dó… h'on…   Three…. two… one…

tseo   this, this is (see phrases)

uiscebai   strong liquor found in the Realm, similar to whiskey

veissin   knockout drug found in the Realm, causes headaches

viant   desired one. A Fae endearment.

Useful phrases:

...tseo mo mhinn ollúnta.   This is my solemn oath.

G'féalaidh sibh i do cónai fada le céle, gan a marú a céle.
"May you live long together, and not kill one another."
A Fae blessing, sometimes bestowed upon those Fae foolhardy enough to undertake some form of exclusive relationship. Definite "uh huh, good luck with that" overtones.

bragan a lae   "toy of the day". The plaything of a highly distractable Fae.

Fai dara tú pian beag. Ach tú a sabail dom ó pian I bhad nís mo.
You cause a slight pain. But you are the healing of more.

Cein fa buil tu ag'eachan' orm ar-seo?   Why do you look at me this way?

Dóchais laurha, dóchais briste.   Hope spoken is hope broken.

Bod lofa dubh.   Lit. "black rotted dick". Not a polite phrase.

Scílim g'fua lom tú.   I think I hate you.

S'vra lom tú.   I love you.

Sus do thón.   Up your ass.

D'súil do na pracháin, d'croí do na gaoirn, d'anam do n-oí gan derea.
"Your eyes for the crows, your heart for the wolves, your soul for the eternal night." There is only one stronger vow of enmity in the Fae language, and trust me, you don't want to hear that one.

Lámagh tú an batagar; 'se seo torq a'gur fola d'fach.
"You shot the arrow; this wounded boar is yours." The equivalent *as'Faein* of "You broke it; you buy it." Often used in its shortened form, "*Lámagh tú an batagar.*" (or "*Lámagh sádh an batagar*" for "they shot". It's probably only a matter of time before some Fae in the human world, taking his cue from "NMP" for "not my problem", comes up with "LTB".

Tá dócas le scian inas fonn, nach milat g'matann an garta dí g'meidh tú folath.
Fae proverb: Hope is a knife so keen, you don't feel the cut until you bleed.

G'ra ma agadh.   Thank you.

Tam g'fuil aon-arc desúcan an lanhuil damast I d'asal. G'mall.
"May a unicorn repair your hemorrhoids. Slowly." One can only imagine….

Magairl a'Ridiabhal.   Satan's balls.

Se an'agean flua, a'deir n'abhann.

The ocean is wet, says the river. The pot calling the kettle black.

galtanas deich meloi
"promise of ten thousand". A promise given by a Fae, to give ten thousand of something to another, usually something that can only be given over time. Considered an extravagant, even irrational showing of devotion.

Támid faoi ceangal ag a'slabra ceant.   We are bound by the same chains.

Né seo a'manach   This isn't for me.

mo phan s'darr lear sa masa   my favorite pain in the ass

Dúrt me lath mars'n   I told you so

Bual g'mai, aris.   Well met, again.

About the Author

Rory Ni Coileain majored in creative writing, back when Respectable Colleges didn't offer such a major. She had to design it herself, at a university which boasted one professor willing to teach creative writing: a British surrealist who went nuts over students writing dancing bananas in the snow but did not take well to high fantasy. Graduating Phi Beta Kappa at the age of nineteen, she sent off her first short story to an anthology that was being assembled by an author she idolized, and received one of those rejection letters that puts therapists' kids through college. For the next thirty years or so she found other things to do, such as going to law school, ballet dancing (at more or less the same time), volunteering as a lawyer with Gay Men's Health Crisis, and nightclub singing, until her stories started whispering to her. Currently, she's a lawyer and a legal editor; the proud mother of a proud Brony and budding filmmaker; and is busily wedding her love of myth and legend to her passion for m/m romance. She is the winner of the Rainbow Books Award. She is a three-time Rainbow Award finalist.

Books in this Series by Rory Ni Coileain:

Hard as Stone
Book One of the SoulShares Series

Gale Force
Book Two of the SoulShares Series

Deep Plunge
Book Three of the SoulShares Series

Other Riverdale Avenue Books You May Like:

The Siren and the Sword: Book One of the Magic
University Series
by Cecilia Tan

The Tower and the Tears: Book Two of the Magic
University Series
by Cecilia Tan

The Incubus and the Angel: Book Three of the Magic
University Series
by Cecilia Tan

Mordred and the King
by John Michael Curlovich

Collaring the Saber-Tooth: Book One of the Masters
of Cats Series
by Trinity Blacio

Dee's Hard Limits: Book Two of the Masters of Cats Series
by Trinity Blacio

Caging the Bengal Tiger: Book Three of the Masters of Cats Series
by Trinity Blacio

Made in the USA
Las Vegas, NV
26 November 2021